ISMARIL'S SWORD

· · · ··· ··· ··· ··· ··· ··· ··· ··· ··· ··· ··· ····

WES PENRE

Book Three in the Trilogy,
Ismaril's Journey

Previous book in this series:
Book 1: *The Book of Secrets (2021)*
Book 2: *The Underworld (2022)*

Copyright © 2023 by Wes Penre

All rights reserved. This book or any portion thereof may not be reproduced or used in any manner whatsoever without the expressed written permission of the publisher, except for the use of brief quotations in a book review.

First Edition: 2023

Cover licensed through
SelfPubBookCovers.com/Joetherasakdhi

https://wespenrebooks.com

Acknowledgement

I want to dedicate this book to all my wonderful friends, patrons, and forum members who have supported me through the entire writing process. Your support has been a massive inspiration for me.

A special dedication to the Lady of Fire, who personally encouraged and aided me with such enthusiasm. You also know who you are. Your commitment is very much appreciated and has greatly helped me through the process of writing this book.

Synopsis

This is the third part of the trilogy, *Ismaril's Journey*.

In the first part, *The Book of Secrets,* a small village called Eldholt, where people usually mind their own business, is being invaded by an army of Wolfmen, led by Yongahur, an angelic emissary of Gormoth, which is a realm in the northeastern part of Taëlia. There, Azezakel the Black is the king, and Ishtanagul, his Bride, is the queen.

Yongahur and his army of Wolfmen are looking for a person who lives in Eldholt, going by the name Ismaril Farrider. Yongahur and the Wolfmen burn the village and kill many of its people when the villagers of Eldholt refuse to tell Yongahur where their friend Ismaril is.

When Ismaril returns to his home, he finds out his wife Maerion and his little son Erestian were killed in the raid. Furious and beside himself with grief, he wishes to retaliate, and he brings three friends on a journey east to find Yongahur. Their names are Sigyn (who lost her fiancé in the Wolfman attack), Gideon, and Zale of Merriwater.

But Ismaril carries deep secrets.

During the previous Wolfman War, he stole a magic sword made from the Unicorn's horn; a Divine and holy creature that Azezakel's men had killed. The horn was then forged into a sword.

During the Wolfman War, a captain of the Khanduran army stole the weapon from Azezakel's men. He understood the importance of the sword and urgently tried to deliver it to King Barakus of Khandur. Being ordered by the Court to prioritize his mission, he failed to save the life of Ismaril's brother, who was killed by Wolfmen. Ismaril heard the captain neglected to save his brother's life, and he retaliated. He found the captain wounded, killed him, and took the sword, without knowing that it had magic powers.

Ismaril named the sword *Gahil*, the *Demon Slayer*.

On his journey to find the murderous Yongahur, Master Raeglin, a pilgrim of Divine origin, confronts Ismaril outside Merriwater. He claims to be in the service of the Mother Goddess, thought by many to be the Creator of the Universe.

Azezakel, son of the Goddess, manifested in Taëlia ages ago, declaring himself to be the Father of humankind. Since he and his angelic sons, whom the humans call the Dark Kings, and of whom Yongahur is one, they told the humans they had always tried to make peace with them, but all humanity could see, when looking back at their own history, was perpetual wars between humans and gods, continuing up to this day. Now, both humans and gods are preparing for the *Last Battle* to establish who shall be the rulers of Taëlia, considering the world will survive the war.

When confronting Ismaril in Merriwater, Master Raeglin notices something special and mysterious about Ismaril and tells him to seek the Book of Secrets, which, according to legend, lies hidden somewhere inside the Snowy Mountains at the Gormothan border. The pilgrim has reasons to believe Ismaril is the right person to open the Book and get magic insights from it.

On their travels from Eldholt to Gormoth, Azezakel's realm, they experience many adventures, and Ismaril loses three friends on his journey: Gideon, a man named Holgar, and Zale, his childhood friend. With much help from Master Raeglin and the earth spirit, Kirbakin the Gnome, Ismaril finds the Book of Secrets, opens it, and reads a poem within, pertaining to him, telling him what to do next. The poem tells him to go on a journey into the Underworld, where he will learn what he must learn before he can be of help in the Last Battle.

After much hesitation, Ismaril and Sigyn find a boat by a river, running through the same cave in which they found the Book of Secrets. The two companions say farewell to Raeglin and Kirbakin, who no longer will follow them on their ongoing journey.

The first book ends when Ismaril and Sigyn disappear deeper into the cave, using the boat and the underground river to reach the Underworld.

In the second book, The Underworld, Ismaril and Sigyn journey through the Underworld, where they experience many adventures, getting Ismaril ready for the task before him—to eliminate the Dark Kings of Gormoth and thus save the world from Evil. They encounter more and more obstacles the farther they travel, and the more exhausted they get, until it seems inevitable that they will succumb. In a tunnel system deep underground, a demonic being curses Sigyn.

Up on the surface, the world is preparing for war. King Barakus of the Divine Kingdom of Khandur finds his realm under siege by Wolfmen, Birdmen, and other abominable creatures, and a devastating battle takes place, where Khandur is the victor, but not without suffering great losses. His second son, Prince Exxarion, travels north to Anúria, a colony of Khandur, and becomes the governor there. But the prince has lofty ambitions that might jeopardize the future of the entire Taëlia.

While all this is happening, an odd fellow who calls himself "Hoodlum" shows up in the northwest, in a kingdom called Urandor. He has little memory of his past, and people in Urandor shun him and drive him out of the country. There he joins a band of pirates from Piscas Urash, the Pirate Island, on their way to Gormoth to join Azezakel in the coming Last War, predicted in Prophecy. Hoodlum is gifted with a special kind of magic, with which he can summon animals. The pirates treat him badly, and when he has had enough, he summons the Grimms from Hell, who kill most of the pirates. From there, Hoodlum loses his mind and thinks he is a preacher and a spokesperson for the One and Only God, whom he considers being King Azezakel. Wherever he goes, disaster follows. He travels east on his black mare, who is his best friend, but the horse was killed by the pirates. The mare, Stormcloud, appears to

Hoodlum as an apparition that he can ride and interact with. His goal is to reach Gormoth before the Last Battle starts.

Only two pirates, The Revenger and Tomlin, survive the Grimm attack on the pirate crew, and the two also travel east to join forces with Gormoth.

After an encounter with Queen Ishtanagul, the Queen of the Underworld, and King Azezakel's Bride, Ismaril and Sigyn find themselves on an endless, barren field without water and food.

Book two ends when Ismaril and Sigyn give up on the barren heath in the Underworld, ready to die.

The Poem

*Life in fury, life in pain
much seems lost, though not in vain
The only shadows being real
are those that you thyself conceal.*

*Go through life with open eyes
bring light to Darkness, live no lies
For Darkness is not what you view;
it dwells in depth inside of you.*

*Where Darkness roams, you still must go
where stakes are high, and hope is low
where worst of horrors once been hurled;
journey through the Underworld.*

*Bring thy strength and bring thy weak
tame thy fury, feed the meek,
that dwells within but buried deep
Your roaring waves you still must keep
for yet some time for you to use
until it is time for you to choose.*

*Calm it gently, let it go
when sword and arrow, knife and bow
no more shall serve you on your quest,
put them down. Lay down to rest*

*what troubles you, for that shall be
but far-gone tears and misery.*

*Far you traveled for these lines
seen death and danger, troubled times
Bring what is yours but still not yours
and learn its will and tame its force.
Use it wisely, not with scorn
'come fresh, anew, once more reborn.*

*Last, not least, now keep in mind
with Wisdom you must lead the Blind.
As hopeless as your quest might seem
it is on your shoulders to redeem
some who live in endless night
without Glory, void of Light.*

*For all the wise and for the fool
for shadows dark, for those who rule;
for those which hope since long is gone
and joy is foreign, faith is none
For all those, shine, be a star
and light the Darkness, near and far.*

CONTENTS

Synopsis i
The Poem v
Chapter 1 From Friends to Foes 1
Chapter 2 Up from Way Under 10
Chapter 3 Spellbound 17
Chapter 4 The Doomsday Prophet 24
Chapter 5 Another Time and Space 29
Chapter 6 Red Sails and Longboats 40
Chapter 7 Ulves 51
Chapter 8 Caëgrun 62
Chapter 9 The Journey East 73
Chapter 10 Setting Sails 82
Chapter 11 That Which is Buried 93
Chapter 12 Misthorn 102
Chapter 13 Through Forest Deep 109
Chapter 14 The Dream Master of Kingshold 119
Chapter 15 Whispering Island 124
Chapter 16 Ishtarion 136
Chapter 17 The Recruits 149
Chapter 18 Reunion 155
Chapter 19: Two Brothers 163

Chapter 20 The Ancients	172
Chapter 21 Treacherous Planning	183
Chapter 22 The Battle for Khurad-Resh	187
Chapter 23 The Fall of Emoria	203
Chapter 24 The Road North	213
Chapter 25 The March of Giants	220
Chapter 26 Wilderness of Ice and Snow	231
Chapter 27 Wasteforge	247
Chapter 28 Two Dark Kings	260
Chapter 29 Confrontation	270
Chapter 30 An Unexpected Encounter	274
Chapter 31 Azezakel's Voice	284
Chapter 32 The Treshandor Battle	290
Chapter 33 Grimcast	299
Chapter 34 Divine Combat	309
Chapter 35 The Dragon Whisperer	315
Chapter 36 At the Camp	320
Chapter 37 The Mind of a Demon	331
Chapter 38 Turning of the Tide	346
Chapter 39 A Heroine's Last Journey	352
Chapter 40 The Council	362
Chapter 41 Another Time, Another World	374
MAPS	385

Chapter 1
From Friends to Foes

It was a wounded city that met the three horsemen when they reached the heart of Khandur. On this day, women wept in the streets of Ringhall, and children were running about, asking for food from aimless wanderers who had nothing. Corteges blocked the main roads, carrying the remains of courageous officers who had sacrificed their young lives for a cause that most likely would never be accomplished.

People mourned and chanted and were so overwhelmed by grief over fallen husbands, lovers, or parents that they failed to notice the three riders. Nor saw they it was their Prince sitting on the back of the white stallion; even fewer noticed the two odd fellers who followed him: one on a regular-sized horse, clad in many bright colors, whilst the other rode a little pony that appeared too big for him—the little feller looked like a fairytale character from another world. Few townspeople had seen a Gnome before, and yet they paid him no attention.

Dragon fire had twice swept the streets of the Capital, and many homes were still burning, causing many casualties and homelessness. Prince Xandur studied his people as he rode and never wanted to see war again—ever. Yet he knew this was merely wishful thinking.

The road leading to King Barakus' palace appeared endless, and the horsemen's pace was slow to prevent running over someone in the crowded streets. In their path, a desperate young woman grabbed Xandur's reins and stopped his horse.

"Young man, sir," she sobbed. "Please give me a coin or two so I can get something to eat. I lost my husband in the…" She noticed too late that the young man she had halted was the Heir of Khandur. Shocked, she went down on hands and knees and bowed her head until her forehead touched the stone. "Forgive me, my Prince. Please pardon me. I knew not it was you. I hope I address you properly."

"Stand, young lady," Xandur said, and his voice was mild. "You did nothing wrong, and you are hungry. Do you have children?"

"Two boys of five and seven, and a little girl of two, Sir." She stood up now, face dirty, hair hanging in ringlets.

"May the Goddess bless you, ma'am. Here is for you and your children." The prince gave her a leather purse with coins, likely to buy her food for weeks. She bowed, and her gratitude was heartfelt.

While the procession of three closed in on the Royal Palace, Xandur was in deep thoughts, thinking of all the things Queen Astéamat of Emoria had told him about war and peace, and how to accomplish and maintain a paradise like hers. *No one wants war less than I do'* he thought, *but how can we achieve peace? Certainly not by laying down weapons and inviting the enemy to come. Sometimes, we must do evil to do good.*

"I have been a fool," Raeglin said, pondering similar thoughts. "Queen Astéamat was right; I am too involved in human affairs. I should be more concerned with the affairs of my own kind."

"Who are…?" the prince asked.

"The Dark Kings."

"But you are not a Dark King?"

"At first, neither were they. I was unaware that living too long in Taëlia has affected me, making me develop dark traits, melding with the blackness that dwells here. The Queen shockingly reminded me. To some extent, I have neglected my mission."

Prince Xandur looked at the pilgrim curiously. Then he said, "So, what is your plan?"

Raeglin shook his head and said nothing in reply, and the three continued in silence. Before them, the Royal Palace still stood proud, soaring as they approached. Xandur was eager to see his father.

It pleased the companions to see the king was on the mend. When they arrived in the palace, he sat on his throne, dressed in a purple royal outfit, but there was only one hand on the armrest. It was still a shock to see one of the king's arms missing.

The company bowed before him.

"I am glad to see you are back in your chair again, father," the prince said. "Strong must be your will, for you are mending fast."

"Perhaps so," King Barakus said. "Yet, I should not be in this chair but leading an army. The flame burning inside me as a young man is swiftly fading. I have seen wars, and in some I fought; but never have I seen or heard of times like these. They are unprecedented, and I carry little hope. I have failed as a monarch, for my son has betrayed me and little did I see it coming. Exxarion is leading Anúria to destruction, and here I sit on a worthless throne, maimed and tired. We lost many men in the battle, Xandur."

"We did, father, but we were victorious. One victory may lead to another, and yet another."

"Not in the void of allies. And allies we have none. It is up to me, and it is up to us, the Khandurans, to save the world now. The odds are exceedingly against us."

"Yes, we are the saviors now, and although it appears to be a hopeless task to fight against Azezakel's hellish forces, our courage and our victory may inspire other nations to rise to the task; even those that previously refused."

There was an emptiness in Barakus' eyes when he met his son's glance. In only a few weeks' time, his face had grown so much older; his skin was gray and his face hollow. Gone was the erect posture, otherwise so typical of a proud regent. Now, his body was bent like an old tree, and his head was heavy, like filled with gravel.

"You have yet to tell me about Emoria, which you visited without my permission," he said, piercing the three companions with a stern gaze. "Do we have Queen Astéamat's allegiance?"

Xandur looked aside, unwilling to meet his father's stare.

"Forgive me, Sire," Raeglin said. "If I may, I shall speak to that."

"Go ahead. My son appears too embarrassed to face me. It

gladdens me someone is brave enough to speak up. I believe I can expect bad news, so give it to me with no roundabouts."

The pilgrim bowed. "I shall be brief, to the point, and truthful. The Queen will not let her Mazosian army take part in Taëlia's liberation. On one hand, this is disappointing, considering their ferocity as female warriors in times agone, but after having an awakening conversation with her, I realized she was right. Emoria is the last oasis of freedom and peace in the world, and its people need to stay in tune with that. Without them and their Queendom, nothing balances things out, and our hopelessness would be well-founded indeed. The three of us were there for only a brief moment, but their paradise slowly withered in our presence. This shows me a bitter truth: Humankind has fallen so deep from its original state it can no longer return to its former paradise unless a change occurs within them. The gap between Emoria and the peoples of the world is monumental."

"If true, this is bad news," the king said. "Then I was right; there is little to no hope."

"Hope must be the last thing to leave us," Kirbakin said. "And we are not at that point yet."

Barakus scoffed. "Here I sit, listening to a pilgrim and a Gnome. Is that what it has come down to? Are you the best source of advice I can get these days?"

"The Gnome is correct," Raeglin insisted. "We still have an important move to make."

"Enlighten me," Barakus said, not without sarcasm.

"We must find Ismaril Farrider."

The king raised his eyebrows. "The thief and the murderer? We *are* trying to find him, too, so we can bring him to justice, but thus far, we have been unsuccessful. Why is it important for you to find him, and what significance does he play in this scheme?"

"Perhaps more than you think, Your Majesty," the pilgrim said. "The sword he took plays a central role in this entire war and the outcome thereof. As you well know, it's a Unicorn sword—the only one of its kind. It is Divine and tightly woven into the Prophecy."

Barakus' voice turned to a clap of thunder, and his eyes to lightning. "If so, it is now in the hands of a thief and a murderer. Woe to us all! If you are speaking the truth, I can see why it is imperative to find this Farrider and take the sword from him. The blade must be delivered to me. I said I would go to war once more, and perhaps there is a higher purpose driving me. Could it be that the sword, in my hands, will turn our unlikely success into victory?" The king sat back on his throne, and his fiery blood cooled off.

"Sire, the sword is not for you to carry," Raeglin said. "It is true it was stolen, and a fine knight of Khandur had his life spoiled because of it—highly unfortunate—but perhaps it must be that way, so the sword would go to its right owner—"

"The right owner? Why do you support a criminal, whom I will not hesitate to execute when I get my hands on him? The Divine Sword in the hands of a criminal?"

"Sire, please let me finish." The king reluctantly sat back, muttering between his teeth. "Farrider has been tested, and he passed the test; let us leave it with that for now. To fulfill the Prophecy, he must travel through the Underworld for a second test—a test that judges his character—and that is where I left him. Now, I have a distinct feeling he might be back from there."

"You sent him to the Underworld with the Sword?" Barakus exploded again, and in his peripheral, Raeglin saw even Prince Xandur's baffled face turning red. "You sent the Divine Sword to the Enemy. Does that not make you an enemy, warlock? Whose side are you on, or are you playing both?"

"I do not take sides, Sire. My mission is to help to bring peace to these lands, regardless of what it takes. To accomplish that goal, it has been more beneficial to associate with humans than with the Dark Kings. But this means I sometimes must take chances. Not necessarily because I wish to do so, but because Prophecy requires it. King Barakus, I am aware of the odds, and I am aware that the path to victory is narrow; but we inhabit a divine weapon, and literally so. We must use it, relying upon that the weapon-bearer is the correct person to use it."

"This is insanity! You have betrayed me, you have betrayed the Divine Kingdom of Khandur, and you have deceived the rest of the free peoples of Taëlia. You are a traitor."

"Not so, Your Majesty. And when we visited Emoria, Queen Moëlia reminded us of our options. She knows what she knows, and that is without us mentioning Ismaril Farrider or the Sword."

Barakus sneered. "Moëlia! How dare you mention her in this

context, as if she is a significant voice? She is not willing to help our people; she would rather see the world in flames than lift an eyebrow. Why would I listen to her, and why should you? Indeed, I was right, and I have been too trusting. Here I sit, listening to a warlock and a Gnome, the latter who has spoken only once, and foolishly at that. You may be crazy, but perhaps I am the craziest one."

Raeglin stood his ground. "I trust my instinct, and my instinct tells me Farrider is the correct person to fulfill the Prophecy. If it were not so, he would have failed the first test."

"What test?"

"He opened the Book of Secrets, and he read the instructions he must follow. No one else but the Sword-Bearer could do that, and thus, he must be the right person for the task. One such instruction was to travel through the Underworld to prove himself worthy."

The king sat in silence for a while, staring at the pilgrim. Then he said, "You are a two-faced sorcerer. Do not expect me to support either your mission or this fugitive… Farrider. You try to lure me with your covert actions to change sides and support Azezakel's cause and lose the war."

"I ask you to support nothing, King. I merely feel it is time for you and your son to know what is happening behind the scenes. The truth of the matter is that the Enemy is not even interested in keeping the Sword for themselves, for they are well-versed in Prophecy. They have no use for it in battle or otherwise; it is not for them to carry it or for use. They merely want to keep a prying eye on Farrider's whereabouts for now and to discourage him and us. The enemy will hit when the time is right. They follow the Prophecy, albeit they work hard to alter it; but they believe in it. I suggest you consider doing the same. They cannot take the Sword from Ismaril, or they will face their own demise. Now, when the Blade is in the right hands, it is a part of the Sword-Bearer. I say it again: It is Divine, and it gives him Divine Powers that he must find within himself. His personality must align with the power of the Sword. Thus, he needs to go through hardship to merge with the Divine; yet his destitution has merely begun, and he knows it not."

"Divine Powers?" Barakus shook his head, and his voice was bitter. "The Divine Powers of a thief and a killer? Now, when

Ayasis has fallen, the Divine Powers lie with me, and therefore, the Sword belongs to me!"

"It is well enough that Divine Powers lie with a king, but kings are merely representatives for the people. For battles to be victorious, the power must come from the bottom up, with or without divine swords. Yes, even from a thief and a murderer, as it may be. The powers of the Dark Kings are impressive, and hence, we must counteract with the greatest power we have— that of common men. Aye, even of the *imperfect* common men. Among those, Farrider is the representative."

"I am sitting on this throne for a reason, and my sons are of my blood; the same blood that has run through the veins of ruling kings, and kings in exile, for thousands of years. We are pure-blood."

"And that is precisely why you must not carry the Divine Sword," Raeglin said. "If you possessed it, only those of pure blood would stand a chance of surviving this war. This is exactly what the Black King wants. People on your streets would not survive. Ismaril Farrider was chosen for a reason, and we must protect him with all the might we have."

"I shall protect no outlaw," King Barakus said. "If we find him, his head will roll."

"Then I must also protect him from you," Raeglin said.

"And thus, we are enemies," the king said.

A long silence followed. The king and the pilgrim locked eyes as if they were measuring their strength against each other. Then Barakus looked away, and he said in a low, resentful voice, "I should have you executed for this. You and that Gnome you bring with you everywhere. But I shall spare you this time because of how you fought with us in the battle and perhaps saved my life. I might have owed you, but now I have repaid my debt, for I will spare your life in return."

Then the king raised his voice. "Behold, for this is an act of mercy. You must now leave my kingdom and never put your foot here again whilst I am alive. This applies to you both. And if we meet once more, I will see that you both be decapitated. You will be anyone's game, and my soldiers and knights I shall order to kill you if you cross their path. This time alone shall I show mercy. You must exit my halls, my city, and my country immediately. You will be under escort until you have passed through the gates of my kingdom!"

Barakus grabbed a club and hit it three times against his table. Three guards instantly entered.

"Go get another dozens of men and escort these two figures out of Khandur. They must not be allowed to return!"

Two guards chained Raeglin's and Kirbakin's hands to each other and forced them out of the chamber.

"I will follow them out of the castle, father, making sure they leave" Xandur said, and left with the exiled.

In the courtyard, a dozen knights joined, and they threw the pilgrim and the Gnome onto a cart drawn by two horses. Before the escort took off, Prince Xandur signaled to the commanding sergeant to wait. Then he put his hands on the cart railing and gazed at the two figures he had considered friends. His face was stern, and in his eyes, Raeglin could behold a trace of sorrow.

"Thus, our friendship has come to an end," the prince said. "I have been a fool; and like an idiot, I traveled with you, fought by your sides, and I had faith in you. Now I hope we shall never meet again."

Raeglin raised his head and met Xandur's gaze. "Alas!" he said. "Dark indeed are the times when friends fight against friends. Evil plays tricks on us all; and for good to prevail, the darkness inside each of us first must perish. Hence, we all need to cast out our demons and find clarity. But a time shall come if destiny will have it when darkness gives way for the light to enter, and all shall be revealed. Until then, fare thee well, Prince. You may no longer hold faith in me, but I hold faith in you. More so than in your father."

Xandur's lips tightened. He said nothing, but kept his eyes locked on Raeglin. Then he smacked one horse on his back, and the escort started moving toward the castle gates. Meanwhile, two knights had taken the pilgrim's horse and the Gnome's pony from the stable and brought them on. Raeglin saw the prince stand amid the courtyard, following the escort with his gaze until the gates slammed closed.

With the wagon rocking and stumbling along the cobblestone, Kirbakin spoke.

"What now?"

"Our task must be to find Ismaril and Sigyn. Something tells me they are alive and back from the Underworld. I could be wrong, but my intuition is strong."

Kirbakin nodded. "Aye, I feel the same way."

Raeglin turned toward the Gnome and smiled. "Good!" he said. "That may confirm I am correct. It gives me hope."

"After that, then what?"

"Even if Ismaril and Sigyn are alive, we do not know where they are, and we do not know the condition they are in. Did they pass the test? All is unknown, but at one point or another, I need to go north to the Frostlands. There live a certain people, and if I can gain their trust, they might go to war against Azezakel. Yet, I know not which side they are on, if on any. I may not be welcome there."

"I will come with you," Kirbakin said.

"That may be very dangerous."

Kirbakin laughed, and his face wrinkled. "Do not talk to me of danger, warlock. I am an Elemental, and it is my duty to save the land. I am not afraid of danger."

Raeglin smiled. "I expected nothing else from you."

Thus, the escort closed in on the city gates. Raeglin got his horse back, and Kirbakin his pony. Behind them, as they trotted, the Ringhall city gates slammed shut, and neither of the two would see that city again from the inside.

Chapter 2
Up from Way Under

NOT WITHOUT EFFORT, Ismaril opened his eyes, only to find they were burning like lava. Before he could locate himself, he remembered the desolate landscape in hell that appeared to continue forever. Real or imagined, he smelled the death scent that had been so prevalent for the last few days as they were wandering across the barren fields. The agony, like a parasite devouring him, flared up to its fullest, and he wanted to die. As he step-by-step regained his senses, he noticed how weak his body was, from starvation and thirst.

When he became conscious enough, he noticed he was halfway sitting up against a stone wall, and he could hear water gurgle somewhere yonder. Beside him on the ground, stretched out on her back, Sigyn lay, and she moved not. Was she still breathing? He was too weak to move there to investigate. When he further looked around, he noticed they were in a cave, and no longer on the heaths of death, where they both had passed out from lack of water. Where was this?

Then it dawned on him. Before he fell unconscious, he dreamed about this exact cave, hearing running water in the background. He tried to clear his foggy mind to make sense of this, thinking he must have recurring dreams. *I wonder if this often happens when you are dying,* he thought. *I must be dying, for my life force is leaving me...*

After having penetrated his foggy mind, he decided he was

awake and not dreaming. But the dream he had on the heath of death had apparently turned real. Leaning against the wall, he moved his head to the right, and in the far distance, he saw a tunnel opening, which appeared to lead to the outside world. On his left, the tunnel or cave continued farther in, but it was from there the sound of gurgling water came, with some dripping and dropping attached to it, echoing through the tunnel.

"I must go there," he said to himself. "If this is indeed real, we need water. Sigyn is dying or is dead, and I am close to death myself."

It took him a lifetime to get to his feet, convulsively holding onto the cave wall. Once upright, his head was dizzy, his knees weak, and his breathing shallow. With each breath, his dry and swollen tongue was burning. Each thought told him to sit again to rest, but then there was that little spark inside him, forcing him to disobey the urge. For another moment, he hesitated whether to check Sigyn's condition, but chose not to—not yet. If he did, he would bend down, and he likely could not get up again. Instead, he attempted to save them both by holding onto the cave wall and slowly forcing himself farther down the tunnel, where he heard running water. If this was anything like his previous dream, there should be a stream of water pouring from the wall deeper down the cave. He fumbled for his headband and then put it on, lopsided, but he cared not. The precious stone shone in the otherwise pitch-dark tunnel, and he could more safely find his way forward.

Although he must have walked merely a few hundred paces, it felt like a league. Then and there he saw the stream of fresh, cold water coming out from cracks in the wall, creating an subterranean brook, meandering the downslope farther into the cave, which from there narrowed into a black tunnel. Ismaril gratefully sobbed and fell to his knees before the stream.

The dream had indeed given him a glimpse of the future.

With his last effort, he put his lips to the wall and started drinking. He remembered the dream, in which he vomited from drinking too fast, but he could not be bothered; he had no willpower to restrain himself. After vomiting, and after some additional gasping, he continued inhaling the water, and this time he could keep it down. It was cold and divine. He thought this must be Heaven; he could think of nothing more pleasurable than drinking from this stream.

When he could drink no more, he felt his strength returning, the fog in his head dispersing, and his life force rejuvenating his body. He fervently pulled up the two canteens he carried and filled them to the brim. Then he returned to Sigyn as quickly as he could.

There she lay, in the same position he had left her. He crouched and felt her pulse. She was still alive, but barely. He shook her to wake her, softly at first, only to rock her more violently. Yet, he could not help but think she was better off dead than alive. The last few days had worn him out.

"Sigyn! Wake up!"

Her response was naught. He slapped her cheeks, but it accomplished nothing. Nervously, he poured some water into his palm and wetted her cracked lips. Then he sat her up against the wall to prevent her from choking on the water he forced into her mouth. Only a little to hydrate her swollen tongue, so it was easier to breathe. Over and over, he repeated it, and after not too long, her body jerked, and a moan came through her throat. Then her eyes opened, and she sighed. She tried to talk, but her voice could not carry the words yet.

"Do not talk," Ismaril said. "Let me help you until you have recovered."

Soon, Sigyn took her first sip and swallowed, followed by a weak cough. She wanted more, but Ismaril was careful not to overdo it. In her condition, he wanted her not to vomit. It took some time, but once she could tolerate more water, her strength returned, and she gave him a vague smile.

"So, we are alive?" she whispered. "I had such disturbing dreams. I thought I was in Hell…"

"You were… we were. And we are probably still there; we yet need to find out."

"Are we in a tunnel? This is not where we were when I lost myself. Did you carry me here?"

"I did not, and I don't know where we are. After losing my consciousness, I woke up here. I dreamed about this place, and the dream was foreboding this location. Regardless of where we are, this place saved our lives, for here is water. It is a miracle I woke up at all. Let us rest a little, and then we must see what is outside this cave. I hope it's not worse than before, but I am not holding my breath."

Before they left the cave, Ismaril returned to refill their canteens. He realized how hungry he was, but they had no food. They could do without for yet a few days, he reckoned, but no longer than that. He closed his eyes and prayed there would be something to eat outside the cave. Then he returned to Sigyn, who by now was on her feet, slowly walking around to try her legs. Ismaril saw them shake, but he knew she would soon regain her strength. He watched her for a while from a distance, and a warm wave of powerful emotions rushed through him. She was more than a shield maiden to him now. He must teach himself how to show it to her. Yet, he did not think he deserved her after all he had done.

"Are you ready?" he asked her in a soft voice.

She stopped and looked at him, and her face was tired and her skin pale.

"I think so," she said.

―――

It was daylight outside the cave, and once they passed the entrance, a bright sun blinded them after having lived in a shadowy world for so long. When their eyes got used to the light, Sigyn laughed.

"This is fantastic! It's beautiful! Sunlight and warmth. Ismaril, are we back on the surface?"

"Speaking of beautiful," Ismaril made a wide arm gesture. "Behold!"

As they looked to their left and to their right, they saw themselves standing on an outdented, hanging cliff, high above the ground. Far beneath, a seemingly endless forest spread out in every direction like a sea of green, with treetops swaying in a mild summer wind. The scent of pine trees and something else they could not identify reached their noses and filled them with gladness and hope. The land before them was stunning, even magical, as if no evil could enter this land. But there was yet another feeling that rushed over them at the same time—that of anguish, melancholy, and despair.

"I never felt such conflicting feelings before," Ismaril said.

"It is like having my inside torn apart," Sigyn said. "There is this height of exhilaration at the same time as I feel the deepest despair. I want to laugh and cry at once."

A brisk breeze caught Ismaril's long hair and washed his face, refreshing after the long journey in twilight.

"I know not why we feel so conflicted," he said, "but I believe we might be on the surface again."

For a moment, they faced each other, exchanging glances. Abruptly, they laughed full-heartedly and merged in a long, warm embrace. Tears of joy and relief wetted the other one's cheeks.

Then the conflicted feelings overtook them again.

"I think we need to leave this place and go down to the forest," Ismaril said. "These hills and this cave are gloomy and frightening. Yet, we have no other place to go than down, for I wish not to go down through the tunnel to the Underworld again. And over there, the forest is everywhere."

"But how do we get there? We are above the treetops, and the hillside is rocky and steep."

"Behold!" Ismaril said and pointed. "I think I see a path."

Path was an overstatement; rather, it was a narrowness leading downward a few yards from where they had positioned, but it looked unstable and dangerous to tread. Looking down, they saw not whether the frail constriction continued or ended unexpectedly. Sigyn glanced at her companion with a frown.

"Come," he said. "It is the only way down from here that we can see. We got to try."

And thus, they strode their way down the hillside, with Ismaril taking the lead. Their pace was slow, as the risk of falling was great. Sometimes, the path was so narrow they had to squeeze themselves sideways between rocks, whilst holding their backpacks up high. Other times, the path was a little wider, but the rocks on the ground were unpredictable, rolling off beneath their feet, and they sometimes fell on their backs. The slope was steep, making a fall hazardous; and when entering a dangerous area, Ismaril grabbed Sigyn's hand, helping her through. Thus, they eventually reached the hill's bottom.

In front of them was a short field with rocks, stones, and gravel, void of flowers and any kind of undergrowth. It was dead and barren, and Sigyn shivered. This reminded too much of the landscape they had just left in the Underworld.

But across the field, there was a wall of beautiful trees, sparkling in the intense sunlight, growing so close together that the forest appeared impossible to penetrate as if the trees themselves were the guardians of the forest. The suffocating sense of doom and gloom once more welled up, and halfway across the desolate field, they stopped and gasped for air.

"I feel hopeless," Sigyn said. "I do not want to continue. Let us go back…"

"Yes, let us go back," Ismaril said and turned around toward the hills they had just left behind. He walked a few paces in that direction, but then stopped once more. "No," he said. "We can't go back. Why would we go back?"

"I don't know," Sigyn said, and there was a desperate tone to her voice. "I just don't seem capable of continuing."

"Me neither. Something tells me we should enter the forest, yet something else tells me we should not. I don't know how to proceed, Sigyn. I am lost."

He faced his companion, noticing her face expressed the same desperation. She gasped, and her eyes widened.

"Ismaril!" she cried. "Your sword!"

He felt a sting in his heart and grabbed for the sword, thinking he had lost his weapon on the way, and that Sigyn just noticed. But the blade was there.

"What is wrong with my sword?" he asked.

"Nothing! Just draw it. I sense… well, just draw it!"

Confused, Ismaril hesitated, but then he did what she asked. A swooshing metallic sound from the sheath cut through the compact and suspenseful silence, and then Ismaril raised Gahil toward the sun. Sparks of silvery light reflected on the black surface, spreading bright beams about. A great calm came over the two wayfarers as they stood, and their conflicts and worries wore off.

"Fantastic," Ismaril said.

"Keep it drawn," Sigyn said. "And now, let's continue into the forest."

This time, the push and pull they had experienced earlier was nearly gone, but they must yet force themselves forward until they stood before the thicket of trees. But there was no path leading into the forest; the trees stood narrow, and the undergrowth was too massive—there was no place to enter.

"This is a dead end," Ismaril said.

At that same moment, a part of the forest before them dissolved and turned fuzzy, floating in waves, back and forth, like a mirage flickering in the sunlight. The two companions took a step back, and Ismaril held his sword in front of him with both hands. Suddenly, an arch appeared and turned solid. It was high and impressive, and wide enough for three people to walk abreast; and interwoven branches, decorated with the brightest and most beautiful flowers in many colors, created the shape of the arch. Beyond it, a bright light pulsated, and so brilliant was it that the two spectators could see nothing of what was beyond it. But none of that light entered the field of woes upon which they stood.

"A portal," Ismaril whispered. A surge of immense love hit him deep inside and spread through his body and mind. There was nothing he wanted more than entering through the arch. Sigyn appeared just as mesmerized.

"Is… is this a trap?" she said.

"I don't know. The forest wants us to enter. Perhaps we are still in the Underworld, and this is yet another trick. But it's the only path. Either way, I do not want to go back." For a moment, the flash of his dear friend Zale going through the Portal in Gormoth flushed over him like a river of mud, and he was anguished.

Sigyn nodded. "Usually there is no way back. Every time we have tried, the path whence we came was blocked."

"Then we must not linger here anymore."

A stream of blue light emanated from Gahil and surrounded the two companions. The light was warm and easy on the eye, but within short, it faded out of phase, into a dimension beyond what their eyes could see; but they could still feel its presence around them as if it tried to protect them.

The two travelers exchanged another long gaze to find encouragement in each other's presence. Then Ismaril took a step ahead, holding Gahil as a protective shield, with Sigyn following suit.

And then the forest swallowed them up.

Chapter 3
Spellbound

QUEEN MOËLIA OF AYASIS was furious. How dare someone betray her like this? She just got the news and was pacing the floor. Her maidens rushed in, one after the other, eager to please her, but she dismissed them as soon as they rushed in. The only people allowed in were the council, and when they had all arrived, scattered and upset, the Queen smashed the door to her chamber closed.

"How did this happen?" she cried. "How was it even allowed?"

Then spoke Vrilya, now the Queen's First Seer, "I think we could not have predicted this, Milady. Nothing of this nature and magnitude has ever been done before."

"But the signs were there," another council member, Celestia, said. "There was always a rebel within her."

"She stole Cloudwing, my Chief Dragon," Moëlia said and hammered her fist against the table. "When I get hold of her, I will give her the death penalty. She has betrayed me and the Queendom and made me look like a fool."

The others spoke not, awaiting what they knew would follow.

"And because of her betrayal, Khandur won the battle," the Queen said. "This means I will look less empathetic and compassionate in the eyes of the world. She has destroyed my reputation!"

Silence; heads down.

"Because of her, it will make it more difficult for me to be accepted by my people and other peoples after the war is over."

"My Queen—" Vrilya's voice was low and timid.

"She was to me like a daughter. I am hurt and upset. We must find her and bring her back. I have already sent out guards to protect the other Dragons. This must never happen again!"

"My Queen!" This time, Vrilya's voice was demanding, and the Queen halted her long rant.

"What?"

Vrilya cleared her throat. "We have bigger problems than Naisha."

"Speak out!"

"The people. The congregation outside the palace…"

"Congregation?"

"Yes, Milady. Your maids tried to tell you, but you dismissed them."

"What do they want?"

"They… are not happy with our decision to join the enemy."

"Enemy?" Moëlia cried. "Gormoth is no longer our enemy. They are our allies. We have signed a contract; a peace treaty."

"That is exactly the problem. Our people don't understand. They don't agree to the alliance."

"How many people are there outside?"

"Unknown. A few hundred, perhaps a thousand… We must act."

"They are ignorant fools," the Queen said. "They know not what is best for them and for the Queendom."

"Nonetheless…"

"Yes, yes! I will handle it. I shall tell them a memorandum is on its way and I will post it all over the Queendom for everyone to read."

"How will it be worded?"

Moëlia hesitated ere she spoke. "It will be straightforward and firm in notion. I shall tell our people the peace contract with Gormoth is the best option for us all. It will save the Queendom from destruction and from all our demise. An alliance was the answer, and we will hold up our end of the bargain—pridefully so. I will add that protesting the alliance will lead to a death penalty from here on."

Vrilya gasped when hearing these harsh words, but then something within her calmed her down, and an inner voice told her the Queen was right.

"Adjourned," Moëlia said, and the council accompanied her when she left the chamber. "I still want Naisha," she added as they walked down the hall.

When entering the next floor down, they could all hear it. Outside, the masses were loud. The Queen sighed impatiently and stopped. "Let us behold."

The council changed direction and took the stairs up to the tower and watched the crowd. Indeed, a crowd it was. A large congregation had surrounded the Dragon Court, and they were talking over each other. When some of them spotted the Queen and her council in the tower's balcony area, they pointed and raised their voices some more. The stronger voices repeatedly conveyed the same message, "No alliance with the Dark King!"

Moëlia swept her garment tighter around her, for the winter was bitter. She glanced over at the crowd but said naught. Her head was high, and her eyes, usually mild and compassionate, were now colder than the snow below. The people on the ground turned louder when they got no response from their regent.

Celestia pointed at something beyond the crowd.

"See!" she said, abruptly.

Moëlia leaned forward. And alas! As far away as eyes could behold, a lonesome rider sat upright on a white horse. She quickly grabbed a monocular and zoomed in on the stranger. Then she lowered it and faced her sisters on the council.

"It is him," she said in a deep voice. "The messenger has returned."

Vrilya's eyes and mouth opened wide. "He arrives at an inconvenient time. What does he want? Why is he here?"

"I would presume he is not happy," the Queen said. "Gormoth lost the Battle of Khandur, partly because of us. That is why he is here."

While the sisters of the council studied him, the rider came closer, and his horse kept a slow but steady gait. A wind blew from the east as he approached, and it was suddenly getting colder. His long hair flowed sideward in the wind, and the Gormothan banner he held flapped in the wind, and the wind stirred up light snow about him. In the foreground, people in the congregation stood closer together to endure the unexpected eastern wind, and they refused to disperse. The rider wore neither a helmet nor a hood, but the chilly wind appeared not to bother him. When he reached the crowd, the Ayasisians made room for him, without a second thought, as if their minds were owned. And although the rider carried the flag of Gormoth, with the Dragon and the Sword, no one seemed to notice.

The rider reined his horse before the gates and gazed at the women in the tower.

"Flaradhir, a Messenger of Gormoth, seeking audition!" he said in a sharp and authoritative voice, heard well above the crowd. And thus spoke the Queen, "Let him in!" Her voice reached the gatekeepers, and the gates opened.

The sisterhood descended the stairs to meet Flaradhir in the courtyard. When they arrived, the messenger sat still in his saddle in the middle of the yard, waiting to be honored. Two guards took care of his magnificent horse, and Flaradhir stuck his banner into the ground with dominant force, and no one had the courage to remove it. His lips were merely a thin, straight line, and his eyes, constantly shifting colors, were fixed on Moëlia. No words came through his mouth, and everybody standing in the courtyard felt an intense wave of fear running through them. But the Queen stood straight, inferior but not overly bothered. He was like kin to her, merely there to reprimand and set records straight.

After the group entered the conference room, the Queen offered the messenger a seat, but he declined.

There was a long silence, and Flaradhir kept steady eye contact with the Queen until her breathing became heavier.

"Hail Flaradhir, Messenger of Azezakel," she said. "This is unexpected. What brings you back so soon?" Of course, she knew the answer.

"Well met again," Flaradhir replied, but his tone was frosty and unfriendly, unlike the smoothness he had presented during his last visit. "My King is not pleased with the outcome of the battle outside the gates of Khandur. He implies your Queendom had something to do with the outcome."

The Queen swallowed hard. "We are investigating this as we speak. I have been notified of a betrayal, and we will find the perpetrator and punish her accordingly."

"No!" The courier's harsh reply came instantly. "When she

is found, we want her."

Moëlia hesitated. "Does this imply you know her whereabouts?"

"Of course! She is still in Khandur, believing herself to be safe there. She is not!"

The Queen nodded. "As you wish. If we capture her, we will inform you."

"Do not bother. Leave that to us."

"As you wish."

"What about the crowd outside?"

"I will respond to them."

"Worry not. They will obey you. I expect them to have a change of mindset very soon. No need for you to interfere. Our contract is binding, so we will keep our word. This means we will help handle obstacles on our common path. One day soon, you shall regain full sovereignty and reign in peace. It is merely a matter of time."

The messenger crossed his hands behind his back and started walking in circles around the room.

"Your little traitor and the crowd outside your gates should not be your primary concerns," the Messenger said with eminent authority. "You should direct them toward Emoria."

"Emoria?" the Queen said. "Why is that?"

"You who are present in this room know as well as I do you and your people are the True Originals, the superior spirit of humankind. It is imperative you keep this truth alive through the rough times ahead before we can bring peace to the world. Taëlia needs your strength and your innate power. And it needs your Dragons. News has reached King Azezakel's ears that the Mazosians of Emoria are about to declare their own Divinity and their superiority over you, and they will do it loud and clear. They are planning to go to war against you to prove it, considering you imposters and frauds. And you know from history how ferocious the female Mazosian warriors are."

No words came over Moëlia's lips. How was this possible? The Mazosians had kept themselves outside the wars and politics for millennia.

Gathering her thoughts, she said, "What made them want to take such a drastic step, if it is indeed true?"

"True it is, and their plans are well in progress. If you let them proceed and mobilize, you know they will defeat you, with or without Dragons."

"And what action do you suggest we take?" Vrilya asked.

"Strike before they do!" Flaradhir said.

The sisterhood mumbled between each other and exchanged glances.

"There is no evidence of such an aggression on Emoria's part," Moëlia said. "It is correct they consider themselves the True Originals, but we know better, and so long as they keep themselves in their woods, there is no reason for us to act. We do not want to go to war against Queen Astéamat."

"Evidence?" the Messenger said. "Whose errands do you think Naisha ran? Why was your council in agreement to sign the contract but Naisha was not? When you signed our agreement, should she not have accepted the council's decision as declared by law? She did not. Instead, she stole the Dragons to fight Gormoth's armies; and she succeeded. Forget not the alliance between our countries, Queen. An alliance goes both ways. Naisha's treacherous act was a direct hit not only against Gormoth but against your Queendom. It was she who turned the battle from victory to defeat because of her wicked act. Do you really think Naisha worked on her own?"

The Queen's face turned white. "What are you implying?"

"I am implying nothing. I am wording the exact thing you are thinking: It was Emoria and Queen Astéamat who made her do it. Naisha is working for Emoria, and Queen Astéamat is joining the war, which will delay peace, and possibly prevent it from befalling unless she is stopped."

Many sisters of the council stood up, and they all talked above each other, each one expressing her own feelings. The courier from Gormoth waited until they had calmed down.

"Think about it, Sisters of the Wise Council of Ayasis. Doubt it not. Naisha worked as a spy. She would not single-handedly have done something so foolish as to use your Dragons against us. Emoria has a spell on her; she is their asset and their agent and has been for some time. I should also mention that Khandur is aware of her treason, and they welcome it. Mighty Queen, they are laughing behind your back. Alas! They make a fool of you, and Naisha is boasting about how easy it was to steal the Dragons; and she will do it ten times over if she must!"

The silence in the room was deafening.

"But that is not all," Flaradhir said, and his voice softened. "We have our seers, too, just like you. They have evidently seen what is going to happen. We saw a small group from Khandur, led by Prince Xandur himself, visit Emoria to negotiate. While Khandur concentrates their efforts toward Gormoth, the prince wants Emoria to take on Ayasis."

"This is difficult to believe," Moëlia said. "I do not mean to be skeptical of Gormoth's ability to see the future, but this has yet to happen, if ever. We cannot act on something that may or may not happen in the future."

"This is wise thinking, Milady, and we expected from you to convey that wisdom. Gormoth understands and agrees. Bide your time and see if I am correct. If a Khanduran group visits Emoria soon, you know why. We suggest you send out a few of your scouts close to Emoria's border seven days from now. Let them stay there for yet another week or two and see what happens. When there is no longer any doubt, act accordingly. Does this sound fair?"

What the Messenger had told them now rang true, but something inside the Queen made her refuse to believe.

"Very well," she said. "We shall take you up on it. I will send a few of my people to Emoria's border."

"You are showing your loyalty to our alliance, Queen. Gormoth will remember. And I must add: *Be prepared for war!*"

He bowed before the council, and then he said, "Now, show me the way out. It is time for my departure. My visit here is over."

The council escorted Flaradhir out to the courtyard, and the Messenger mounted his horse.

"Follow me outside," he said.

"We cannot," the Queen said. "The masses by the gate would storm the castle."

Flaradhir grabbed the Gormoth banner he had stuck into the ground and smiled wryly. "They will not. Trust me and come with me to say farewell."

The sisters looked at each other and chose to trust the courier. With a creak and the rattling of chains, the gates opened, and Flaradhir passed through it. The council members reluctantly followed. stopping by the gate.

The congregation that had roamed outside was gone.

Chapter 4
The Doomsday Prophet

ESHAMBLIN WAS A BUSY fishing town on the western shore of the Bay of Aldaer. Those who had heard about it knew it was inhabited by independent, self-sufficient people, hardened to survive under challenging conditions. The town was built over 800 years ago by a tribe of wayfarers who had traveled through the northern wilderness for a long time, living on what the environment could bring them. They were not of the same nomad group as those of Yomar's tribe, but they had the traveling mindset in common. The group found a home for themselves when their journeys led them to the shores of Aldaer Bay. Forests surrounded the area, in which there was game in abundance, and the sea was rich in marine life. Over time, Eshamblin was founded, for the little group of nomads grew, and they built a small village, soon growing into a middle-sized town.

Eshamblin was not for everybody. The town did not see many strangers, except for a few passing through on their journey to somewhere else. Yet, it was not amidst any trail or main road, so few people had errands there. Likewise, merchandise was usually not asked for; the townspeople had what they needed and were known for not mindlessly trusting strangers. Here, everybody attended to their business, but they were yet a tight-knit group, going back a long way, all of them related by blood. Therefore, the stranger who showed up there one day caught the attention of many settlers.

Hoodlum, bent over on Stormcloud in his usual fashion, rode slowly through town. Anyone who came from outside would smell the distinct scent of recently caught fish, but Hoodlum paid no attention to such things anymore. He wore his hood up, and his long beard was all people could see from his face. To anyone who glanced at him in passing saw a vagabond who might fall off his horse at any time from exhaustion, or perhaps because of some illness. Nor did he notice people stopped their chores and followed him with their gaze as he continued east on the main street. People addressed him and attempted to talk to him, but he ignored them and kept riding. There were those who paid enough attention to notice that the horse's hooves left no clattering noise, only silence, and an odor of rotten flesh reached their nostrils when the wind was coming from that direction.

On the outskirts of town, close to the harbor, and with a stunning view over the bay, there were open areas where people could gather and join. Around, there were many inns, where they served fish, meat, and alcoholic beverages, and along the shoreline, there were many massive fountains with stone benches in circles. As dusk was oncoming, the inns were getting populated, and along with an increasing number of alcoholic drinks, voices turned louder. On this evening, a breeze blowing on and off brought a fresh scent of saltwater across until Hoodlum and Stormcloud entered the square.

People sitting around were already intoxicated, so only a very few took notice of the stranger, and those who did failed to pay much attention. The curious rider, hidden under his hood, bothered not to dismount; he merely stopped amid the square and sat still on horseback, watching the crowd there assembled.

As it turned a little darker, the townspeople started pointing at the mysterious rider, who idly sat there, and they commented on his bizarre manners.

"Why are you sitting there, staring at us?"

"Who are you, and what are you doing in our town?"

"Speak up! And what is that stink?"

Hoodlum pulled back his hood and showed his face. His eyes appeared to be glowing.

"Speak you say?" he cried in a high-pitched voice, and with a great impact. Most people stopped talking and watched him. Hoodlum rose in his saddle and pierced people in the crowd with his intense gaze. "Then I shall speak."

The silence that fell was noteworthy, save for some spontaneous murmuring here and there.

"Behold!" Hoodlum said, and his voice shivered. "Behold, for you know not what is awaiting. You sit here, indulging yourselves without care. The end is nigh, and you pretend times are not changing. God is at war, and this war is raging above and below. For eons, God has watched over you and given you this magnificent town to live in. But now, peace and freedom are at stake, and it is time for you to take heed. I say it is time to go to war to defend your benevolent God against forces that plan to do you harm. Your participation is needed and asked for. I am the Harbinger!"

Then Hoodlum's voice got a louder and darker tone to it, demonic and trancelike as he continued.

"I have seen the depth of the Underworld in my visions," he said. "I know what is dwelling there. And all of you shall end there unless you listen up now and act. Are you for or against your God? Fight on his side against evil or be devoured in hell!"

Someone in the crowd, who had had a little more to drink than the rest, said, "Hey, stop preaching, will ya? We're trying to have a merry time here."

"The end is nigh! In these times, good times are bad times!" Hoodlum's answer followed quickly. "Good times mean indulgence and void of care. In Hell shall you burn for voicing such ill manners! By all means, enjoy your last days. For the rest, I am here to summon you. This is the last chance of repentance!"

A few spread laughs came from the crowd, finding Hoodlum's preaching eerie but amusing.

"I don't know how much you've been drinking," one person hollered, "More than me, obviously, for you're not making sense!"

Hoodlum continued as if he had not heard. "The end is nigh! Salvation is across the bay, and you sit here as if nothing was afoot. Our True God, who descended to MAEDIN for you, needs your presence in the imminent war against the infidels. Only through him can you gain your freedom and peace! Grab weapons, set sails, and navigate to Gormoth to take part in the Holy War. You are *all* summoned! For behold, the end is nigh!"

"Hey, stranger, this is getting old," another man said. "Stop your bemusing preaching and leave us alone. It's been a long day."

"Once I was a lost soul," Hoodlum said. "I wandered aimlessly, having nobody. I was an outcast because of my gift, and they shunned me wherever I went. Then I awoke from my long sleep, and I found the light and the truth. It is now my mission to wake others up. I am the Harbinger, and my time has come!"

A young woman, tired of the preacher's manic rant, grabbed a stone from the ground, and drunk from too much wine, threw it toward Hoodlum. The stone barely missed him and landed on the ground behind him. Hoodlum turned silent and raised in his saddle, madly staring at the woman on the bench. He took a deep breath, but the wrath that flooded him from inside was impossible to tame. He yelled from the top of his lungs and pointed a finger at the woman. What happened next silenced the entire crew, who watched in astonishment. The woman levitated above the crowd, screaming in fear. Then Hoodlum stretched his arm forward, and the woman flew into the massive fountain pillar behind. So great was the impact that she broke her neck and fell dead into the water beneath. The crowd jumped up and ran away in many directions, shouting as they went, "Sorcery! Sorcery! God help us!"

"God's mercy is exhausted," Hoodlum cried behind them.

Suddenly, the bay area was void of people many hundred yards north and south, and Hoodlum, ignoring the dead woman in the fountain, calmly rode south along the shoreline, as if little had happened. As he closed in on some inns in the distance, where no one knew what had just occurred, people noticed the lonesome horseman approaching, and some heads turned his way, glancing at him in passing.

Then the unfathomable happened. The few who witnessed it went silent, but then pointed at the stranger and what they beheld. People rose from their chairs with their mouths open, thinking they were dreaming. It was almost dark outside now where they sat, and only the oil lamps were flickering, leaving a spooky light. Some thought it was the darkness that played tricks on them, but others were more convinced that what they saw was real. There were those who were convinced pure evil had visited Eshamblin that night, whilst others insisted it was an act of God.

Before their eyes, and without paying the crowd any attention, Hoodlum steered his old mare toward the dock. Although there was a shift in elevation between the quayside and the waterline below, he rode over the edge and disappeared. No splash followed. The beholders thought the rider was drunk and was now drowning, so they rushed to see. But when they looked out over the water, they sighted the stranger ride out on the bay, away from them. The horse's hooves did not touch the water.

Chapter 5
Another Time and Space

WITH GAHIL DRAWN and held up in front of him, Ismaril, heeled by Sigyn, moved into the forest. When Sigyn looked back, she noticed the entrance disappear behind trees and bushes, and the trees moved closer together, completely covering the portal. Once they entered the forest, they could not go back.

A blue hue encompassed the woodland, and the two wanderers looked about in awe at what they saw. They had encountered many forests on their travels, and they had mostly been magical and frightening, but this was extraordinary. It was a mixed forest, but few of the trees, bushes, or flowers were familiar to them. It was like they had entered a portal into another world, and so uplifted were they that they must stop and inhale from the environment.

A clear path, free from leaves, with a golden-colored quality to the soil, cut further into the forest, with no other paths branching off on either side. The trunks and branches were in silver and purple, but needles and leaves were blue and turquoise, and there was a shimmer to them, with an occult source they could not detect. Everywhere was birdsong, creating the most wonderful harmonies, but although Ismaril and Sigyn tried to get a glimpse of them, they showed themselves not to the wayfarers. The sunbeams, searching for a way through the overhang, were greenish-yellow and emitted a perfect temperature, so the wanderers did not get hot or cold. This was indeed a magic place.

"I don't know where we are or where we are going," Sigyn said, and her voice was soft, as if she wanted not to disturb the peace in the forest.

"This is the most beautiful place I have ever seen," Ismaril said in a dreamlike voice. "I wish I could make this my home." Then he glanced at his sword, and a wave of shame washed over him. Quickly, he put Gahil back in its sheath and covered the hilt with his cape. There was no glamor in carrying a weapon in here.

"There is only one problem," Sigyn said. "I see nothing here we can eat."

"I am starving. If these trees at least would bear fruits—"

And behold! Suddenly, many trees around them grew fruits of all kinds. They gasped and exchanged glances.

"How is this possible?" Sigyn said. "These fruits were not there a moment ago. Do dreams and thoughts come true at this place?"

Ismaril carefully removed one that was round and with a yellow embedding peel from its branch. He squeezed it lightly, smelled it, and looked at his companion.

"I wonder if it is edible."

"Of course it is. You wished it into existence, remember? Let us both try it."

The peel came off easily, and the juicy fruit was red and inviting. Without further ado, they dug into it with great enthusiasm. Tasting like a mix of orange and lemon, it was delicious, and it stilled their hunger and quenched their thirst. Each cell lit up with an inner fire, and all tiredness vanished.

"I have never felt so good and uplifted in my life," Sigyn said and laughed.

"I wonder what else I can wish for," Ismaril said. "Perhaps I should ask for something like…"

"No!" Sigyn grabbed his arm and squeezed it hard, and she got serious. "I have a feeling we should not ask in vain. Our hunger is stilled, and so is our thirst. Let us show gratitude and not ask for more."

Ismaril nodded. She was right.

As they strode farther into the woods, the golden soil turned into stones, placed in the ground in complex patterns; but inside them was a luster so bright that it must be magnificent to behold when the day darkened, and they shone in all the colors of the rainbow. After following the path for not too long, it took on three different directions—straight, left, and right. In front of the three-way crossroads, and hither, there rose a golden fountain with a stream of water sprouting a few inches up into the air. At the brim sat small, many-colored birds, dipping their beaks into the water. When noticing the two wanderers, they tilted their heads and looked at them curiously, and without fear. Beyond the fountain, the three pathways led to a tall hedgerow, stretching left and right as far as they could see, and each one vanished into a portal in the hedgerow. Great white light emanated from them, making it impossible to know what was beyond.

The wanderers stopped at the fork in the path.

"What now?" Sigyn said.

Ismaril shrugged. "I guess one choice is as good as the other. We have no way of telling one from another. I say, let us pick the one amidst."

But it let him not pass. When he put his hand to the portal, the white light turned into a mirror. He watched himself and jumped back. What he saw was not what he expected. His face in the mirror was grotesque and frightening. The eyes were flashing red, and his mouth twisted in a demonic pose, full of wrath and vengeance. His voice growled back at him, and the reflection drew Gahil and lashed out to kill. Ismaril shrieked and fled backward. Slowly, the reflection dissolved.

―

"Fear not," said a voice. "Nothing here will harm you."

Ismaril and Sigyn spun around, and behind them stood five of the most impressive figures. Extraordinary in stature, they reached over seven feet in height, red-haired, and strong-armed to the eye. And they were all women. They wore no clothing, save for skirts made of flowers around their waists, and their skin had a golden-brown luster to it. They gave the impression of giant warriors, but they carried no weapons. Although Ismaril knew how to fight and felt intimidated by these five figures, it occurred not to him to draw his sword. He and Sigyn stood frozen, staring at the five strangers.

Although she was not the tallest of them, one woman at once stood out as a leader, and she wore a band of yellow flowers in her hair.

Her green eyes were mild when she spoke.

"Welcome, Ismaril Farrider and Sigyn Archesdaughter."

Ismaril tensed up. "How do you know our names?"

The woman smiled. "You expected you, worried whether you would be in the right mindset to enter our land, but you have both done well enough."

"Who are you, and where are we?" Sigyn asked.

"Pardon me," the woman said. "My name is Ayashakim, and I am Queen Astéamat's land captain. You have entered the Enchanted Woods of Emoria from the eastern passageway."

"Emoria!?" Ismaril and Sigyn said in chorus. "But we are regular humans. How can we enter your land?"

"Normally, you cannot," Ayashakim said. "You need permission for that, and you must not take too much low frequency with you into this realm. But enough of this now. Queen Astéamat wants to meet with you."

Ayashakim made a hand gesture, and the two visitors turned and kept going; but when they did, they noticed there was no hedgerow anymore, and there were no portals. Instead, the forest and the path continued as before, deeper into the unknown.

"Where did the hedge go?" Ismaril said.

"It was never there," the leader said. "You created it with your mind. Perhaps you thought you should not be here in our forest, and your own thoughts created an obstacle."

"Then what is actually real and what is my creation?"

Ayashakim laughed. "That is an excellent question. You may ponder that."

"And the mirror? The attack?"

"It takes some time to get used to Emoria when coming here from the lesser lands. You were facing your own fears and demons. More things for you to think about."

Ayashakim smiled and took the lead, followed by Ismaril and Sigyn. The other four Mazosians formed the tail. The path they followed was astonishing. In awe, Ismaril watched twinkling yellow lights popping up on both sides of the pathway, and he learned they were Elementals—ether spirits, often called *Dream Weavers*. He recalled the Dream Weavers in Dreamwood, and it seemed so long ago. He shivered at the thought. Although he had later learned from Kirbakin that these spirits were not evil, they filled him with fear and an urge to recluse. But these Dream

Weavers were different; they had no intention of waylaying or manipulating wayfarers. He glanced at Sigyn, and her eyes told him she felt the same way.

"The Dream Weavers are, to a large extent, responsible for keeping this realm intact," Ayashakim clarified. "The ether spirits are the leading Elementals, overseeing the other four, those of water, earth, air, and fire. In Emoria, all of them are in balance, and thus, these forests can continue to exist in this dimension. It is then our human task to act under Elemental Laws."

"Is that not difficult?" Sigyn asked.

"No, it is much more difficult to act in your ways in your sphere of existence and influence. To us, our ways are natural and require little effort."

"If all the Elemental forces are present here, are here Gnomes, too?"

"Yes." Ayashakim pointed at a pine tree with a massive trunk on the right side of the trail. Sigyn laughed hastily, reminded of the gigantic oak trees growing on and about Green Peaks, where they first encountered Kirbakin. There was a sting in her heart when thinking about the little charming being, so faithfully following them all the way to the cave with the Book of Secrets. Her mind returned to the moment of their departure, and a moment of grief pierced her. On the pine trunk was a tiny door leading to the interior of the tree. It was the same kind of door she had seen at Green Peaks. She told the Mazosians briefly about their adventures in Dreamwood and at Green Peaks.

"The Dream Weavers of Dreamwood differ from those who live here," Ayashakim said. "The ones you encountered are from your world, and over time, the evil that resides there has corrupted them. Not to say they are evil, but they have forgotten some of their original purpose."

"Then what about the Gnomes in our world?"

"We just had the honor of meeting one of them. The same Kirbakin you so kindly told me about just now. Your dense world has affected even him."

"Kirbakin was here?" Ismaril stopped, making everybody else halt. "What was he doing here, and when was this?" Beside him, Sigyn gasped in anticipation.

"He accompanied a pilgrim. You know him. His name is Raeglin. They were here only a few weeks ago, based on how you count time, but they left for Khandur, from what we understand. They wanted us to join them in their war."

Ismaril spontaneously grabbed the Mazosian's arm, and his eyes locked with hers.

"Are you joining?"

Ayashakim shook herself loose, and Ismaril realized his mistake and stepped back.

"We once were warriors, but no more. If we engaged in human wars, our realm would fall. We worked hard before we could stabilize Emoria in this dimension. Now when we have found the equilibrium, we will not go back to your world of evil."

Ismaril's shoulders drooped, but he said no more about it. He thought he understood, but had hoped for another answer.

The group continued into the forest. After a quick stride, they came upon a stream, rushing on its path between the thicket, and it appeared and vanished, to and fro as the group continued. Soon, the water turned wider and forceful, but the sound of the rapid was soothing to Sigyn's ears, and her spirit soared. When she mentioned this to Ayashakim, the Mazosian said, "You feel the lifting energies of this place now, do you not? It takes a while for strangers to connect with it. You shall notice that all the worries and burdens of your life outside this realm will wash away whilst following the path of the water. The Nymphs will wash them off you."

"The Nymphs?"

"Yes, the freshwater spirits, in contrast to the Maermaids, who are saltwater spirits, residing in seas and oceans."

Indeed, when Sigyn gazed upon the running water, some larger waves seemed to ascend above the surface in a crescent-like figuration. A wonder to her eyes it was to see these waves turn into humanlike female beings, shaped by the water, forming entire bodies. From surfing graciously on top of the stream in elevated formations, they occasionally fell back and merged again with the river, only to once more rise above it; and thus, it happened over and over. Whilst watching them, a ripple of joy spread within Sigyn.

Ayashakim noticed it. "Now you sense it," she said. "The wave inside you. Your body comprises water, and the water signifies a substantial part of your spirit. The Nymphs help you connect to it."

"I feel it, too!" Ismaril said with a smile.

"Those with a heart will experience it."

The Mazosian's last statement pinched him. He never thought he had *hearts*, at least not in a good sense. He noticed Ayashakim studying him and his reaction, but she remained silent. Instead, she changed subjects.

"Come now," she said. "This is not the route we would normally take. We have moved westward from Hallow Peaks, where you entered our realm; but only so you could get cleansed by the Nymphs. It was not for your benefit alone that we sidetracked; it was also for ours. The more cleansed you are, the less danger Emoria will be in by allowing your presence. You are not of the same vibration as we are, and it will noticeably affect our forests. Now, we are heading south to see our Queen."

After having passed through an area of mixed forest, the trees now turned into what Ismaril could best describe as androgynous. Each tree comprised both leaves and needles, as if deciduous and coniferous trees had merged. A greenish-yellowish hue blanketed the forest; and close together the trees stood, rising like divine thrones from the rich undergrowth of blue grass and colorful flowers, with branches and boughs bent over the trail, giving a sense of walking through a vault or a tunnel with no end in sight. The leaves and needles sprouted in the most unusual color patterns, almost as if they were glowing. Although the sunlight could not pass through the thick overhang, the forest was bathing in light from these amazing colors, enhanced by the sparks of the Dream Weavers floating about through sparse spaces between trees. Ismaril inhaled the fragrance from the environment. It reminded him of pine and the many fresh flowers growing in the childhood forests of Lindhost; all the places he loved to wander about in solitude long ago. Yet the fragrance in this forest was so much stronger. Ismaril's spirit was unusually uplifted, and the yearning in his heart transformed into an odd recognition. Ever since his childhood, when hiking through the woods, an abstract and agonizing longing always resided within—a wish to go home, but he knew not what or where home was. It was too nebulous to grasp. Now it felt like home was here, and he wished to be nowhere else. All concerns seemed to be from another lifetime, or something he had only heard of in tales but was experienced by someone else. The sorrows of the world seemed not to bother him anymore, and all he could experience was delight.

And it filled the wood with birdsong he had never heard. As if they were all connected, they seemed to sing in chorus with one another, regardless of species. Here were no conflicts, and he could perceive there was no death, only harmony. He understood why these people wanted nothing to do with the cold and emotionally barren world outside this heavenly construct. It was like exiting a place of howling winds, biting blizzards, and devilish cold, void of love and compassion, only to enter a place of eternal bliss, where the garment of the old world washed away, not to return.

In this magical place, time seemed to not exist; neither did hunger nor thirst or tiredness. The path rolled its carpet of cobbled stones, plowing through the thicket of the forest, which seemed to embrace them with love and compassion rather than imposing. Although magical, the sense was natural, as if this environment had always been embracing them, albeit only in the invisible world. And the deeper into the forest they strode, the more euphoric their minds were.

There appeared to be no dusk here, nor any dawn or nighttime. The forest was always lit with the same entrancing energies, encouraging the wanderers to linger here. After having walked for what seemed to be a full day, the overhanging trees retreated to either side of the trail, as if they graciously, and in amazement, opened to a much wider space of wonderment. Once more, the sun, with its green light, shone from an open sky, and the landscape shifted before their sight., They now stood at the top of a hill, gazing down over a valley or the bluest, most shimmering grassy slope and canyon where few trees grew; but a creek dividing the land ran across from east to west. Here the company stopped, and the Mazosians sat down in the grass, watching the newcomers gasping at what they beheld: Across the canyon, another hill ascended, but it was higher than the one from which they gazed. Yet, that was not what caught their attention. When they looked upward, above the hill's summit, they saw an entire city emerging among the clouds. Half cloaked and half visible, it appeared to be hanging in the air without support. Tall towers, castles, and buildings of the most magnificent architecture tickled their eyes and soothed their weary souls; for this was a city of majesty and wonder, and not a city of busyness. Here was a city of thriving and glory. In emerald, the buildings shone as if polished with the most impeccable thoroughness and in the very minute of details. But most astonishing was the music. Out from this city, in the clouds emerged the most harmonious sounds, forming a melody so elevating and eloquent that Ismaril and Sigyn stilled in their movements and just listened. It was not a loud symphony; it was a simple movement, perfect for the ear, vibrating such that it affected both spirit and soul. Tears streamed down Sigyn's cheeks, and Ismaril had a lump in his throat. Were they in Heaven?

"Not in Heaven," one Mazosian laughed as if she could read their minds. "You're still in MAEDIN, mind you; we are yet in your world, and you are in ours. But all you have experienced in the realm you once had but you forsook. Those in control made you do so—it was part of a plan, orchestrated by those who had merely their own interests in mind. Yet remember, you fell for the sake of it. Your fault it was not, but you exited Paradise."

"What is this place?" Ismaril whispered in a deep out-breath and opened his arms to make the gesture.

"Over there is Caëgrun," Ayashakim said. "It is also called Elverstone in the common tongue. Few are those outside Emoria who have heard of it. Queen Astéamat must hold you in high regard."

"Caëgrun..." Sigyn pondered over the name. "What is it?"

"It is Queen Astéamat's city, of course," said Ayashakim and laughed. "This is where her palace is. That is where we are heading."

"But... but it is in the clouds," Sigyn said.

Ayashakim's eyes twinkled as she met Sigyn's confused gaze. "So? Is that a hindrance?"

"Well..."

"Look, I understand your confusion, but please do not be concerned. I am here, my people are here with you, and we go there often. Again, shred your fears."

"Azezakel's Dragons must easily spot Caëgrun," Ismaril said, and his voice was dry. "Why don't they target it?"

"Do you think Azezakel's Dragons have any impact here?" Ayashakim said. "I told you when we met, we are concerned about the level at which the two of you vibrate, for you are not up to par with the frequency of this realm. Yet you vibrate higher than Azezakel and his Dragons. Unless we allow you, you have no access to this realm, and no quality to experience it the way it truly is. Why do you think the Black King and his servants can even recognize what is there when they, in their ignorance, fly over our lands? To them, it is merely a forest. They know where we dwell, but they can gain no access here, nor can they perceive our reality. Once, the entire world was inaccessible to them, but alas! They manipulated you, and in your naivety, you invited them here."

"Then why is your realm safe?" Ismaril asked. "Were you not once one of us?"

"After being the most ferocious warriors that ever existed in the world, our tribe realized war is not the answer, but we refused to be manipulated, for we saw through the evil in the depths of the Dark Kings' minds, so we saved Emoria from influences and strengthened it with our creative magic. And we solidified the borders. Ever since, Emoria has been a closed-in part of Taëlia."

"So, you are indeed the true Originals?"

"This is what those from Outside call us. Yes, we are in our original form, and we have sustained our creative abilities in that we can still create with our minds and can mostly manifest what we create. Now, even this realm has declined a little, affected as we are part of the environment outside. Yet we do not differ from you, for even you are Originals, but you fell and created a world for yourself through aggression and vengeance, until your innate creative abilities got lost."

"And the Ayasisians? They claim to be the remaining Originals, and so do you."

Ayashakim sighed. "Yet they live in your realm, do they not? How then can they be the Originals, such as you define the term? They cannot practice creative magic in your realm; for it is too dense and emotionally polluted. Their magic happens outside their minds; they need assistance to practice it, making it far more inferior. Even they lost much of their abilities."

"Was that what I did before you came?" Ismaril said, now sitting up straight. "You said I created the hedge."

The five Mazosians laughed in chorus. "So you did," Ayashakim said. "You regain some abilities when you are here, but behold, for you can just as easily lose them; it has everything to do with how in tune you are with nature around you. Here, the

Elementals are greatly active, and it is through the elements you manifest your mind's creations, using imagination and thought."

Ismaril sat in his own thoughts for a moment and gazed far out into the clouds and the city. To his astonishment, a huge white bird, resembling an eagle, but with a wingspan like a Dragon's, flew under the clouds, and on its back sat a Mazosian. Then it soared and disappeared into the clouds toward the city.

"That was not a Dragon," Ismaril said.

"No, that was a Khibi," Ayashakim said. "They live only here in Emoria and cannot live anywhere else, for they are native to this environment. Should they leave our realm, they would die. Horses we have not, but the Khibis are to us what horses are to you, and they will joyfully carry us on their backs so we can quickly fly from one part of our realm to another. Often, though, we prefer to walk, for we love the environments we have created, and we merge nature with who we are."

Sigyn looked around, nervously. "How do we get to Elverstone?" she said. "I see no road, no bridges, or any other form of entrance. And none of us can fly."

Ayashakim smiled, and her green eyes sparkled as she spoke. "Or maybe you can? Indeed, you must fly, or you cannot enter Caëgrun. Get on your feet, and I will show you how to get there…"

Chapter 6
Red Sails and Longboats

KING BARAKUS STOOD bent and stern, gazing north from the tallest tower. Whilst in deep thought, he watched the snow melt on the mountainsides, busy ridding themselves of the burden of excessive unfrozen water; and many rushing streams and forceful waterfalls formed, throwing themselves down from the heights with ferocity into the gaping abyss. A mild breeze came in from the west; a promise of re-approaching summer; and in the open sky, a warm, caressing sun shone over the lands. Yet, it gladdened him not. His mind returned to the time of his youth before wars and grief knocked on his door and let themselves in, uninvited. His heart weighed heavy, his body showed itself to be torn and crippled, and more than all that, he mourned the betrayal of his youngest son. Exxarion had always been strong-willed, but who suspected such darkness and jealousy dwelling in his son's heart? *I have failed as a just father when raising my sons,* he thought, lacking the guiding hand of a loving wife and the nurturing mindset of a mother; for alas! The queen had died at childbirth, forcing him to raise them alone.

Resentment and bitterness disturbed his thoughts. He had failed not only as a father but also as a regent and a vigorous leader, for he was not as powerful and courageous as his praised ancestors; scared and insecure in battle, and too many times making ill decisions. The Battle of Khandur turned out victorious, but would have been lost unless one person had intervened and defeated the Enemy. What all his troops failed to do under his leadership, a female sorcerer from Ayasis and her Dragons accomplished in an instant. During his darkest moments, Barakus considered it might have been best if Khandur went down, and he with it. Now, his people praised Naisha as their savior, and they saluted her in the streets, while they barely mentioned their king's name. There was no glory and pride reserved for him, and it clouded his heart with shame.

Amidst his deepest thoughts, one of the king's chief officers, a major, joined him in the tower and took the attention away from his troubled mind.

"My King," the major said, "I have news."

Barakus glanced at his officer, but his eyes showed no keen interest. "If so, may it bring us hope," he said.

"This we do not know yet, Your Majesty. But your intervention is called for."

The king sighed. "Say it!"

"Halfway up Gray River, farmers spotted three black longboats with red sails moving upstream."

"Rhiandorian pirate ships," Barakus said in a whisper. "What are they doing on our land? Are they here to declare war?"

The major shrugged. "It could be."

Barakus thought for a while. "Gather two hundred horsemen. I am riding out, and Prince Xandur will join me."

"But Sire, you are still on the mend," the major said. "You cannot possibly—"

"Tell me not what I can or cannot do," the king barked. "I am your King, damn it! Get out of here and execute my order! The afternoon sun shall watch me leave, and I will confront the trespassing pirates ere they reach the mountain range. If they are here to declare war, none of them shall see their homeland again. Not one! Now, hurry!"

—

The king's men, with the monarch in the front and with Prince Xandur on his right, rode south in great haste down Kingshold Road. It was barely past midday when they left Ringhall, and it was the king's intent to reach Gray River via the Road to Ayasis by sunset. Then they would encamp for the night and await the longboats from there. The road was drying up after being covered with melting snow for days. There was no Spring looming, for the curse of winter had lifted, and the season returned to what it had been before the curse was cast—late summer.

Barakus sat straight in his saddle, clinching his jaws not to show his men he was hurting. The phantom pain in his lost arm was excruciating, and the mending wound, where they amputated it, pulsated and ached as if struck over and over with a hot iron. And it got worse the longer he was on horseback. The monarch knew his son noticed, but he appreciated Xandur's silence.

After a few hours, the company reached the three-way crossing and turned west on the Road to Ayasis. Here were only open fields, clad in sparse vegetation: Low thorny gray bushes with some green in spreads grew in patches to the south and to the west, and in the north, the foothills of the Western Mountains stood like pointy gray arrowheads, still shaking off the overcoats of a merciless winter. There was no wind, which pleased the king, for this meant the Rhiandorian ships must slow down, and the sailors take to the oars. Thus, Barakus' men would have the advantage of reaching the upper part of the river ahead of the pirates.

It was already past sundown when the knights of Khandur could hear the Gray River roar somewhere before them in the dark. Barakus spurred on his horse to cover the last distance, and when they reached the bank of the river, the company stopped. Xandur jumped off his horse and helped his one-armed father off his stallion. The river moved fast here, so close to the mountains, hurrying on its way to the sea in the south; and the wind was chilly when the sun had closed its warming eye and left the night watch to the moon and the stars. The king ordered his men to raise the tents, and he put a few on guard, should the pirates show up before dawn. Yet, this was highly unlikely, for the river was deceptive in places, and even experienced seamen, which these pirates were, would not risk their boats running aground in the dark. The fleet had more than likely anchored somewhere along the way.

Barakus and Xandur sat awake outside the purple Royal Tent for a little while. Two oil lamps burned, creating a ghostly flicker in the dark. There they sat in silence, contemplating, and Xandur spoke first.

"Father, your face is tense and your eyes distant. Is there anything I can do to ease your pain?"

"Yes," Barakus said, and his voice was low but firm. "You can avoid talking about it. A wounded child, I am not, and I prefer not being treated as such."

Xandur knew better than to insist.

"Then, let us speak of plans," he said. "Little do we know what the longboats want, but if they want war against Khandur, we may be in trouble. We lost many soldiers in the battle, and we are not as prepared as we used to be."

The king stared out into the night, and he frowned. "This so-called fleet is here to give us a message. They do not have manpower enough to attack with the few oarsmen they sent. They are here to talk." The monarch hesitated, "But if war against our Kingdom is what they wish for, I stand by my word. None of these emissaries shall then return to Rhiandor. No more will I allow insults against me and my people. I will consider the smallest sign of such a declaration of war."

"Father, we must tread lightly. The pirates are warriors at heart. Though they may have been peaceful for many long years now, they were once of the infamous pirate tribe of Piscas Urash. They parted ways with them in the past, but that same pirate's blood runs through their veins, and blood can be thick. Perhaps they have formed a new alliance. The Pirate Island villains are few in comparison, but it is the intention that counts. If the two tribes merge, we have a powerful enemy, operating in the south and in the west."

"Two in the west," Barakus objected. "Forget not the Queendom of Ayasis."

To that, Xandur said nothing and let his father continue.

"Do you understand what all this means?" the king said. "Khandur stands alone against enemies lurking in all directions. My people were so concerned when the enemy surrounded us before the Battle of Khandur. Yet we cannot underestimate the allusive siege we have been under thereafter. Azezakel has indeed been tactful. He has recruited all the nations, kingdoms, and queendoms in all quarters. Thus, we are under a passive siege, unable to move in any direction. They have surrounded us, Xandur. Alas! We have already lost the war."

Barakus sighed and took a deep breath. "One more time shall I go to battle, and when I do, I am going to give it all, one-armed as I am. And my people shall fight with me. Even if everything is in vain, our defeat shall at least cost them!"

There was nothing Xandur could say to that. He knew his father was most likely correct, and if they lost, no one was going to sing their praise and write poems about their last bitter fight for freedom that never came to be. In contrast to his father, the prince refused to give up. Although he did not know why, hope had yet to leave him.

"Let us go to bed, father," he said. "The night is late, and tomorrow we will possibly encounter the pirates."

"You go to bed," the king said. "My thoughts are too vivid, and sleep will not take me. Perhaps later."

The next morning came, and when Xandur awoke, King Barakus still sat outside the tent where he had left him.

"Father, did you not get any sleep?"

"No, I have too much on my mind." Then the king stood and gazed toward the horizon. "We will get another cloudless day," he said, and his voice was now loud and forceful. "This means we can see the ships clearly as they arrive." He glared down the river, running in a straight line for perhaps another eight-hundred paces, before it took a left turn and disappeared behind trees and brush.

Xandur went off to wake the soldiers, and the rest of the morning they spent waiting. Then, when the sun had left its position in zenith, one soldier pointed to where the river bent.

"Ships!" he cried.

Barakus and Xandur rushed closer to the riverbank to see the first longboat coming up the river. The wind had abated once more, so the sailors had folded the sail, and many oars stuck out from the sides of the longboat, forcing it forward toward the Khandurans by strong-armed oarsmen. Soon, two more ships showed behind the first, and after them, there were no others.

Black and threatening, the longboats approached, gliding upstream against the current. In the fore, the carved face of a Dragon stared ahead, grim and unforgiving. With the ships well proportioned, they left the impression they could cross a mighty ocean when called for. Amidst the decks were elevated wooden cabins, and each ship hosted fifty powerful men, a hundred and fifty altogether. On the shore, two hundred Barakus' men stood lined up in silence, prepared to meet the southerners.

When the first longboat closed in, Barakus ordered his men to draw their weapons and hook arrows to the bowstrings. Then he stepped forward and raised his arm with the palm of his hand put forward.

"Halt in the name of the Divine Kingdom of Khandur!" he said, and his voice was deep and authoritative. The foreign oarsmen stopped rowing, and the front longboat came to a stop in line with the monarch and his soldiers, and all three ships cast anchors. The oarsmen remained seated, and a few, who appeared to be officers because of their wide-brimmed black hats decorated with white eagle feathers, stood up on the decks. One officer, who seemed in charge of the front ship, positioned himself a few steps before the others and spoke.

"Hail, King Barakus of the Kingdom of Khandur," he said in a gruff voice. A sudden wind took his black, braided hair, falling long to his waist, and his thick, drooping mustache, braided at the edges, made him appear stern and dangerous. His left hand rested on the hilt of a saber that was attached to a broad golden belt made of fine silk fastened around the waist of his long, black coat. "We come in peace if you want it."

"That remains to be seen," Barakus said. "Many years have passed since we last saw each other, Lord Zarabaster, and now, unexpected and suddenly, you have trespassed into our Kingdom without permission, accompanied by a large group of your armed sailors, an action more warlike than peaceful."

"For this, I apologize," Lord Zarabaster said. "We intended not to trespass, but I regret to say that your border is ill-guarded. There was no one from whom we could get counsel. In fact, the border was wide open. Thus, we continued up the river until someone had the courtesy of stopping us."

"It may not have dawned on you down there in the south, but we were attacked, and a great battle took place outside our north gate," Barakus said. "We expected not any invasion from Rhíandor, so we guard more pertinent locations instead."

"No reason to be hostile," Zarabaster said. "We come not to invade. I traveled here in person, as you can see, and with a great risk for my safety, would you choose to confront us in battle. We are quite aware of what happened outside your borders, King, and therefore we are here. As I said, we come in peace."

"So you say, but peace is hardly a word that has relevance

these days. You choose to see me when the battle is over, after my people suffered death and despair on the battlefield in a fight we nearly lost. Great would your support have been if you would have come to our aid then. But nonetheless, the relationship between our nations has always been lukewarm at best and hostile at worst, albeit we have had no serious conflicts. Why are you approaching me now?"

"The times call for that we all must act. War will come upon us all, perhaps later than sooner, to our land, but it will come. It is better to unite, even if our foreign relation has more to wish for and our ideals differ. We are here to aid, Your Majesty. Let me and my men step ashore, and we can speak without the need to raise our voices."

The king was quiet for a moment, and then he spoke. "Very well, but on one condition: leave your weapons onboard."

"That we refuse to do! You trust us not, you say, but trust is always mutual, not so? If you don't trust us, why would we trust you?"

"Not a good start of a negotiation."

"This is not a negotiation, it's an offer to help. Admittedly, the intention is not only to assist but also to secure our own borders should Gormoth attack us in the future. We shall keep our weapons when we leave our longboats, and if that is a problem, we must turn and sail back home with mission inept."

Prince Xandur glanced at his father and nodded subtly, suggesting his father would accept.

"I will allow it," Barakus said. "But if anyone attempts to even subtly reach for their hilts, we will act accordingly."

It was an impressive group of pirates that stood in front of the Khanduran knights. Although dressed in casual clothing, wearing white, blue, or gray linen shirts and baggy trousers, strung at the ankles, they looked at least as capable of fighting battles as the armored knights.

"Let us stay close to our boats for now," Zarabaster said. "We want to keep an eye on them at all times."

"Then let us sit right here," the king said. "This place is as good as any."

Both groups sat down in a circle next to the riverbank with the Lord Zarabaster, King Barakus, and Prince Xandur in the midst.

"My commiserations," the Lord said. "Did you lose your arm in battle?"

"So I did," the king said. "But I still have my sword arm, and it is yet as strong as in my youth."

"This is good to hear, for you will need it. We failed to aid you in the battle, for we are no longer pirating or taking part in conflicts and wars unless absolutely needed to save our great nation."

"And you have no alliance with the pirates on Piscas Urash?" the king asked.

"That we have not!" said Zarabaster, puffing up his chest. "If necessity calls, we will rather fight them than to negotiate. They are savages, and they side with Azezakel!"

Barakus raised his brows. "So, you are in with the Goddess? Your adherence to the religion of NIN.AYA is good news."

"I must disappoint you," Zarabaster said. "We acknowledge no Sky God or Sky Goddess, as little as any other deity. The only *God* we know is Azezakel, and he is of the Underworld. For him, we feel nothing but spite. My proud people have learned that if anything needs to be done, we must do it ourselves, and not rely on a deity that does not exist or wishes to harm us. We are a practical people; that is how we survive and thrive. We usually negotiate or partner with nobody. Therefore, us coming here is a privilege; but we come for selfish reasons more than anything else. We care little about other nations than our own. Their business is their business, but strange are these times, and exceptions are called for."

"If so, how can you help?"

"We intended to ask you that same question. How can we serve best?"

King Barakus studied the Lord's crew, one by one, where they sat beside each other in the ring, facing him. Gruesome and fearless they appeared, and their gaze was penetrating and as cold as the winter that was. None of them spoke, and neither of them moved as he watched them.

"How many men does Rhíandor have at its convenience?" he asked.

"Maybe 12,000."

"And they all know how to sail?"

Zarabaster's dark-skinned face turned darker. "Insult me

not," he said. "We are seafarers. You should know that!"

"Then you can be of great help. Anúria, our colony in the northeast, is in great danger. The Commander General of the colony has rebelled and is now planning on invading Rhuir on his own. It is a treacherous act, but also bound to fail, and then we lose our most important outpost, so close to Gormoth. The Commander General must be stopped, but not killed. I want him sent to me unharmed, but the invasion of Rhuir must be evaded, and if it is too late, your 12,000 men might be what we need to take on Rhuir."

"Rebellion, you say. And who is this rebellious Commander you speak of?"

Barakus hesitated, and his eyes stared into nothing. "He is my son, Exxarion."

Zarabaster sat up straight, and his eyes widened. Then he said with a wry smile, "Your son, indeed?" He turned around and waved at two men from his crew. "Earlham and Royden, come over here!" he commanded. Two young men stood and stepped forward. Both resembled the Lord in looks, but younger.

"These are my two eldest sons," Zarabaster said, and his black eyes gleamed when he put his arms around them. "Earlham is my firstborn, and Royden came second, with six more waiting at home. Never would any of them betray me, not even under the cruelest torture. Is that not true?" He poked his eyes into them, one first, and then the other.

"This is true, father," they said, and they seemed to mean it.

Zarabaster nodded and locked eyes with Barakus. "Aye! I raise my children firmly to be faithful. If fate will have it, one of them shall succeed me one day, but what good would it be if he cannot rule justly and with honor?"

Barakus' face hardened. "You may raise them to be faithful, but you raise them with terror. I can see it in their gaze, and that will make inefficient leaders…"

Earlham and Royden stood up, at the same time grabbing the hilts of their sabers. In response, a dozen Khanduran knights knocked their arrows. For a moment, the atmosphere was tense and threatening, one party waiting for the other to act further. Then Zarabaster signaled to the boys to sit, which they reluctantly did.

"Enow," the Lord said. "Let us return to the proper

discussion, for our people and yours are not on good terms with each other, save for a common goal. So, you want us to rescue Anúria for you, and remove from the Kingdom a reckless Commander, who happens to be your second-born. Why would I put my men's life at risk for such a task that does not concern us?"

"Well, it would indeed benefit us both. If Anúria can be saved, or an invasion of Rhuir will be successful, we have gained much ground. We can hold on to our outpost and keep a watching eye on Azezakel and his son, Nibrazul, King of Rhuir. It would be ideal if you and your men would remain in that region, which is a good strategic move; it would make Azezakel think twice before invading Anúria, and we here in Khandur have time to recoup and regroup after the battle we just endured, preparing my army for further defense or attack."

Zarabaster picked up a pipe from his pocket and lit it. A mild scent of tobacco lingered amidst the circle of men.

"As you well know, we are seamen, and we live on what comes out of the sea and the ocean. We often sail far and wide to catch good, fat fish. Lately, our sailors have had company on some of their trips."

"What kind of company?"

"Maermaids."

"Elementals!" King Barakus' attention increased. "Are they bringing news?"

"Yes, news of evil tidings. The Maermaids watch over the seas and the oceans, and they know what happens in the waters, far and wide, from north to south, and from west to east. The fish are dying for no reason, and it is harder for us to find food. It is the work of Azezakel, the Black King. The Maermaids do what they can, but there are very dark forces at play. This, too, must stop. I am concerned about what will happen to my nation if we have less access to marine life. It concerns if we are away from home for too long. This means we have fewer fishermen who can bring food to the tables from an already decreasing food supply, and my people will starve. I will take you up on your plan, but in return, we need your help. We need you to share your food supplies with the soldiers I send to Anúria, and we need you to share supplies with the people left behind—our elderly, women, and children."

Barakus nodded. "That can be arranged," he said. "Anything

else?"

Zarabaster shrugged and shook his head.

"Then I am expressing my gratitude to you and your people," Barakus said. "When can you leave?"

"I need about a week after our return to Rhíandor. I will lead my fleet, and these two sons of mine will be my captains. My nation is going to war."

Prince Xandur looked at his father, and he said, "I will go with them with your permission. I know we are short of people, but I would like to use our own fleet, or a section thereof, and join the Lord. Exxarion is my brother, and I want to handle this matter with him in person, if possible. As you mentioned, to secure his safety."

"Then you have my permission," Barakus said. "I want Exxarion returned here. I care not whether you bring him to me in chains and in a cage, so long as he is alive and not harmed. You can use four ships and a crew for each, but that is all we can spare."

"And that is all I need."

"Very well," Zarabaster said. "We will sail ten days from now. Our fleets shall merge at the southern tip of the peninsula, where Belofast meets Urasamo Bay. Whoever arrives there first awaits the others."

Thus, the meeting was over.

Chapter 7
Ulves

AFTER FOUR DAYS of traveling, Raeglin and Kirbakin had passed Moon Hills and now trotted north on horse and pony-back along Anzabar Road. Once more, they had taken the path through Dimwood and diverted to the north through the thick forest a few leagues before Anzabar Bridge at the edge of the wood. From there, they passed the Hills and went back on the lowlands.

The journey was smooth and without incidents. No Wolfmen or other enemies had crossed their path, and it convinced them both the beasts were off licking their wounds after the Big Battle. All snow had melted, and the sun glared from a worry-free sea-blue sky. Even the nights had been mild, with summer around the corner.

"Enjoy it while you can and let it embrace you," Raeglin said. "Summer might be nigh, but we are not riding to meet and greet it. We are going north and will find winter again."

"It bothers me not," Kirbakin laughed. "Earth spirits do not distinguish; the soil is our domain and our element, regardless of season."

"Lucky you. Without a thick fur coat, I cannot travel through the Frostlands."

As they continued across the plains, where short grass grew, and a sparse number of awakening flowers bloomed, Emoria's Enchanted Woods spread out a thick line of trees on their left, like a never-ending carpet of green and blue; and on their right, but too far to behold, the mighty Great River of Anzabar flowed, rushing north toward the Bay of Aldaer. Nature, still in shock after the abrupt winter coming and going, was still not quite ready to transform into summer again, and the mild breeze brought up no scents from the heath beneath them. No birds chirped, and no animals crossed their path or showed themselves on the open plains. It was as if the two riders were alone in the world.

Soon, Moon Hills shrunk under the horizon behind them, and the flatland went on as far as eyes could gaze. Nights fell late here, and the morning sun rose early in this barren, abandoned wilderness.

"This is the part of our journey I was the most concerned about," Raeglin said. "As much as we can see what happens leagues ahead in most directions and prepare, we are also vulnerable; others may notice us from afar, and we have no place to find shelter out in the open."

"From what I hear, you have traveled here before," Kirbakin said.

"Yes, but those times are far gone. I have been to most places, save the Frostlands."

The Gnome scratched his wrinkled forehead. "Uh… that is not very comforting. The Frostlands are wide and confusing. It is easy to get lost there."

Raeglin laughed. "Therefore, I brought a Gnome."

"I am flattered, but I might not be of much help. Nothing about the Frostlands is familiar to me, other than what I have heard from other Gnomes in times long past."

"I expected not that you know that territory. But you may still be useful."

"And it fails me how far the heaths reach, as well. From what I can tell, they seem to go on forever more."

"By tomorrow, we should reach an arboreal area. Although I am happy that we are alone in the open, it makes me nervous. The warrior in me prefers encircling trees."

As the evening drew nigh, a distant isolated howl disturbed the days of peace and silence. Yet another responded to the first.

"Those are no wolves," Kirbakin said.

"Certainly not."

They looked at each other and spoke at the same time.

"Ulves!"

"How far?"

"Hard to say."

The Gnome sat like a statue in his saddle, carefully listening. "Perhaps three or four leagues," he said. "The howls are coming from the north. It is dark, so we see them not, but they are still in the far."

"The Mounds of Sleeping Giants…," Raeglin said to himself. "That could be where they are. If they are already aware of our presence, we will have them over us in not too long, and there is nothing we can do about it out here. It sounds as if they are calling out to others to reassemble. The howls are coming from slightly different locations."

"We must not stay here."

"You are right. We want no Ulv encounters out in the open. No sleep tonight. We need to get to the forested area. If I must fight them, I prefer to do it with my back against a tree or two."

"The forest is my primary domain," Kirbakin said, anything but enthusiastic.

The companions spurred their horses as fast as they could carry their riders, while the last glimpse of the sun over the horizon left extended ghostly shadows over the vastness, and its long red and white beams flashed and twinkled in the dusk. Raeglin anxiously expected to see the silhouette of an Ulv against the vanishing light and the shadows, but so far, no living creature showed. For yet a couple of hours they rode, whilst the howling became more intense and sounded closer. By that time, the sun was asleep, but a moon, almost full, lit up the darkness enough for the riders to notice trees appearing to their left and to their right; sparse at first until the forest appeared denser about them. They continued well into the forest before the pilgrim drew rein and Kirbakin stopped behind him.

Ahead was a clearing, encircling about a hundred paces. From the sky, moonlight fell straight into the open area. The grass grew wild and dark, bowing to spurts of winds. The road continued through and disappeared among the trees on the opposite side.

"Let us stay among these trees and wait," Raeglin whispered. "Here, we can oversee the clearing, and the forest will cover us for now. The Ulves may not yet know we are here. There could be many reasons for the howls, but it is best to be prepared."

The two travelers tied the animals to a couple of trees and moved away from them, merging with the blind forest. The howls were now increasing in volume, and more Ulves replied to the initial call.

"They are coming our way," Kirbakin whispered.

Raeglin kept his eyes focused on the clearing. He expected to see the first Ulv at any moment coming out of the forest. It was quiet for a little while, save from an owl hooting twice. No wind disturbed the silence. The suspense of the sudden stillness made them both nervous. Raeglin would have preferred the howls. Why had the Ulves stopped howling? Perhaps they had gathered and gone for their hunt, likely involving the two travelers.

As on command, what seemed like an entire pack of Ulves started howling in unison, and the cacophony was nearing. The howls turned into growls and cries. Raeglin pushed the back of his head closer to a tree and stood ready with his sword. He knew this could be his last battle. It always felt that way. Yet, from the sound of it, there were too many Ulves to defeat on his own.

Next, the sound of running feet to their right. Or was it running paws? A shadow swooshed by in the dark like a ghost a few dozen yards away and disappeared among the trees. Then another one, and another. Raeglin turned his head in all directions to have all sides covered, ready to be attacked by anything hidden. Growls turned louder close to the clearing, but still in the forest across. The howls and growls were different now: they were more aggressive, more agonized, like there was a titanic battle somewhere near and among the trees. The whimpering from dying Ulves reached them, but there was something else; humans were shouting. Then there were branches cracking, and men screaming from afar, almost inaudible among the loud growls from the Ulven beasts.

Out into the clearing ran four Ulves, side by side. No signs of Wolfmen. *Wild Ulves!* At great speed, the beasts ran toward the pilgrim and the Gnome. Slime, dark in the light of the flaming moon, dripped from their jaws, and their red eyes impinged with an insane glow. Adrenaline ran through Raeglin's body when he saw the size of them. The Ulves Wolfmen rode were always impressive, but these were gigantic, almost twice in size, and much more ferocious. Raeglin glanced at Kirbakin, standing beside him with a short knife drawn, not nearly big enough to create an impact. *I will be alone in this*, the pilgrim thought. *I must defend both Kirbakin and me.*

At a close range, something swooshed past Raeglin's ear. Then again. One Ulv cried out in pain and fell on his nose. The body tweaked a few times and lay still. A second Ulv fell on its side and moved no more. The two beasts that remained stopped in their charge, confused, until an arrow hit one in the side. The creature wobbled but remained standing. Together, the two beasts crossed the clearing and flew into the forest, right into the arms of the pilgrim and the Gnome. Raeglin buried his sword into the throat of the unwounded Ulv. Warm acidic blood spurted out of the wound and hit the pilgrim's arm and burned it through the clothing. Then the Ulv fell where it stood, kicking Raeglin over, and then it died. The impact emptied the pilgrim's lungs. Close by, the wounded, furious Ulv attacked Kirbakin. He fought for his life, waving his little weapon as if it were a useless pocketknife. Raeglin, still gasping for air, wobbled to his feet to help his friend. But before he could swing his sword, a flurry of arrows hit the beast until it looked like a porcupine. The Ulv left the Gnome alone and spun around to meet his new nebulous enemies. But the wounds were too deep and too fatal; the monster fell dead after merely a few steps.

Confused, and with his sword still drawn, Raeglin looked everywhere in the dark to see whence the arrows came. Friends or foes? With legs widely spread, and with the sword in front of him, he stood before Kirbakin to protect him from any arrow attacks.

"Are you alright?" he said, glancing at his friend with a quick head movement.

"Yes," the Gnome said. "A little shaken up. A couple of shallow flesh wounds, that's all…"

"Who is there?" the pilgrim cried into the dark unseen.

Silence. There was that owl again, hooting from afar. The unconcerned moon was on the move past the clearing, and the night turned darker. No more Ulves howling and growling.

"Show yourselves!" Raeglin demanded. Like a blind man, he fumbled around, trying to make sense of his environment. But no one showed up. No footsteps, no sound of lingering people.

Still highly alert, he put his knee to the ground close to the Gnome and quickly glanced over his friend's body to locate any wounds. There was a flesh wound on his left arm from a scratch of the Ulv's claw, and a similar mark on his cheek.

"Is that all?" he said.

"Yes, I am fine."

Raeglin used some drinking water to clean the wounds and put a bandage around Kirbakin's arm, and then he sat down beside him against the tree.

"I will not close my eyes until the archers have shown themselves," he said. "They saved our lives, and it seems they scared the Ulves off. Yet, they could still be unfriendly. They refuse to show, and I know not why."

"I think they study us," Kirbakin said, groaning in pain. "I can feel their eyes watching us from a distance."

Raeglin nodded.

―

Dawn arrived, and yet there were no signs of the archers. A few feet away lay the dead Ulv with his jaws open, showing a long line of sharp teeth, some of them broken. The red eyes that had glowed so intensively in the dark were now pale and lifeless. Kirbakin shuddered. It had been a close call.

"At least our horses are unspoiled," the pilgrim said. "You can hear them neighing thither." He kept looking about. "It seems the bowmen will not show up. They might be far from here now. If they wanted us dead, we would not sit here talking now. After breakfast, we should move on. We will not get any sleep until tonight, so it will be a long day."

After eating a quick dried meal, they prepared to leave. They brushed the soil off their clothes, but when they looked up, they jumped. Before them, without having made a sound, eight bowmen stood, staring at them, but they held their bows casually in one hand, and the arrows were still in the quivers. They gazed curiously at the two strangers.

Raeglin grabbed for the hilt of his sword, but the bowmen just stood there, making no attempts to reach for their quivers. The archers were light-skinned and wore their raven hair shoulder-long, and their eyes were brown, impenetrable in the light of the morning. Tall were they and clad in pale green and dirt-brown garments, blending well with the environment. That, and their skills of moving about quietly, prevented the pilgrim and the Gnome from noticing them until face-to-face.

Raeglin and the archers stood frozen, studying each other for a while. Then Raeglin spoke.

"Hail, bowmen and Ulv slayers," he said. "We have you to thank for being alive. Who are you?"

One bowman spoke. "Our leader wants to see you. Join us. We know who *you* are. And you are not prisoners."

Surprised, Raeglin and Kirbakin glared at each other.

"Very well," the pilgrim said. "I presume we owe you."

They followed the group of men across the clearing and into the forest beyond, where the path continued into more forest. Here and there, dead Ulves lay spread. It impressed the pilgrim. These beasts were difficult to defeat because they were unafraid and late to retreat when in battles.

They wandered for a long time in the same direction Raeglin and Kirbakin would have taken. Shortly after midday, the forested area ceased, and open fields unfolded before them. All this time, the bowmen said nothing, merely striding on. Now, before them all, tall hills arose, covered with ankle-tall grass.

"We are almost at the journey's end." These were the first words anyone had uttered since the walk began. The archer continued. "In front are the Mounds of the Sleeping Giants. It is said that there are Giants at rest underneath these hills, and they will awake when the end is nigh. They have been asleep for many long years, but the day is drawing nigh when they will awake. If you walk too far to the east, as I am sure you know, is Northgrave, an outpost of Azezakel's. We are going neither nor. The person who wants to see you is not far."

Soon, they reached a place where the Mounds rooted into the encompassing high grass. The company turned east and entered an upward slope, where cypresses grew sparsely, pridefully showing off their admirable crowns as if they were unaware that summer had not fully transformed into adulthood yet. A biting wind blew westward, bringing the cold saltwater air from the Bay of Aldaer. Raeglin watched every move the group of strangers made, but soon, he relaxed; it seemed this group was not hostile, merely secretive. He knew them not, yet they appeared familiar.

Then, at once, the company stopped. A man, seemingly in charge, signaled to the pilgrim and the Gnome. "Wait here!" The man walked forth, accompanied by another, and they were gone for a while. When they returned, they again attended to Raeglin and Kirbakin. "You are awaited."

There, where the Mounds created an overhang that was covered with moss and short grass, a few men sat against a rock face. The company that had brought the pilgrim and the Gnome made a pathway between them, letting the two come forth. A man in the midst of stood up and looked Raeglin in the eyes.

"Well met again, my friend," he said in a burst of heartfelt laughter.

Raeglin's jaws dropped, and his eyes widened when he saw who was before him.

"Yomar!" Raeglin said. "Am I dreaming?"

The two old friends embraced and patted each other's backs.

"Yes, the good old Nomads, remember?" Yomar said. "Little did I expect we would meet once more, and less did I know we would rejoin here of all places!"

They stood for a long time, grabbing shoulders, gazing into each other. Then Yomar spoke again.

"When we met at the feet of the Foggy Mountains not too long ago, a group of people accompanied you. Now, you show together with a Gnome. Where are the rest? From what I understood, you were on an important mission."

"So we were," Raeglin said. "And thus, I still am." The wrinkles of joy disappeared from the pilgrim's face, and his heart sank. "Much has happened in a short period. Some of those in my group are where they are supposed to be, whilst others are no longer among the living. The times are challenging and confusing."

Yomar nodded. "Indeed. Much has changed. The people here who led you to me are not the same people you met in the camp under the Foggy Mountains, as you have well noticed. These people belong to a different nomadic tribe, dwelling north of here. The rest of my tribe is still by the Foggy Mountains. Times are tight, and I need to be where my heart leads me. But please sit down, both of you. Your friends are my friends, and it is a true honor for us to have a Gnome keeping us company."

"Kirbakin at your service."

"Yomar, your humble servant," the Nomad said and bowed.

"You saved our lives last night," Raeglin said. "We would have fought those beasts on our own, to no avail. I hope you lost very few men; indeed, I hope you lost none."

"Each man is a major loss," Yomar sighed. "I yet must get the latest update, but from what I know so far, we lost six men—six *good* men. Still, it could have been worse. These were wild Ulves, and there were, fortunately, no Wolfmen about. That made it easier. I am glad I could help. Care for a nomadic meal?"

"We would be fools to say no," Raeglin said.

An hour later, they sat around a small fire, eating roasted wild swine. They ate in silence, and when they were done, the sun had disappeared behind the Mounds that rose about them like shadowy triangular pillars, attempting to reach the sky.

"What are you doing up here?" Yomar asked.

"Remember Ismaril?" Raeglin said. "He journeyed *down under*, if you know what I mean. He has shown himself to be the one who might help to turn this war around. A big burden on him it is, but he and Sigyn, his companion, went where no living being would dare to tread. Now, we are looking for them."

"Yes, I remember," Yomar said. "Ismaril and Sigyn. Ismaril was not too keen on us, and he trusted neither me nor my people, I recall." The nomad laughed.

"It helped him not that I needed to disappear and leave their group," the pilgrim said. "Ismaril thought I betrayed him, and because of it, to him, you became the enemy. I meant not for that to happen, but it was a lesson for him as it was for me."

"And you expect to find him here?"

"I am uncertain where he is, or whether he is still in the Underworld, but my heart tells me he is alive and no longer underground. My intuitive feeling led me here, but my search is not yet over. I will seek until I find him and Sigyn. Where are you heading with your people?"

"The Nomad in me knows no destination, but another part tells me I must act. My people are skilled warriors, and you have seen them in action. There is a war, and it is escalating. We can no longer be bystanders. No one is unaffected by what is happening. The question is where we can help the most."

"Do you plan to stay in this vicinity for a little?" Kirbakin asked.

Yomar shrugged. "Probably for a short time, then we must decide what to do. Why?"

The Gnome exchanged glances with the pilgrim, wearing a mischievous face; then he turned to the nomad again.

"Why not follow us?" the Gnome said.

"Where to?"

Raeglin laughed. "Thank you, Kirbakin," he said. "That is a brilliant idea. Why not come with us to the Frostlands?"

Yomar raised his eyebrows. "To the Frostlands? Why are you going there? Nothing good is dwelling in the northern regions."

"That remains to be seen," the warlock said. "You said you wanted to be of help in the war. Well, here is your chance. The Gnome and I are going up there, trying to recruit the Icemen to hit against Gormoth. If we succeed, they can be of significant help. From there, we will travel east through the Frozen Forest and approach the enemy from the north."

Yomar scratched his head. "That sounds like a desperate plan."

"Yes, it is desperate, but we must look for opportunities where there seem to be none. Khandur stands alone against an enemy that has the entire Underworld for an army, besides what they have conquered on the surface. If we are not bold and creative, the war is already lost. We are doing this without King Barakus' approval because we are both ostracized from his kingdom."

"He expelled you? How did that happen?"

"Well, the king has his own opinion about Ismaril and his mission. He views him as a thief, an outlaw, and an enemy. When I told him Ismaril might play a big part in how this war would end, both the king and Prince Xandur excommunicated us. Now, Kirbakin and I must take things in our own hands."

"That is sad to hear," Yomar sighed. "Now tell me: if the Icemen will follow you, how will you cross the Strait of Aldaer?"

"There are two options," Raeglin said. "The Icemen travel by air, but if we are not allowed that privilege, we will cross the strait on sleds. If you choose to come with us, I presume that is the way we must travel. The ice on the strait should be thick enough; it usually is. And the Icemen have Dragons."

Yomar nodded. "You will need my archers. If the Icemen are hostile, there is little you can do to survive their wrath on your own. My men can help. I will gladly come with you, old friend, but it is not merely up to me. I must talk to my men, if I may call them that; but I am not a leader, only a guide."

"Take your time," Raeglin said. "You and I must part for a

while, for I must find Ismaril and Sigyn. If they are alive, which I expect, they need my help. They are lost in what to do and where to go without me. I assume that is my fault."

"Then I must ask you, why do you wish to head for Gormoth now? Even the Icemen cannot fight Azezakel alone. And you are no longer in good standing with Khandur. It appears a suicide mission, ill-coordinated."

"And yet, this is how the Enemy operates: He turns man against man, preying on man's pride. Man is easily manipulated."

"And what are you going to do about that?"

"I am not a man. I am a warlock."

"But not even a warlock and an army of Icemen can defeat the Black King."

"Khandur will come," Raeglin said. "They will come, and so will Anúria, if things go well. No more battles at Khandur's border. This time, *we* are attacking the enemy!"

Chapter 8
Caëgrun

AYASHAKIM CUPPED her hands around her lips and sang a few notes. Then she repeated them once more. They amplified in the vastness, and soon, five impressive Khibis sailed out of the fuzzy clouds from many directions. Despite their massive stature, they landed gracefully in front of the group of seven and retracted their wings.

Sigyn immediately stepped back, gasping over their sizes and the intensiveness of their presence. They appeared like Dragons, and it was challenging to respond to them, for they seemed to emit both benevolence and malignancy.

What differed them from Dragons were their feathers of many colors, and each of the beasts had different color combinations, making them unique. Like Dragons, their bodies were long and sturdy, but there was no tail. Instead, they sat down on the crescent-shaped end of their bodies. Although it looked unnatural when catching the eye, the creatures' bodies seemed perfectly balanced. Their heads were like hybrids between bird and Dragon, shaped like eagles' heads but lacking beaks. Instead, their jaws were like those of reptiles, and a red, forked tongue rolled over their lips, showing a glimpse of two rows of sharp teeth. But what drew Sigyn's attention the most was their eyes. Something in their gaze scared her when their intense gaze found hers. They resembled regular bird eyes, bright yellow and with black pupils, but the energy these beings emitted through their stare made her heart gallop, and she looked for an escape. Ismaril's comments on the beauty of these birds seemed absurd to her. Was it wrong what she felt? How could she experience their presence so differently from his?

"There are seven of us, but only five Khibis," Ayashakim said. "Ride with me, Ismaril. Sit up behind me. And you, Sigyn, ride together with Etiel."

Ayashakim showed the two visitors how to mount the birds and stretched out her arm to help Ismaril up. Etiel mounted her bird last and signaled for Sigyn to come, but she hesitated.

"Do not fear," Etiel said. "I will help you up."

Sigyn took a step toward the Khibi, trying not to meet the bird's gaze.

Suddenly, the giant bird opened its mouth and lashed out toward her with a loud and vicious squeal. Sigyn cried out in fear, stepped back, and fell. The bird made a new attempt to attack. In a trance, Sigyn heard the commotion about her. Etiel's voice rang louder than the others while grabbing the bird's neck to stop its ravaging.

With much effort, Etiel held back the bird, who reluctantly calmed down, scratching its claws, stirring up moss and soil. Etiel dismounted and ran to Sigyn's aid.

"I am so sorry," she said. "I expected not for this to happen. This is troublesome, and so unlike the Khibis. Are you alright?"

Sigyn breathed fast and shallow, and she stared at the bird with wide-open eyes, making sure she kept Etiel between herself and the bird.

"Yes. But I will not set my foot near one of these. Your bird dislikes me."

Etiel turned back to her Khibi and used a hand signal to make her bird bow down. Then she whispered something in its ear. The animal grunted and frowned.

"Come to me," Etiel said in a friendly voice and waved at Sigyn. "It will not happen again. I promise!"

Sigyn stood still for some time before she found the courage to approach once more, but moved in an extra-long circle around the beast. This time, there was no reaction from the bird, and the Mazosian helped her up on its back. Sigyn's entire body shook.

Thus, all five birds took off. Sigyn held Etiel in a tight grip around the waist, while the ground fell under them, and the sky came closer. The Khibi was swift and moved upward with long wing flaps, flying far distances with merely a few swooshing wing movements. Sometimes, it did not move its wings at all, gliding on undercurrents while the sky ascended. Soon they flew into a cloud, and the rest of the company faded into the fog. When flying through the cotton balls, sunbeams now and then gleamed in between.

Soon, the Khibi stopped flapping and let itself fall through the air, out of the clouds to where the sky was bright and blue again. Sigyn felt a knot in her stomach from the sudden fall. She buried her nails in Etiel's garment.

With little courage left, Sigyn peeked beneath, and there was Elverstone, an island floating on a sea of air. As the bird tilted, the city appeared to follow, creating the illusion there were no up and no down. And lo-and-behold! As the sun gifted the sky with its light, the entire city appeared to pulsate in shifting colors, radiating waves of energy, coming out of the building structures in spurts. There were low buildings, tall buildings, lofty towers, and ponds with transparent blue water; even rivers flowed here in midair, and the entire city seemed so ethereal, almost as if a few people could lift it with their bare arms. The mere sight of this magic place blew Sigyn's anxiety off. And as they descended, she could see people moving around down there. She looked about her, and there were the other Khibis ahead, already hovering over the city below. From the color of the bird, she could distinguish Ayashakim's Khibi in the lead, and there sat Ismaril like a little stiff mannequin from a child's play kit. She laughed to herself, almost in a revengeful manner, realizing she was not the only one uncomfortable with the ride.

Sigyn and Etiel landed with the others on a large open field amidst the city, where blue grass grew, maintained, and shaved. And white trees with leaves sparkling in fall colors spread out in orchestrated patterns across the field; and from their branches, yellow, oval-shaped fruits with thin peels hung. Ayashakim picked two of them and gave one each to the two guests.

"These are ciessar fruits," she said. "They are delicious and will give you extra strength." Then she glanced at Etiel's Khibi and turned toward Sigyn.

"Feeling better now?"

"Yes, I have overcome. Thank you!"

Sigyn took a bite of the fruit, and a wave of pleasure moved through her body. This was even better than the fruit they consumed earlier. It had a sweet and sour flavor in a perfect blend, and even for somebody who was not thirsty, the fruit triggered a sense of thirst that was pleasant. Although her energy level was high merely by being in Emoria, the ciessar fruit elevated her to a new level. She looked at Ismaril with a mischievous grin. He had just taken a bite, and the juices from the fruit leaked from the side of his mouth and poured down his chest. He noticed her glance, and he tried to turn around, not to show his embarrassment. Then he laughed.

"Cannot eat fast enough, I suppose," he said, trying to gloss it over.

"No manners," Sigyn said and laughed with him.

"Come with me," Ayashakim said. "The Queen is waiting for you. It is over there."

And up front, a palace distinguished itself from every other building near and far, appearing out of nowhere. Sigyn could swear that it was not there before. It sparkled in white, red, and yellow in rapid succession, resembling something borrowed from the old fairytales that parents told their children in the villages of Lindhost; but this was even more magnificent. Not overpoweringly, but artfully constructed; translucent, perhaps manifested by imaginary minds of excellence, something no one could replicate in the world outside Emoria. Like a little child, she was once again ready to explore an imaginary world.

"Look, Ismaril!" she said and pointed. "The tower over there… I can see through it!"

Ismaril glanced in her direction and focused. "I see it now. It looks solid to me," he said.

The Mazosians laughed, and Ayashakim said, "Welcome to Caëgrun, where everything is real, but only in your mind. Not two people can experience our city with the same set of eyes. You see only what you interpret with your mind. This city is not solid, per your definition. It is our common creation, manifested directly from our mind's eye. You add to it and subtract from it with your own creative imagination."

"But if it is not solid, it cannot be real," Ismaril objected. "That would mean we stand in midair now. Why do we not fall to the ground far below?"

Ayashakim smiled mysteriously. "Consider this: What is real and what is not? Is our world real? Is yours? Is anything real, or is it all merely in your mind? If you would be your mind and you look into a mirror, is the reflection real?"

"If our world, beyond Emoria, is also a creation of minds, why is there so much suffering in our world but not here?"

"Both our worlds are continually created with the common effort of the collective minds inhabiting the two worlds, respectively. You see, thoughts also have a range of solidity to them. If your collective minds are more solid, and you work against each other's best interests to elevate individual interests over others, you end up in a world of conflicts, wars, suffering, and decay. You create, using your thoughts and emotions destructively. Then you reap what you sow. But if you join and create something beautiful and lasting; something everybody can benefit from, the mutual creation will be like ours. You have forgotten about the power of the mind. You think conflicts are external, but they are not."

"This is fantastic," Sigyn said, and her face lit up. "I am the creator of what I see. I made the tower transparent. See, there it is again!" Ismaril glared at Ayashakim and Sigyn and scowled.

Ayashakim continued talking as the company walked toward the castle, but Sigyn heard her not. Here were no high gates, guarded by stern armed knights in armor. Nor was there any solid fence of solid rock surrounding the building. Instead, a low fence in pale light purple encompassed the castle, merely high enough not to jump over. Upon it were short pillars, topped off with white, cone-shaped peaks. The white wooden gate was only high enough to let the tallest Mazosian walk through upright. As they approached, the gate opened by itself. Inside, a long pathway of white bricks led straight to the castle. The path ran through a magnificent garden; not well-structured but left sole for nature to shape. The colors of the flowers were as bright as those a child would picture in a most intriguing saga, encompassing flowers unique to there. The fragrance was enchanting, and although scents blended, Sigyn could separate the fragrances when she focused. And there was no buzzing of bumblebees or other insects, but there were small turquoise birds of an unknown species sucking nectar from the petals. Although some flew near them, they were not shy or threatened by anybody's presence. Stunned by her experience, and within a fleeting moment, she wondered why

Ismaril was so unaffected and kept talking to the Mazosians.

Not even at the main gate of the castle were there any guards. Once more, the brown wooden doors shot open, and the company entered with Ayashakim in front. A breeze, resembling that coming from a salty ocean, hit Sigyn's nose as they walked into the castle; yet there was no ocean nearby. Here, the magic was immensely potent. No wars, no conflicts, and no deaths and suffering. If there ever was a Paradise, this must be it. Then a brief wave of anxiety washed over her. This was like being in a childhood that never was, but she wished she had experienced. She did not even understand how she could envision such a childhood when no one outside Emoria could experience it. Now, it seemed more real than anything she had ever encountered. In a haze, she heard the surrounding voices, and someone called her name.

"Sigyn, is everything alright?"

She recognized Ismaril's concerned voice. A flash of irritation passed through her mind. How dare he interrupt her thoughts now?

"It is perfect," she said. When glancing at Ismaril, she noticed he was unconvinced, but at this moment, it bothered her not. *Just keep walking and leave me alone,* she thought.

To her, the inside of the castle was just as impressive. The walls appeared to float in wavelike patterns, switching between different pictures in motion as if telling a story: Resembled images creating visions inside minds, vivid, like in a child. First, there was an ocean upon which a magnificent golden ship, sails of silver, was bobbing, then shifting to a mighty mountain range over which a confident, majestic eagle flew. Abruptly, the perspective changed, and she saw the landscape from the eagle's eyes, hovering high above the untouched, forested, and proud mountains, and the deep valleys. For a moment, she and the bird were one.

Ismaril now walked in silence beside Ayashakim. To him, the walls seemed to shift, sparkling in the most astonishing colors, only to change into a more solid white, and so it switched back and forth. There were no sceneries shifting, but he seemed to pay little attention to any of it.

Sigyn gasped: Now, everything became unfocused. The floors morphed from black marble to glass, whilst leaving no reflection. The walls turned translucent, and Sigyn could see the garden bleed through. In waves it went, to and fro, from solid to transparent. Astonished, it did not even occur to Sigyn to ask questions.

And behold! There it was: a throne built from what nature could spare. The seat, carved from the stump of a trunk, gleamed white as of shiny gold. Below was a footstool of short-shaven blue grass, only high enough to rest your feet. An arch of white branches encircled the seat, decorated with leaves in yellow, red, blue, and green. Purple flowers, alive as if they were still growing in the wild, blended magnificently with the leaves of many colors. A fragrant mix of spring flowers from Lindhost, carried on by a mild fleeting breeze, empowered Sigyn's inner senses, and her eyes wetted. What would she not sacrifice to be home again? Could she ever return? These thoughts were brief but caused a swift mood swing, followed by a great joy at being here in this heavenly place. Her emotions were chaotic.

But the throne was empty.

The small company halted before the royal seat. None of the Originals spoke, and although Sigyn had many questions, she kept silent. Now was not the time to ask.

Out of nowhere, an apparition took form on the throne; a white orb at first, bright and enigmatic, came into shape, and lo! Before them sat a tall and erect woman, wearing a glorious crown of flowers. Her large, green eyes pierced the two newcomers like Dragon Fire, but Sigyn had no fear. A warm calmness overtook her, and the smile that welled up inside emanated from her soul. Sigyn and Ismaril did not need to be reminded; following their learned customs when standing before royalty, they bowed before her, but the rest of the Mazosians stood erect, saying nothing.

"Please stand," the Queen said, and her voice was mild and stern within the same breath, yet not unpleasant. She sat in silence for a moment, while further observing the two guests.

"You have come a long way," she said, "and trouble has beset your travels. I know who you are, of course, or you would not be here. I am Queen Astéamat. Welcome to Emoria."

Sigyn and Ismaril bowed again, and then Ismaril spoke.

"Never have I seen such beauty," he said. "You are exceeding my wildest imagination, Your Majesty."

"Your tongue is fair, Ismaril Farrider," Astéamat said. "I have expected you both for some time. Yet we could not know for certain whether you would survive the journey through the

Underworld. You did, but not without paying a price." She gave Sigyn a quick glance. "But let us move to a more informal location, where we can talk."

Suddenly, the castle dispersed before their eyes, and for a split moment, Sigyn perceived herself to be in two places at once. The castle blended with the wild forest from afar and disappeared. As in a dream, they all sat in the grass amid a clearing, surrounded by deep forest, lit by a green sun. Amidst, encircled by the Mazosians and her two guests, Astéamat sat on the same throne still, waiting for Sigyn and Ismaril to recover from the shock of the transition.

Then she smiled at them. "You seem surprised," she said. "Well, you yet have to learn what minds are about. As much as minds can create worlds, if ready for it, they can also deceive. I intended not to meet you in the castle, nor do I own one. I do not live in castles, and there are none in Emoria. It was entirely your creation, and my escort went along for it. This is the place at which I proposed to meet you."

"The castle was not real?" Ismaril cried. "What else we have experienced here is not real? What about the Khibi birds? The city itself? And what of this forest in which we are now seated?"

"It is good that you question what is real," the Queen said. "This world is *our* common reality, and into our creation, I have invited you both. Mostly, you experience it the way we do, but because of the transparency of our world, powered by our collective minds, it also allows you to create here with *your* minds. The problem is you have difficulties separating what you create inside and what already exists outside, created by others, and shared by the same. Yet, what we have created and maintained can only exist here; taking this into your world, we cannot, and likewise, your world cannot embrace our reality. They exist on different planes of existence and the two do not mix. Our world would perish in yours, and your world would not recognize ours. But try not to be confused, this forest and this clearing both exist here and now."

Then she turned toward Sigyn. "I sense that you have questions. Now is the time to ask them."

"Yes, I have one question for now. Why did the Khibi attack me?" She was not sure she wanted to hear the answer.

"For two reasons," she said. "These birds are sensitive and can feel other's emotions, thoughts, and energies. If there is something they dislike, they respond with aggression."

"But what have I done? Is there something wrong with me? They accepted Ismaril."

"No, Sigyn Archesdaughter, nothing is wrong with you, but your journey down under has affected you. Do you recall what happened there?" The Queen pierced her with her gaze.

"Well, there were a series of events... What do you mean?"

"The curse..."

Sigyn lowered her gaze. "Aye, the curse. It is bad, is it not?"

"It is serious, but you might have the power to overcome it. I say not that it is going to be easy, but you can override if your mind is strong. Yet you will live its complications throughout. It is merely the ending that is open and not predestined."

Sigyn sat straight, and a subtle shiver of discomfort waved through her body. "This is terrible! Can you help? Can you break the spell? Please...?"

"That I cannot do. These curses are strong and sticky. Usually, only the person who gave it to you can break it. The hope for a good outcome is your will. You shall be tested, but how well can you challenge your fate? You know not until you have met what lies before you."

Ismaril grabbed Sigyn's hand. She tried to keep it still, but she was shaking.

"What is the worst scenario?" Ismaril asked.

The Queen shook her head and hesitated. "Death, I suppose..."

"But that is not all, is it?" Ismaril insisted.

"I do not know. We are dealing with the darkest of forces. I know not what this curse entails. When I try to envision the outcome, there is a wall I cannot penetrate. Be careful, daughter of Arches."

"Alas, and woe to us all!" Ismaril said. "Yet I shall protect her. Sigyn and I have been to Hell and back, and even so, we stand here before you among the living."

"Yes, this is a monumental accomplishment. Yet your journey is not over. You both need to know what awaits you and what you must overcome. And be careful judging those who mean you well, Ismaril. In the end, the decision is always yours."

Sigyn gazed at Astéamat whilst sitting quietly for a long time before daring to convey what else bothered her.

"There is more, is there not?" she said in a low voice, and she swallowed hard.

"There is," the Queen said. "Something else happened in the Lower Realms, did it not? Something between the two of you?"

Sigyn and Ismaril locked eyes, and Sigyn spaced a moment of shame.

"Yes," they both said at the same time.

"Sigyn, you are pregnant!"

A thousand thoughts ran through Sigyn's head, and in her peripheral, she barely noticed Ismaril jumping and gasping. Her world fell apart. *Not now!* she thought. They were only intimate once, and it was not during a time when she would be particularly fertile. Yet she could not deny that she had felt something strange inside her recently. Never had she been pregnant, so how could she tell? Ismaril's eyes stared into nothing, and his lips were two thin lines. No words came from his tongue.

"What shall I do?" she said, desperately. "How can I travel through the wilderness in such a condition? What when the baby is born?"

"The pregnancy is in its infancy," Astéamat said. "You can return to Lindhost and give birth, and Ismaril continues his journey alone. Or you may follow him until the end. If you choose the latter, the Day of Judgment, when all is said and done is nigh, and it will be over long before the baby is born or grows beyond your capacity. I cannot advise you, dear lady. If you go with Ismaril, you may jeopardize the child, and yourself with that."

"I know not what to do!" Sigyn covered her face with her palms and wept.

Ismaril grabbed her shoulders. "Go home," he said. "Return to Eldholt and give birth to our child. Astéamat is right. This war is mounting and will soon reach its culmination. When all is over, I shall come to you, and we'll raise the child together. I am so sorry. I have made so many mistakes, with this being the worst! Alas! I should not have taken you with me, as little as I should have let the rest of my friends join me. Look at them! Most are dead, which is because of my doings! And now I have failed you."

Sigyn faced him. "How can you say that? After everything we have gone through together. Have I not been of any assistance to you? Have I merely been burdensome?"

Then Ismaril wept. "No, of course not. But I carry so much

guilt. How can I ever repay my debts to those whose lives I spilled? I cannot! And now I have put you in an unbearable situation. Perhaps we should both return to Eldholt."

Sigyn dried her tears. Then, with a face carved in stone, she held her head high, and she said, "Nay! None of us shall return to Eldholt. At least not yet. You can't go back. Too much is at stake if the Prophecy tells it as it is. And I must not return, either."

"Of course you must," Ismaril said. "For the baby's sake, and for yours." Then his voice sank. "And for mine."

He raised his arms to the sky. "Cursed is this world, and cursed are all who live in it!" he shouted. "Woe to us all, for the end if nigh, and there is no hope!"

In response, a sudden breeze blew, and the leaves on the trees across rustled. A handful fell dead and crisp to the ground.

"Watch your tongue, Ismaril Farrider," the Queen said. "Your emotions bring death to our realm. Calm yourself. You gain nothing from your outbursts."

Then Sigyn spoke, and her voice was steady. "I must come with you, Ismaril. I was presented with a choice, but for me, there is none. It appears my destiny is to follow through. There is a curse put upon me, which I do not know how to overcome. But my intuition tells me I cannot overcome if I return to Eldholt."

"Sigyn, that is nonsense!" Ismaril cried.

"But she is right, Ismaril," the Queen said. "This is also what my intuition tells me. I believe returning to Eldholt will be detrimental for all three of you; the baby included. There is no other path to walk but that which leads ahead."

Ismaril sat down abruptly.

"Then so be it," he said and stared at the grass before him. He had nothing more to say.

Chapter 9
The Journey East

THE REVENGER'S FACE WAS red and his breathing shallow where he sat, rocking back and forth to the irregular rhythm of the creaking cart. The Northern Highroad east of Dimwood was muddy and porous, and the horses' backs were frothy as they worked themselves to exhaustion, with the cartwheels sinking deeper into the mud.

"Now you have really put us in a dreadful situation," he said. "The snow has melted, and that's only two days after we left Barren Hills!"

"So?" Tomlin said, snapping the whip in the air above the horses.

"If you had listened to me ere we spoke to the Ghost King, we would have gone north, passing the hills with no problems. Now, there's a curse upon us and an oath we need to fulfill… thanks to you."

"What are you talking about? You know as well as I do that the snow was still high, and we could never have passed through there, with or without the cart."

"It's of no consequence. What I'm saying is that if you had listened to me, we wouldn't encounter the ghost, and the snow would have melted within short. My point is you don't listen to me."

"That doesn't even make sense. And I will not argue with you and your deranged brain. Things are what they are, and we can't do a damn thing about it. The road will hopefully soon dry up, so we can travel faster."

It was past midday on the second day since they met the Ghost King, and the eastern wilderness laid flat about them as far as eyes could see. The Northern Highroad cut through the plain, looking more like a muddy river than a road; and the heath was like a mire after the snowbrowth. Sudden stenches of stalled marsh water hit Tomlin on the coach box, and he pondered whether it was going to get worse or better. The trip since Lahrs' Inn had been a nightmare with no end to it.

One horse, in frustration, suddenly kicked his legs in the dirt, splashing up sludge in Tomlin's face and soaking his clothes. He spat and hissed and wiped his lips free from some of it.

"That's it!" he said and drew back the reins. "We can go no further. The horses are consumed, and the road is awful."

The Revenger peeked over the cart railing and saw the left wheel buried in the gruel, making the cart tilt.

"Aye! We're stuck," he said.

Tomlin jumped down from the coach box and landed in the mud with a splash. He studied the sunken wheel and groaned.

"This is not working." He gazed at the bleak sun, shyly peeking through the clouds to and fro, being of no help. Then he turned east and gazed toward the horizon, not in favor of what he saw. "I see no shore beyond this muddy ocean, Revenger. It might take days before this dries up, and who knows if there will be rain before then? We can't sit here and wait for that to happen. The cart is too heavy for this terrain."

"Are you saying we should leave the cart here?"

"We have no choice. We must continue on horseback."

"But what about our victuals?"

Tomlin shrugged. "We'll take with us what we can and leave the rest. I would say we are about three days' riding distance from Gormoth's border. You can see the mountains yonder. That's where we're heading. But riding through this marchland will not be a simple task; we probably need five days or more. I figure we could bring a week's worth of food and necessities."

The Revenger glared at his companion. "And you call me stupid? When we left the slaughter site where our comrades fell, we left with seven horses: four in the lead and three tied behind the cart. Now we only have the four before the cart, for you stubbornly set the others free. They would certainly come in handy now, wouldn't they? I was against letting them loose, remember?"

"We couldn't feed them. You know that. Do you see any grass for them to eat here? There is barely enough food in the cart to feed three animals. We've already discussed this to exhaustion."

"Three? What about the fourth? Are you setting him free, too?"

"Aye. We don't need him; he's just deadweight."

"Well, let's pack and leave then," the Revenger said, ready to jump off the cart.

"The horses need a break. If we let them rest until tomorrow morning, they will be in a better shape and can carry us longer."

The next morning, the two pirates untied the horses from the cart, and when they had packed everything, they let the weakest horse free and then mounted, letting the third horse carry the provisions.

The journey was faster now, but slower than they had wished for. Tomlin rode first and decided the pace, but he dared not push his animal too hard on the muddy road, afraid of slip falls. In the late morning hour, the clouds dispersed, and the sun got braver, showing a warmer and kinder face. In the afternoon, the road was a little better, and more comfortable for the horses.

So they stood before a crossroads, and Tomlin halted. One road continued east, whilst the other disappeared on a northerly path.

"What now?" the Revenger said.

"We continue east," Tomlin said. "The north road must be the road to Zebadhim. We could go there, but something tells me not to. The town is one of Gormoth's outposts, but I think we should ride straight to Gormoth."

The Revenger looked about, anxiously. "It is so quiet everywhere, as if we are the only people alive. We haven't met a soul since the two of us started our journey. Don't misunderstand me; I do not want to meet anybody if I can avoid it; but it's queer, and quite eerie, too."

"I've thought the same," Tomlin said. "Well, let's take advantage of the silence and continue as far as we can ere dusk."

It was difficult to find a place dry enough to camp out that night. Then they came upon a rocky spot by the wayside, with baldheaded gray stones sticking up from the mossy terrain.

"It will do for a hard bed," Tomlin said. "But I prefer that before the wetland."

They were both tired after a long day's ride, and despite the solid stone bed, they fell asleep immediately after dinner, shortly after the sun went down.

—

The Revenger shouting out woke Tomlin up. When opening his eyes, he noticed the morning light but barely paid any attention to it. He swiftly sat, and a shockwave flushed through him. On the road, a dozen Wolfmen sat silently on massive, drooling Ulves, staring at the two pirates. Yet, it was not the Wolfmen who caught Tomlin's eyes. Amidst sat a tall man on a Giant Boar. His long, sandy hair blew over a clean-shaven face carved in rock. Not much could scare Tomlin, but this man's steel-blue eyes were atrocious and merciless, void of any human emotions, save hate and contempt. When Tomlin met his gaze, his body shivered, and his heartbeat sped up. He sensed this man was much more dangerous than all the Wolfmen together.

The loud, high-pitched scream from the Boar woke Tomlin from his trance. He wanted to pull his weapon, but chose not to. He wanted no battle with this small army of bloodthirsty killing machines.

Then the tall man spoke. "You are a dreadful sight," he said in a sarcastic voice. "Have you children played in the dirt?"

Both Tomlin and the Revenger rose and stood in salute as if they were the tall man's soldiers. His own reaction surprised Tomlin.

"So, who are you?" the tall man asked.

"Tomlin and the Re… Iorwain," Tomlin said.

The man on the Boar pierced them from top to toe. "You wear sabers. What are you? Pirates?"

Tomlin knew not what was safe to say and what to withhold, but chose to tell the truth as much as he dared. It seemed to be the right thing to do in front of this uncomfortable man.

"Aye! We are… were. We have left our tribe and travel alone, Iorwain and I."

"So, you are the spokesperson. Then what brings you so close to Gormoth's borders? Or are you on your way to Anúria, perhaps?" His voice turned as cold as the breath of an Ice Dragon.

Tomlin glanced at the line of Wolfmen, and then he said, "We are going to Gormoth to join King Azezakel's army."

"You traveled all the way from Piscas Urash, Pirate Island, to join forces with Gormoth?"

"Aye, sir!"

The tall man laughed dryly. "You amuse me. What use would we have for two ruffians like yourselves? You leave tracks that an infant could follow. We come from Zebadhim and instantly saw your hoofprints in the mud. With your level of stupidity, what good would you be? Your ignorance could be detrimental to us."

"It… it was impossible to hide our hoofprints on the muddy road," the Revenger said.

"Because of that, now you must deal with us, mustn't you?"

"No, no, we're on the same side," the Revenger said, nervously. "We are ex-pirates, and we've come a long way to fight the war with your men."

A mumble went through the row of Wolfmen, and some growled and showed their teeth.

"Careful," the tall man said. "You upset my crew. None of them wishes to be called a man. Man is their enemy; on men, they merely seek revenge. Were I not here to stop them, you would be dead now for your careless blather."

Tomlin kicked the Revenger on the side of his ankle, urging him to be quiet.

"Know you aught what we can do, sir?" Tomlin said, trying to stay calm, but inside, there was turmoil. What had he gotten himself into?

"To Gormoth you are journeying, say you?" the tall man replied. "Yet you know not who I am. If you are so eager to join, why know you not my name?"

The two pirates looked down at their feet, wondering how this was going to end.

The tall figure fluffed up his chest. "I am King Yongahur of Zebadhim, and henceforth, my name you shall never forget."

Oddly, this gave Tomlin hope. It sounded as if Yongahur was going to let them live—at least for some time.

"So, tell me!" Yongahur leaned forward in his Boar saddle. "What are you two good at, save creating disasters? And be quick and loud, for I have little time!"

The Revenger opened his mouth to speak, but Tomlin kicked his ankle, so it hurt, and he said,

"We can fight, and we can sail. We are excellent boatsmen, Sire Yongahur."

"Of course you can sail if you are pirates, but can you also command a fleet?"

Tomlin almost swallowed in the wrong pipe. "Very much so, Sire."

Yongahur seemed to look right into Tomlin's soul for what felt like an eternity, and then he spoke. "For your own sake, I hope you are not lying. If you are, the punishment shall be so harsh you wish death will take you."

I am not a ship commander, Tomlin thought, and in the peripheral, he noticed the Revenger staring at him with surprise and agony written all over his face. Never had he seen a man sweat like that.

Yongahur dismounted and walked up to the pirates. Tomlin could not understand what made him so terrified before this tall man, but every cell in his body shook in his presence.

"Very well," the Dark King said. "Then I shall dub you officers of the Fleet. You will report to the Watchtower at the border of Gormoth, and they will transport you to Khurad-Resh in Rhuir, by the sea. There our main fleet lies waiting. They will assign to you a ship each under your command, but not until you show you can handle it. If not…"

Tomlin found it difficult to breathe, and his head spun. They were doomed. Neither he nor Iorwain had ever commanded a ship; they had both been oarsmen. He could imagine how demanding it must be as a captain of Azezakel's fleet.

"How… how do they know in the Tower who we are?" Tomlin stuttered.

Yongahur drew a short blade from its sheath. "This will speak volumes," he said. A thin flame suddenly ignited at the edge of the long-knife, and he directed it at Tomlin's forehead, using the fire to carve something into his flesh. Tomlin cried out in great pain, and he smelled his own burned flesh. The Dark King stopped a little and then continued carving. Tomlin thought his entire head was on fire.

When the pirate could stand it no more, Yongahur stopped

and admired his creation. Then he put the width of the blade against the burn. The weapon was now cold as ice, increasing the pain.

"There we go," Yongahur said. "This will keep the tattoo intact for as long as you live. Show this to the Watchtower, and they will know what to do." Next, the Dark King turned to the Revenger.

"Your turn."

With his head pounding in pain, Tomlin wished there was snow on the ground so he could put it against his wound. In a haze, he watched his comrade as Yongahur approached, and he noticed how the Revenger's face turned as white as in death, and his eyes expressed pure horror. Yongahur raised his knife but hesitated.

"Hm, about you, I know not. You freeze in fear. Is that how you will react when you are a Ship Commander, too?"

"N… no, Sire," the Revenger whispered, not capable of speaking, for his mouth was too dry. "I can handle it… Sire."

Yongahur's eyes narrowed, and he leaned over until his face was almost touching that of the horrified pirate. He forced the Revenger to lock eyes with him, and when he did, Tomlin could almost see the life energy leaving his comrade.

Yongahur laughed wryly and started the fire procedure. Already pumped up with as much terror as a man could endure, the Revenger's legs shook when the pain came. Even Tomlin tensed up, afraid his partner would not make it, and Yongahur would kill them both. Ere the Dark King had finished the first carving, Iorwain's legs finally failed him, and he fell to his knees. In the background, the Wolfmen shouted and egged their Commander on, and the Ulves gave up ear-shattering growls. Yongahur stepped back a little and raised his left arm without touching the pirate. The Revenger's body levitated a few feet off the ground and froze in a position where the Dark King could comfortably finish the tattoo and freeze it in place with the width of his blade.

Then he let go of his victim, who fell to the ground and landed on his back. Tomlin, shaking like a leave, could now read what Yongahur carved onto Iorwain's forehead, and it said,

A Z S C

Yongahur noticed the confusion on Tomlin's face.

"It means, 'Azezakel's Ship Captain,'" he said. "Now you are both branded, and you remain Gormoth's property until death will take you. Welcome to Gormoth!"

Then the Dark King glanced at the Revenger with scorn, watching him try his best to stand, forcing his legs to carry him. Then the Commander turned to the other pirate.

"I can detect an ounce of guts in you, Ship Commander Tomlin," he said, "but with your comrade, I am uncertain. Thus, I also put you in command of him to better ensure he will be successful. If he fails, it will be your failure, too. Do you understand, or do I need to spell it out?"

"No, Sire, I understand," Tomlin said. "If he fails, we both die."

"I like you. You are smarter than the other one." Yongahur snarled and returned to his Boar and mounted.

"I command both of you to ride to the Watchtower, which is not too far off to the east. There you report to Guard Commander Hútlof, and you tell him what I have told you. Say they must transfer you to Khurad-Resh forthwith. He will understand what to do. You are now officers of the Fleet of Gormoth, and I am your First Commander. Now, get ready and leave!"

Yongahur pulled the rein of his Boar and rode west, heeled by his crew of Wolfmen. Then they increased their pace and soon became small dots in the distance. The two pirates sat down abruptly with their mouths open and took deep breaths.

"That was a close call," Tomlin said.

"Close call?" the Revenger said, on the brink of tears. "Now we are really in trouble."

"So, you have changed your mind?" Tomlin said. "Burning head and cold feet?"

"I think we have made a mistake. That man means Big Trouble."

"He is not a man, he's a God."

"This was the first time I've seen one of them. He nearly killed me with his gaze alone. I preferred the Wolfmen... yes, even the Ulves."

Tomlin nodded. "Aye."

"How can we get peace and freedom with a Commander like that? If the rest are anything like him, our mission scares me.

Perhaps we should turn back and go home to the Island?"

"With Gormoth's sigil tattooed all over our foreheads? They will kill us. Nah, we are at war, you know. To stand a chance of victory, the Commander must be brutal. You understand that, don't you? Our own captains on Piscas Urash were brutal, too, or our tribe would be no more." Tomlin was not so sure he believed his own words, but it mattered not. It felt better to think about it that way.

Chapter 10
Setting Sails

FROM THE RINGHALL CASTLE, Prince Xandur stood on a balcony, pointing to the north. Far like a hawk, his gaze reached, but his focus was not on prey. Before him were mostly open plains, stretching for many a league, with the Cascade Mountains peaking yonder. From his lofty position, he glimpsed the Falls, forcing themselves down the edgy mountainside, accentuated in their majestic rampage by the sun, hanging low in the west. Yet another day was soon to pass, and the day of departure drew nigh.

With his mind wandering to places of depth, he noticed not when someone suddenly came up beside him, showered and veiled in the sharp evening sunlight. He stood back and saw it was Naisha. He gave her a vague smile and refocused on the distant mountains.

"My Prince," she said. "For two long days now, you have stood here in solitude and said no word to anyone. Your mind is aloft and yonder, and you are troubled. Can I help?"

"I am thinking of the world," Xandur said, and his voice was dreamlike. "For the world, the chances are meager. I am going to war once more, and though hope is the last thing that usually leaves me, it is now hanging onto a thread that is about to break. Many are the enemies, eager to slay, but significant is also the number of friends I have lost; not all of them in battle."

"You are thinking about your brother, I presume," Naisha

said.

"Not only my brother. I also lost two friends I thought would assist me and my people, fighting by my side in whatever battles were to come. Now, they are no longer welcome in the Kingdom of Khandur."

Naisha laid a soft hand on his shoulder. "Master Raeglin and Kirbakin the Gnome…"

Xandur nodded. "Alas! Sometimes I wonder if the worst enemy is not Azezakel and the Dark Kings, but the traitors within."

"Trust yourself, Prince. Do you feel it was wrong to banish the pilgrim and the Gnome?"

Xandur stood silent for a while, and then he said, "They were like the brothers I never had. Exxarion and I were not close; we are so different. My two former friends were closer to my heart. Then that happened…"

"My purpose is not to make your already troubled mind more troubled, but what if they are right?"

"About Ismaril? No! He is a thief and a murderer. I am shocked these two not only support his actions, but believe Ismaril can somehow turn the war into victory. A remorseless thief and a murderer? Those who side with such a man are themselves guilty of the same crimes. Thus, they are no longer friends of mine."

"You have heard the expression, 'an Ulv in a man's clothing.' But the contrary can sometimes be true. Colors come in shades, and what seems dark at night brightens with sunlight."

The prince's voice became snappier. "What is there for me to do? Take them back? Dub them as knights and place them in my legion?"

"No. I merely ask you to have your mind open and not completely slam the door shut. Make not the same mistakes so many rulers and top officers did before you, whose minds were rigid and unforgiving. Such rulers often lead their people astray. Greatest are those who show compassion and mercy—even toward their opponents. Not to embrace them when they are evil, but to show compassion and empathy to understand them. Thenceforth, you truly know in your heart how to act and react."

Xandur looked at her in awe. "Your words are sensible," he said. "Indeed, Queen Moëlia has lost a wise counselor in you. Yet I cannot call Raeglin and Kirbakin back; nor would the King allow it. It would force me to keep my guard up, studying their every move, always suspecting treacherous acts. My focus must be on other things."

They stood there for a while without speaking. Then a sting of sadness unexpectedly pierced Xandur's heart.

"I must leave two days from now for Port Urasamo," he said. "My fleet is waiting for their Commander. Will you stay here in Ringhall? You would be safe from any retaliation that might be plotted against you."

Naisha smiled and locked eyes with him, and his mind got lost in the moment. "I am not afraid of retaliation," she said. "A bird in a cage I am no longer; it tore me asunder. Men think this is their war to fight, whilst maidens of eagerness must stay chained and idle. For many, staying passive might be their fate and their duty, but that is not for me. Too long have I and my people sat idle. Now this bird has flown, and free she must remain."

"Then what is your plan, fair lady?"

"Do you not need a seer on your ship? I wish to fare with you."

"No, milady," he said, playing with his finger. "A seer I already have. And if you follow where I am going, you might share my fate; for I may not return."

"It is not for you to decide my fate, Prince. That responsibility is mine. Yet I must ask for your permission to board your sea vessel."

She hesitated, and then continued, "A seer you already have, you say. Who is she?"

Xandur thought he noticed an ounce of jealousy in her voice, and he said, "Nobody. My seer is not a live person."

He removed his hand from the finger he had played with and showed her a ring sitting on his right index finger. And lo! It was of pure silver, with many tiny diamonds inserted all around, reflecting the fading sunlight in prisms, with lights in shifting colors spreading about. On top was a pearl, appearing light blue in its essence, but even that changed when the elongated sunbeams hit. Naisha raised her eyebrows in wonder.

"That is a beautiful ring," she whispered. "It almost has its own life. I can feel it!"

Xandur nodded. "Yes, you could say it is alive. From many generations agone, they passed it down onto me; always to the firstborn when he came to age. It is indeed a seer's ring, but it only has as much power as the owner gives it. It is said to contain the bearer's own life energy within its glamor, and it transforms the ancestral memories of the person and reads potential fates, destinies, and events yet to come."

"How accurate is it?"

"It depends on me. My thoughts are influential, too. My mindset."

"If I may be so bold as to ask: How did it come into your ancestors' possession?"

"It has been handed down from Irvannion, our first king. A female warlock gave it to him. Yet I must learn to use it."

Naisha took his hand in hers and lifted his wrist for a better glance. Then she smiled gently. "This warlock, of whom you speak, was not any warlock, Prince. She was of our kind. No, in fact, she was of the true Originals."

Xandur gasped. "I believe that to be true. But why, milady, do you say, 'true Originals,' as if you distinguish them from yourself and your kind?"

Naisha's gaze wandered, and she sighed. "Because we, the Ayasisians, are not the true Originals. The Emorians are. They are the Mazosians, the Female Warriors and Warlocks of times long agone."

"Then you say it is true: Those of your Queendom are not the Originals?"

"Of sorts, we are. But we fell. The Emorians did not. This I know, for I have studied our history, denied by my kind for thousands of years. My people are proud; so much that they became blind to who they are."

Xandur studied her from top to toe. "You are a wonder, Lady Naisha," he said in a tender voice. "How come you can see, and they cannot?"

She laughed from her heart. "Because I am a seer, of course. Is that not obvious?"

"But there are other seers in your Queendom. Do they not see?"

She shrugged. "This is the reason I wish to come with you. I can be of help."

Again, they stood silent, but the silence was not unpleasant, and the prince wished it to linger. Yet he finally spoke.

"Very well," he said. "You have convinced me, milady. You

can come with me. We shall leave Ringhall at dawn the day after tomorrow."

Not until then did Naisha reluctantly let go of his hand. The sun had withdrawn its last beams, giving room for a starlit night; but the two companions had noticed no passing of time. Together, they left the balcony and returned inside.

Two days later, and by dawn, Prince Xandur left Ringhall with a cavalcade of 150 men, and yet another 1500 were awaiting at Port Urasamo by the Bay, 30 leagues south of there. The prince rode in front, dressed in purple and white, and with a silver helmet on his head, topped with a plume in red and white. Beside him rode the flag bearer, carrying the dark blue banner of Khandur with the castle and the Dragon against a full moon. Forthwith behind them, Naisha rode a black mare, dressed as a man, in a dark green garment, and her head was bare. Her fire-red hair fell long and thick on her back, and she rode as straight and well as any man. Tall and proud, her head raised higher than any of the mighty men who followed suit, for thus was the stature of the Ayasisians. In a sheath fastened to a brown belt, a full-length Khanduran sword rested, and across her shoulders, a quiver and a sturdy bow hung. Naisha was ready to meet aught was to come.

Before them lay the wide heaths, laid with small hamlets, which they quickly passed. In some of them, the villagers ran inside and locked their doors, thinking they were the enemy attacking. Others saluted them as they rode by, happy to see their beloved prince, but ignorant of what was happening and where the soldiers were heading. In other settlements that had been less fortunate, where the war had struck them harder, people's faces reflected weariness and sadness, and they cared not to greet the troops, for these women, men, and children were still mourning.

A drizzle hit the soldiers by midday, right where the road to Oldguard crossed their path, but they kept their pace, only stopping once to eat and to let the horses drink at a ford over a traversing creek. Betwixt River Falluin and River Eastwald, a sparse forest of fir trees lined the road on either side, while the rain fell harder upon the company. But the road was well maintained, and it did not slow them down. It was still raining when they reached the River Eastwald bridge, and by then, the hour was late, with dusk approaching. Here, they stopped for the night and encamped, raising their tents in the land's wetness.

On the morning that followed, a warm sun awoke them. The clouds had withered, and as the early dawn evolved, the sky cleared. As the procession continued down Fort Dongill Road, ere the day was old, the creeks and rivers became sparse and the land dry. Nothing much grew here, aside from groups of thorny bushes spread out, and some brush here and there. The Barren Heaths, lasting for many leagues, were named so for a good reason. Through this desert, the road kept winding. Afar, and increasing as they neared, a naked mountain touched the sky, lonesome and out of place, it seemed.

Later, and farther south, the Barren Heaths ended, and the land became fertile once more, with green grass, sparse at first, but soon thickening and growing taller. In the afternoon, they rode into a ravine, where the road narrowed into a path, allowing only two men to ride side by side. On their left, they had the gray Hills of Annumael, and on their right, Mount Anum, erstwhile spotted from afar, steep, ragged, and void of foliage. Here they stopped for a little to stretch their legs and rest their horses.

"We will reach the small town of Rior ere too long. It sits at the fork between the Southern River and its tributary. There, we can rest for a night, again sleeping in proper beds, and tomorrow afternoon, if the weather will have it, we should reach Port Urasamo, where ships and crew are waiting."

The Company reached Rior before dusk and spread out, booking rooms at different inns where there were vacancies. After a good night's sleep, they left early and rode south, crossing a ford where the Southern River split in two. On the far side of the singing water, continuing south, a thick forest grew. There were mostly fir and pine, mixed with some lime and birch trees. The limes and birches were already blooming, although the snow had barely melted and fallen from their boughs and branches. Azezakel's magic had indeed weakened after the Khanduran victory in the recent battle.

The forest reached many leagues to the south and to the east, and in the west, it soon mixed with the vast Southern Wildforests, largely unexplored territory, being no one's land. The foliage was so thick there that it was a hazard to travel; and it had its unique wildlife, quite different from other forests along the southern coasts of Taëlia. Occasionally, or so it was rumored, queer beasts appeared close to the villages, dark in minds, and frightening at sight. Although many people were hunters in this part of the kingdom, no one placed a foot inside the Southern Wildforests and had not done so since the start of the Age, according to legend. Whether there was any truth in those stories, someone brave must enter deep into these woods and return to find out.

Following a day's ride, the prince's legion galloped into Urasamo by the Bay. As soon as they entered the town, there was the smell of saltwater reaching Prince Xandur's nose from afar, creating a nebulous yearning in his heart. He was not a mariner, but he had always loved the seas and the shores, the freshness of the ocean winds, and the vast, open spaces. As a child, he had been eager and excited when his father let him and his brother join on long trips far from shore, where mysterious lands and islands, often covered with forests and hills, floated by as the ships passed. On these trips, the officers taught him and Exxarion everything they needed to know about ships and sea life, and how to command a crew; something kings and princes must learn. These were fond memories, and a fleeting sadness hit when he thought of his brother as of now. In their youth, they enjoyed many things in each other's company. And never would he forget the seagulls squawking when the ships returned to the shore. Even now, from across town, their soothing noise touched him, and his heart galloped with joy.

On worn, uneven, and weather-bitten cobblestones, the cavalcade trotted across town, reaching the harbor and the quay. There, along the whole side of the harbor, twelve massive warships rocked on the whipping waves, splashing over the quay in late afternoon winds, rolling in from the blue-green sea yonder. Many gulls and other seabirds flew about everywhere, when they were not sitting on top of masts or on the quay near ships, hoping to snatch a fish or two.

The horsemen stopped and spread out in a long row, in line with the harbor and on either side of the prince. Before them, the ship crews waved and hollered, happy to see the prince and his men come to. Many threw their hats in the air, others drew their swords and raised their arms in honor of the prince, and on the decks, the officers stood in salute before their Chief Commander.

~ Setting Sails ~

Xandur was proud of the Khandur navy, and the Khanduran shipwrights were the masters of trade at building sturdy warships. He had seen these ships before, but he was yet in awe, and his eyes glistered. Built with the best cedar and oak, growing in abundance about Port Urasamo, the ships sailed sturdily and pridefully on any water. In the bow of each ship, the shipwrights had wrought a massive head of a Fire Dragon, and in the abaft, a Dragon's tail was carved, making the entire ship rise aloft like an enormous Dragon. An armada of these ships had scared many enemies to flee in past battles by their mere appearance. Near the bow, forecastles ascended from the decks, and in the aft, the stern castles with a quarterdeck rose. Two massive masts mounted from the mid decks, but the dark blue sails with the fire-breathing Dragon in white were now folded for the high winds. Xandur dismounted and walked on board the main ship, anchored amidst—the vessel over which he would be the Commander—and he greeted the crew.

"Welcome to Urasamo, Admiral and High-Prince Xandur," the ship commander said. "I am Captain Ethenwulf, and I shall be your Second in Command on Stormwind."

"Hail, Captain," Xandur said. "When we are at sea, you can title me Admiral." He sighed and smiled absently, caressing the railing. "It was on Stormwind, this exact ship that I learned to navigate at sea, as well as did my brother, Prince Exxarion. It is a pleasure to walk these decks once more after so much time past. Is everything prepared for departure tomorrow morning?"

"Aye, Sir! Whenever you are ready. How many men have you brought?"

"One-hundred and fifty."

"Very well, Admiral Xandur. The armada has room for them all."

"Then let everybody know we are sailing two hours past sunrise," the prince said and returned to his men, waiting on the quay.

When the prince's entire crew had been accommodated on different ships, he and Naisha went ashore alone and sat on a bench by the water, while the sun slowly sank beneath the horizon, leaving a flickering light mirrored in the water.

She faced him and spoke.

"This is a beautiful place. Are you as fond of the waters as I am? I must admit, I have never been at sea."

Xandur met her gaze and smiled.

"Since I was merely a child, I wished to be a mariner," he confessed in a dreamlike voice. "But I was born for something different. Yet, now I can go to sea again, as I did many years ago. I only wish it was during better circumstances. We are born in evil times over which we have little control; we can only do the best of what we have to meet the challenges ahead, of which we know little. The ones with the most strength may succumb, while a good deal of the weak may survive. There is no telling who will live and who will die."

"Are you amongst the strongest, Prince?" she asked.

"Yah and nay," was his answer. "I was born royal, born to rule. This makes me no better or worse than any other man. Each man and each woman have their destiny. We choose not our destiny; it is already decided for us. Yet, in the hand we are given, we have choices to make, but we know not whether they are wise until we have made them and acted upon them. Destiny is not fate, and we can still change the path we are on."

Naisha nodded. "So it is," she said. "And a choice I have made is unlikely for someone like me. I am not of your people, yet I feel a belonging that I never felt amongst my kind."

"Nonetheless, we are all human, are we not? It saddens me we are the same, yet so different. How many times have I not wondered why we must be divided when all we wish for is the same? Do we not all want peace and freedom?"

"Not all do, or perhaps I should say we all do, but such words ring differently for different people and species. Even the Dark Kings want peace, do they not?"

"Same goal, different motives."

"And therefore, there are wars. Even my people want peace, my Queen included. Thus, she made a peace pact with Gormoth, thinking that would save the Queendom and hopefully bring global peace. She is not evil, Xandur, she is merely concerned."

"You addressed me without my title," Xandur said and turned toward her. "I like that."

Their gazes met for just a little, but the prince was first to look astray.

"It was not purposefully," she said, "but I appreciate I can speak freely. What I meant to say was that Queen Moëlia and her entire Council, of which I was a part, mean well. Yet, they are blind to what is truthfully happening. Ayasis could have saved the lives of many a good knight if we had come to your aid."

"But *you* did," Xandur said. "Your action was heroic, brave, and yet wise, for it won the battle. Now say to me, why are you here? You could have waited for another moment that surely will come; war, not peace, is written in the cards."

She was quiet for a moment, and then she looked him in the eyes.

"Is that not obvious… Xandur?" she said, and her voice was but a whisper.

He said nothing in return, but his gaze was now steadier, and they both saw the depth in each other's eyes, drowning, not knowing whose gaze was whose, for they appeared to merge. Until now, the rhythm of the washing waves had soothed them, but the sound now seemed to diminish and vanish. Left was a melding between the two. Then they closed in on each other, and they kissed. The sun had sunk out of sight for long, and the only light left was the moon and the gaslight from the lamps burning on the porches of the houses nearby. Yet the prince knew their feelings could never be substantiated, for the Ayasisians and the rest of the human races could not mix.

―

By sunrise, all men had boarded the ships, with an average of 125 men on each schooner. Prince Xandur stood tall and proud on Stormwind's quarterdeck with Naisha by his side. The sails were rigged, and a moderate wind blew from land. Over on the forecastle, the horn blower stood prepared, waiting for the signal.

"Roll in the anchors!" Xandur cried, and the man at the bow blew his horn, and its great voice spread across the harbor, and each ship knew to follow.

With Stormwind going first, the armada of twelve mighty schooners and roughly 1,500 good men left Port Urasamo and sailed out on the bay in a wing formation, ready to take on the great sea beyond and join the pirate ships from Rhiandor farther out. Thus, the Kingdom of Khandur went on the offense, closing in on the Enemy's nest. Xandur grabbed the wooden quarterdeck railing and raised his chin. As expected, he wore a large black hat, and in its brim, many long feathers in blue and white were stuck and spliced, moving to and fro in the wind. Then he glanced at

Naisha beside him, and he smiled inside. She was the taller of the two and dressed as a soldier she was, wearing gray armor appropriate for private soldiers and foreigners. But her head was bare, and her green eyes shone in her black face. Her tall stature and assertive gaze gave her the notion of a skilled warrior.

"What does the seer see, Milady?" the prince asked.

She stretched where she stood and gazed out over the wide and troubled water.

"I see war," she said. "A devastating war!"

Chapter 11
That Which is Buried

QUEEN ASTÉAMAT LOOKED at her two guests.
"Come," she said. "I want to show you something."
Ismaril and Sigyn followed into the forest whence they had arrived, and soon they reached the southern bank of the magic River Ossova.

"Magic it is," Astéamat said. "It can do things you would never dream of, but this is not why I took you here. Some of us have studied you, and in some ways even guarded you. A journey through the Underworld is teeming with traps and illusions, amidst real, horrific things. It gladdens me you passed the test and returned alive, which is an impressive accomplishment. Your comradeship may have been a life savior at times. But now I am asking you, Ismaril, what you learned on your journey."

Ismaril said nothing for a long time, staring into space before him.

"I have had little time to reflect yet," he said, knowing very well this was not true.

"If so, your time is now, since you are in a safe environment. Let me hear of your experiences."

"Well," Ismaril said, reluctantly. "There was this man on the pole…"

"This is not what I mean. Did the journey change you inside? Have you changed, Ismaril Farrider?"

"Perhaps… I am humbler, and perhaps more compassionate,

but only Sigyn would know for sure. There are some regrets…"

"Such as?"

"This soldier I killed when I stole the sword so long ago. I met him among the dead." His voice turned into a whisper. "He had a family… I was … I am a murderer and a thief, like so many have told me. Holding back my temper, I could not."

"And now?"

He shook his head and looked down. "Nay! The anger is yet inside me, and it merely waits to surface. I still carry resentment. I hate King Yongahur and the headsmen for murdering my wife and my little boy. How can I forget?"

"You cannot forget, nor should you," the Queen said. "But rage and revenge will not bring them back to life—"

"—Yet it sits better with me if justice will be applied!"

"That sort of thinking has started many wars. The result will be more families losing each other. You opened the Book of Secret, so you possess the likelihood of improving; so what are you going to do with what has been given to you? The sword… Gahil? What did the Poem say in the Book of Secrets? For instance, what about the shadows it talks about?"

The entire poem was burned into Ismaril's mind, and he remembered it from top to bottom.

The only shadows real
are those that you thyself conceal…

"Go on," the Queen demanded.

Go through life with open eyes
bring light to Darkness, live no lies
for Darkness is not what you view
it dwells in depth inside of you.

"Now read me the verse about the sword."

Far you traveled for these lines
seen death and danger, troubled times
bring what is yours but still not yours

and learn its will and tame its force
Use it wisely, not with scorn
'come fresh, anew, once more reborn.

"Take heed, Ismaril," Astéamat said. "It is all in there. In Gahil, you are the owner of the mightiest weapon in Taëlia, but do you understand how to use it? By now, I think you have seen a few minor tricks your weapon can do, and lo! The enemy is afraid of it; even Ishtanagul shuns it. With that sword, you can kill the Dark Kings, but it can do much more than that if its master can use its magic. Yet, Gahil must not slay Azezakel."

"So, how do I use it?" Ismaril asked.

"You have killed with Gahil, is that not so?"

"Aye."

"I would refrain myself from using the blade in battle or man-to-man combats. Do not use it to destroy and extinguish lives as much as you can avoid it," the Queen said. "If you use it unwisely, it might take your life, too. For the sword mirrors you and becomes a reflection of you. Thus, what you let out using this weapon will also be used on you. It works both ways. Thus, you must not kill the Dark Kings with it."

"But then the sword is of evil," Ismaril said.

"No, it merely mirrors the traits of its destined owner."

"Then why me?" Ismaril said, and his voice got louder. "I have done unforgivable things. Why do possess such a weapon—a weapon I cannot even control?"

"You cannot control it until you can control yourself. The blade sought you, for you possess challenges that are necessary to overcome to tame the sword and to heal the world. Dark challenges lurking inside you are not unique to you. Many are those who carry similar darkness inside. Through you, this obscurity can disperse, and only then can you distinguish yourself from the Dark Kings. They cannot endure the Divine Light, and hence, they need to keep you in the dark. You represent your species now, Ismaril. I say not that humanity's fate is entirely in your hands, for it is not, but not even the strongest and most ferocious warrior is more powerful than he who can control the sword, Gahil. One day, I might explain more."

"Little do I understand why I am here," Ismaril said. "Did I go through all this in vain? My heart carries much sorrow and pain, and in my possession, I have the mightiest sword in the world. Yet I cannot retaliate, and I am supposed not to use the blade. How they will I defeat Azezakel?"

"Never did I suggest you should not make use of the blade," the Queen said. "On the contrary: One could say Gahil chose you as its owner so you can use it. Albeit not for evil."

"I am confused. I am not a warlock."

"Nay, you are not a warlock; that is for Raeglin and a few others. You are a wizard, and that is for more."

Ismaril frowned. "I am not a wizard. I do not use magic, and I know not how to."

"If you are a human, you are a wizard," Astéamat insisted. "All humans are wizards. I will show you."

She pointed to an open area between a few ash trees. Ismaril noticed a few dead yellow leaves had fallen there, and for a moment he wondered why that was. There should be no death in this realm, or so he was told.

"Now, both of you, in your mind, imagine a cup—any cup. Do you see the cup?" Both nodded. "Now imagine the cup to manifest thither, between those two trees, without forcing it. Merely place them there with your mind."

The Queen barely finished the sentence ere two cups, one of tin and one of terracotta, decorated with white flowers, were displayed on the ground. Ismaril and Sigyn looked at each other in awe.

"That was easy, was it not?" the Queen said.

"How is this possible?" Ismaril whispered. "Never have I been able to do this."

"But your old ancestors could do it when the world was young, ere the Dark Kings descended on Taëlia. Humans outside Emoria have forgotten their own power, for it stopped working when your world went dark. Yet you can do it here in our realm."

"Are… are they real?" Sigyn asked, astonished. She hurried over to the cups and held them both to show Ismaril. "Behold! They are real!"

"And thus, you created the mirror, Ismaril, and all that you saw in it when my people encountered you in our forest," Astéamat said. "It was your own doing."

Ismaril was in disbelief. "Had I not seen it with my own eyes…," he said. "So, where does my blade come into the story?"

"Out there, you cannot manifest as easily as you can here.

But the sword is Divine and was once the horn of the one and only Unicorn. It has magic properties that work even in your world. But it is your task to tame it, Ismaril. In the wrong hands, it is a very dangerous weapon. The Dark Kings have learned by now that if they use it, it will kill them."

The pathfinder sighed. "I think Sigyn would be a more appropriate carrier of the blade," he said. "She has none of my flaws."

"No one is flawless," the Queen said. "Not even I and the Mazosians. What you see is a paradise, compared to yours, and we built it. Yet we are not without flaws, and things here are not perfect; we are still working on that. Sigyn has her flaws, yet they are not the same as yours. The sword chose you, for you have what you need to fulfill its purpose."

"*Its* purpose? So, I am merely a vessel, and the sword is my master?"

"The master is you, for Gahil cannot fulfill its purpose unless you master it and control it with your will. Remember, Dark Kings and Wolfmen alike fear the blade, but more so he who carries it."

"Are you saying they are afraid of me? They showed no fear in my encounter with them, except perhaps once in the beginning of my journey. I was the one who was frightened."

Astéamat nodded and pierced Ismaril with her green, bright eyes.

"And this is my point: so long as you fear them, they feel safe and in control. So, they exaggerate their aggression, preventing you from using the true abilities you inhabit through Gahil. Henceforth, you must learn to prevail over your fear of them. Not until then shall you master your powerful tool; for the strength and the power must come through you and into the sword."

"What will the sword do?"

"Aught you wish it to do. You are the master, remember? But do not use it mindlessly, or it will come back and hurt you."

Ismaril drew Gahil and studied the blade with new respect. It was as if he saw the blade for the first time. Black as the darkest hour it was, but the green sunlight over the Enchanted Woods reflected in it, and for a while, it changed color to hazel, almost green. For a moment, he caught his own reflection in the blade, and his inner strength increased. Then he pointed the sword toward the ground in front of him and thought of a water canteen, expecting it to manifest there. Nothing happened. He tried again, yet the result was nil. Thrice he tried, and for each time, he put in more effort.

"It is not working!"

"That is because you have not yet mastered it."

"But I could do it without Gahil."

"Much so, but then you created without tools, and aside from your own energy, you used that which was around you in support. When you use the sword, it is you and Gahil working in unison. You must funnel your thought, your energy, your imagination alike, and your intent must flow through the blade."

"How?"

"You must learn how to open up to your emotions again," the Queen said. "Your rigidness and your unwillingness to unlock your mind are your biggest obstacles. You are not allowing yourself to live and to be who you truly are."

Ismaril knew it was true, but he had the right to be shut down. Why open the doors to all the pain inside? What he saw once he looked suffocated him. Life must go on.

"I know not who I am anymore," he said. "Long ago, I locked my emotions in, and I forgot where I put the key. I have not even bothered to look for it. This is how I survive; everything else is too painful."

"And thus, revenge replaces the genuine emotions you refuse to process. Do you see a little better now why Gahil chose you? Your locked-in suffering is not something isolated to you. Humankind is suffering, and you can help. But only if you make a great effort; and what is now locked inside you can be of great use through the sword if your emotions are under control."

Ismaril shook his head. "I am only one person. How much can one man do?"

"Many have asked themselves that question, and thenceforth, they gave up. Had they proceeded regardless, the world might be a little brighter today. But they inhabited no unicorn sword as you do. Learn to control it, and you can ultimately control wars and peace and bring about either or."

The Queen went silent. Ismaril felt as if she was trying to penetrate his mind, and he worked hard to prevent her. Then the intrusion stopped.

"Alas!" Astéamat said. "I was testing you. Ye are so protective of your mind that I cannot reach there. Do you see what you are doing?"

"Aye," Ismaril said, and his eyes glazed over. "I possess so much shame and so much guilt. All the things I have done… every time I have created disasters, both for me and for others… how my actions have set a chain of events in motion; and none of it I wished for to happen. But I was not always like this. My thoughtless actions and reactions even led to the death of my family."

He forced Gahil deep into the soil, and then he sat, burying his head in the palms of his hands. "I know not why I did all the things I did. They are like memories from another lifetime or don't belong to me. Yet I know I am responsible for them all."

"Not all," the Queen said, "but many of them. Yet it is not too late to put things right again."

Ismaril's anger bubbled up from inside. "Not too late? How can any action I'm taking now give me my family back? How can anything I do bring back those who died because of me? Aught I do will bring none of them to life!"

"Perhaps not, but it would surprise you what it *can* do. As unfair as it may sound, there are bigger things at stake than your own grief, Ismaril. Your grief is valid, but your people, and other species with them, suffer too, and like an evil plague, it grows until it encompasses the entire world. Never has Taëlia been so close to extinction, and unheard of is the despair of the human collective mind. The world is in great anguish. The Unicorn allowed itself to be sacrificed so she could best assist humankind in the war she knew was inevitable, and thus, she fooled the Dark Kings who slayed her. Little did they know they were pawns in a bigger game, and the slaying was the first step toward their own defeat. Ismaril Farrider, you must put aside your own suffering for some time if the wellbeing of your fellow man is at all concerning to you; for you *can* do something about it."

"It all sounds so unreal," Ismaril said. "Yet the Book of Secret allowed me to read the pages that were dedicated to me alone, and the sword came to me. I cannot explain that."

Quietly, he sat in deep thoughts. He saw his entire life flash by like a long story inside his head, and many times in his life, he felt shame and guilt. But he looked at each of them as they appeared to him, even the most painful ones, and they made him gasp for air, and his heart pumped so fast it was about to burst in his chest.

He sat for a long time, and Astéamat and Sigyn said none, waiting patiently for him to go through his inner turmoil. Amid the contemplation, a flood of self-pity rushed through his mind and body, upsetting, and next to unbearable to face. There was the sense of no one understanding him, of being alone in a world where no one cared about his pain and suffering.

Then he came to an insight: People had cared about him all this time, but he had refused to let them in. Instead, he had pushed them away as if he wanted his suffering to linger, so he would never forget. Even when so, they had stayed and tried to help, but he never noticed. And his biggest supporter, who refused to leave his side, stood there right before him.

Then he raised his head and in tears, and he locked them with Sigyn's. Arduously, he stood, walked up to her and embraced her, while he wept like a child. She embraced him back in such a way that he was comforted. His body felt so good close to hers, and a heavy load washed off his shoulders; and a garment, like a burdensome weight, fell off his chest where they stood. Most of his life he had carried a burden too heavy to be his, and he understood not how much it had affected him and worn him down.

"Sigyn, Sigyn," he wept. "Alas! How can you stand me? Next to nothing have I given you of what you need, and I have refused to embrace your love and your compassion. I am so sorry. I must be the most selfish person who has ever walked upon the soil of Taëlia!"

She squeezed him harder. "I felt your pain," she said, "for my pain is in some sense similar. We have both lost what mattered the most to us. Yet your path was different, and my losses were fewer. Entwined we are in this, Ismaril, and soon we will have a child to raise, and we shall raise this child well in a world that will be more peaceful than this one. And we shall see to that."

He slowly pulled back, put his hands on her shoulders, and looked her in the eyes. "So it must be, and for the world, and for the sake of our unborn child, I shall do my best to help bring peace into this darkness. I do not want our child to see the world as we see it. Everything must change."

Then Astéamat put their hands in hers and smiled.

"Well done, dear Ismaril," she said. "Albeit your inner suffering will remain for times to come, you have achieved great insights that will help you on the last part of your journey."

She paused, and then she said, "Now look on the ground where you manifested the cups. Were there not dead leaves on the ground only minutes ago?"

"Yes, I noticed," Ismaril said. "I wondered about them."

"Lo-and-behold!" Sigyn cried. "They are no longer there."

Chapter 12
Misthorn

Exxarion had no patience for long meetings. There was no need for them, for he had always chosen the course ere he called upon his generals and other higher officers. It was more of an impatient gesture to win them over and avoid unnecessary conflicts within the Council. Erstwhile, he summoned all higher officers and relevant servants belonging to the court, but this always led to excessive discussions. Thus, he had now reduced the number of the Council members to four; himself being number five. These members comprised two generals, his adviser, and his personal secretary. The latter expected to be quiet during the meetings.

This morning, the prince held a conference at dawn, summering the Council with short notice. One by one, the members of the Council showed up, a few more awake than others. No one wanted to be the last to arrive, though someone must; The Adviser was the last person to show.

"And what excuses you for being late?" Prince Exxarion said harshly, albeit the poor old man showed merely a moment after member number three had arrived.

"I am sorry, Sire," the old man said, out of breath. "You said, as soon as you can, and I did, Sire."

Exxarion gave him a long look.

"Well, let us begin," he said. "I have made an important decision, which will make sculptures raise monuments in my honor.

I want my fleet to be ready to leave Misthorn seven days from now, and we are sailing to Khurad-Resh. We shall take the city, drive King Nibrazul out of his castle, slay Wolfmen and Birdmen, and take over Rhuir. We can expect no help from Khandur, so we must do it on our own. Questions?"

The Council members exchanged hard looks, but they all knew better than objecting at this point.

"Very well," Exxarion said. "I am glad we agree. We cannot sit here idle; it makes me nervous and bored. It is like sitting waiting. Waiting for what? An invasion? No, I am not the leader who sits and expects to be invaded. I do not defend myself—I attack! Nibrazul and Azezakel think they have us in their cage or coffin, closing the lid, and having us scream in terror while buried alive. It might be my father's strategy to be defensive, as well as my brother's, but it is not my way. Is staying idle what we want?"

There was a moment's silence, and then the Council said, echoing each other, "No, Sire!"

"Right! So, what do we want?"

"We want to attack!"

"Exactly!" Exxarion slammed his fist against the table, as was his way of emphasizing his power. "Thus, let us plan. The Anúrian fleet is not big, but it matters. Yet, we will not fight the battle at sea. We shall bring our knights and soldiers on board, using all our ships and all our might, none being excluded. This is a onetime hit, and we are in it for victory and glory. We either win or we lose. If we win, I will go to the annals. I shall be the Rebel Prince who saved the Kingdom and humankind from the world's end, despite restrictive directives from higher up. If we lose, it is the end of the world; for we have no defense left in Anúria once I put my fleet in motion. It is everything or nothing. After our victory, we will take Gormoth. Is this understood?"

Silence, then a mutual nod.

"I trust our knights," Exxarion said, now in a calmer voice. "If I want to give credit to my father, at least he trained my knights well. I even trust our soldiers to some extent. We can use them as shields, attacking in the frontline, with the rest of us coming in from behind. In a bold move like this, it is crucial that I, as your leader, am not being killed. Who would then lead you? After all, it is *my* plan."

More silence. Yet, no one raised their voice.

"I count on that I can be bold and straightforward with you. Therefore, I say what I must say: It will be you, my dear generals, who will gather the army and arrange for our departure from Misthorn. Now I need your input."

After additional silence, a gray-haired general spoke up.

"Can I speak freely?"

"Of course," the prince said.

"Let me be practical," the general said. "The plan, as I understand it, is to take the enemy by surprise. No one is expecting us to attack from the sea. All well. But when we get ashore, we do not have any horses. It is almost two leagues from the point where we anchor to Khurad-Resh. This means we must travel on foot from the shore to the city. I am concerned we will draw a lot of attention to ourselves and be ambushed, whether by alien infantry, cavalry, or Dragons."

Exxarion moved around in his chair. "It would be ideal if we could bring horses for everybody," he said, "but we all know we do not have room for that. Yes, we are bringing horses, but only for officers, and for me, as your leader. Even our trained cavalry will be part of the infantry during this military maneuver."

"Would it not be easier to have our cavalry and infantry cross Eldermount Peaks and attack from the west? Perhaps letting our fleet attack from the sea at the same time?"

"No!" Prince Exxarion said. "That takes away the surprise moment, and all could be lost. I was trained as a strategist under my father, the King, but already early on, I knew I could do things better. I am not like any other strategist you know of, and that is my strength, for I am unpredictable. If we do things the regular way, we lose."

"Sire," said the Adviser. "If we follow your lead, and of course, I am not saying we should not, we will have the entire Khandur Kingdom against us." He bowed gracefully, trying not to annoy the prince too much.

"You are not listening!" Exxarion said. "Here I spend my precious time trying to tell you all, in as simple words as possible, and yet you are struggling to comprehend. Of course, the Kingdom will not approve. But here in Anúria, I am the ruler, and I expect your loyalty. Without it, we can accomplish nothing. United we stand!"

"Of course, Sire," the Adviser said.

"Anything else?" The prince scanned the members, one-by-one.

"Can you give us more details about the strategy, please?" the first general said, sounding somewhat confused.

Exxarion's face turned red. "What else do you need to know? Is this question supposed to come from one of my top generals? It is *your* job, and *your* duty, to execute my ideas. I am merely a brilliant strategist. I bring ideas to the table, and you execute them. Is that so difficult to understand?"

"No, of course not, Sire," the general said. "I beg your pardon."

Exxarion sighed loudly. "The meeting is adjourned. Make sure everything is set up according to my plan exactly seven days from now and do not fail. Quickly recruit as many capable men as possible in the province and draft them. We are going to war, and we are expanding the Khandur Empire. Khandur for now, but soon, this province will be self-sufficient and run under my authority, and we shall prosper! How does that sound? We do not need old men with old ideas running our Kingdom in times of global war. We need young minds, new ideas, and BRILLIANCE!"

The Council members stood up and bowed, quick to leave the meeting.

—

When Prince Exxarion set out for Misthorn, eight- and one-half leagues south of Eldermount, his officers had drafted over 6,000 men to follow on foot, whilst the prince and his officers rode on strong and sturdy steeds. In the mountain range, the snow prevailed, making the journey slow and cumbersome for the foot soldiers. Exxarion, riding in front, often caught himself ahead of his troops, and when he noticed, his impatience showed.

"Hurry!" he commanded. "We have a long way to go before we reach the harbor!"

The travel through the mountain pass lasted that entire day, and by the evening, they arrive at the lowlands, where the snow was absent, and the road was easier to trek. There, among trees and bushes, they encamped for the night. The men gathered sticks and cut branches to create bonfires, and soon they had some friendly fires going for them. Exxarion sat with his group of officers away from the rest, but no one spoke. The atmosphere was tense, and no officer showed signs of wishing to be there, although they were too afraid to speak up.

"Fourteen days from now, Rhuir will have fallen into our hands," Exxarion said in a dreamy voice. "Never has such a thing been accomplished; there are no annals speaking of anything as courageous and bold. All those who take part in the invasion, standing or fallen, shall be remembered as heroes in chronicles the world across. This move will be the most important contribution to our ultimate victory over the dark forces."

After a moment's silence, one of his generals found the courage.

"I only wish we had Khandur's blessing," he said. "Some will consider our action treasonous."

The prince snorted. "The elders will arrive when the young and strong have done the hard work. Why put me in charge of Anúria if I lack authority? If anything, I wish I had my brother's blessing, but he must have aged before his time or listened to those whose wisdom encourages idleness. That is cowardly, and that is treason. I am a strategist, and that skill is embarrassingly uncommon. The Enemy is never idle, General. They are constantly on the move, and they count on that we are not. But we will show them. I would give a pot of gold to see Azezakel's face when Khurad-Resh is fallen."

―

The next day, when the sun was at its highest, the army crossed a ford where the river Englir met the Spring of Emhorn. With Englir gurgling in the background, the march went on, out onto the Fields of Glories. The main road slithered through high grass and groves of beautiful willows and lime trees. Here, summer was in full bloom. The sun shone from an open sky, as casually as it always did, despite the hardship of those whom it shone upon. Human hardship was a *human* problem.

Content, Prince Exxarion turned around on his horse and saw the long line of soldiers and knights marching behind him as far as his eyes could see. The scorching sun almost made his body boil under his armor, but he noticed it not, for his attention was not on that, but on accomplishment, victory, and glamor. Nor did he notice that the officers behind him suffered under the blistering sun. Not once, the prince suggested his men could relieve some of their garments.

He could never be a legitimate king so long as his father and brother were alive, but now his grandiosity and entitlement elevated him above all that; now he *was* a king (albeit without a crown), ready to become a God. In his mind, nothing could stop him from achieving his goals, big or small. He had his own army now, and they bowed to his authority.

Later that afternoon, one of his officers galloped to the front and held in by the prince's side.

"Sir… eh, Sire," he said. "One of our men is sick. He fell in his own tracks. Can we halt for a little?"

"What is wrong with him?" Exxarion wanted to know.

"We don't know, Prince… uh, Sire." He bowed upon his horse as if he were ashamed. Exxarion gave him a vicious look, thinking the officer should know better by now than to call him anything but Sire or His Majesty; for in Anúria, he was the King and the God. "He is not far back in the row. Would Your Highness mind visiting him?"

Exxarion sighed and reversed to take a glance. A hundred paces back, a soldier lay on his back in the grass, surrounded by concerned knights and soldiers, trying to be of help.

"Disperse!" Exxarion cried, and the men made room for him when he entered on his albino stallion. From the horseback, he looked down at the man on the ground, who was grunting and with his helmet removed.

"What is this?" the prince exhaled and looked about at the crowd. "This is an old man. What is he doing in my army?"

After a moment's silence, a general stepped forth.

"Sire, you said we should gather all men we could find in the province who could fight. This man appeared to be fit…"

"Fit?" Exxarion said, now spitting out his words. "This man is on the ground, long before the battle has begun. How can he be fit?"

"I… I am sorry, Sire," the General said and bowed. "He was a volunteer. I remember he…"

"Enow! Embarrass me not! My father appointed you, General, not I. Remember this all of you! Who else have you recruited who is not fit to fight? In truth, how big is my army? A hundred capable men? Two hundred? What of the rest of the 6,000? Elderly cripples all of them?"

"No Sire, of course, no, Sire," the General said. "This is not what I am saying—"

"So. what *are* you saying?"

No answer.

"All of you, take your helms off!" the prince commanded.

Without hesitation, those who could hear abided forthwith. Those who did not hear appeared confused, but watched their companions and followed their example.

Exxarion gazed hither and thither and spotted some elderly among the troops. Those who stood next to him saw the fury in his eyes, and his face turning red.

"For the sake of us all!"

Exxarion's voice impeached like that of a judge, as his voice rolled out its authority amongst the troops. "Those past the age of fifty immediately return to Eldermount! We have no use for you here. What is wrong with you people? This is not a game—it is bloody serious. Turn around NOW! And take your sick fellow with you! When we reach Misthorn and I see *one* soldier or knight sick, or someone beyond the age of fifty, I will hang him! This is the war of the young and fit, not that of the Elder and the cripple. Do not once again attempt to slow me down on my mission! Dismissed!"

The prince turned and galloped past the stationary army to take the lead once again. Looking behind him, and to his dismay, he saw about five hundred men turning around, walking back to Eldermount with head in hand.

When this is passed, Exxarion thought, *someone must pay for it. I am engulfed by fools.*

Enraged, he commanded his troops to move quicker, bearing in mind that once he got the elderly out of the way, it would enhance the progress. Someone's head was at stake, and they knew who they were. Prince Exxarion was not of the kind who forgot or forgave.

———

The morning after, the army reached Misthorn, one of the two most important Anúria havens. In the company of 5,500 able knights and soldiers, the assembly gathered the largest fleet that Anúria had seen since time immemorial; and in charge of perhaps the boldest army in the history of the Kingdom of Khandur was the Prince of Gods, Exxarion, son of Barakus.

Chapter 13
Through Forest Deep

IN THE ENCHANTED WOODS of Emoria, there was indeed no sense of time. Although there were sunsets and sunrises, night and day, these shifts between light and dark seemed to have little impact on those who were dwelling here, including Ismaril and Sigyn.

"If you can create all this magic merely with your minds, how come you let there be night?" Ismaril asked. "Night is darkness."

Queen Astéamat laughed. "Even darkness can be beautiful, and not all that is dark is of evil. If there was no night, there would be no sunset and no sunrise, is that not so? And are they not both beautiful to behold?"

The days had come and gone. It seemed impossible to keep them apart; many of them arrived, and many passed as they melded. They might have spent a week here, or perhaps a month; they could not tell. And never did they wish to leave and return to the world of suffering outside the Queendom. Yet, there is an end to everything, and one morning, the Queen joined them for breakfast, comprising delicious fruits of many sorts, and there were berries, warm bread, butter, and a lot of fresh juices to drink. While they ate, the Queen spoke.

"It is time for me to take you," she said.

"Take us where Milady?" Sigyn asked.

"Someone wants to meet you. Someone very special."

Ismaril raised his eyebrows. "And who would that be?"

"Ishtárion."

She paused for a moment ere she spoke again. "Ishtárion is a Gold Dragon."

The guests stopped eating and stared at the Queen in disbelief.

"A... Gold Dragon?" Sigyn said. "But there are no such creatures anymore. They were extinct at the end of the previous Age."

"This is true," the Queen said. "There is only one such Dragon left in the world; he lives immediately outside our Queendom and under our protection. If the Dark Kings knew of him, they would hunt him down to kill him. He is very, very old, and he is the last of his kind. Many millennia have come and gone, and he has seen plenty of them. These days, he is mostly lying in his den and not moving much. But do not be fooled; he is yet powerful, being of the most magnificent and mightiest species of Dragons the world has ever seen."

"But why does he want to meet us?" Ismaril asked.

"On that, I cannot speak," Astéamat said. "Not even we can impede with a Gold Dragon's affairs. If we did, and his business pertained not to us, he would refuse to speak. Even to us."

"Yes, they speak, do they not?" Ismaril said. "At least, that is what the legends say."

"Gold Dragons have many magical qualities. They speak, but they also read minds if it inclines them to."

"Oh, they do?" Suddenly, Ismaril moved around in his chair, restless and uncomfortable. He was no longer so eager to meet this beast.

"We must not linger at this place for too long," the Queen said. "Although time here passes differently than in the world yonder, the two of you have stayed here longer than was planned. Outside, the world goes on, and I believe you are both needed there. Hence, we should leave today, and as soon as possible. It is a long walk, and we will not reach Ishtárion's lair until tomorrow."

"Why not ride the Khibis?" Ismaril said. "We could be there much sooner." In the peripherals, he noticed the horror in Sigyn's face, and she waved with her arms, telling him to be quiet.

The Queen shook her head. "I wish to walk you there. The trail is beautiful. Although time is of the essence, I want you to carry the experience when you leave Emoria. It will give you strength and something to strive for. This is how your world could be if you let it. The den is very close to Mount Essna, from which you entered our Queendom. The Dragon dwells in Hallow Peaks, but I will not follow you all the way; for I must not leave the Queendom and enter your world, or my powers will diminish. Yet I will follow you until the end of the forest."

From the open space where Ismaril and Sigyn had spent most of their time, a trail led into the forest to the east. Queen Astéamat took the lead, with the two visitors following closely. The opening into the forest was like the entrance to a tunnel, albeit this was not a mountain but a forest: A wide trail led straight into the woods, and above their heads, gigantic and mixed trees bent over and created a ceiling above their heads as if they were protecting the path below. Here, the tree trunks were thick and sturdy, in a mix of green and brown, and the crowns were abundant with leaves and flowers in all unthinkable colors. Although the green sun could not fully pierce, beams of green light with shades of yellow came through the leafage, and the trees cast long shadows across. All the surrounding colors made for a magical stride down the tunnel of trees, and musical birds were singing their own distinctive melodies here and there, not the least shy. The Queen knew them all by name, and now and then she called them to her; and they came and sat on her stretched arm or on her shoulders, chirping and twittering. While on the march, Ismaril inhaled the myriad of fragrances, many of them reminding him of the forests back home. Everything in Emoria was extravagant, and to his senses, it was like inhaling childhood scents, though even more pleasant. Here it was neither hot nor cold; for the sunlight that caressed the skin was of a perfect temperature.

"Are there not any challenges in your world?" Ismaril asked. "Everything here seems so perfect. I am certainly not complaining; I could stay here for an eternity, yet I am used to always being on guard."

"We have challenges," the Queen said, "but they are not the same as yours. We are in a constant state of creation, and our biggest challenge might be how and what to improve, and what to create. For with creation, we grow to higher states of being, where more and even better creations are waiting for us to employ and explore. These challenges are positive; they do not include threats to our survival. The only threat is the world outside, knocking to come in. It requires some effort to keep it out."

Here and there, springs and small rivers crossed their paths or ran in a line with it. Again, water nymphs ascended on the waves, forming humanlike, female bodies, dancing and swirling on top of the water, only to merge once more with the stream or river. They paid little attention to the striders, engaged as they were in their own amusement. Between trees and flowers, butterflies flew, glittering in the sunlight, all having unique colors; and on a glade, a bit into the forest to the north, a white deer saw the trio approaching, studying them curiously and without fear.

On and off, other paths slithered into the forest on either side and disappeared between the trees and in the undergrowth, but the Queen stayed firmly on the main trail. And before Ismaril and Sigyn knew, the sun was sinking in the west, and in effect, the forest was changing color.

"This is defying all logic," Ismaril whispered and glanced at Sigyn, but she was seemingly so overwhelmed with what she saw she heard him not.

As the sun slowly sank between the trees, Ismaril noticed the entire forest shift. Trees with leaves and crowns in green and light blue now turned pink, red, and orange, and they glistened in the sunset. If his mind was ever enmeshed in the forest's magic, this took on a new proportion, turning from fairytale to saga. His mind was in an eternal present, and he could experience any moment in his life as if it happened right now. He described to Sigyn what he saw.

"No," she said. "The crowns and the leaves are not of those colors; they are pink and white."

The Queen laughed. "It is all about how you perceive them," she said. "For two people, they are not the same; you interpret these environments, depending on your individual minds."

Ismaril's eyes were wide, and he studied the forest in wonder. The path had now turned violet before his feet, and on either side, mushrooms, half his height, grew. The stems and the caps were of a bluish tint, but the gills seemed to shine with their own light in yellow and bright green. Blue rocks ascended on the slopes on either side of the path, but they could only be seen for a while before the forest took over and covered the rest with trees and blue grass, from which flowers with large white petals grew.

When the last sunbeam was about to withdraw its light, the Queen stopped.

"Behold!" she said. "Over there to the left is a bit of a clearing where we can spend the night."

Thus, they left the path and walked a hundred paces into the woods. Before them, an empty glade stretched less than twenty-five paces and squared. As Ismaril and Sigyn watched, two thick mattresses with fluffy pillows appeared from nowhere.

Sigyn laughed out loud. "Thank you, Milady," she said. "I wish I could do that."

"One day, Sigyn. One day you will, if everything goes well."

"Where is your mattress, then?"

"I need none," Astéamat said. "I prefer to rest in the grass."

A warm breeze brought the most pleasant fragrance from the trees about them into the glade. Ismaril could not imagine a better place to spend the night. At that moment, his stomach was rumbling, and a table appeared between the two mattresses, filled with the most delicious food.

"Eat as much as you wish," the Queen said, and she sat down on the mattress, close to Sigyn.

They ate in silence, while a bright moon appeared in the sky, spreading its shimmer over the meadow, igniting the top section of the grass in yellow, as were they on fire. Between the trees, the light in the undergrowth spread out and shimmered in light blue, and what appeared to be fireflies flew, playfully bouncing into each other and then detaching.

"Not fireflies," Astéamat objected. "These are sylphs, Elementals of the Air. They are our Helpers, together with other Elementals. When we, the Originals, create our world, they help us maintain it the way we want it to be. They can manipulate and reshape the airways as we instruct them. But they are free and happy; they see it not as a duty but a pleasure. The ignitions you see in the grass are Salamanders. They are Elementals of Fire, to whom we have granted a part of our Spirit Fire. They help keep the Spirit of the Forest intact and alive. There is a science behind everything."

"This is unbelievable!" Ismaril exclaimed.

The sparkling light in the Queen's eyes dimmed when she said, "The Elementals exist in your world, as well as here. The difference is that you perceive them as distinct from yourselves, and you pay them little attention. You have forgotten how to interact with Nature. You were born to be one with Nature, but now you see it as something threatening you must defend yourself from. We have created Emoria from within our minds, and we can instantaneously manifest our inner creations in the outer world. You can do this to some extent whilst staying here. But forget not that you are still creating your own world. Yet you dislike what you have created, and therefore, you assign ownership of your creations to someone else, such as the Dark Kings. Please understand, my friends, that you can never stop creating; your thoughts and your imagination shape your perception of reality. It is still magic, you see, but it is so much darker than the magic we use here. Also, we create consciously, and with responsibility, while humans outside our realm create with little forethought. You manifest what is in your minds, regardless, and you can always see from studying your environment and your world what your minds focus upon, and that is what your thoughts manifest."

Ismaril narrowed his brows. "I think I understand what you are telling us," he said, "but is it not equally true that the Dark Kings are manifesting their dark thoughts into our world? Why put the responsibility on us humans? Perhaps we have a part in it, but our world was a better place before they arrived. They must have the major part in it."

The Queen shook her head and locked eyes with Ismaril. He could suddenly see the deep sadness in her eyes, and he was drawn into them as into the Great Void, yet it was not an unpleasant feeling.

"Not so," she said. "As unbelievable as it might sound, the Dark Kings cannot create; they no longer possess such abilities. But you can."

"I am sorry, but I don't understand…"

"The Dark Kings are Divine in the sense that they are all children of the Great Mother, the Creatrix of the Universe, and the reconstructor of the Void. They were once her Divine Helpers until they rebelled; but when they did, they were also stripped of the creative parts of their minds. They could not be allowed to create, using the four Divine Elements: the building blocks of all creation. They never possessed the Fifth Element, the Spirit Fire, but were cosmic master manipulators of the other four elements.

After the rebellion, the Cosmic Mother could no longer allow that, or they would be a threat to the entire Universe. But they found a way to bypass their lack of creativity; they came here and let *you* create for them."

Ismaril's jaw dropped. "Are you saying...?"

The Queen nodded. "Yes, Ismaril. Things worsened here after they arrived, as you mentioned, but they only indirectly turned Taëlia into evil. By manipulating you, who inhabit creative abilities, they slowly had you agree to their view on how this world should be. Thus, you created it for them; unbeknown to you, I should add that the Dark Kings could not do it; you must do it for them. Thus, you created your own nightmare."

Ismaril and Sigyn sat in silence for a long time, stunned at what they heard.

"So, the suffering and the pain in our world, we ourselves created collectively?" Sigyn said.

"So it is," Astéamat said. "Unfortunately, few humans, if any, can understand this. Hence, there is no change for the better, and now, the Dark Kings are close to taking over the world."

"Why did the Dark Kings rebel?" Sigyn asked.

"Because the Cosmic Queen spent a lot of time with humankind after she created you and MAEDIN, your world. She loved you dearly, and indeed, she still does. The Angels, who became the Dark Kings, felt neglected, and they viewed you as a threat to them. So, they invaded, and they took you as hostages." The Queen's eyes teared up.

"You say they cannot create," Ismaril said. "How then could they create the Wolfmen, the Ulves, the Birdmen, and all the other monsters from the Underworld?"

"They created them not—you did!"

"No, we would never do that!" Ismaril objected.

"Not wittingly," the Queen admitted. "The Dark King put the idea of those beasts in your minds, and you created and manifested them. *That is your power!* The Dark Kings are magicians no more, albeit they claim to be. *You* are, or were, the true magicians."

Ismaril gasped and said in a low voice, "Then we are doomed. There is nothing we can do."

"Yet there is hope," Astéamat said. "But somebody must turn things around. As I mentioned earlier, I am not suggesting it should burden only one man's shoulder, for it is everybody's responsibility. Yet there is only one man who possesses the ability to defeat the invaders and help people wake up from their illusionary world they have created. He must show them it is all a lie they themselves manifested. Only one man has the tools to do so... if it is at all possible."

Ismaril shook his head with eyes widened. "I don't know," he said. "It is too much. I know not how to do that."

"Since we last spoke, have you already forgotten the Poem from the Book of Secrets? Are you not possessing the Sword of the Unicorn?"

"Yes, but I do not understand how I can accomplish so much through my blade; and that is regardless of what you have told me."

"You must learn to be in symbiosis with Gahil the Builder, not Gahil the Destroyer—or *Iguhl*, 'Death by Sword,' as some call it. Why *Death by Sword*? It is the name Azezakel gave it, for he came to understand the sword can destroy him. His sole weapon against it is manipulation and more manipulation, making you believe you cannot do it. He knows by now he must not possess Iguhl, or it would burn him from within. He tried once to possess it, but you got hold of it in a twist of fate. Or was it? The blade chose *you*, Ismaril Farrider, and not the other way around. It was meant to be that way. You are bound to it now. It is Destiny. At one point, Azezakel and his Bride understood the danger of possessing Iguhl, so they changed tactics and instead increased the manipulation and projected more illusions onto you. Does the Poem not tell you to use Gahil wisely? Yet the blade is merely a tool. You, as a creator, are the one who puts your creative energies into it and makes it work. Beware, for you are Gahil's Master; you are the mind behind the weapon. It will react to your mind's thoughts. Do you understand this?"

She paused, and then continued, "You are not a wicked man, Ismaril, but you let behaviors from your dark side surface; and instead of gaining control over them, you act out on them, sometimes in ways detrimental to yourself and others. But you already know this, and you have changed from passing through the Underworld. You were chosen because of who you are, possessing a range of characteristics, from your most noble to your darkest. You manifest the range of aspects of humankind in a way that makes you the best candidate. Thus, you can draw anyone's attention if you put your mind to it. Had someone else been chosen, their mission would, believe it or not, have been even more difficult than yours."

Sigyn inflicted, "That is a tremendous burden to bear."

The Queen looked around. "Do not look at the trees, look at the forest," she said. "Embrace the possibilities rather than what seems not possible. There is hope. And you are right; it is indeed an immense burden to bear, Sigyn."

Then she turned to Ismaril again. "There is no guarantee of success; the chances are faint, but this is a hand we must play. It is all you can do, Farrider. Do what you must and do it well; if you fail, you did what you could."

"I never asked to do this," Ismaril said, staring at the grass before his feet.

"This may be difficult to understand, but it is destiny. You were chosen before you were born into this life because of your soul attributes, but you were also given free will to work against your destiny."

"And that is hardly freewill at all."

"Restricted—yes. It may sound cruel to you, but someone must do it. You still do not know what power you possess, Ismaril. If you could help save the world, would you not do it?"

"Perhaps, but I had no choice in the matter. I wish I would have been asked…"

"Are you sure you were not?"

"No one asked me."

"On the contrary. As I mentioned, this was decided before your birth, and the True Divine had a say in it. You were eager to accept your destiny. Yet in the density of your human body, and from the sorrows of your world, you have forgotten. Still, you have free will to return home and abort your mission. I think no one would blame you."

Somewhere inside, Ismaril felt the queen was right: He had agreed to do this ere he was born, but it must have been easy to agree to such a thing while in a higher realm where suffering and pain seemed so far away. Everything is easy when viewed from a place of peace and safety. Now, the burden was almost unbearable.

"Milady," Sigyn said. "May I ask you? How do you know all

this? You seem to know everything about Ismaril, about me, and what is going on in Taëlia. You must be powerful, indeed."

Queen Astéamat met Sigyn's gaze with a slight smile.

"You have both spent a lot of time with me since you entered my Queendom. Yet you know not who I am."

Sigyn looked confused.

"You are Queen Astéamat, the main Creatrix of this Realm."

"Not only of this Realm, Sigyn Archesdaughter, but of all realms."

Ismaril became suddenly alert and looked up. He noticed Sigyn's face turning ash gray in the moon's light. She tried to speak, but no words came through her mouth.

"Yes, I am the Cosmic Mother," Astéamat said. "A part of me is manifested here amongst my children, the Originals. I created Emoria to protect the last of your primordial kind from the Evil that manifested here. I gathered those who refused to fall for the manipulation of the Dark Ones. The rest I could not protect—it was too late. But I grieve constantly, and I weep for the part of humankind who fell. But I am here not only to protect the Originals. I am also here to oversee what is happening in Taëlia and the rest of MAEDIN."

"Q… Queen NIN.AYA?" Sigyn whispered.

"Yes, this is me."

Both Ismaril and Sigyn got to their knees and bowed deeply.

"Forgive me," Ismaril said. "Little did I know. I am embarrassed."

Astéamat grabbed their shoulders.

"Please do not worship me," she said. "I do not need and do not want the powers you are giving away worshipping me. Your powers are yours, and yours alone. You need them, so do not give them to me, for they are not mine to take. Now, please stand."

Ismaril and Sigyn stood, but the astonishment was so great that no more words came from their lips.

"Now go to bed," the Queen said. "Tomorrow you shall meet Ishtárion."

Chapter 14
The Dream Master of Kingshold

KING BARAKUS ONEARM, escorted by three knights, rode in a spur line toward Kingshold in the south region of Khandur, a city second in size only to Ringhall. A few days earlier, a Seer had approached him in the Citadel, telling him she had received an urgent message from the Dream Master of Kingshold, who needed to see him immediately.

The king was in no mood to take on the one-and-a-half-day ride after everything that had happened in the last couple of months, and the phantom pain from his severed arm was yet throbbing. The road trip did nothing good to his agony, but he knew the Dream Master was immobile and could not come to him in Ringhall.

Fortunately, the summer had returned, and the meadows and the grassy fields were in bloom again, and the weather was dry, which helped some for the suffering in his shield arm. Barakus rode light, dressed in a royal-purple cape, and round his head he wore a headband of gold, decorated with many precious stones.

After a day and a half, the four riders entered Kingshold, where they were greeted on the street by the townspeople, ignorant of the purpose of the king's visit. Unsurprisingly, Barakus noticed the people seemed to wonder why their king visited unannounced, dressed in casual clothing, and followed by only four knights. What might be his errand? The faces of a good number of townspeople expressed anxiety when the foursome passed, suspecting this was not good news.

But the king stayed not at any quarter in Kingshold. Instead, he rode straight through, heading east toward the river, running between Spiderlake and Ulmáren, a couple of leagues outside the city. The road here was ill-maintained and narrow, with thick pines rising to great heights on either side. Then, to their right, they saw a small cottage out in the nowhere, and thus, they had reached their destination. This was the abode of the Dream Master.

The king and his men dismounted next to the cottage, and two ragged men, wearing brown, with black leather caps plastering their shaved scalps, took the horses. The house was small and low, with pine trunks stacked upon each other, insulated with mud, and with a roof ill-maintained, in need of serious restoration. Barakus thought the people living here must have suffered during Azezakel's winter, for this far south, the snow rarely fell, and few were prepared for such serious weather. The two ragged men said nothing, walking in a bent forward position, refusing to look up. One man, striding with his back toward him, waved at the king and his knights to follow him inside.

The abode had only one room. The windows were tiny and let in little sunlight, making shadows long and ghastly, veiling the corners of the room. There was a whiff of mold mixed with a subtle odor of sweat and old incense. No windows were open, making the room uncomfortably warm this early afternoon.

In a chair, next to a brick-laid fireplace, sat an old man, dressed in a long and worn brown robe, and his aged hands grabbed the armrests so tightly that his bony knuckles turned white. His scrawny underarms, sticking out from underneath his cloak, were shaking. His head was bare and almost bold; merely a few long strings of unwashed hair, thin and far between, fell over his slumping shoulders, and his face was leathered with many lines intersecting like crossing highroads.

But most noticeable were his eyes, or rather, the lack thereof. This man was not merely blind; he had no eyes at all, only sockets where his eyes had once been. The few people who knew him knew that this man had plucked out his own eyes to become a better Seer; for only if he excluded the physical world could he accomplish his tasks.

"Welcome, King," the man said, and his voice was high in

pitch, shivering from age.

"Greetings, Dream Master," King Barakus said.

"So, you brought three men with you?" the Dream Master said. Barakus had forgotten that the old Seer could see very well without his eyes, using other senses.

"This I did," said the king. "I came as fast as I could, for I know that when you call for attention, it is urgent."

The Dream Master moved about in his chair, gasping, making noises, as if the king's comment stroked him sideways. But then he said, "Aye! My visions and my dreams have been bothersome as of late, and I must not ignore such signs."

"What have you seen?"

"Let my servants give you something humble to eat first. Then I must focus on a new dream with you as my sole company, Sire. But first thing first…"

The two avoidant servants made the table located at the far side of the room and served the visitors bread, butter, fruits, and homemade cheese. The king and his men ate in silence, and when they were done, Barakus told the knights to go outside, so he could be alone with the Dream Master. Even the servants left the room.

Barakus borrowed a chair from the table and put it close to the blind man, and then he sat, facing him.

"Very well," the old man said. "Your time is precious, but I sense that my message to you will be of importance. I must now go to sleep for as long as it takes for a dream to manifest and play out. For this to work as intended, you must sit before me the entire time."

The king nodded, although the Dream Master saw it not. "I shall be here," he said.

The Dream Master leaned backward in his chair and drew a deep sigh. With his neck turned back and his wrinkled mouth open, he fell asleep.

Whilst Barakus was waiting for the Master to wake up, his thoughts wandered, revisiting his memories of what he had heard of this mysterious man. People had talked about him now and again throughout his life, and his father before him had sometimes consulted with him, noticing the Seer was almost always correct. When Barakus' father visited, the Dream Master had already come of age, which now made him ancient, having been the Dream

Master of Kingshold for three generations of kings. No one knew exactly how this old man gained his abilities and why, and it was unknown who his parents were or whence he came. Superstitious people in town rumored he had no parents, and that he merely manifested here from thin air in a time agone. On any of this, the Master never wished to speak, clouding his existence in mystery. Barakus' father once told Barakus that the servants had been with him for centuries, and that they, too, seemed to live extended lives, if they at all could die from natural causes.

During sleep, the Dream Master gasped many times and moved about in his chair. The king frowned, wondering what nightmares this old man might have, and what they meant. Then the Seer woke with a jolt and moaned. Again, he grabbed his armrests as hard as he could and breathed heavily, gazing at Barakus with his empty eye sockets.

"Is everything alright?" the king asked.

"Nay!" the Dream Master cried. "Nay, everything is not alright. Alas! My dream has acknowledged my fears and my foreboding. But there is yet time…!"

"Time for what?"

"Time to mobilize. Sire, your kingdom is in great danger. In my dream, I saw great armies of the most abominable beasts and creatures marching. There were so many that there was no chance to gain a victory against them. Woe to us all! The End of Time is nigh!"

The king's eyes narrowed. "When will all this happen?"

"Soon, soon!" The old man rasped and coughed. "You must muster your knights and soldiers, and within a couple of weeks, you must ride to war. Use forethought, use intuition… Your intuition will become more important than anything else. Discard not what is on your inside, for your kingdom stands and falls with it."

"But this is not the time," Barakus said. "It is too early. Khandur has no staunch allies. If we ride to Gormoth, we ride into a death trap."

"Allies, you have," the Dream Master whispered, and his voice barely carried him. "More allies than you think, and they mobilize across Taëlia. If you attack soon, you will run to their aid, rather than them running to yours; for of pain and slavery many have now had enow. The world is arising from slumber,

King. Behold! There is still time, but speed is of the essence."

Barakus swallowed hard. Could this old, blind man, who had purposefully clawed out his own eyes, be trusted? Or would he, the Great King Barakus of the Divine Kingdom of Khandur, foolishly follow a crazy man's advice and run straight into the arms of the enemy, letting all his brave men be slaughtered?

As if the Dream Master had heard his thoughts, he relaxed in his chair and leaned forward.

"Trust me or trust me not," he croaked. "Follow your inner guidance, Sire. Only you know what is right to do for your people and for the world. Think of how your father acted upon my advice and take that to consider; but think long and hard, for whatever your decision shall be, it will have great impact."

The two men sat silently, facing each other. The king tried to make sense of the dire message, whilst the blind man studied him, still leaning forward. Then he fell back in his chair again and grabbed his armrest.

"Now leave me, Sire," he said. "For what I have told you is it, and it is all. I have no more to convey. The dream exhausted me, and I now must rest. Return to Ringhall and ponder what I have delivered. Choose your future, choose for your kingdom, and do it wisely."

Following that, the Dream Maker fell into a deep and peaceful sleep.

Chapter 15
Whispering Island

For several days, Prince Exxarion and his mighty fleet fought against a turbulent Maere, the great sea in the east. The prince demanded they sail far out, away from the bay and the shores, out of sight of Rhuir's coastline, or they would lose their surprise moment. A ferocious storm hit as soon as they left Maermaid Bay and reached open waters, and it had been ongoing for several days, with little to no sleep for anybody on board.

"This is not normal!" Exxarion's First Admiral cried over the whipping storm, joining the prince on the quarterdeck. "We know not where we are because we can see nothing through this unweather!"

The dangerous situation did not bother Exxarion.

"We have a compass, do we not, Admiral Mundo?" he shouted back, arrogantly, staring at the water, while the heavy rain lashed in his face. "Keep north, that is all!"

"Aye, Sire!" Admiral Mundo said. "But need to find land soon, or we will not make it through the storm!"

"It is your job to sight an island where we can anchor and find shelter!" Exxarion said. "You are my First Admiral, so keep looking instead of whining to me!"

Mundo gave a salute and wobbled down the stairs to the main deck, aware there was nothing he could do but to keep a steady north.

By that afternoon, the weather was so terrible that they could not see the rest of the fleet; and the following night was unprecedented. The entire crew worked for their lives to keep the warship afloat.

———

At dawn, the storm finally subsided, and the rain stopped. Maere withdrew her hungry waves, and soon the sea was like a mirror. Heavy clouds dispersed, and a pale sun beamed through. The crew fell where they stood, exhausted. For now, the nightmare was over.

But Admiral Mundo did not rest; he was all too quick to please his superior, sensing he was in constant trouble with the prince. Starboard, he spotted a tiny island, so he went to get a map and the sextant in the orlop and started measuring the sun's position on the horizon, trying to establish where they were. Exxarion watched him from the quarterdeck, noticing the Admiral's content face. The senior officer glanced up toward the deck and noticed how the prince studied him. He ran up the stairs and approached his superior.

"Good news, Sire," he said. "We have held a steady course north, and we are now merely a few nautical leagues journey from Whispering Island. From there, if sailing straight to the west, we will hit Dragon River, next to our target, Khurad-Resh."

Exxarion showed no facial expressions, annoyed by the Admiral's unprofessional enthusiasm. Instead, he looked out over the sea, noticing that all ships, though spread out, were in one piece and on course. He could see land nowhere, only water and more water.

Then he turned toward his First Admiral. *If I had time, I would fire you on the spot,* he thought. *But I must wait until after the invasion. Perhaps I may have you go on the plank…*

"We need a base at sea if something goes wrong," the prince said. "Set sails for Whispering Island. There, we can also fill up our water supplies and get some rest before we take on Khurad-Resh."

Admiral Mundo's face turned white, and he tensed up, knowing not what to say. Then, only the Goddess knew where from; he found some courage.

"Sire, with respect… We cannot go there. The island is cursed. It would be suicide or worse."

Exxarion exploded. "That is ridiculous! We are grown men, not children who are listening to our mother reading us fairytales. Everybody knows it is just a stupid myth. The island is fine, and even if it would be cursed, I expect my men to be strong and brave enough to resist!"

"Sire, I beg you to reconsider. We might not get out of there alive if we can even get ashore."

"Enow! Set sails for the island!"

Poisoned arrows shot out from Exxarion's eyes when he locked them with Mundo's, and the Admiral immediately bowed.

"Aye, aye, Sire!" he said. "I will see to that, Sire!" He could not hurry down the stairs fast enough, wishing himself as far away from the prince as possible.

―

As the sun moved across the sky, the crew heard the squawking of seagulls at a distance, and Exxarion walked over to the bow to get a better view. A crew member climbed the shroud and jumped into the crow's nest, peering out over the horizon. Soon, sea birds settled down on the mast tops and on the ship's rail, with a promise of land ahead. Ere midday that same day, the sailors heard what they had been waiting for.

"Land ho!" the man in the crow's nest hollered. Exxarion peeked through a monocular, and there it was: a long landmass rising above the horizon.

Carried on a strong wind, the warships cleaved the water, and soon they closed in on the island with the prince's ship in the spear front. A few mountains ascended from the southern shore, and Admiral Mundo commanded the ships to turn eastward to explore the eastern shoreline. Thickets grew there, and toward the inland, a wild forest overtook. Betwixt the trees ran a quick stream.

"Let us anchor over there, close to where the freshwater is!" Exxarion said, and the ships steered at the eastern bay.

As they got closer, the wind subsided. The air went still and the water was calm; not the tiniest breeze blew wind in the sails anymore, and the ships slowed down to a halt before they reached the bay. An eerie silence swept over the surroundings, and there were no more seagulls squawking; the silence was compact. The ship crew spoke not, simply listening to the silence. A wave of terror swept through the entire fleet, but no one could say whence it originated.

"Let us turn, Sire," Mundo said in as low a voice as possible. "Many things have they told me about this place, and none of it is good. There are other islands nearby; smaller, yet friendlier than this one."

The prince rolled his eyes. "My men are going to war against Wolfmen and Dark Kings within days, and you are telling me it must horrify us to go ashore on a deserted island? You are disgusting to me, Admiral. Very much so!"

"But look at our men, Sire. They freeze in terror."

"For the Goddess' sake, Mundo! The more important you stay strong and assertive. It goes beyond me how my father could have made you an Admiral. A greater coward I have never seen!"

Exxarion turned around and faced the men who had gathered on the main deck.

"To the oars, everybody!" he yelled. "We are going ashore!" Shaking and with great reluctance, the crew followed orders, and for a while, the fleet continued toward the bay.

Suddenly, a siren went off inside Exxarion's head; low at first, but then with an increasing pitch, until it was nearly unbearable. Then it stopped. Confused, he spun around and noticed that others shared his confusion.

"What was that?" the Admiral said, and his face was as pale as that of a dead man. Exxarion kept silent. He grabbed a monocular and gazed toward the inland, but everything appeared normal. The stream was sparking in white and blue, reflecting the sunlight, and the trees were still, since there was no wind. No birds, no wildlife.

"Row on!" he commanded, but his voice fell flat, making him doubt whether his words carried far enough weight for the crew to hear. They must have, for the ship started moving.

Then there were the whispers.

They all heard the murmurs, but no wind carried them; they manifested inside their minds. Exxarion could distinguish no words, only an unintelligible mumbling between several voices inside his head. The whispers came in waves, increasing and decreasing in volume. Down on the main deck, a few men put their hands over their ears, though there was no outside noise. Others walked around in circles, moaning and groaning, as if they were about to go insane.

"Focus!" Exxarion roared. "Listen not to the voices. Focus on your tasks, and they will go away!"

"They will not," Admiral Mundo said. "This, people have told me. The whispers that will drive people mad. We must turn around, Sire, before too late. *We must!*"

Exxarion was about to say something when a foreign voice inside him became distinguishable and raised above the mumbling.

Turn around!

The prince's eyes widened, and he slowly twisted his head left and right, trying to make sense of what was happening.

Do not enter the island!

A splash!

It came from the starboard.

Exxarion ran over there and stared into the water. Two Maermaids and one Maerman swam to and fro between bow and stern. When they saw Exxarion beholding them from the deck, they threaded water with their fishtails and stayed still, looking up. Without uttering a word, one of them sent thoughts into the prince's mind.

This island is off-limits. If you go ashore, your lives will be endangered. Dark forces run this island. This is a warning! We are the guardians.

"The guardians?" Exxarion spoke out loud, although the Maermaid had not voiced a sound, and probably could not. "I fear no forces, ill-intended as they might be. I am King Exxarion of Anúria, and I am entering this island."

We cannot let you pass. We repeat: We are here to prevent sailors from going ashore!

"Nonsense! How are two Maermaids and one Maerman supposed to stop me?"

The three creatures swam toward the island, reaching beyond the bow of Exxarion's ship, where they stayed in a line as if trying to prevent the schooner from proceeding.

The prince laughed dryly. "Are you serious? Now aside, so we can pass without running you over."

The beings said nothing but stayed put. A wave of rage ran through Exxarion, and he could feel the heartbeats in his temples while his face turned red.

"For the last time, MOVE!" he shouted from the top of his

lungs.

"Sire…" The Admiral tried to calm his superior down, and he put a hand on his shoulder. Exxarion shook, reached for a bow a few paces away, and without hesitation shot the Maerman in his throat. The creature made no sound, shivered, and sank under the surface. The two Maermaids sat frozen in their positions—shocked and terrified.

"Leave now, or one more will die!"

The Maermaids dived and returned to the surface no more. They were gone.

Every man on the ship stood in silence, as frozen as the three Maermaids. Then, in unison, they took a few steps back to increase the distance between themselves and their crazy commander.

"S…Sire!" the Admiral said. "You just killed a Maerman."

"Shut up!" Exxarion yelled. "Of course I killed a Maerman. No one may stop Exxarion the Great!"

"This is a bad omen," someone on the main deck mumbled.

Exxarion turned. "Who said that?" No answer, only silence. "I am embarrassed by your superstition. I thought I had the best knights and soldiers the world can bring, but watch yourselves! You shiver like little children who are afraid of the dark. What is wrong with you? I had a glorious vision of success in the upcoming battle, but now I have my doubts. To the oars! The fleet will steer toward the island again in five minutes, or someone is going to pay for it!"

"You heard the Sire," one of the lower-ranked officers said. "Get to work! We want to be on solid ground before the afternoon declines!"

Soon, the armada of warships was moving again into the bay area. With the men at the oars, the prince's ship was halfway across the bay where a peninsula ended, and they sighted a smaller bay within the bay. There, ahead, close to the peninsula beach, sat a capsized ship, sunken into the sand in the slush, where land and water met. It sat solidly tilted, with its masts broken, and a large hole in the hull gaped on the port side. When Exxarion used the monocular, he noticed from the rotten wood the ship had been sitting there for years agone.

"That is not an Anúria or a Khandur ship," the prince said to Admiral Mundo, who stood beside him, nervously moving his fingers. "Perhaps it is from the vast lands in the east, across Maere. All ships, cast anchor!"

The Admiral let his voice be heard, and the oarsmen held up their oars. The rattle from the anchor roared like thunder in the compact silence about them. From the crow's nest, the man on the lookout made a sign to the ship behind them to do the same. All the while, the soldiers heard the constant whispers inside their heads.

Prince Exxarion turned toward a few officers standing by the port's rail.

"Captain, you come with me," the prince said, "and bring a strong oarsman with you, able also to fight if needed. The three of us are going over there to explore."

Prince Exxarion, a captain, and a brawny man with a yellow, bushy beard and thick eyebrows took a seat in a. The brawny man grabbed the oars, and the trio parted from the main ship, steering at the wreck. Exxarion had thrown a bow across his shoulder, as well as a quiver filled with arrows, in case they were running into trouble. He also brought a monocular, which he used frequently whilst sitting at the stern. From what he could detect, using the looking glass, there was yet no sign of life, and if there were birds on the island, they were eerily quiet.

They parked the cockboat alongside the hull of the wrecked ship, where the large hole gaped. The split wood pieces encompassing the gaping mouth were like Ulves' teeth, ready to devour them. The murmurs in the prince's head turned louder and became increasingly difficult to endure. He glanced at his two companions and noticed their discomfort. Yet none of them dared to bring up the subject.

The oarsman secured the oars and threw the anchor into the shallow water with a splash. Exxarion lifted himself up through the massive hole in the hull, heeled by the captain, and last, the oarsman.

It was early afternoon, and the sun spared enough light to hurl the darkness out, in that the trio could see well enough. In an old wreck like this, there could be no survivors, but other creatures could have found refuge inside the ghostly carcass. Thus, they drew their swords and stood still for a while, listening. Yet, there was nothing to hear. It was as if the entire world around them had gone silent, save the noise from their creaking footsteps against the half-rotten planks. When they stood, only their heavy breathing amplified in the absence of sound. Even Exxarion, fancying himself as being fearless, had goosebumps on his bare arms, and he recognized the terror in his companions' stares. The prince put a finger across his lips, signaling that they must remain silent.

Carefully, the three moved across the bilge. The smell of damp, rotten wood got stronger as they moved farther into the ship's interior. Tossed all about were full and empty, and they often must step over them. Yet, there was nothing of value to explore here; it seemed to be merely an old, abandoned shipwreck. The crew must have settled on the island, and perhaps they were still there. The companions took the stairs toward the upper decks but needed to be careful when they stepped on the rotten stair planks.

When they arrived at the berth, they stopped there to explore. As they ascended within the ship, the whispering in Exxarion's head seemed to be transitioned from there to the surroundings. Suddenly, the voices in his head were gone, but they were all around, ghastly, lurking in shadows. His two companions stopped, stunned at the change.

"The voices seem to come from inside this ship," the captain whispered in an unsteady voice, "What are they? Are they demons from Hell?"

"I am happy the voices in my head are gone," the brawny man said, "but I think not that this is better. It freezes my blood."

Exxarion gave them a quick glance but said nothing. There was nothing to add.

The group moved about in the berth area when the captain suddenly exclaimed and pointed, "Lo! Over there!"

Leaning against the wall sat the skeleton of a man, still holding a sword with a blackened blade in his hand. He was dressed in foreign clothing, unknown to the three explorers. He must have died, fighting.

"There are more!" the oarsman said, and his voice cracked and shivered.

Indeed, there were dead men spread all over the berth. Against the wall, in a long row, they sat, all holding swords in the same position.

"Someone lined them up as part of some bizarre ritual," the brawny man said.

"And who might this 'someone' be, I wonder?" the captain said. "Is this 'someone' still around?"

Exxarion stared at the unbelievable scene. There must be at least fifty men against the wall. The trio stood there, unable to move, and their minds got weaker, unable to turn their focus away from what had unfurled. As they stood there, frozen in time, the murmurs turned into vicious laughter, moving hither and thither. Exxarion wanted to scream but he could not. No sound came out. His scream got locked up inside, and an unbearable panic attack arose within him.

Then the whispers became so low they could barely be heard. Instead, a voice that seemed to come from the depth of the Void roared across the deck.

Death liberates, death is peace
But no peace shall be gained.
Join the Undead and walk in the Freeze.
See those before ye now are chained:
Peaceful seem they, quick to rot,
but that which man sees, it is not...

Another wave of rage, brought on by the terror he experienced deep inside, rushed through Exxarion's system, breaking the spell, and he spoke.

"Who are you?"

The voice disregarded him and continued, *Are you brave or foolish? It matters not. No one has entered here after these men came, but their pride allowed us to devour on their souls. These fools thought they could overcome. And lo-and-behold! You bring us not a ship but an armada. Man's foolish pride was always his nemesis... nemesis... nemesis...*

The voice echoed out through the void, repeating the last word until it faded out. This broke the spell, and the three men gasped for air.

"Sire, let us get out of here, while we still can!" the captain said in a desperate voice, and with pearls of sweat on his forehead.

"Yes, please... Sire," the oarsman said.

Exxarion's eyes were dark, and his face grim. He hated any thoughts of retreat, but this was too much. His mind signaled "danger, danger!" He sheathed his blade and strode back down the stairs, furious and without a word, immediately followed by the other two; but the goosebumps on his arms refused to go away. He felt anything but safe, and wherever they went, the whispers followed them.

"I cannot endure much longer," the oarsman said, as they hurried toward the gap in the hull whence they came. They threw themselves in the boat, and the oarsman used all his strength and speed to get out of there. He turned his head around over and over, making certain they made progress toward their own ship. Soon, they bumped into the hull of Prince Exxarion's ship, and the on-board crew heaved them up. The captain tried his best to hide the horror on his face, but the oarsman was less successful; and the brawny man sank down against the rail of the ship and broke into tears, face in palms. Exxarion was the only one who seemed emotionally untouched.

"Sire, what happened?" Admiral Mundo asked, obviously frightened. "The whispers are gone from our heads, but they are yet all around."

"I know," Exxarion said, visually agitated. "We are leaving. Pull up the anchors and start rowing until we reach open water. Perhaps we shall find some friendly winds there."

The oarsmen turned the ship around and rowed for their lives toward the open sea. The prince called on his officers to follow him to his aft cabin for a short briefing. He had three officers sitting down around a massive oak table amidst the cabin, and the prince opened a cabinet. From there, he grabbed some glasses and a bottle of fine white rum and served it to his officers.

"After everything we have gone through, I think we need a drink or two," Exxarion said, and his men happily agreed. They sat there for a while, sipping on the liquor, and they spoke not.

After some time, the prince said, "We must not yet go to battle. Exhaustion has overtaken our men after this recent endeavor, and they need rest. According to the navigation map, there is a small island northwest of here. We should go there and rest for a day. It is *this* one!" He tapped with his finger at a small landmass on the map. "Who knows anything about it?"

Whispers.

Many oars hit the water.

Ship moving.

A lieutenant spoke. "Deserted Island. I know about it, but I have never been there. As the name suggests, it is a barren, and often windy place. Small mounds, but no fresh water or wildlife."

"We should have enough water to get to Rhuir," Exxarion said, while the whispers increased in volume. He became more and more agitated at the disruption, finding it difficult to think. "I suggest we…"

The whispering voices swirled across the air, moving hither and thither. It was impossible to continue a meaningful discussion.

"Damn it!" Exxarion slammed his fist on the table. "We should be close to the open sea again. Why are the whispers not stopping?"

He flew from his chair, stepped out of his cabin, and with with long strides, he entered the deck. Still no wind, and the water round the ship splashed from the many oars. The ship moved at a steady pace, but the island did not decrease in size. Gazing out from starboard, he could see the bay where the shipwreck sat stuck in the mud.

"Hell, we have not moved an inch!" he said out loud to no one in particular, or the island is following us. "Why are we not moving?"

He rushed over to the cockswain. "What is going on?"

The man at the helm shook his head. "I was about to tell you, Sire, but I wanted not to interrupt your meeting. The men have rowed for a while now; we appear to move with good speed, but we seem to go nowhere, even though we should be. I mean…"

The prince's body turned stiff, and the blood disappeared from his face.

"You should have interrupted the meeting!" he said in a harsh tone.

"I… I am so sorry, Sire," the cockswain said. "I cannot think straight. All these voices…"

Exxarion gave the cockswain a long look, and then he yelled as loud as he could, so the oarsmen would hear him.

"Halt the ship!" he commanded, and the oarsmen stopped rowing. The prince did not want them to exhaust themselves in vain; he needed their strength later if they ever were to leave this goddess-forsaken island. "Cast anchor!"

Few were the moments in Prince Exxarion's life when he

was unsure of what actions to take: He considered himself an impeccable leader, in full control, and with a quick and accurate mind. Yet this was one of those few moments he knew not what to do next, and he knew of no antidote to the magic at play here. He desperately gazed in different directions. His armada filled up parts of the bay, but they were stuck.

Admiral Mundo entered the quarterdeck and stood beside the prince with his arms on his back; but he dared not say anything, for he had no solution, either. Exxarion bothered him not, for he understood the Admiral could not help him. A moment's shame and regret washed over him for having brought his men to this place, against sound advice, but then he waved it off. *I am not to blame;* he thought. *If the crew from the stranded ship had not fallen for these hideous entities and let themselves be cursed, we would not have faced this dilemma. That crew was weak, giving away their minds to the demons that took them.* Then his face turned pale again. *That is what the demons want to do with us! They want to devour our souls, like they did with the stranded crew. Why did I not see that before? It's these damned murmurs… I cannot think! We are becoming like living dead! Yet, in my brilliance, I was the first to figure that out…*

The whispers now became more hypnotic. The prince fought against them with all his might, for he understood what this was about, and he resented it. Yet it became more and more difficult to resist, and his mind became increasingly unfocused, shifting into a dreamlike state. Against his will, he floated into a twilight zone and was barely aware. Then he took a scant breath and banged his fist against the rail to stay awake, but there was no pain; he could not feel his hand. The whispers moved into his head and through him, and then they spun around and entered his mind again, now from the other side. *I am awake!* He did his best to convince himself he was still in control. *No forces from Hell can take over Exxarion's mind. No one! I am in control! I am stronger… I am the strongest. Yes, this is correct. I am stronger than any malevolent force. Now I am fully awake again. See? I could do it!*

Then he fell where he stood, and his mind failed him.

Chapter 16
Ishtarion

THIS WAS NOT A GOOD NIGHT for Ismaril and Sigyn. The following day would force them to leave this amazing and heavenly Queendom. Never could Ismaril have believed he would miss something so much. Queen Astéamat noticed their sadness, and she spoke wisely.

"I am not telling you not to mourn, or otherwise disregard your feelings; for intending to detach from that which is evil is hard, but detaching from that which gives you joy and pleasure is harder still. It is helpful to find your peace in both. If you can do this, you may one day return here. But first, there are things you must accomplish on the outside."

Although these words bore little consolation at the moment they were uttered, they both knew deep inside the Queen was correct.

The next morning, they ate breakfast in silence, and the Queen let them have their moment. Then they continued their last stride through the Emorian forests. The closer they came to the end of the deep woods, the closer the trees grouped together; the vault over their heads closed again and formed the tunnel that allowed only limited sunlight in, but the forest emanated its own inner light, magically dim and pulsating as it shifted slightly in color from white to yellow, and sometimes to faint blue.

Soon, they reached the end of the forest and stood before a

portal decorated with arched branches, leaves, and flowers in many colors. The forest here was so dense they could not see what was beyond the trees; and the opening amidst the vault was nebulous and veiled, floating and swirling in white and light blue. The shine it emitted was bright to look at, to the point it was hurting their eyes, and they must look away.

"Thus, we have arrived at the end of your visit to Emoria," Queen Astéamat said. She smiled gently, and round her gestalt was a light, ethereal shimmer, mesmerizing and irresistible to behold. Her thick, fire-red hair flew in waves to her waist. A black face with eyes of endless depth gave Ismaril a sense of immortality and an abundance of wisdom and compassion.

Ismaril and Sigyn said nothing. Their eyes were glazed, and tears fell down Sigyn's cheeks. The Queen put her hands on their shoulders and pierced them with her divine gaze.

"Grieve not," she said. "If all goes well, we shall meet again; perhaps sooner than you think. You know your quest, Ismaril Farrider. You have had important insights lately, which I expect will be of great help to you in the last part of your journey. Do not doubt yourself and try not to think too much about your past. You may not yet understand, but the only way to change the past is to change the present. Time is fluid, even in your world, and nothing is as solid as it seems. Live your inner truth, follow your guidance, and the reward will be greater than in your wildest dreams. Let no one divert you from your path. Your future, and that of humankind, may depend on it.

"And to you, Sigyn Archesdaughter, I have this to say: Shield maiden you are his safety and security on your joint mission, and with this, you have done excellent work. You are wise in the most practical way, and it has had an enormous impact at times. In this, digress not from your part. You are pregnant, and there is a curse on you I cannot break for reasons I am not to reveal, or it will make things worse. Only you can overcome, and you alone know how, albeit not yet. When the time comes, you too will stand before a choice, Sigyn. Choose and choose wisely, daughter of mankind."

Astéamat turned silent and locked sad eyes with Sigyn.

"You have said nothing about our child, Milady," Sigyn said. "How come?"

The Queen removed her hands from their shoulders and

sighed.

"Of daunting possibilities, there are many, but not all possibilities are of evil. Care for your unborn with love and compassion. Stay focused on the tasks at hand and follow your inner guidance. Do so, and the outcome may still be bright."

Ismaril glanced at his companion, and he noticed this was not the reassurance she had wished for. For reasons vague, by the Queen's words, he felt a sting and a deep sadness at heart.

"Now go through the vault into your own world," the Queen said. "You will see Hallow Peaks straight ahead. Approach, and you shall find the entrance to the Dragon's lair. She is awaiting you, and she knows you are here. Listen to Ishtarion with care, for she is wise and can advise further. If you focus on her words, you may get a clearer sense of your mission and where to go next."

She studied them, back and forth, and then she said, "Two friends of yours were here just recently."

"Who?" Ismaril and Sigyn said in chorus.

"You call them Master Raeglin and Kirbakin, the Gnome. They were my guests for a brief period, wishing for my help in the war to come. I declined on behalf of my people. We have left our warrior ways behind for long, and being the only oasis in Taëlia, the mere place there is yet peace and harmony, we shall not let this dwelling sink back into the shadows again."

"Where went they?" Ismaril asked.

"They were searching for the two of you. My intuition tells me they are not far, and you may run into them at some point. As always, they can be of great help, but beware! Although Master Raeglin is of the Divine, he has spent a long time in your realm. Kirbakin is an Elemental, and he has spent even more time there. Taëlia changes humans and Divine visitors alike, and their minds can become duller in your dense world. I believe you can trust them, but foremost, trust yourselves."

She turned toward the magic vault. "Now go," she said. "The world out there is waiting for you. Fare thee well, my precious guests. But ere you go, look around. No leaves are falling, and nothing here is dying. You have not lowered our realm in the least. Thus, keep a steady course, and keep evil off your true selves. Fight not with hate or vengeance but with love and compassion. Not to forgive and forget, but to keep your mind focused.

Hate and vengeance blind and degrade, whilst love and compassion make for clear vision. This is my advice. Queen Astéamat has spoken."

With heavy hearts, Ismaril went into the vault opening, followed by Sigyn. There was a short sensation of floating in a void, and then they appeared on the other side.

The shock was excruciating, and their gazes met in astonishment. For Ismaril, it was like dwelling timelessly in a warm and comfortable place by a cracking fireplace, where there was no evil, and amongst the best of friends, only to be flung out into the devilish cold, where ravenous wolves were howling and monsters shrieking.

But it was not cold, and nor where there any ravenous wolves, only a sense of death and doom. Before him, there was barren land stretching east on either side of two peaking mountains with a flat summit. To the north and to the south, the forest spread, but they could enter no more.

"Odd it is," he said. "I do not remember our world being so harsh and devastating to the heart."

"It is the contrast," Sigyn said, wiping off tears of grief from the departure. "Now I understand what Queen Astéamat tried to say: We can have what the Originals have if we do it right… if only we can do it right."

Ismaril nodded. "Or die in the attempt. I now have a difficult time continuing in this hellish world. They say that if we do nothing, the Dark Kings will win and take over. But alas! They already have! Look about you, Sigyn. Do you feel the pain and hopelessness inside you? We have suffered since birth, but we were unaware to which extent, until in Emoria we experienced peace and harmony. The Black King has infected us all with his darkness in such that the entire world has turned into a shadowy ghost land."

"And such it has been for long ages agone."

Ismaril sighed. "I wish I knew better what to do. The future seems veiled in mists of sorrow that I fail to see through. With Gahil, I try to cut it open, but to no avail; the impenetrable mist prevails. After all the advice I have received, I am yet shrouded in darkness."

Sigyn grabbed his shoulder and kissed him. "We have a baby

on its way," she said, voice as smooth as the flow of an Emorian river. "Our child shall not grow up in a world like this. We'll do what we can; nothing more and nothing less. I think the Queen tried to tell us to pay little attention to this physical world and instead trust intuition, imagination, and strong inner will and conviction. I believe that is how we can regain our world. If we humans change, the world changes, too, for good or for bad."

Ismaril raised his head and gazed at the twin mountains yonder.

"Thither are Hallow Peaks," he said. "To there, we must stride."

And so they took a breath and stomped through the barren land. A scorching sun from above stirred up a cloud of dust and left a dry smell each time they put their feet down. No wind and no birds singing; it was like walking through nothingness—a place uncharted to any journeyman.

When they reached closer to the heights, short brush and thickets spread across the land, dry and thorny; rains seemed far between here. They reached the closest of the two mountains and saw a magnificent entrance into the depths beyond. It was as high as fifteen grown men, and nearly as wide. A strange odor, albeit not unpleasant, hit them when they peeked in.

"So, this is the Dragon's lair," Sigyn whispered. "What do we do now? The Dragon has not invited us in."

"There is no gate," Ismaril said. "Nothing to stop us from entering. Does that not make the Dragon vulnerable?"

He took a few steps inside the cave and leaned forward to get a better view. "Appears we can walk right in."

Sigyn hesitated. "I hope she does not attack…"

Ismaril stepped inside, and Sigyn slowly followed. He knew not to draw his weapon, though he had the impulse to do so. It was dark, impossible to tell what was happening around them. There was complete silence, no water dripping, no sounds, and no signs of a Dragon, save for the queer odor getting stronger the farther in they went. Then the tunnel took a sharp turn to the left, and a light, vague at first, appeared farther down. With hearts pounding and breathing shallow, they courageously strode on.

The tunnel ended, and the wayfarers stepped into an immense hall, lit up by brilliant wall decorations of precious stones in thinkable and unthinkable colors and nuances. A hue of ancient magic filled the hall, and images of times far gone rushed through their heads. Here were no magnificent treasures: No gold, necklaces, diamonds, or other valuables covered the ground, otherwise so common in a wild Dragons' den. The floor was bare, save for an astonishing Dragon!

Massive she was, Ishtarion, spreading out on her belly. Nowhere in the world was there such an impressive Dragon in their days. She was more than twice the size of Azezakel's Dragons, and three times the size of those of Ayasis, whom Ismaril encountered during the Wolfman War. She was shining as of purest gold, and her wings, folded against her enormous body, were like white gold, with a span that must be wider than any other living creature imagined. The Dragon would have overwhelmed the two companions with terror if it were not for her eyes, glaring at them where they stood. They were green like emeralds with black slits in the midst; but they were mild as a mother's gaze upon her newborn, emanating compassion and an abundance of ancient wisdom. When locking with them, all fear at once washed off the travelers.

Then there were the enormous jaws that normally would make the bravest knight freeze in horror, but she had them closed and brought into a warm smile. There was nothing threatening about this beast unless you were her enemy.

Ismaril bowed first, with Sigyn following forthwith.

"Hail, Ishtarion," Ismaril said in a deep, mature voice. "Never have we seen such magnificent."

"No need to flatter me, Ismaril Farrider," the Dragon said, and her voice was rich and colorful, filling the entire hall. "You are both expected, and I have been waiting for you."

"We are sorry, Mighty Ishtarion," Sigyn said. "We were delayed in Emoria. It was too wonderful a place to leave."

"Such it is, I hear," Ishtarion said. "But time spent in those forests is not the same as being spent here. Worry not, you are on time."

"The entrance to your cave is open. Are you not afraid of trespassers?" Ismaril asked.

The Dragon's deep and heartfelt laughter bounced against the walls. "I let no one in unless I invite them first," she said. "Be it humans, Originals, or Wolfmen. Few are those who can pass my invisible gates without my permission. They were open when you arrived, for I had left them open for you."

Ismaril cleared his throat. "From what we took away from Queen Astéamat, it is urgent that we meet."

"Urgent, perhaps," the Dragon said, "but what is not urgent these days? An apocalyptic war is drawing nigh, and you two wayfarers have a role to play in it. I am old, and my time is almost for naught. I have seen ages come and go, and the many years have both weighed on me but also helped me gain wisdom. History being told and history that truly is are not one and the same. I have watched humankind decline, and the entire world with them. My next of kin are no more, for I am the last, if that matters. I guess it does, if for nothing else but for the memories and the wisdom I gained and carry: Wisdom I can share as I see apt."

Ishtarion sat up from her lying position and shook her heavy body. A wave of sadness washed over Ismaril, for the Dragon was old and stiff, having lost much of her erstwhile strength and power. But her voice was yet strong and steady.

"I know of your blade, Ismaril. Azezakel slew the Unicorn, the One and Only, but that was predestined. The Enemy was aware, but he thought in his pride that he could bypass Destiny. He realized too late that he may not. In vain, he attempted to possess the sword against the odds, but it slipped away from his grip, and he lost it to humans until it found its right owner—you. Things are as they should. Though older than many mountains, I still have farsight and foresight. You passed the crucial tests predestined for you, Ismaril Farrider, but the most challenging test is ahead."

"This is true," Ismaril said, "yet I know not how to proceed."

"But have you not been told? The Queen conveyed it to you. Emoria still stands, for the last of the Originals refuse to go to war. Tell me the difference between slaying your enemy and the art of spiritual peacefare."

"I know the difference, but how can I win a war if no killing takes place? The Wolfmen will surely do their best to kill me and others, so how can I defeat them if I do not defend myself?"

Ishtarion locked eyes with Ismaril. "Erstwhile I told you I am old, and my days numbered. I shall soon go to where my ancestor dwell. My joints are stiff, and my flight is not as swift as fore." She stood up straight now, looking down at the two humans many feet below. "See my belly? Yes, down there, where the dark gold turns light. Stab me there, Ismaril. Let your blade sink deep into my hide, just where the heart is. Draw Gahil and let it work for you."

Ismaril's blood ran into his stomach. "No, I cannot do that?"

"Why not? Do it!"

"But that will probably kill you!"

"It will if I let you do it. And I *shall* let you do it."

"I... no! You are not my enemy. Besides, you have something to tell us."

"Maybe I asked you to come only to accomplish this task?" Ishtarion said. "Perhaps, by killing me, you will accomplish something essential that is needed for a future purpose? Maybe it is a part of Destiny?"

Ismaril swallowed hard.

"Call it a mercy killing if you wish," the Dragon said. "I suffer, but it will yet take a while ere my time is up. I would be honored to die by the blade of the Unicorn."

Ishtarion stretched some more to make it easier for her bane man to slay her.

"I am waiting," the Dragon said.

Indecisively, Ismaril drew his sword.

"No!!!" Sigyn cried behind him. "Ismaril, no!"

The pathfinder took a few steps forward until he reached the point beneath Ishtarion's giant underbelly, where she was the most vulnerable. She sat still, not moving an inch, waiting for her slayer to proceed.

A sense of hopelessness and unbearable agony overwhelmed Ismaril, and before he could restrain himself, he screamed as loud as he could, and fell to his knees, throwing Gahil away across the hall. It hit the wall with a metallic clonk.

"Stand, Ismaril," the Dragon said. "You did well."

His heavy breathing amplified in the great hall, and he looked up, confused, but all he saw was the Dragon's underbelly.

"Come out from there," Ishtarion said.

Ismaril got to his feet, and on legs unsteady, he backed off; and once more he stood before the Dragon's gaze.

"Do you see now?" the Dragon said. "You experienced a horrible dilemma: You showed empathy for my suffering, and thus, you wanted to end it because of my wish. You showed compassion. Yet you could not kill me. But it was compassion that drew your hand back: You could not kill someone who is not your adversary, even though I begged you to. Whatever choice, even if you would have killed me, would be driven by compassion. Yet you spared a life rather than taking it."

"Sometimes, we do not have that same choice," Ismaril said. "You did not threaten to kill me. It is different."

"Yes, but that is not what I tried to teach you. You can control your own mind, and the choices you make are powerful, for they always manifest eventually. Mindset is key. Why do you think you will die if you do not kill? Because you are afraid, Ismaril. Terrified. Fear is the Enemy's strongest tool; for if they can induce fear in you, they have won more than half the battle. Think and recall. The Enemy seldom attacks suddenly and without warning. They first intimidate, and it works each time. When the Enemy then attacks, they do so from a coign of vantage.

"I am not telling you that you must not kill when the situation so requires. I am telling you not to fear, Farrider. For alas! Your emotions transfer to your blade, and your blade will act according to her master's state of mind. Be revengeful, raging, and with slaughter in mind, and Gahil will abide, but beware, for it will come back on the master. Show grace and wisdom, and that is what the sword will return to you."

"Yet this tells me nothing about how to defend myself, should someone attack me," Ismaril said.

"But it does," Ishtarion said. "You must overcome your fear. The trip through the Underworld was a test. You did well, for you meandered betwixt the threats, killing nobody. Instead, you used your mind to overcome obstacles. Thus, you are still here, and you are alive. Yet you do not have the full insight into what it entails. Your mind, Ismaril, your mind…"

In his head, he pictured himself face-to-face with Yongahur or Azezakel. How might he use his mind against such powerful gods? For gods, they were. Once more, he fell into hopelessness and despair, and a sudden thought came to mind: Was the death of his former companions a consequence of those Gahil had slain, steered by his fearful hand? Had Gahil returned the outlet of his terror? Then he veiled those thoughts, for they were too difficult to face.

The Dragon seemed to perceive what happened.

"Fret not, soldier," she said. "For a soldier you must be—a

Soldier of the Mind. Humans attribute all this magic to the Dark Kings and their cohorts, and you believe they own it. They own nothing of the sort, but you do. Most of it, they stole from you. Your entire species were made to create magic. Magic is merely what you can do with your mind and manifest, for magic is creation, and creation is magic. When your thoughts and imagination go toward defeat, defeat manifests. Thus, you believe that is normal and the way it should be. When you think positively and wish for good things to befall, those will manifest, and you think it is *like magic.* Funny that."

Ishtarion lowered her head and gazed into Ismaril's eyes. And he felt like an open book for the Dragon to read, and nothing remained hidden or secret. So long as she penetrated his mind, all the erstwhile shame and guilt that had torn him asunder haunted him no more.

The Dragon snorted, and puffs of smoke came from her nostrils.

"Past, present, future… they are all one," Ishtarion said. "Humans dwell on their past and deeds they wish undone. Yet you believe you cannot change them. You can! But you must not return to the past as something that befell erstwhile. Instead, you must change your past in the present by changing yourself and your beliefs. Then your past will change, and your troubles and worries will leave you. Forgiveness, Ismaril, forgiveness. If you cannot forgive yourself, you cannot live, and you stop thriving. You hold on to a past agone, which you solidify in your present, making it more important than proper tasks at hand, and you are not even aware. Thus, your present and your past merge and become one, whilst the past takes the lead upon which you force your decisions, hindering you from making sound choices based on what lies before you. *Use your mind, Ismaril!* Murderous wars have no winners, for even the victors must live with their misdeeds, and they know not how. Woe to humans, for they know not what they are doing. You have powers not even I possess—you carry the Magic of the Universe, for you are the descendants of the Divine Goddess, and you indeed met a manifestation of Her in Queen Astéamat.

"Believe in yourself wholeheartedly, Farrider. Show your true strength! You are an excellent archer and a skilled swordsman, and you know how to slay; but you act in fear and call it defense. Yes, you fend for your own life by taking someone else's, and you call it good; yet your mind merely learns to store more shame and guilt. You even feel guilty for other people's deeds and misdeeds, and you carry their responsibilities and misfortunes. Whilst carrying their burdens, how can you then cleanse yourself of your own? Own your mind, Ismaril, and Gahil will be your best friend."

Ismaril sighed. "All that sounds good, but how do I accomplish such a monumental task?"

"By addressing the Goddess inside you. Know thyself. The end is nigh, and time is short, but you already know how to do it because you already did it. Reflect, or your journey through the Underworld was to little avail. Learn from your experiences and expand on them. I saw through your mind, and I would not tell you all this if I knew you could not accomplish what you set out yourself out to do. Yet it is up to you to find *your* way. Trust intuition and your inner guidance, for they are there to assist you, and not to mislead. Only your entrained lower mind makes you react impulsively and misleadingly. This is the time to let that which was buried surface and lead. In the end, you shall stand at two roads crossing, and you must choose between them: One may lead to victory, while the other may not. It will be one of the hardest choices you will ever make (but not the only one), and yet all you need to do is to choose and act. In all its complexity, the choice is simple, for the complexity is merely a bag of beliefs you have collected, and most of them behoove you not. Penetrate your shadows; see them for what they are, and you shall know what to do and how to act."

Like lightning, striking inside Ismaril's mind, a heavy rock split in two. Deep inside, he felt, on one hand, the wisdom in the Dragon's words, whilst another part of him rejected it as if his life depended on it. He realized that the former was his courage and the latter his fear.

"I have faith in you where you currently lack it," Ishtarion said. "I possess my own magic, but it is not as strong as yours; yours is merely more hidden. You may think your task impossible, and I blame you not for it; but I trust on the day when it counts, it will all come to you. Meanwhile, ponder my words and prepare your mind; for the time *will* come, and it will come soon, when you must make the choice."

"Wise are your words, Ishtarion the Magnificent," Ismaril said. "In the chasm of my mind, I know your wisdom. I shall do my best." He put his hand across his chest and bowed deep.

The Dragon seemed pleased. "Very well," she said. "And for you, dear Sigyn Archesdaughter, I have this to say: Your wisdom is deeper than you think, and your love is as strong as iron. You are of tremendous support to Ismaril, and he knows it. Stick together, for you will need each other. Be his shield maiden, but also lift his courage when he needs it the most. Give him affirmation when he succeeds and encouragement when he fails. You must realize your role in this is as important as his."

Then the Dragon stopped herself for a moment, watching Sigyn closely, and her eyes dulled, as if a great sadness manifested in their depth.

"Be careful, my dear Sigyn, for your path will not be an easy one. You carry a child inside, and malison is upon you, not to be taken lightly. Even you have choices to make, no less difficult than Ismaril's. To you, I have little advice to give, for your path is shrouded, and I cannot see. Yet my heart tells me to advise you not to let your emotions lead you too far; they can sometimes be ill advisers. Thus, trust your heart, always, which is your intuition; and follow only the emotions feel you can control."

The Dragon lowered her head all the way to the floor. "Now leave," she said. "You will always be in my mind, as long as I live, and you will sense my presence on your journey. Go east to the Mounds of Sleeping Giants. Awaken those who have dreamt for eons. To behold! Their time is now in the coming! They have their own destiny to fulfill."

"How can we find them?" Sigyn asked.

"You will… Go east."

Sigyn trotted forward and gave the Dragon a hug. Surprisingly, the scales were softer than she had imagined. Then Ismaril bowed once more.

"Thus, we shall leave," he said. "Farewell, Mighty Ishtarion, and thank you for your counsel. The road ahead weighs heavily on me, as I know it does on Sigyn, but we must prevail. I now can see where before I could not. I shall no longer resist, as far as my destiny goes, and if I fail, I must die in the attempt and with courage. It is not what I have to lose or what I have lost that is important. What does all that matter if we lose the world?" There was a lump in his throat, making it difficult to speak, for he disliked farewells. "Perhaps, if destiny permits, we shall meet again."

"It is a pleasant thought," Ishtarion said. "Yet our destinies, mine and yours, are not in our favor, as far as that goes."

Chapter 17
The Recruits

Reaching the crossroads by the Dead Forest, where Ismaril and his fellowship had passed before them, the two pirates could look at a blue sky, and they held back their horses.

"What now?" the Revenger said. "Which way to go? And don't look like that. You know the way, don't you?"

"This Yongahur figure was right," Tomlin mumbled. "I am smarter than you. Think, Iorwain, think! The sun rose in the east, so east is that way. Obviously, we are not going east, or it will take us to Anúria. If so, that road, meandering over there, must be the northeast. Don't wanna go there; it leads into that unappealing forest you can see thither. One road remains, leading northwest. Wanna go there. Woe to me! How could you survive the Grimm massacre, when smarter men did not?"

"You are the one who puts us in trouble all the time!" the Revenger said. "How smart is that? Now we have a curse upon us, throbbing tattoos on our foreheads, and a lifelong strive in Azezakel's service, reporting back to the most vicious man I've ever met, and I've met many. Upon that, I feel our lives will be significantly shortened. All this happened on your watch. And why do you suddenly call me by my birth name? No one does that."

Tomlin sighed. "Do you really want to go to Gormoth calling yourself the Revenger? How would that come across? From here on, you are Iorwain; I got to get used to it, and so do you. Now, take heed, for the mud has stiffened, and our journey will be swifter. Ere too long we should be at the Watchtower."

"It's not too late to turn around," Iorwain said.

"Aye! And where would we go? Into the wilderness, spending the rest of our lives in each other's company, you and me? No, thank you! We have burned our ships, as our saying goes. There is no other way but forward. Enough of all this nonsense talk. Let's move!"

He put his heels into his horse's sides and took off on a spur. Iorwain followed, having little choice. All the while, his forehead was burning.

The farther they rode, the colder it was, and in the east, the Snowy Mountains, at the border of Azezakel's Gormoth, stretched their voracious, ragged peaks, like a row of open jaws, ready to consume even the surrounding air.

"Well, we're not entering that way, at least," said Iorwain to himself.

That afternoon, snow that never thawed replaced the brown and gray soil, and a bitter wind blew from the Bay of Aldaer in the west, building icicles in the horses' manes.

There, before them, rose the Watchtower, closer and closer, pulling them in; but out here on the snowy heaths, there was no place to hide. Iorwain doubted not that the guards of the lofty tower had discovered them already. The more they closed in on the tower, the more nervous he became, while Tomlin seemed unaffected as if on a pleasant afternoon picnic. Iorwain wished they had never left Piscas Urash to begin with.

When the afternoon came, the two journeymen stopped in front of the gigantic tower, but no one came to meet them, and no one shot at them; there was only silence, save for the icy wind that was whistling between the mountains.

They looked at each other.

"What now? said Iorwain, and his body was shivering; not solely from the cold.

Tomlin shrugged, seemingly unconcerned. "I guess we'll knock on the gate."

A deep growl made them both spin about in their saddles. Behind them sat a couple dozens of Wolfmen on Ulves, silently studying the two newcomers, staring. The two pirates stared back, and Iorwain froze.

This awkward moment lasted a while, and then a Wolfman, appearing as the leader, holding a long spear, departed from the crowd, and closed in on the two wayfarers. A few paces away, he held his Ulv back. A nauseating odor from the ragged animal reached Iorwain's nostrils, and he swallowed hard, whilst watching the beast drooling and growling, wishing to eat him alive at the sole mercy of its rider. The Wolfman tilted his head, letting his gaze scan them from top to bottom. Then he snarled and snorted and told his Ulv to move closer until Iorwain could feel the Ulv's bristles against his leg. His horse became restless and difficult to control. The Wolfman carefully studied the tattoos on their foreheads and leaned forward to sniff on them, letter by letter.

"Yongahur!" the Wolfman snarled. "Yongahur did this."

"Aye, Sir," Tomlin said.

"What do you want?"

"To see Hútlof. We were told to report to Hútlof."

"Hútlof, huh? Do you know him?"

"Nay, Sir!"

The Wolfman laughed hoarsely. "Well, you will."

That did not sound promising, and Iorwain's heart pounded faster. What was he doing in this horrible place?

"Follow us," the Wolfman said and waved to the others to move. Half the crew passed, and the rest stopped. Yet no signs were given, verbal or otherwise, but the pirates understood what to do and fell in line amid the group of Wolfmen. The leader knocked on the gate with his spear and the two massive oak doors cracked open.

Iorwain studied the Watchtower as they proceeded. The mortal was ancient and worn, whipped by many storm winds, in need of restoration, yet holding up against decay. He shook his head. Who had built something like this? It must have taken ages. Then he realized: slave labor. He swallowed. *I hope Yongahur keeps his word and lets us join the fleet, and not put us somewhere else, building towers.*

—

There were good reasons to suspect Hútlof being unpleasant. Standing before them, in the tower's loft, stood an abominable figure. Iorwain had expected a Wolfman, or perhaps a Birdman, but Hútlof was neither. This being was twice as tall as the tallest human, and he resembled a crossbreed between a Wolfman and an Ulv. Iorwain had never seen one before, but he intuitively knew this was a Werewolf. Dressed in a tunic that was more like a breastplate with an overhang, leaving his fury, brawny arms bare, he looked like an unbeatable wild animal, capable of defeating half a brigade on his own. Amid the indescribable horror this creature expressed, Iorwain caught himself thinking, *I wonder if this being can shapeshift into a human—or is it the other way around?* The creature's eyes were red as burning coal, and his snout was like that of a wolf; and from the side of his jaws, two sharp tusks stuck out, like those of a wild boar. He rustled with each breath as if his lungs were full of water, yet he looked strong and healthy.

His office was oval-shaped and sparse. It had no resemblance to an officer's suite; it looked more like something put up in a hurry and created by someone who cared little. There was a desk made of granite at the back of the room, and he sat on a granite chair, carved out of the bedrock. There were no other chairs in the room. A long, vertical glass window, like the slit eye of a Dragon, let enough light in to distinguish between light and dark, but nothing more and nothing less. The rest of the room was empty. Iorwain could not help but think that this being would not care; for he was not an administrator; he was a warrior and an executioner.

With a long, vicious snarl, Hútlof stood up from his throne, greatly impressive. Instead of feet, he had hooves like a goat, clattering against the solid floor, and with heavy, determined steps, he walked over to the pirates, putting his arms behind his back, circling round them. Then he stopped and studied their tattoos like the Wolfman did.

"Yongahur!" His voice was deeper and more vibrant than any voice that the pirates had ever heard. "Indeed, these are authentic. What did he tell you?"

Tomlin and Iorwain looked at each other, and Iorwain knew better by now than to speak on important matters. He gave the word to Tomlin.

"We... I... He told us we would be commanders of your ships, Most Highly Respected Sir!"

"Hmm...," Hútlof said. "You have Yongahur's navy seal. Yet, what makes you capable of commanding one of our magnificent ships?"

"We are pirates… eh, ex-pirates, Sir," Tomin said. "We are qualified…"

Iorwain's legs almost failed him. *No, we are not;* he thought. *We are in big trouble. Look what you have gotten us into!*

Next, Hútlof lifted him with his brawny arm, as if he was of pure air, pulling him close.

"Name?" The voice vibrated in Iorwain's head.

"Ah… The Rev… Iorwain, Sir!"

"The Reviorwain?"

"Only Iorwain, Sir. Sorry, Sir."

Hútlof let go, and Iorwain fell to the floor like a sack of garbage. Then, the Werewolf grabbed Tomlin.

"And you?"

"Tomlin, Sir. Aerok Tomlin."

Iorwain, yet trying to get to his shaky legs, was astounded by Tomlin's ability to stay calm.

The Werewolf dropped Tomlin, who landed on Iorwain.

Hútlof scoffed. "You are pathetic, the both of you. Well, I guess Yongahur has his reasons, and I shall not oppose his will; no way I will. But I have my personal doubts about you two. Tell him that if you wish. Although I mistrust your loyalty, I will not act upon it, for it is not in my authority to do so. You shall both become captains of your own warship, and to war you shall go." He locked eyes with them. "Hmm…" he rustled. "You seem okay, Tomlin. But I do not know what to think of you, scum. Yes, I am referring to you… Reviorwain. You seem more like a liability, perhaps even a threat."

Iorwain stood in salute, expecting the worst.

Then Hútlof spoke again, "It is not for me to judge. What do I know? I am just the Captain of the Watchtower." He growled and showed more of his sharp yellow teeth. "Only a few words of advice: If any of you two even show the least of disloyalty towards Gormoth, Azezakel the Great, King Yongahur, or myself, you shall not merely be killed, but I will see to that you burn in the Lake of Fire for as long as MAEDIN exists! Is that understood?"

They both gasped.

"Yes, Sir!" Tomlin said.

Iorwain hesitated, but although no one knew him as the

smartest amongst a group of pirates, he knew he had little choice, and he hated it.

"Yes, Sir!" he said.

Hútlof nodded. "Good then! I will send you to Elphaz for training. There will be inspections, and I expect excellency!"

Iorwain glanced at Tomlin and halfway opened his mouth. He wanted to say they must see King Azezakel to break the curse of the Ghost Kings, but he dared not. Now they were truly in trouble.

Chapter 18
Reunion

ON THE FIRST NIGHT since they left the Dragon's lair, Ismaril and Sigyn encamped beneath a clear and starry sky. All day, they had stridden through a sparsely forested area. Most of it was pine and fir this far up north, but sometimes mixed with lime and birch. They headed northeast now, toward the Mounds of Sleeping Giants, though they could not yet see the hills.

Before they slept, they lay on their backs, close together, while gazing at the spangled heaven, lost in their personal thoughts.

"How is our baby?" Ismaril said after some silence.

Sigyn grinned. "Fine, I think," she said. "I have not yet had any real discomfort."

He bent over, put his ear against her stomach, and listened.

"He is not kicking," he said. "Should he not do that?"

"I am not sure. Perhaps it is too early. How do you know it is a boy? It could be a girl."

"I think it is a boy. Yes, definitely a boy." He laughed.

Sigyn laughed. "Yes, I know. It feels like that to me, too. Is that good?"

"It is good."

He turned over on his back again, and they remained silent for a moment. Then Sigyn asked, "Are you worried?"

He sighed and put his arms behind his neck. "Yes, of course," he said. "Our time with the Queen and the Dragon has been fantastic and enlightening, and once I changed my attitude, my task seemed easier, so long as I was in an uplifting environment. Now, as we are out in the cold again, everything seems hopeless."

"This world brings us down, doesn't it?" Sigyn said. "The difference is alarming. We humans have come a long way low since we were like the Originals. It's like another universe."

"And, in a way, it is. It is hard to fathom that this world can ever reach the heights of Emoria. All we think about here is attack and defense, and we are always on watch for what could wait around the next corner. And here I am, a thief and a murderer, carrying a magic sword I am not supposed to slay with if I can help it. Yet, I am supposed to assist the world in the transition from where we are now to something like Emoria. It's elusive to me."

She grabbed his hand. "I know. But that is all we have, and it's all well. If we give up, we are certainly not going to make any changes. And if we fall along the way, at least we tried. It's better to do something than nothing. At least then, life has some kind of meaning."

He knew she was right, and he had not given up, yet the task seemed so unobtainable and abstract. He had no magical powers he knew of; aside from being a thief and a killer, he was an ordinary person, not even an outstanding soldier. He could scout, but that was about it. Yongahur was the only Dark King he had encountered, but if the rest of them were anything like him, how could he defeat anybody like that? And Azezakel?

He slept poorly that night.

———

The next day was mainly overcast, but the two wayfarers welcomed it. It was easier to travel when it was not hot. All day, they had been on their feet. The Originals gave them no horses to ride, for there was nothing they could bring from that realm down to here. Likewise, they could carry with them no food from the Enchanted Woods, so all they had was small rations of dried meat and dried fruits; but the sparse forest was rich in berries and delivered a strange and bitter fruit, barely edible, yet stilling their hunger.

This land had few paths, and those that existed were narrow animal trails, half overgrown, sometimes ending abruptly in nowhere. Therefore, most of the time they strived on their way through a wild undergrowth, where long and thick snakes lured, swiftly slithering off as the travelers unbeknown closed in on them. A drizzle whipped the travelers' faces in the afternoon, soon making the soil wet and sunken, giving off the sudden odor of marshland. Large birds of unfamiliar kinds flew up from the trees when Ismaril and Sigyn approached, by which the foliage above released its heavy water, splashing over the travelers. It was a wet march the rest of that day.

The drizzle stopped before darkness. It was impossible to find a dry spot that night, and although it was summer, the wetness made them cold and uncomfortable, with the damp texture from their sleeping bags stuck to their bodies.

A few hours into the following day, the landscape took an upward slope. Here, the forest turned coniferous, comprising only pines and firs, and the wood got denser.

"We must have reached the Mounds," Ismaril said. "I welcome it, for there is no undergrowth to plow through."

"Aye, but where do we go next?" Sigyn said. "How do we find the Giants?"

Ismaril shrugged. "The Queen said we must not worry, and that we will find them. I do not know how, but we will find them; I am sure we will."

The ascending slope got steeper, and the sun now gazed from a blue sky, making it hot and tiresome to walk. They took many breaks under overshadowing trees, but mostly, they were striding downhill and uphill, hither, and thither, with no obvious destination in mind. And nowhere did they find signs of Giants or entrances to some mysterious caves. When afternoon arrived, they were mighty tired and had lost most of their hope.

"I think we might have gone round in circles," Ismaril said. "These hills seem without end, and one hill is like another. It is soon getting dark, and after that, we will find nothing."

Sigyn gazed at the sky. "We have yet another hour or so ere sundown," she said. "Let us not give up; there's still a chance…"

But the hour came and went. The sun quickly sank beyond the hills and trees behind them, and the night darkened.

"Well, I guess we must give it another day," Ismaril said. "If we make no progress after tomorrow, we should reconsider."

"But the Queen stressed the importance of finding the

Giants."

Ismaril raised his voice. "I know, damn it!" Then he lowered his head. "Sorry, I am tired and dismayed. No one is giving us explicit instructions, and we are always fumbling in the dark, hoping we are doing the right thing. Now it is pitch black again, and we must find a place to sleep."

"Not pitch black," Sigyn whispered. She grabbed his arm and pointed. "Shh! Look over there!"

And behold! Beyond the next hill, a light flickered hither and thither. Then it disappeared for a moment and then reappeared, to and fro.

"Looks like a fire," Ismaril whispered back. "Perhaps Wolfmen or Birdmen… or worse."

Sigyn pulled his arm. "Let us walk the other way to avoid them."

"Well, they seem to have settled for the night, and I want to know whom we are up against. I want no surprises. Wait here, and I will find out—"

"No, please stay!"

He shook himself loose. "I will be careful. Wait here!"

He ran uphill, looking left and right, veiled by the moonless night. When he reached the summit, he went down on his stomach and crawled over the top. Slowly and carefully, he raised his head and peeked.

In a small depression between the ridges, a sizable bonfire burned, licking the air in the shy night breeze. In a circle sat a large group of shadowy figures, impossible to distinguish. They did not resemble Wolfmen or Birdmen, and the few words he could extract from their muffled voices sounded human, but with a distinct dialect. Ismaril took a deep breath of relief. He knew not yet who they were, and though they might be human, they could be hostile and untrustworthy. Strange folks roamed in the north, or so he was told. Yet the conversation they had was joyous, and laughter filled the night air.

Then one man stood before the fire as if preparing a speech, making him distinguishable. Ismaril ducked but kept his gaze. Then he gasped, dropping his jaw. The man's gold-colored boots shone and glistered in the fire's light, and his purple cloak with all its circular patterns was one of a kind. And now, beside him, a much smaller figure, half his size, stood, wearing a hat, long and brown, and a white beard encircled his fleshy face.

Ismaril stood up and waved his arms. "Raeglin, Kirbakin! It is me, Ismaril! Sigyn, come over here!"

The conversation by the fire stopped immediately, and all men stood up; and for a moment, there was the clanking of weapons being drawn. Some grabbed bows and nocked their arrows, aiming at him.

"Who is there?" said a harsh voice amid the crowd.

"Hold your fire, brave Nomads," Ismaril said. "For Nomads you are, is that not so? I recognize your voice, Yomar. I have Sigyn Archesdaughter with me, and we are both coming down!"

"Hold it! Shoot not!" the man with the gold-colored boots cried. "I recognize his voice. It is truly Ismaril. For the Goddess' sake, come down—both of you!"

Much laughter enhanced the gladness in everybody's heart during the reunion, and they shed many tears of joy; not even Kirbakin's eyes were dry. The embrace was lengthy and heartfelt, and many compassionate words they spoke.

After the first excitement had settled, Ismaril approached Yomar, and they stood there, exchanging gazes for a while. Then Ismaril held out his hand, and he said, "I apologize for how our previous encounter ended. I doubted you, and I was wrong. I have hopefully come a long way since then."

Yomar took his hand, and then he pulled Ismaril onto him and embraced him. "No hard feelings," he said. "You had reasons to be suspicious. You would have been foolish not to be careful. Let us celebrate this joyful moment. Lo! There is deer, hot and ready to eat. You and Sigyn must be starving." *That is an understatement,* Ismaril thought. *Of skin and bones am I, and that's all...*

The two travelers sat before the fire and ate until their stomachs could handle no more. Thereafter, Ismaril spoke again.

"This is unbelievable," he said. "How come we find each other in the wilderness after having been apart for so long? It can't be coincident."

"No such thing," Raeglin said. "There are plans within plans, and upon that, there is a Grand Design that is Divine. There are no coincidences. Many things we have little control over."

"Indeed!" Ismaril said. "And now, when we finally meet, I

know not where to begin. So much has happened. What are you all doing here?"

Kirbakin laughed. "What are *you* doing here?" he said, and his eyes glowed in the contrast betwixt the fire and dark of night. "Why not let the two of you tell *your* story first? I think that is of greater significance. Unless you are too tired, of course."

"For Sigyn I can't speak, but tired I am no more," Ismaril said. "There will be little sleep for me tonight, for I welcome your company. We shall speak on this if Sigyn allows."

And so, Ismaril and Sigyn told what they could remember, one following the voice of the other, beginning on the day they disappeared into the tunnel in their boat, entering the Underworld, their adventures there, how they came back to the surface, and last, their meeting with the Queen of Emoria and the rest of the Originals. But Ismaril left out what Queen Astéamat had told him about Gahil, and they said nothing about their meeting with the Gold Dragon. When they reached these parts of the story, they fell silent, glancing at each other. Merely by exchanging gazes, they formed agreements not to mention some incidents. They knew not why.

When Ismaril looked at Raeglin, he knew the pilgrim noticed the sudden silence.

"I am delighted to see you alive, and you seem to do well, despite the circumstances," he said after Ismaril and Sigyn finished. "Yet I am concerned about the pregnancy, but particularly the curse, Sigyn. We need to keep a watch on both."

"Aye," Sigyn said. "Fortunately, I have had no problems with either the pregnancy or the curse. Perhaps we need not worry."

Raeglin nodded vaguely, but his eyes revealed further concern. Yet he left the subject. "And the Queen told you to wake the Giants?"

"That is why we are here," Sigyn said. "When we found you, I thought you were here for the same reason. Are you?"

Raeglin shook his head. "No, I was not aware it was time for them to wake up. This means the last hour draws nigh, when Taëlia's fate shall be sealed, and the Ending War of the Ages be upon us. We have less time than I thought, and we can no longer drag. Did the Queen tell you anything else of importance that you might have excluded from your story?" He looked at Ismaril curiously.

"Nay," he said, but lowering his gaze. "That is all we can tell."

Sigyn quickly spoke to disperse the sudden tension. "Why are you here, and where are you going?"

Raeglin was in deep thought and gave no answer. Instead, Kirbakin spoke. "We are going up north to the Frostlands." And he told them everything of significance that had happened since Sigyn and Ismaril left the group. He spoke on the Battle of Khandur, the victory, Ayasis' betrayal, and about his and Raeglin's dispute with King Barakus and Prince Xandur, leading to expulsion from the kingdom. He further told them about Prince Exxarion's betrayal, their own encounter with Queen Astéamat, and their purpose with the meeting.

"The allied nations are few, and the armies, ready to meet King Azezakel in battle, are rare and far between," the Gnome continued. "We are desperately trying to recruit the free people round and about, willing to help regain power over Taëlia. We know little about what success we will have, but we shall do our best to recruit the Icemen of the north. They have Dragons, and they are powerful people. The problem is we know not on which side they are, if any."

Raeglin was alert now. "This leads to the next question," he said. "Where are the two of you going? Following the Giants?"

Ismaril winced. Unbeknownst, he had not yet thought of that and was embarrassed to admit to himself he had no plans past the awakening of the Giants.

"Unless you have any plan," Raeglin said, "will you join us? There is little the two of you can do on your own. You could follow the Giants, of course, if that rings true to you—your choice. If we can get the Icemen with their Ice Dragons on our side, we must then hurry to Gormoth, coming in from the north as soon as the time is right."

"How do we know when the time is right?" Ismaril asked.

"Ravens," Yomar inflicted. "Not all of them are Azezakel's spies; some are our messengers. We must wait for Khandur to march, which I am sure they will soon; for they have little choice otherwise. We must not join them, for the king and the prince do not support the two of you, as little as they support Master Raeglin and Kirbakin—or me, for that matter. Thus, we must march to Gormoth with a separate army. Barakus will come in from the south, and we shall come from the north if we are lucky enough to get the Icemen mobilized."

Ismaril locked eyes with Sigyn, who nodded.

"Very well," he said. "We will come with you. It sounds like the best plan."

Raeglin and Kirbakin both smiled, and Yomar spoke again. "Excellent! And I will help you search for the Giants, taking a few men with me."

"Kirbakin and I will join in, too," Raeglin said. "Are we not, Master Gnome?"

"Aye, we are!" Kirbakin said. "You could not stop me, even if you called for the world to fall asunder."

"There is one more thing," Ismaril said. "Queen Ishtanagul left us with a message. She said we must find King Barakus and Prince Xandur, telling them Gormoth wants peace. She wants a meeting between all nations to discuss the matter."

Raeglin snarled. "It is a trap," he said. "It is true they want peace, but on their terms. I smell an ambush. It sounds like the enemy is nervous, though, or they would not have told you this."

"Besides, it is no longer possible," Kirbakin said. "Neither Ismaril nor Sigyn is welcome in Khandur."

"Well, then it is time for us all to sleep through the rest of the night," Raeglin said, and he stood up. "We will start looking for the Giants in the early morn."

Ismaril and Sigyn rolled out their sleeping bags away from the rest, and before they fell asleep, Ismaril said, "Can you feel it, Sigyn?"

She looked at him with her gray, glittering eyes and smiled. "Aye," she said. "I feel the Gold Dragon's presence. Ishtarion is thinking about us."

Chapter 19:
Two Brothers

Lord Zarabaster's fleet, combined with that of Prince Xandur, had scouted the Rhuirian coastline over, once and again, having learned from Misthorn natives that Prince Exxarion had sailed for Rhuir. But nowhere could they find the docked Anúrian ships or any signs of upheaval. Often, Xandur felt they sailed too close to the Rhuirian coastline, concerned they would be detected from land by the enemy.

After a few days of intense searching, the combined fleet anchored outside a tiny, nameless island, a few nautical leagues east of the Rhuirian coast, where the ocean was shallower. Ashore on the deserted island, Prince Xandur visited Lord Zarabaster to have counsel. His heart weighed heavy, and in his stomach, he had an imminent sense of a forthcoming disaster. Something was askew, and he knew not what it was. As an army man, he had never experienced such an intense sense of doom and gloom, knowing he must take such signs seriously.

—

Prince Exxarion woke up and winced in panic. Disoriented, like a drunk waking from a toxic snooze, he stumbled and got to his feet, knowing not where he was and what had befallen.

Cold and wet from rain and heavy saltwater, he gazed over the rail. A low sun in the east blinded him, and he couped his hand above his eyes. He looked north and south, and thereafter, he looked to the east, seeing only water—no land. Then he remembered Whispering Island and the mind-altering voices. He stopped and listened. There were no voices inside his head anymore, nor were there any around and about, and the island was nowhere nearby. What had happened? He must have fallen asleep suddenly.

About him, many men lay spread on the main deck, as if there had been a gigantic party the night before, all falling asleep where they stood. Slowly, they awoke, one after the other. Exxarion ran to and fro across the deck, until he found Admiral Mundo on his hands and knees near the mizzenmast, about to get to his feet.

"Admiral," Exxarion cried. "What is going on? Hurry from there and get back to work!"

Mundo mumbled something unintelligible and got up on unsteady feet. His Admiral Hat was gone, never again to be found; it must have blown overboard. His hair stood in all directions, in need of a brush.

When he regained his composure, he uttered a regretful, "My apologies, Your Highness. I must have passed out. I do not understand…"

"We all passed out," Exxarion said impatiently. "You are of little help to me. The voices are no more, the island is gone, and things appear to be back to normal. But where are we? Our ships are floating amid nowhere. Find out our position! I am no sailor; that is your job."

The Admiral saluted and hurried on his way, groggy and stumbling. Whilst waiting for his First Commander to return, the prince picked up a monocular and gazed out across the water. Ships were drifting hither and thither with their bows pointing here and there; but one by one, their crew members must have awoken, for the vessels suddenly changed course, yet with their sails folded.

"I cannot tell exactly where we are, Your Majesty," Mundo said with a flushed face when he returned. "All we can do is to keep west, and we should then see the mainland in due time."

Exxarion waved him off, giving permission for the Admiral to go ahead.

Once the entire fleet was in line with Prince Exxarion's ship, the prince ran up to the quarterdeck and voiced to the crew for attention.

"We are now on course again! In not too long, we will hit Rhuir's coast and sail up Dragon River to Khurad-Resh. The curse upon us by the island is no more. If anyone hears whispering voices, I want to know." If someone did, he must throw them overboard. "In perhaps a day or two, we will be in battle, as planned!"

His men cheered, raised their fists in the air, and they hailed their commander. "War! War!" they cried in unison. "Kill! Kill!" The frenzy worsened, and the men got louder, as if in a trance. Erstwhile being reluctant about going to battle, following the prince out of fear, the entire crew was now eager to kill and plunder. Exxarion stretched where he stood and pridefully raised his chin.

—

"Many ships approaching in the south!" a man in the crow's nest shouted to his comrades on the island.

Prince Xandur and Lord Zarabaster ran up the hillside, which abruptly ended with a cliff that fell straight into the foamy, splashy waves below, perpetually whipping the bedrock. From up here, the two commanders had a better outlook. They glanced southward through their monoculars and saw an armada steering west, about a nautical league in the distance. Xandur lowered his looking tube.

"That is Exxarion," he said, locking eyes with Zarabaster. "They are Anúrian ships, headed for Rhuir."

The pirate lord nodded. "They must have visited one of the many islands east of here."

"Quick! We must pull anchors and meet them. I need to talk to my brother, for we must stop him!"

In great haste, the joint Khanduran-Rhíandorian navy sailed out to meet the Anúrian fleet.

After a short sail, Lord Zarabaster said, while looking through a monocular, "They have seen us, and they are changing course."

Prince Xandur confirmed, using his own monocular. The front ship, likely being his brother's, changed course and sailed onto them. The remaining Anúrian armada folded sails and cast anchor shortly before they reached the Khanduran-Rhíandorian navy. Thus, in that pale afternoon, and in calm waters, the two brothers' ships anchored side by side. For a long time, the brothers stared at each other, but neither of them spoke. On the quarterdeck, with his hands on the rail, Exxarion rose, resembling a pirate better than any of Zarabaster's crew members. Xandur felt the tension increase. When he opened his mouth to speak, Exxarion preceded him.

"What brings you?" Exxarion asked harshly. "Not on a fishing trip, I reckon!"

"No fishing trip," Xandur cried. "Neither are you, brother. I know where you are heading."

"Of course you do. And as usual, you do not answer my questions. You know where I am headed, so what is *your* errand? Are you trying to stop me?"

"We need to talk. I either come over to you, or you come to me."

"Neither. I am good from here, and to my ship, I do not invite you. If you have something to say, speak while I am patient enow to hear you."

"These ships do not belong to you. They are Khanduran property and are owned by the Crown. As the elder of us two, and upon that being the heir to the Kingdom, I command you to abandon your plan, sail back to Anúria, and return the fleet to me as the senior representative of the Divine Kingdom of Khandur."

"Skip the formalities, brother. Anúria belongs to Khandur no more! I have declared Anúria sovereign, and I am its first king. We both wish for Azezakel's defeat and demise and thus, I shall bring victory effectively and magnificently to the world. May the old bury the old and let that which is buried turn to dust. Make room for the New Ways, for thus, we shall win the war. I am tired of old men's passiveness. Attacking is the answer, and attack is now!"

"Beware, Exxarion, for this is treason, and upon that, death is the penalty! I give you the last chance to surrender the fleet and come with me back to Ringhall. Thus, your life we shall spare."

"Enow! Your words are nil to me and my men. Behold, my brother! See you not how large my armada is? These men are as dedicated as I am. None of them want Khanduran rulership anymore. They want me, Xandur!"

"Are these your last words?"

"Aye! And I hope they are the last words I shall ever utter your way. If you threaten me with capital punishment for winning the war for you, so be it! For if we had met in Anúria rather than on the open ocean, I would have had you executed. Now, make way for me, for I come in fury and with great power. Within short, Rhuir will lie before my feet."

"And what then, Exxarion? If you are successful at invading Rhuir, what then? Have you now forgotten about the Gormothan Dragons and Azezakel's armies, comprising endless legions?"

Exxarion laughed. "Whilst yet in the Eldermount Palace, I had a dream. The Goddess came unto me, promising me success and support. Thus, I fear no armies, and I fear no Dark King; not even the Black One. For I am King Exxarion, and as Exxarion the Great, the annals shall remember me, the king who defeated Gormoth's armies all on his own."

"Alas! Then you are indeed a fool and out of your mind. Rethink your decision, for your actions will bring doom to us all. There is yet time to stop this madness. Brother, come to your senses ere too late!" Xandur's voice sank at the end of the sentence, for he knew he spoke to deaf ears.

Prince Exxarion turned his gaze toward the ship's main deck and made a sign. Then he stood in salute, keeping his eyes on the mainmast, while his men raised a flag to the mast top, picturing the white, prancing Unicorn on a black background, resembling the Royal Flag of the Province of Anúria; but the banner they had changed: the background was green no more, but black.

A murmur went through Xandur's crew, and Prince Exxarion ended his salute, again turning toward Xandur. "See that?" he said. "This is the Banner of the Sovereign Kingdom of Anúria, and the black background is a direct challenge to the Black King. Thus, King Exxarion the Great has spoken!" And alas! On deck, his crew cheered and shouted in chorus, saluting their new king.

Prince Xandur's body became heavy as a rock, and all hope left him. His brother was indeed madder than he could have imagined, and there was no more to say. Now, additional words would make things worse.

"Farewell, brother!" Exxarion cried. "You have no business here. Return to Khandur and pass on the message to our father. If he is brave enow to go to war against Gormoth, he has my blessings; but also tell him there is no need. I can handle this war in the company of these brave men, and with the Goddess' blessings. Perhaps the old man should stay where he is, safe in the

Ringhall Castle, and not shame himself on the battlefield. You despise me now, Xandur, but one day you may fall to your knees, praising and thanking me. Too long, the youthfulness of your body and your apparent vigor have fooled me; for you are but an old traditional man inside, belonging to a dying breed."

Thus, Prince Exxarion laughed in his madness, pulled anchor, and returned to his fleet. Prince Xandur stood speechless on the quarterdeck, watching the Anúrian armada disappear in the west, taking the afternoon sun with them.

―

Naisha joined the prince in the aft, where the Royal Cabin was. They sat quietly for a while; her watching him. His eyes were distant and moist, and there was a veil of sadness engulfing him. She felt his pain as if it were hers, and a deep sadness fell upon her,

Then he focused his gaze and locked eyes with her.

"He is my brother," he whispered. "Mad perhaps, but still a brother, and I love him." He paused, and then continued, "I recall our childhood. He was always dominant, trying to get ahead of me in everything we were doing, were it sports or fencing, but there was a closeness between us—a bond. It is still there within; a bond I cannot easily break. I wished he could repent, and I would have spoken for him, and favored him before the Court of Khandur. I do not know what has gone into his head lately, but he used not to be this way. He was always arrogant, but not like this..."

"Some people cannot handle power," Naisha said. "He appears to be one of them."

The prince nodded. "I still do not understand. When I visited him in Eldermount, he threw me out, but I could yet recognize him. Now, he has changed. But there is more: Did you see his crew? They saluted him and cheered for him, and they seemed to mean each word. He must have a tremendous power over them; a power I did not know he possessed."

"There may be another reason for these behaviors," Naisha said. "I am a Seer, and on Queen Moëlia's initiative, I often looked into the Well. I saw many things; some I understood, some I did not. There is an island, not far, full of dark spells. I confronted it in one of my trances, for it was an opposed force to something we encountered in the Queendom. The name of this place is Whispering Island."

Prince Xandur tensed up. "I have heard of it, too, but I know next to nothing about it. Do you think…?"

"It is possible, taking the crew's behavior into account."

He swallowed hard. "Spells… curses… What happens to those who visit?"

Naisha sighed. "The island is part of a landmass that fell ages ago, in a long-forgotten magic war, and Whispering Island is what remains; yet the dark magic lingers there. Sailors who come too close to that place are warned by Maermaids and Maermen, so if your brother docked at the island, I do not understand why before that, he was not warned. That place alters the visitors' minds. The evil spirits locate a person's worst and most vicious traits, rooted deep inside, or lingering at the surface, and they enhance these behaviors. Thus, if the prince is hungry for power and glory, traits within him, corresponding to that, will enhance. The same applies to his men."

"This would explain the erratic behavior of the entire crew," the prince said. "More than likely, they visited that cursed place and got possessed."

"Not possessed," Naisha said. "Possession is something other. These spirits can alter your mind, that is all. The traits they call to come forth with their whispers already exist within the person. These behaviors are then locked in the forefront, suppressing other urges and needs of a more benevolent kind. It creates an evil person of someone who was not evil before."

Xandur leaned forward. "How can these spells be broken?"

Naisha shook her head and lowered her gaze. "That is not a simple thing to do. I do not know of cures for such spells, for here we are dealing with much older magic than that which I possess. The only thing I am aware of that can break the spell is if the person repents—"

"Then there is hope?"

"There is always hope, but it requires a lot from the cursed person to break through. They must have an iron will to do so, and from what I have seen, your brother does not possess such will, for he already expressed these enhanced traits as a part of his earlier personality."

"Then I have no choice. I must capture him and bring him back to Khandur immediately. The damage he can do is unlimited. There will be no end to his power hunger."

"I am afraid so. You cannot save him from himself."

"Can you foresee what will happen using your Seer's skills?"

"I can, but I must refrain myself from doing so. I wish not to foresee personal events involving conflicts between people, or even inner conflict within one person. If I did, it would break many universal laws; it would affect that person's destiny, and not necessarily in a good way. I am sorry, prince."

She noticed his grief and sense of hopelessness, so she took his hand to comfort him. And there, in her palm, she noticed Xandur's silver ring on his finger. The band was cold to her skin, but the pearl on top was warmer than her hand. She let go, and instead, she gently grabbed his finger to inspect this beautiful artifact. The pearl was constantly shifting between turquoise and ruby red.

"Your ring is magnificent," she breathed. "And I can feel there is magic to it."

"Yes, there is magic," he said.

She said no more about it, but she looked up, meeting his gaze, hoping he would explain.

And he spoke, "It is an old ring, inherited by the eldest of the princes in the Royal Line, and he receives it on his day of manhood to wear throughout his reign until the day he dies. An Angel, sent by the Goddess many thousands of years agone, handed it to our first king, Irvannion, and it has passed on from father to son thenceforth."

"And how does the magic work?" she asked with increased curiosity. "This is also ancient magic, like that of Whispering Island, albeit this magic is more benign. Will you tell me?"

He smiled, but his eyes remained sad. "The Angel told my forefather it was important to keep this ring within the bloodline: for one day, its magic will come to full fruition, and the ring will fulfill its function and its purpose. Its fate is unknown, but tightly connected with its bearer and world events. So, we have carried it for ages, and it has shown us little power, other than giving us strength when in deep inner troubles. Yet, this is not its purpose. The ring's actual power will not show until the end of the Last Age."

"And that is now…"

He nodded. "Aye, that is now, and I am the bearer. I know

not what this will entail, and I am unaware of what to do with it, other than I need to make a choice when the right time comes." He raised his eyebrows and looked at her with a new pair of eyes; this time with more hope.

She shook her head, hearing his thoughts. "No, dear Xandur. I cannot help you find out, and even if I could, I would not. It is not my task to do so, and it would disrupt and distort the power of the ring and your Divine bond with it."

He winced. "I reckoned. I merely needed some hope to cling to."

She grabbed his hand once more, and this time her grip was harder. "You will find your hope, Xandur," she said, and her voice was mild and giving. "And so will I. Perhaps we will find it together…"

Then she stood, walked over to his side of the table, and took both his hands to make him stand. They looked deep into each other's eyes, and Naisha felt their energies swirl in a serpent-like pattern around each other; hers in violet and his in bluish white. When the serpents touched, electricity emerged. Faster and faster, they spun, until their energies turned into sparkling fires that merged. Next, they fell into each other's arms, and all was well.

Chapter 20
The Ancients

ONE NIGHT, ISMARIL had a vivid dream. He saw a colossal door embedded into a steep hillside; and arch-shaped around it, out of the moss, flowers in white and yellow grew on long and entangled pedicles, hiding most of the door from bypassing travelers. The door looked as if it had always been a part of the hillside from the time the knoll rose. In the dream, Ismaril turned to his left and noticed a spring pouring out from inside the hill, continuing an S-shaped path down the slope to the valley below, rippling and clucking. With a trembling hand, he approached a massive stone handle on the right side of the door, trying to open it. But when his hand reached a few inches from the handle, he woke up, gasping.

It was early morning, and the sun had just risen over the hills. Everywhere, Nomads were walking to and fro, minding their morning businesses, and Sigyn's sleeping bag was gone and her spot empty. Soon, he noticed his shield maiden by the bonfire, which was still glowing. There she stood, talking to Raeglin and Kirbakin. Ismaril approached them, groggy, and a little confused after his vivid dream.

"Ah, there you are," Raeglin said. "We were just discussing today's plans. Come and join in!"

"And there is breakfast for you," Kirbakin said.

Ismaril grabbed some cold leftovers from the night before and ate them while Raeglin spoke.

"These hills stretch a lot yonder," he said. "There is much territory to cover if we wish to find an entrance to inside these hills; so, we must spread into small groups to cover more ground. If we are fortunate, we might find an entry before sunset."

"I had a dream," Ismaril said. "It is not clear how valuable it may be, if at all, but it was about a door…"

"A door?" Raeglin said. "Go on!"

Ismaril told them about the arch of overhanging foliage, preventing the door from being discovered easily.

"Hmm," Kirbakin said. "If the dream was an attempt to help us, it is yet too vague. This door, particularly if occluded, will be hard to find."

"In my dream, there was a narrow spring beside the door, and the current was brisk, running down the hillside."

Kirbakin opened his eyes wide, and his face lit up. "That might do it. I noticed such a spring when Master Raeglin and I first entered the mounds. I think I can find the way back there."

"Indeed!" Raeglin said. "If the dream was correct, we might discover a gateway into the Giants' chamber. Let us gather our group and follow you, Mr. Gnome. Your memory serves you better than mine."

Less than an hour's stride from the camp, the entire group of Nomads, now led by the Gnome and Ismaril, came midways upon a stream that emanated from up higher.

"This is it!" Ismaril cried and pointed. "Up there… That is where the door should be if my dream has meaning."

The group climbed up the slope with Ismaril trotting first. He took long steps, eager to find the entrance, and he was soon ahead of Kirbakin, now walking second, struggling to keep the pace on his short, stubby legs.

Before Ismaril, a massive stone door stood, embedded like in his dream's vision. He spun, facing the large group that was still struggling with the steep climb; and with breath in throat, he cried out, "It is here! The door!"

Passing the pilgrim in his effort, and when done climbing, Yomar told his men to wait about 50 paces away, and to Ismaril's side, he rushed, ensued by Master Raeglin, Kirbakin, and Sigyn.

Behold! In front of them, a weathered stonewall ascended, four to five times the height of a full-grown man, and at least wide enough for five men to stand side by side; but it was overgrown and difficult to detect unless its location was erstwhile known. There were no inscriptions on the stone, and nothing showed where the door was leading; it merely stood there amid nowhere.

"Lo!" Ismaril said. "There is the door handle. My dream was a Divine sign, and it was precise!"

Raeglin ran his hand over the rough stone surface. "It was. We are being assisted."

"Queen Astéamat told us we would find the Giants," Sigyn said.

The pilgrim grabbed the handle with both hands. "The door should open outward, so step back a little…"

He put his right foot in line with the door and pulled with all his strength; but it moved not a single inch. He cared not to try twice.

"It is too massive. No man can open this door using strength alone. Such is its nature, and it is not supposed to be unlocked by wayfarers in passing."

"But all signs point to that it is time to wake the Giants," Yomar said. "Ismaril's dream proves it."

"Perhaps so," Kirbakin said. "But this door, as Master Raeglin detailed, will not open by strength alone."

"Then how do we open it?" Yomar asked.

"It is kept closed with magic," the Gnome said. "Ancient magic."

"Ah, a password!"

Kirbakin shook his head. "No password. Think again, folks.

"Who dreamt the dream?
Who told me to find the stream?
Who opened the Book of Secrets among the team?"

Raeglin laughed briefly. "Yes, of course! Ismaril!"

Ismaril raised his brows and gazed helplessly at Raeglin and then at the Gnome. "How would I do that? I know of no such magic."

"And you do not need to," Kirbakin said, waving his short arms in circles. "Merely open the door."

Baffled, Ismaril stepped forward and grabbed the handle. He placed his foot by the door and pulled the handle with all his might, expecting no response. But alas! The door flung open in a blink, needing little of his strength to respond. Bewildered, Ismaril fell backward, and then to the side, swept away by the flinging door. He flew many paces through the air and landed in some thorny brush with a grunt.

"Ha!" Raeglin said, paying little attention to Ismaril, who was cursing while getting to his feet. "The Giants have waited all this time for you, my friend. It is all about the Prophecy."

A musty smell met the companions, hitting from inside the door. Raeglin peaked in, while Ismaril had returned to his friends on stiff legs, with a concerned Sigyn asking him if he was hurt.

"I am glad someone cares," Ismaril mumbled and stared at Raeglin, who was too busy to hear or notice.

"It is very dark in there, as expected," the pilgrim said. "Yet I have my stone to light our way. Come with me. It is time to enter."

Raeglin raised the gemstone above his head, and Ismaril saw a glimpse of a long tunnel leading straight into the mound. He let the pilgrim lead the way, and he followed close behind. Then came Sigyn, Kirbakin, and last Yomar.

As soon as the Nomad had entered, the door closed behind him with a deep rumbling that echoed down the tunnel.

"May the Goddess help us! We are trapped!" Sigyn cried and grabbed Ismaril's arm.

"Worry not," Raeglin said. "The door is operating on magic. It closed so no one else can sneak in while we are here. It is for the Giants' protection."

"How do we get out?" Yomar said.

The pilgrim shrugged, casually. "Let us wake the Giants first. After that, we can concern ourselves with the door."

The five companions continued down the burrow. There was plenty of room above them, for the tunnel was wide. When Raeglin swept about with his gemstone, strange hieroglyphs in a forgotten language became visible, carved into the smooth walls on either side. Ismaril and Sigyn put on their headbands to see better. Perhaps the hieroglyphs were telling the story of those who dwelt here and might yet reside at this place. The door into the tunnel must have been closed for ages, for the air in here was still, with a foul odor of rotting soil to it, tickling their noses. Everything was eerily silent; no dripping water or other typical cave noises, as if no sounds had reached here since eons agone, making one person's breath distinguishable from another.

They soon reached some broad stairs in the dark, leading downward and turning right a little farther down, out of sight. The steps were even and smooth as if carved recently from bedrock. The company followed the pilgrim down and soon reached the bottom. Another tunnel continued straight for a few hundred paces, making a permanent stop in front of yet another door. This one was not as massive as the previous one, and it was ajar.

Raeglin made a sign for the others to stop behind him, and Ismaril saw the warlock peek inside, holding the gem before him. Then he disappeared into the unknown, out of sight.

Ismaril had little patience to stand idle. He glanced through the door slit and distinguished the bluish light from the gem in there, flickering around. Yet it was difficult to notice what else was roaming in the pitch-black darkness.

"You can all come," Raeglin said in a full voice. Ismaril opened the door wide without effort, and thus, the entire group entered a large chamber inside. Raeglin swept the gem in broad gestures across the room, leaving ghastly shadows about.

The chamber was square-shaped, about fifty paces across and thirty feet high, and the walls were not gray like granite, but shimmering white in the light from the pilgrim's stone. The floors near the walls were free from objects, but amid the chamber, twenty-five long sarcophagi lay spread in squares of five; one midst, encased by the other four. Each sarcophagus was at least thirteen feet long and made of the purest gold, polished as if time dared not touch them. There was no dust and no wear; and so shimmering were they that they nearly blinded the visitors when Raeglin's stone shone on them. Though Ismaril knew what they were, he instinctively put his hand on Gahil's hilt and squeezed it.

Raeglin carefully closed in on the nearest sarcophagus, and Ismaril followed abreast. The enormous coffin had a lid made of thick, transparent glass; and when the pilgrim swept with his light over it, Ismaril noticed a giant figure inside, lying on his back, seemingly in a deep sleep. His stern face was pale and at peace, and his long and thick red beard was carefully combed, resting on his chest, curly at the ends. A long hair fell likewise over his chest and ended in line with the beard. The chest was bare, having no sign of body hair; but his arms and torso were massive and muscular, seemingly capable of effortlessly ripping anyone apart. Around his waist, he wore a sharp-blue tunic with golden seams, reaching to his ankles. His eyes were closed, and on his head, he wore a tight and rounded golden helmet, decorated in many interwoven patterns. His hands rested on his torso, gripping the blade of a long sword, with the hilt resting on his right shoulder, and the blade ending at his bare feet. Sigyn gasped when she saw this magnificent being, and Ismaril and Raeglin exchanged glances.

Sigyn put her palm before her mouth and whispered, "He must be at least twelve to thirteen feet tall."

"There are twenty-five of them here," Yomar said, being the last to join the observers. "They are too few to matter. Are there more chambers here somewhere, perhaps?"

Raeglin shook his head. "No. The tunnel ends with this hall. This is the end of it."

"Few or not," Sigyn said. "How do we wake them up?"

"How about making it simple?" Kirbakin said with a twinkle in his eye. "We merely open the lid."

The pilgrim smiled. "There we have our practical Gnome. Let us get to work then."

The five companions gathered around the one sarcophagus to examine how they could open it, but there was no handle or other equipment they could easily recognize as hatches or the like.

"What now?" Sigyn said.

"Let me try to push it open," Yomar said and pressed on the dome-shaped glass window. To his surprise, his hands went right through, and he almost lost his balance. Gasping, he instantly removed himself from the container.

"Ah, more magic," Kirbakin said. "I am too short for this. Can someone try to touch him?"

Raeglin attempted, but his arm faced an invisible barrier a few inches above the giant body in stasis.

"This will not do," the Gnome said. "Well, here we go again. Ismaril."

The pathfinder swallowed hard, not eager to touch the silent body. Slowly, he lowered his arm into the sarcophagus, but he also ran into the barrier, and he quickly withdrew. Looking at Sigyn, he said, "As you said, what now?"

Raeglin frowned and took yet another look, but got no

wiser. The body had not yet moved. Ismaril went to inspect other sarcophagi, in which bodies, almost identical to the first, lay at rest and in the same position; all of them with a blade along their torsos and legs.

"Every casket looks the same," he said, trying to touch them, one by one. "There must be a mechanism somewhere. Perhaps it is elsewhere in the chamber…"

Iguhl… The original name of Ismaril's blade popped up in his mind, distinct and clear, as if a voice inserted itself into his head. Confused, he looked about, first thinking it came from outside. *Use your blade.* Someone was communicating with him. His gaze focused on one sarcophagus. Was this possible? Did a Giant communicate with him via his mind?

Ismaril moved toward the container whence he thought the voice had come. Inside was a Giant, almost identical to the first one they encountered, save his hair and his beard that were black. *I must be crazy,* Ismaril thought, *but here we go: What do you want me to do with Iguhl?*

First, there was silence, and then a deep voice inside Ismaril's head said: *Lay it in line with my blade and rest it on my left shoulder.*

Ismaril shrugged, drew Gahil, and placed it upon the invisible boundary close to the body, and in the exact position the voice had suggested. Then he stepped back and watched.

The Giant's pale skin instantly gained color when his heart started pumping, and his eyelids opened, exposing two large, yellow eyes, locking with Ismaril, who jumped. Then, like ice breaking, the invisible boundary on top of the body must have shattered into a thousand pieces from the sound of it, but no glass or ice was visible to Ismaril's gaze.

The Giant grunted, and his voice was like thunder as he sat up in his sarcophagus. He rocked his head violently so that his long, black hair almost whipped Ismaril's face where he stood. Then he grabbed Gahil and his own sword, one in each hand, and stood up in the casket. He was twice as tall as the tallest human, and his muscles played under his skin when he moved about.

The five companions backed up some more when the gigantic beast stepped out of his ancient bed. With legs far apart under his blue tunic, he kept his gaze locked with Ismaril, whose heart battered like a hammer against an anvil.

I presume this sword is yours.

Ismaril heard the Giant clearly, but there were no words coming from his lips; it was all in Ismaril's head.

"Aye," Ismaril said out loud. "It is Gahil."

Gahil? The Giant continued transferring his thoughts. *That is a better name than Iguhl.* The colossal man handed back the blade to Ismaril.

Next, ear-shattering to all, the noise of splitting ice was everywhere. One by one, the caskets opened, and soon, twenty-five Giants of enormous stature stood tall in the chamber with swords in hand. Ismaril tensed; were these beasts friendly? Did they have a temper? How should he act? He stayed still and quiet.

For a while, the Giants stood idle, until the red-haired, whom the wayfarers had spotted first, stepped forward and stopped a couple of paces from Ismaril, who looked like a small child before him.

Then it is time, the Giant said inside Ismaril's head. *You have awoken us, and there is only one man who can do so. The End of Times is upon us, and we must act. If the time is right, we have been in stasis for thousands of years. My name is Arraok, and I am the Lord of the Zemlins, by which we are renown, but we call ourselves the Ÿadeth-Oëmin.*

I am Ismaril…

You can use your voice. We do not use voices, but we understand your tongue. My thoughts reach both you and your friends, but yours do not. Hence, it is better for you to speak.

"We know very little about your people," Ismaril said. "I was told we must wake you up, and that the time is now."

Said who?

"The Queen… Queen Astéamat."

The Lord Arraok's eyes expressed content. *Very good. Then all is in order.*

"Well, I would not go that far," Ismaril said. "The Black King has a significant advantage." He swallowed before he continued. "I can see you are powerful men and can be helpful in battle, but you are only a handful. I mean no disrespect, but the enemies are many."

Arraok seemed to laugh, although no sound came through his mouth. *We are not so few. If we all survived our long sleep, we would be three thousand powerful men. And they are all about* to wake up now, resting in other mounds around here.

"This is excellent news!" Yomar said. "Now we have an army and a powerful one at that."

"But why have you been hiding in these mounds?" Sigyn asked.

It is a long story, Arraok said. *We have little time to tell it now, but I shall do my best to be brief. Once we were a much larger group of people than we are now. At the peak of our civilization, we lived in the land Kaz-Maír, ere Gormoth invaded it. They burned the giant forests covering our land, and most of our people died in the flames. Azezakel used Fire Dragons to do the job. Surprise took us, and we must flee. Those of us who survived found shelter under Emoria's trees, where Gormoth's Dragons could not follow. Queen Astéamat took us under her wings, and we seemed to disappear from the world.*

After living in Emoria's timeless realm for what seemed an eternity but was not, the Queen spoke of Taëlia's destiny and the End of Days. She told us we must not stay in Emoria much longer, for we are not of its vibrations; and alas! Trees and plants withered in our presence. Thus, she asked if we wished to have a part in defeating the Enemy once and for all when the time arrives. We hesitated not, for the Black King had murdered almost all our kind, save three thousand men. The Dragons and the Wolfinen went for our women, and they deliberately killed them all, so we can procreate no more; thus, we are a dying species.

Therefore, the Queen suggested we go into stasis, only to be awoken in the future when we can be of help. We agreed, and the Mazosians buried us in these mounds, so we would not die off before the Great War.

"But why did the Queen prepare you for war when the Emorians are a peaceful people, refusing violence?" Sigyn asked. "For that is what the Queen told us."

On that, we cannot speak. When the Queen put us in stasis, she spoke of war, though the Mazosians were no longer a warlike people.

Kirbakin cleared his throat to draw attention. "From the little I know and understand, the Mazosians were not warlike then: They did not shun war if war was necessary, but they sought it not. The Queen has foresight enough to see what will come of Destiny, and she wanted to prepare to change it. Since then, she and her people have become completely peaceful; but since she already put the spell on the Ÿadeth-Oëmin, the Queen cannot reverse it. Astéamat knows war is inevitable; not even she can stop it. All she can do is to impact the outcome. She puts a lot of hope in you, Sigyn, and in Ismaril. That much I have understood."

"Your words are wise, Kirbakin," Raeglin said, "and I believe them to be true. These are sorrowful times, and many who are now alive will not be so when the war is over. We all wish it was different."

And we must waste no time. The Ÿadeth-Oëmin must go to war. Are you following us?

"Where are you going?" Raeglin said.

Straight to Gormoth. If the world looks anything like when we walked the lands, we shall find our way.

"Then we also must hurry," Raeglin said. "You shall go, but we will not follow. We are going north to the Frostlands to build yet another army. We shall take them on, charging from the north."

Very well, Arraok said. *Then, let us dwell here no more!*

The group of twenty-five Giants left the chamber, heeled by Ismaril and his companions. But when they came close to the front door, Ismaril smelled smoke. Arraok, who was in the lead, opened the door with little effort.

Outside it was almost dark, and as far as Ismaril's eyes could see, there were many Giants gathered on the mound. It seemed all three thousand had awoken, ready to march.

But something was wrong. Ismaril gave the army of Giants a mere glimpse, for elsewhere, something horrible must have happened. Smoke from a tremendous fire lay thick and heavy in the air, and way yonder to the west, the sky was lit in a most dreadful way. Aside from the smoke, there was a distinct smell of burning trees.

No one moved, and even the Giants stood still, watching the scenario before them, and tears fell on Ismaril's and Sigyn's cheeks.

"Woe to us all!" Ismaril shouted out, and his voice cracked. "Emoria! Emoria is on fire!"

"Alas! Alas!" Raeglin cried. "Emoria has fallen!"

Sigyn rushed over to Ismaril and grabbed both his arms.

"Ishtarion!" she wept. "I sense her no more. She is no longer in my mind!"

Ismaril closed his eyes, and a stream of tears rolled down his cheeks. "You are right. I feel her not…"

Chapter 21
Treacherous Planning

AT THIS TIME OF THE YEAR, when midsummer had passed, Queen Moëlia and her sisterhood usually spent time in the northern part of the Western Mountains, in Astar, the capitol of The Queendom of Ayasis. Albeit this year, worries were many and pleasures few. The sorrows of the world weighed heavily on the queen. Vrilya, her new Seer, replacing Naisha after her alleged betrayal, tried to comfort Moëlia, but to no avail. The Queen stood often in the highest tower, looking out, and her words were few.

Then, one day, her scouts returned. Four women on horseback rode on a spur toward Astar, coming in from the west. The Queen's heart jumped. What news would they bring? Had Flaradhir, the courier from Gormoth, been correct? Deep within her heart, she hoped he had not. She paced to and fro across the tower balcony, waiting for the scouts to arrive.

Once inside the castle, the scouts were eager to see the Queen and the council. Although they were dirty and covered with dust, guards escorted them to the Hall of Counsels, where the entire sisterhood had assembled. Breathless and nervous, the four tall women bowed before their Queen and the Council.

"Magnificent Queen," said their lieutenant. "We have news."

"Good or bad?" Moëlia asked.

"I regret to say they are bad, Milady."

The sisterhood exchanged glances, and there was fear in their gaze.

"Go on…"

"Yes, Milady. As you assigned us to do, we stayed close to Emoria's border for two weeks and patrolled it to and fro. From the first week, we have nothing to report, but on the tenth day…" The lieutenant lowered her gaze. "I am reluctant to say that on the tenth day, a small group, comprising three horsemen, approached Queen Astéamat's border between Moon Hills and Moonlake River, coming out from Dimwood. They asked for an audition, which they were granted."

Silence. Then the Queen said, in a low voice, as if she wished not to know the answer. "Who were they?"

"One resembled a warlock, and yet another was a Gnome, for certain. The third…" The lieutenant hesitated again.

"Yes?" Moëlia said, impatiently.

"The third one was … Prince Xandur, the Heir of the Kingdom of Khandur…"

A buzz went through the congregation, and Queen Moëlia's face turned ash gray. She stared at her lieutenant with such intensity that the scout leader must bow down, unable to meet her impinging gaze. The Queen's heart fell heavy like a stone, and her mind filled her with thoughts most unwished for. A profound sadness grew inside her, mixed with an approaching rage, rolling up from the depth of her mind.

Moëlia adjusted her posture and held her head straight. "Anything else?" she asked, and her voice was authoritarian once more.

"No, Milady. The three in company disappeared amongst the trees, and that was the last we saw of them."

The Queen dismissed the scouts, so the sisterhood could be private.

"Flaradhir was right," Moëlia said in a deep voice. "I must admit I doubted him, but all this time, he has spoken the truth. And Naisha is with the Emorians. How can I have been so ignorant?"

Vrilya put her hand on the Queen's shoulder.

"We were all deceived," she said, consoling. "And Naisha played her treacherous role well."

"Naisha!" Moëlia snorted. "Never has our Queendom seen

such a traitor. One day, I will see her again, and I shall watch her execution in person. I always trusted her as a true sister: Always righteous, honest, and loyal; or so I thought. Now I know she was everything but—"

"What now?" another sister asked. "Perhaps Flaradhir returns."

"It matters not whether he returns, for I have decided." The aggression in her voice now became prominent, and her words filled up the hall. "We are going to war against Emoria!"

"But how?" Vrilya said. "Emoria is hidden and can only be accessed by invitation."

"There is another way," the Queen said, and her eyes were cold and merciless. "Our Dragons!"

The sisters looked at her, confused. "What can the Dragons do?" Celestia asked. "Gormoth wants us to keep them idle, and even if we use them, of what help would they be?"

"Is that not obvious?" Moëlia said. "Queen Astéamat has secluded her Queendom, so we cannot reach there. But mind you, our Dragons were once hers, given to us a long time ago, when there was peace in the world. Our Dragons still have access to her Queendom."

"So, should we…?" Vrilya said, and her voice trembled.

The Queen nodded. "Indeed. We let the Fire Dragons do the job. We shall send them over Astéamat's wide and enchanted forests and burn them all down to ashes."

"Milady," Celesta said, visually shocked. "We cannot do that… We must not destroy Emoria. Astéamat's Queendom creates balance in Taëlia, as much as that is possible. Without her queendom, we are doomed."

"Nonsense!" the Queen cried. "Astéamat is preparing for war, so she creates her own imbalance. About that, we can do nothing. But I shall not sit idle and wait for her to come and destroy our beloved Queendom! We shall surprise her, for we will strike first."

"Should we not talk to her first… negotiate?" Vrilya said.

"Negotiate?" Moëlia's eyes were like Dragon Fire. "She is planning on attacking us unprovoked and letting surprise take us, but now we have powerful friends in Gormoth, and by them, we have been warned. I negotiate not with such an enemy as Queen Astéamat. I refuse to show weakness!"

Then she stood, and she cried out, loud and clear, "Prepare for war! Let loose the Dragons!"

Chapter 22
The Battle for Khurad-Resh

EXXARION'S FLEET CAME in from northeast and approached Rhuir where the kingdom was the least populated. In great numbers, like dragon ships from the Underworld, they exposed themselves across the coastline; and treacherous men ashore, the Er-Ekhanim, ran for all they were worth.

The prince stood at the bow, sword in hand, fist clinched around the hilt, and with the tip of the blade resting on the deck. With the remaining fleet growing apace, the armada cleaved the Dragon River. A northeastern wind took Exxarion's hair, and it blew freely in the wind, occasionally whipping his face; for his hair had grown very long, and so had his beard. Majestic, he appeared, larger than life, making his mere presence terrifying to the people beholding him. Tall and broad-chested, he stood, resembling a barbaric pirate lord rather than a Khanduran prince. But Exxarion cared little about the petty folks on the shores, for he had grander plans. He knew that about two leagues up the river, the city of Khurad-Resh stood, and there he hoped to encounter King Nibrazul himself and take him as hostage. Grand and arrogant were his plans, but lesser men had succeeded in their quests using a hard head.

This far north, the wind was biting, breathing unmercifully from the Ocean of Ice, and the sun was blistering; white, and cold. As they sailed up the river, the land on either side was hither and thither deserted and plain, and elsewhither sparsely forested with pine and fir. The river was wide and striding on its run toward the Sea, and there were smells and tastes of fresh saltwater carried upon the wind. The chill from the north empowered the prince, and in his mind, he was like King Irvannion of old, gazing out over the fields, way up in the north and nigh to the Frostlands. Albeit King Irvannion had been great in his time, Exxarion's time was now, and his Greatness was even grander than that of his heroic forefather; for as a self-proclaimed King of Anúria, invading one of Azezakel's most strategic colonies, he would write history, thereby exceeding Irvannion by plenty. He had planned his mission well and passed it on to the crews on board each schooner, so every man knew what to do ere the battle started and continued throughout.

As they neared their destination, the prince noticed random groups of Wolfmen and Birdmen studying the armada from afar, but with too few warriors to intervene, they remained idle. A few hurried northwards: some on foot and others on Ulves, rushing to warn the city ere too late. And there were no Dragons in sight, perhaps busy elsewhere, not expecting an attack from the Sea. Yet, Exxarion understood it was orderly to haste.

Soon, fir and pine grew denser and turned into a deeper forest, and as the late afternoon sun cast long shadows over the land, the magnificent watchtowers of Khurad-Resh appeared over the treetops to the north, with their rutile quartz shimmering in many vibrant colors. From these towers, the guards must have noticed the armada coming up the water, even though the forest might have hidden the ships long enow.

At close range to the city, Prince Exxarion ordered his fleet to cast anchors at the northern shore and prepare for their assail. He grabbed a monocular and zoomed in on the massive black marble wall and its surroundings. Everything was quiet and deserted as if no one lived there. Were the city ill-maintained, it could be considered a ghost town, but the prince knew it was populated.

"They are biding their time," Exxarion said to Admiral Mundo. "They wait for us to make our move so they can arrow us down."

He smiled wryly, gazing at the man in the crow's nest above and made the sign. The man in the mast climbed to the mast top, where he put a red flag seamed to a pole and fastened it in a designated place to signal to the rest of the armada to prepare.

"Tell the men to stay on alert," the prince said to his admiral. "This should be a brief and victorious battle."

Mundo opened his mouth to say something but closed it again with a click.

"Speak up, for all's sake!" Exxarion said.

Mundo found his courage. "Even if... I mean, when we have taken the city, what about the Dragons? How do we defend ourselves toward them when they find out and storm in from Gormoth to kill us all?"

"We will use the catapults, of course. We can easily transport them, rolling them down the ship's bridges and eventually convey them into the city."

"But do the citizens have no ravens or crows to send as messengers to Gormoth and warn them?"

"Nay. These citizens are arrogant, and they take for granted the Dragons will catch intruders. I have planned this, Admiral. I know what I am doing. And now is a good time to attack, for the Dragons are elsewhere."

"How do we know that?"

"You do not know, but I do. I am a strategist. It requires a warlord to know one. Gormoth is busy elsewhither. I believe something is happening in the west and possibly in the north. The world is mobilizing; at least those who choose to take part in the war. Try to see my genius in all this and learn, Admiral. We are taking Rhuir by surprise, and we will captivate King Nibrazul and use him as a trade. Thus, we can set the terms."

—

Afternoon turned to evening, and a starry night sky with a faint, waning moon followed thereupon. The first life sign from the city came by sundown, when torches were lit along the top of the wall, but from inside the gate, no communication came. Exxarion smiled, for this bothered him not; he knew the torches would do the townspeople no good, and about the silence, he cared even less. Those inside the fortress expected an attack, so the Rhuirians could shoot them down. Yet the torches would be too dim to expose all the prince's men moving among the trees.

Secluded by nightfall, the crew rolled up many wooden catapults on deck and pointed them at Khurad-Resh. Then they signaled to other ships to follow. Soon, there was a long line of catapults aimed at the city, and the buckets, filled with a mix of saltpeter, sulfur, and oil, would burst into flames on impact. The prince stretched a little extra where he stood, taking credit for this ingenious invention. In Khandur, they knew nothing about his new weapon; it had been Exxarion's secret.

The prince raised his arm and held it for a while, taking a last glance at the target, awaiting the right moment. Then he lowered his arm and shouted as loud as his voice could take it, "FIRE!"

Distinct noises followed when the crew released the restraining ropes of one catapult after the other. The mechanical arms swung fast, and the payloads of liquid bolted through the air. Most liquid reached the target inside the city walls. Yet a few fell short and landed on the ground before the gate, where they set grass and bushes in flames.

Screams in anguish reached the Anúrians' ears from inside the walls when houses and people were caught on fire. Tall flames and smoke from wooden buildings reached above the city wall level where the ship crews could see them. Exxarion laughed hysterically, and with great excitement, his eyes glowed in the dark. "RELOAD!" he shouted. "FIRE!"

A new swarm of liquid flew across the land from many ships, hitting the target once more. The prince jumped up and down. "AYE!" he cried. "This is enow… FORWARD!"

The soldiers on all ships ran ashore in long lines, moving swiftly in serpentine patterns among the trees, trying to avoid retaliation from the city wall and the towers. Some men brought long but foldable ladders. The many trees and the darkness of the night protected them and made for suitable covers, and few were those on their way who fell from piercing arrows. When his entire crew had left the ship, Exxarion followed last.

As the prince's troops closed in and became more visible in the torchlight, the city soldiers let their bowmen loose in great numbers. Many Anúrians fell while charging the wall. But the catapults had done great harm: The city was on fire and in the chaos that followed, the soldiers inside could not mobilize. Trained and efficient in action, the Anúrians unfolded the long ladders and raised them against the wall in many places. In swift succession, the invaders climbed the ladders. Occasionally, the townspeople threw a ladder back with men still climbing, but the

Rhuirians had too few resources to keep up with these ferocious invaders. Soon, many Anúrian troops occupied the city.

Prince Exxarion, reaching the top of a ladder, jumped over the wall, heeled by Admiral Mundo. Hot waves flushed the prince's face, and there were crackling noises from a city on fire. Toxic smoke made Exxarion's eyes burn and tear up, and breathing was hard.

Everywhere, like enormous bonfires, houses stood in flames. On the streets were many corpses, some still burning, and the invaders covered their noses to protect themselves from the terrible stink of burning flesh. Aimless women and children fled to and fro, crying in fear when they saw the advancing Anúrians. But the prince had the sense to spare women and children.

In the city, there were humans, Wolfmen, and Birdmen mixed, now confused and shocked. Thus, the two opposing legions met in battle inside the gate of Khurad-Resh, and this battle would go into history as The Battle for Khurad-Resh. The confrontation was crushing, and the death toll was high.

Screaming and uttering many curses, the armies clashed with each other in a bitter fight, man against man. Wolfmen and Birdmen fell hither and Anúrian knights and soldiers fell thither, and many suffered painful deaths. The metallic flick of blades against blades sang in the air.

An arrow from a desperate Rhuirian watchman, trapped in his tower and engulfed by blue flames, pierced through Exxarion's shoulder. The prince moaned in pain but broke the arrow in half and pulled it out. Warm blood poured down his chest and back. He ignored it. He took a position closer to the demolished gate, searching his way deeper into the city. Two Wolfmen approached, and one pushed him so that he flung back. The beast came upon him, swinging a heavy axe in the air. Swoosh! The axe missed Exxarion's head just about. The axe blade sank deep into the ground. Exxarion, with his sword, cleaved the Wolfman's head from top to shoulder. A cascade of blood and brain spurted, hitting Exxarion and the second Wolfman alike.

The prince was quick to his feet. The Wolfman's blood blurred his vision, and he missed the blade coming. A long cut opened from ear to lip, and he fell once more. Now he noticed the blood and the throbbing pain. Then, the Wolfman's sword rose, aiming to strike.

But no strike came. The Wolfman's head departed, and the beast fell dead. Behind stood Admiral Mundo, drenched in blood. He hurried to the prince's side.

"You alright, Sire?"

Exxarion nodded, but the shoulder pain and his throbbing cheek made him nauseous.

"Stand your ground," the prince said. "I am taking a few men to open the gate. Many of ours are yet outside."

He assembled fifty of his own to ensure his success, and like ferocious gods, they slew their way free to the gate and quickly released the chains. The gate swung open on squeaking hitches, and the Anúrians outside ran in to join the battle.

The morning was breaking, and from afar, Exxarion saw something moving across the river bridge. More Rhuirian troops approached from the southwest, but it was impossible to say how many. The prince's men closed the gate to keep the hostile troops out; and all ladders, still leaning toward the city wall, he ordered to be pulled up to prevent the outside enemies from making use of them.

After half the day, the Anúrians took over Khurad-Resh, and the Wolfmen and Birdmen, who were trained not to surrender, were slain, along with treacherous humans, by many called Er-Ekhanim. The battle for the city was over, and Exxarion was quick to exchange Rhuir's flag with the Anúrian banner.

Great was the victory, and most Anúrian men were still alive. Yet, Exxarion was not pleased: for his success depended upon taking King Nibrazul as hostage, but the king was not there. A prisoner among the Er-Ekhanim told him the Dark King was currently in Gormoth. Without Nibrazul as hostage, Khurad-Resh was extremely vulnerable. Exxarion had no solid plan on how to defend the city when Gormoth would arrive, and he knew they would come shortly.

The flames inside were slowly fading, but water could not put it out, for this hellish liquid burned atop the water. And the smoke lingered over Khurad-Resh, with no wind washing it off. People were coughing, and they wet their eyes with water to rid themselves of the burning effect of the smoke.

But although the city was now under Anúrian command, it was also under siege by the Rhuirian troops who had arrived from across the bridge, lining up outside.

Erstwhile, strong and powerful Anúrian men had successfully rolled most catapults into the city, hidden in the dark of night, but a few cannons they must leave outside. Exxarion was not concerned, for all liquid was inside the city wall. Two other things concerned him the more: There had been no time to safeguard his ships after the battle, and now an army stood between him and his schooners. The enemy could easily lay hands on the vessels or burn them down. The second immediate concern was Gormoth's Dragons. They could show up soon, and he must ensure there was enough liquid to potentially take them out with fire as they arrived, and not use it on the outside army to any significant extent.

From the tower, he watched the army of Wolfmen and human traitors on the ash field there under. They were not a vast army, but strong enough to be a threat to the Anúrians.

Exxarion suddenly interrupted his thoughts, for behold! Up the river, an armada of warships as great as his own came sailing. Most were pirate ships, but a significant number sailed under the Khanduran banner.

Exxarion hurried down the stairs and ordered his men to line up across the ring wall and get ready for battle.

"My brother is coming!" he shouted, and all men, well enough to fight, took position.

—

"Alas!" Prince Xandur cried. "My brother has taken Khurad-Resh."

Through the monocular, he witnessed the trail of slain warriors spread all the way to the city gate; and the trees wailed, some yet on fire, whereas others stood black and in smoke, like empty skeletons bearing witness to something mortifying. And the smell of scorched timber lay thick over the ships as they drew nigh.

The prince handed the monocular to Lord Zarabaster.

"The enemy has put Khurad-Resh under siege," he said. "There are many of them."

"Aye, but not enow. We have plenty of men to take them down, and they have yet to notice our presence. But I wonder what put all this land in flames. Never have I seen anything like it. The enemy must possess powerful weapons, but their efforts were to no avail. If my brother is alive, he is within the city walls."

Thus, it came to pass that Prince Xandur's and Lord

Zarabaster's armies joined in battle at the End of Days, and for the first time in history. With great caution, the large, coupled army sneaked up from the riverbank and from behind, overwhelming the enemy.

Ere the armies were nigh, the Rhuirians did not discover them, and it took them by great surprise. Thus, the enemy must battle against two forces; one in their tail, and one in front; for from the ring wall, Prince Exxarion's men used bowmen to slay the Wolfmen and the Er-Ekhanim below.

Then a battle followed, short but raging. The enemy knew they were in peril as the Khanduran-Rhíandorian armies surrounded them. Wolfmen, thoroughly trained by Azezakel, fought to the bitter end. Many Er-Ekhanim fell before the city that day, but few were the Khanduran-Rhíandorian men who met their fate there. The pirates fought with great skill and hesitated not, and when Xandur's men noticed how well Zarabaster's men battled, they heightened in valor, and in boundless agony, the enemy fell in great numbers. When merely a few dozen Er-Ekhanim still stood, they dropped their weapons, fell to their knees, and asked for mercy; for there was nowhere to escape with the victors encompassing them.

"Spare your arrows, bowmen of Anúria!" Xandur cried to the men on the wall.

Thus, the battle ended as swiftly as it had begun. Prince Xandur stepped into the circle of the captured Er-Ekhanim, still on their knees, facing the ground. Stretched, and with great authority, the prince walked in circles around the prisoner, beholding them in silence. Then he halted and spoke.

"Thus, you have met your fate, men of treason. Horrendous is your crime, and you shall surely die for your betrayal. Now listen, for lying will not behoove you: We will interrogate you thoroughly, and your death may come easily, or it may come hard; the choice is yours. Cooperate, and we let your death be swift and painless; refuse, and we shall drag it out. Raise your treacherous heads and see the man over there. He is Lord Zarabaster, grim and ruthless, descending from the infamous pirates of Piscas Urash. Fear him rightfully, for he shall lead the interrogation."

In the silence that followed, Xandur lifted his gaze to the Anúrians on the city wall, and he said in a powerful voice, "Is my brother there? Let me speak with Prince Exxarion!"

The men on the wall moved about just a little, but no one seemed to make the effort. Xandur waited longer than was called for, and then he spoke again. "Answer me, knights and soldiers of the Kingdom of Khandur! Is my brother alive?"

Then Exxarion showed himself on top of the ring wall.

"Hail, brother!" he said. "My men responded not to your request, for you addressed me falsely and with disrespect. My title is no more Prince Exxarion, for I am King Exxarion of Anúria and Rhuir, and Khurad-Resh is now my domain."

"A king you are not, my brother, for your title is self-proclaimed, and hence, a treacherous act. Now let me and my men in so we can talk."

Exxarion laughed. "Your men and the followers of a simple pirate chief are not welcome in my city. And beware that we could have slain the enemies outside our gates without your help. Now, return whence you came, Xandur. Go home to our father. I am sure he needs all the aid he can get."

"Hear me out, for what will you do when the Dragons come? You and your men must meet the same fate as those I assume burned to death in the city, there perishing in flames. I know not what caused that hellfire, but I sense it is your work."

"Catapults, my dear brother. Catapults. And I added a small invention of mine to the equation. Thus, I could put the entire city on fire: wood, stone, and water alike. You and father have always doubted me, have you not? Little do you recognize a genius and strategist when you see one. But a brilliant mind cannot sit idle: If no one listens, he must act on his own behalf. Behold, for I took the city, and Khurad-Resh is now mine!"

"Aye! You have occupied the city, but for how long shall it remain yours? I am startled the Dragons have not yet come, but when they arrive, what can you do?"

"Use the catapults again, of course! Dragons spit fire, but they can also succumb to fire. If Gormoth dares to send Dragons upon me, the beasts shall not live to regret it. I will use fire against fire."

"These are delusive fantasies, Exxarion."

"You said the same thing when I told you I would invade Khurad-Resh. Now lo-and-behold! Who was right and who was wrong?"

"The entire city is destroyed, and the land you burned down

with it. And you lack sufficient food supplies, I reckon. You will not last long here. Surrender and come with me. This is your best choice now, ere things get worse. Gormoth will not merely send Dragons; they will send Wolfmen and Birdmen, too, and who knows what else? Even if we join you, we stand no chance against Azezakel's armies. They will crush us, for we are few and they are many."

Exxarion shook his head.

"Not in the least do you know me," he said. "Have you heard of scouts? Azezakel is busy elsewhere. He might send the Dragons, but that is all."

"You know that is not true. You counted on taking Nibrazul as hostage, did you not? So, where is he?"

Exxarion was silent.

"You do not have him. You based your success on one thing, and one thing alone: to use Nibrazul against Azezakel. But Nibrazul is not here. So much for your scouting. Now you know not how to proceed." Xandur paused, but his brother said naught.

"Be sensible," Xandur said. "You took the city, you burned it down, and you killed a lot of enemies. Look at it as a victory. Take your men and come with us. It will spare thousands of lives."

"So that you can take me back to Khandur and let the headsman decapitate me?"

"Come by choice, and I will speak for you that your life be spared."

"I rather stay here."

"Take your time until the sun moves from zenith to west, and we shall speak again. If your Anúrian army hears me now, I also accuse them of treason. This is the last call, and your last chance to find redemption and repent." Where after Xandur withdrew his men to hold counsel away from the city walls.

As they departed, Zarabaster drew Xandur nigh, and he said, "I think the Anúrians inside the city will not obey, and I believe I know wherefore…"

"Speak," Xandur said.

"They are spellbound. Remember when we met your brother at Sea? His armada came in from the east, almost in a straight line from Whispering Island."

"So?"

"I am a seafarer, and I am familiar with many waters and

many lands that float upon them. Though I have never visited that island, I know what I have heard from those well-informed. There is a good reason wherefore clever sailors never go near that island, for it is cursed. Evil winds blow there, and upon these winds, dark forces ride. Go nigh and they will possess you."

Xandur's mouth was agape. "Are you saying…?"

Zarabaster nodded. "Aye! I believe Prince Exxarion and his crew are possessed and cursed. The curse of the island makes the worst of what is inside a man, and it will surface and become his principal character. Alas! The entire Anúrian army is cursed. Therefore, they are unreasonable. They will go to great lengths to fulfill what their leader, your brother, has in his mind."

"This is horrific if true!" Xandur cried. "How can we break the spell?"

Zarabaster sighed, and his eyes glazed over. "I do not know if we can."

—

Whilst Prince Xandur spoke with his brother, his officers had interrogated the Er-Ekhanim, and two pirates approached their lord and the prince, dragging one Er-Ekhanim with them.

"My Lord and the Prince," said a pirate, "we suggest you hear this man out, so you can determine his fate. For this is what we quickly have gotten out of him and many others of his kind."

Xandur made a gesture. "Very well, let him speak."

The prisoner's body shook and could not lock eyes with the prince. His head and face were shaved, as was required for all these men. He bowed in submission and spoke in a trembling, broken voice.

"Prince and Lord," he said. "Most likely, my fate is sealed, and so also that of my comrades. But hear me out, Sirs, even if these are the last words I ever utter. For hundreds of years, we have been in bondage to Gormoth and King Azezakel. The world believes we joined your enemy by free will, but not so. My fore fathers they captured, and they forced our kind to join. Little we wished to do so."

Zarabaster's voice was harsh and assertive. "Then, wherefore did you not refuse? Did death frighten you? You rather let yourself be defiled than give up your lives? That is cowardly."

"Indeed, so it may seem, Lord," said the prisoner. "Yet it had little to do with the courage of my forefathers, other than they were compassionate."

"Compassionate? How so? Betrayal and treason are strange ways to show compassion."

"Children, Lord. Our children. We refused to join forces with Evil, but they tortured our children…" The prisoner wept and spoke not for a moment. Then he said, "They could not bear to see their offspring suffer, so they agreed. Azezakel spared the young, with the stipulation that we must promise always to be in liaison with Gormoth. I believe all those you call Er-Ekhanim, the Betrayers, would gladly fight for Khandur and the alliance against Azezakel and his Dark Kings."

"This is no excuse," Prince Xandur said. "You have the priorities wrong!"

But Lord Zarabaster raised his arm in a gesture to intervene. He said, "Are you proposing that you repent?"

"Yes, we do! All of us."

"That is convenient," Xandur said. "Now that you are prisoners, anything goes to save your poor lives. It behooves you not, and it makes me more upset."

"I understand, Prince," the prisoner said. "Then we are ready to take the punishment you choose for us."

"So it shall be," Xandur said. "You and the rest of the prisoners shall die before sunset."

"Can I speak to you in private, Prince?" Zarabaster said.

"You can. Hold on to this prisoner until we are back."

The Lord pulled Xandur aside.

"I have an idea," he said. "How many Er-Ekhanim roam in Rhuir?"

"I know not the numbers," Xandur said, "but they are many. We can count them in the tens of thousands, possibly more."

"That is better than I assumed. We can use them."

"How?"

"We have a good number of prisoners here. Send a few to talk to their own, wherever they roam, and let them bring news that Khandur and Rhíandor give them pardon if they come back and fight with the Alliance against Azezakel. If the prisoner is telling the truth, they can repent and redeem themselves by helping us win the war. If it works, your brother is right: Rhuir is ours, and we have a stronghold here. From here, we can attack Gormoth from the east, and Nibrazul will never see his capital city again."

"They will not abide," the prince said. "Gormoth yet has the power over their children."

"True. But now the world is mobilizing, including Gormoth. My people's ancestors were brutal warriors, and there are things we have not forgotten. If the Er-Ekhanim trade allegiances, there is little time for Azezakel to use the human children against them. I think the Er-Ekhanim are ready to switch back their allegiances."

Prince Xandur sat in silence, pondering. Then he locked eyes with Zarabaster, and he radiated power and strength.

"You may be right. It is worth a try!"

They returned to the prisoner and spoke to him.

"If your tongue is truthful and your mind has resumed true loyalty, send three men of yours to speak to the rest of your people. Tell them Prince Xandur of the Divine Kingdom of Khandur will pardon them if they swear their allegiance to Khandur and Rhíandor. Should they choose to fight by our side against Azezakel, we shall pardon you all, and the past be forgiven. However, if you and these three messengers fail, you will all hang. What say you?"

The prisoner met Xandur's and Zarabaster's gaze, and the tears that filled his eyes swiftly dried, and they glimmered and glowed with pride.

"Prince Xandur and the Lord Zarabaster, bless you both in the name of the Mother Goddess," he said, and now his voice was steady. "Thus, it shall be. I will take my best men to inform the rest of us in this kingdom, and we shall return upon you with a vast army."

"And what about your children?"

The prisoner looked down. "That will be as it may. The children are with us now. Therefore, if they succumb, so do we. We are tired of supporting the wrong side. For long, we have wished to rejoin your forces, but we did not; for we were certain you would not accept our repentance."

"Then go ahead," the prince said. "Leave immediately and tell them speed is of the essence. I want to see the Er-Ekhanim army in the many thousands assembled here before the capital of Rhuir as soon as possible."

"Great is your mercy, Sirs," the prisoners said. "This is a good day!"

Then he disappeared on swift feet.

—

Three days passed without a response from Gormoth, and Prince Xandur paced to and fro in the camp.

"This is of concern," he said. "Whilst waiting for the Er-Ekhanim to return, we are running short of time. Wherefore are Azezakel and Nibrazul not attacking? I am happy they are not, but the silence weighs on me. Trusting the Er-Ekhanim is perilous business, and we know not what they will decide. Our chances are bleak if the Dragons and Wolfmen charge ere the four messengers return."

Zarabaster's eyes glanced at the sky, and he pointed. "Your doubts and concerns aside. They know we are here."

Far aloft, left of the sun, a black spot circled, almost impossible to espy. Xandur went for a monocular and zoomed in.

"A Dragon," he said, and his voice sank.

"Aye, and a scout of that, I reckon," Zarabaster said. "It will return to Gormoth and report."

"Then more Dragons will swarm in over us. And it is too late to retreat."

"Irony is playing us, for our hope is now in our former adversaries: We need the Er-Ekhanim."

"And my brother's cooperation," Xandur added with a scowl.

—

Day four came and went, and all was calm. But behold! On Day five, an immense army stormed in from the west: The Er-Ekhanim returned with thousands of men. Swift on feet and greatly armed, they drew nigh to the camp. Xandur unwittingly put a hand on hilt, unsure whether the army of men would assail or greet them. Then he glanced at the city wall, where his brother stood in the company of many Anúrian knights, ignorant of what was happening below him.

"We are under attack!" Exxarion cried from the wall. "An army of traitors! Gather the bowmen!"

"Hold it, Exxarion!" Xandur shouted back. "They are joining, not charging."

"What say you? These men are traitors, not allies. They must die, and we shall be their executioners. You and I shall join in an alliance against them, brother. We have no choice, or we shall all succumb."

"Hold you men," Xandur said. "Give me some time, and you and I shall talk. Yet it seems you are correct; for you and I must join again, if only for in short."

Xandur's words seemed to make an impact, for Exxarion was silent, although he kept his bowmen in suspense. Meanwhile, the Er-Ekhanim entered the camp, and their spokesperson stepped forward.

He bowed deeply and said, "We had no problem assembling an army. Few were those who refused and remained disloyal, but they we took care of. The army we bring is loyal and willing to die for the cause. Many thousands of us there are, a vast army Nibrazul had long nourished to use in an Anúrian invasion. We are all proud to join you under your banners, Sirs Xandur and Zarabaster."

"You kept your word," Xandur said. "And I shall keep mine."

Then he paused, stretched, and locked eyes with the army, and his voice was impinging and firm.

"Be loyal and fight with us to victory or defeat. Die or survive, be that as it may, and all survivors shall be free from persecution."

The army of men saluted him in one loud voice. "Hurray for the Prince of Khandur and the Lord of Rhíandor! Hurray for our liberators!"

Then the crowd turned silent, and the prince continued, now turning toward the aforesaid messengers.

"Know thy anything of what is occurring in Gormoth? Wherefore this silence?"

"We know not all of it," one man said, "but we know King Azezakel expected no attack from the Sea. When you arrived, we were all unwary. Gormoth had planned to assail you in a future raid, not the reverse. Gormoth has its attention directed toward the north and the west. His enemies, which are now our allies, as well as yours, are mobilizing. The Dark Kings want to charge before they themselves are attacked. Thus, they lack sufficient troops to fight on this front. Later, I reckon; but for now, they cannot."

Xandur looked at Zarabaster. "My brother knew this…"

"… Or he was just lucky," the Lord said.

"If so, we are all lucky."

Forthwith, Prince Xandur addressed his brother on the wall.

"I have brought to us a new army," he said. "We count them in the many thousands, and they are now loyal and willing to defend Khurad-Resh. Traitors they were, but thus enforced. Now, their willingness to defeat Gormoth is as strong as our own. I have given them a chance to repent, and freedom I have granted them, should they fight by our side until the end. This I have done with my authority as the Crown Prince of the Divine Kingdom of Khandur. With their help, we can indeed create a stronghold here."

"I trust them not!" Exxarion said.

"What choice do you have?"

"As soon as they enter this city, they will try to kill us all. Why think you not that they are Azezakel's covert army, and they are double-crossing us? Why think you not that this is Nibrazul's way of taking his city back?"

"Because I, your brother, say they are no longer our enemy. Trust me or not. It is in your hands now. Let us all inside and take your chances, and perhaps your conquest might have been to avail. Oppose and deny us, and we shall all fall short. Divided we will die, but united we might stand. Think swiftly, for the real enemy could be here ere we know."

Prince Exxarion withdrew from the wall and was gone for a time, where after he came back with Admiral Mundo by his side.

"Very well," he said. "I shall let you in, and we will fight together for a while and for the good of all. But forget not! Anúria is yet mine!"

Then Xandur said to an officer beside him, "Send a ship back to Khandur and tell the king what has happened, and that I will stay here for an undisclosed amount of time."

Chapter 23
The Fall of Emoria

WOE BEFELL THE WORLD at the End of Days, with Darkness cast in manners the Greater Realms could not withstand. And the world turned to wars and battles never erstwhile seen in Taëlia. Earthquakes shook its foundation, and cracks opened into horrifying places, from where abominable beasts of wicked realms raved terror and onslaught on the world. Foods swallowed land in places, and many of a sane nature went insane.

But the most mournful onslaught was perhaps that which targeted the Queendom of Emoria ere the Last Battle of the Ages. No one foreboded what was to betide, for it was unprovoked and uncalled for, but a mere consequence of Azezakel's many lies and deceits. Yet, no tale can accurately convey the depth of mourning and suffering that followed and was laid on the lands.

In great numbers they came, and they filled the peaceful air over the Enchanted Woods. Their formation almost blocked the sun, and the leaves in the forest rustled and the trees shook. In awe, the Emorians stared at the heavens as if they were watching a mirage. An evil wind swept through the forests and the lakes, and the peaceful people among the trees below were at a loss; for they had not felt such evil for eons. Thus was the impact of Queen Moëlia's Ayasisian Dragons.

Queen Astéamat could not believe what she now witnessed. Her Queendom was supposed to be safe, hidden from the rest of the world. Yet, and deep within, she knew whence the beasts came. Only the Dragons of Ayasis could enter Emoria's airspace like this, for they were once of Astéamat's realm. Now her body froze; these Dragons came not in peace but were sent to do harm.

Aloft, the beasts circled, and with each circle, they descended, nigher and nigher in their flight, soon hovering over the treetops. The Queen felt air swooshing as a Dragon passed close above her head, blocking the sky with its blue underbelly.

Then there was fire…

At once, the many Dragons, quick and ferocious, spat cascades of flames over the dense and enchanted forests of Emoria. The trees wailed and cried in hurt as they burned. In droves, elementals dissolved with intense agony and pain; and then they were no more. Magic lakes lost their enchantment and flooded without constraint, and rocks and hills shook and withered.

Countless were the tears the Emorians shed that day, and lives were lost. Once eternal they were, but now and forever, they vanished from Taëlia. Others, desperate to save what they could, used their magic against the assaulting Dragons. But alas! The Queendom was already weakened, and their magic was for naught. A mantle of doom fell over Emoria.

"Woe is us, and woe is the world!" the Emorians cried in despair. "What is now to befall us?"

Thus, the glorious Queendom, the Last Paradise, burned; and it fell in density as swiftly as a rock thrown down a precipice, only to crash into pieces. Emoria once more merged with what had become the Realm of Death and Sorrow, which was Taëlia.

In her body, Queen Astéamat thus knew the heaviness of the world, erstwhile spared of such menace. The sun changed hue from green to yellow, and the skies now darkened, aside from the overhanging cloak of smoke from many fires. All grass, yet saved from the flames, turned from blue to green; and from unaffected trees, leaves still fell from their branches and rapidly withered, engulfed by the hungry soil.

The Dragon attack was swift and deadly, and then the beasts took off and flew south as fast as they had come. But the damage was done, and Emoria was no more.

Queen Astéamat seated upon a rock amid what had once been an enchanted garden with flowers and trees of much fragrance. Left was a desolate black field of smoke and random fires.

Her eyes glazed over, and she moved not until long.

Inside her mind, and with an inner vision, Ishtarion, the last of the mighty Gold Dragons in the world, could see the assault on Emoria take place. She lay in her den with eyes closed, and she moved not. Devastated, she grieved the woe that befell the Queendom. There was nothing she could do, for not even a Gold Dragon could enter the Realm of Emoria. In her mind, she saw the forest burning and smelled the smoke lingering; she felt the chaos, the horror, and the pain from bodies in flames, and her inner ears heard the crackling of burning wood and the shrieks from Dragons. Ishtarion was long-lived, even for a Gold Dragon, but never had she experienced so much emotional pain and grief. Although her remaining days might be few, she wept for the world she soon must leave. She was ancient, and her prime was long agone; yet there was strength and power in her worn body, and though defending Emoria she could not, there were other ways.

A little more at ease, she left her lair, and into high air she flew. With wide flaps, her enormous wings took her browsing over the sacred lands of the Queendom into which she could not descend. Below, vast areas were on fire, and above that the Ayasisian Dragons hovered. But she could not reach them.

She shrieked in agony and took a southwest direction. Swift winds bore her across the fields of Hithos and over the Windy Mountains, until she, in great haste, reached the city of Astar in the Queendom of Ayasis. Those who saw her coming stopped and pointed to the sky, for a Dragon of this size they had seldom encountered. Ishtarion hovered over Astar for a while, and the people below fled in fear, and many went to grab their arms.

But Ishtarion was not bothered. Her giant claws grabbed the rail surrounding the pointed top of the Queen's castle. There she placed herself and unfolded her wings; head high and proud, and her reptilian eyes swept over the white city. She spoke not, but powerful were the thoughts she sent into the castle; for so great was the power of her kind that she could communicate both in spoken words and with thought.

"Queen Moëlia of the Queendom of Ayasis, heed me," the Dragon transmitted from her mind. "I am Ishtarion, the Gold Dragon, and I am the Guardian of the Divine Queendom of

Emoria."

Silence, and then thoughts came back into Ishtarion's head. "Why are you here? Are you an emissary?"

"Aye, but self-proclaimed. I am here because of the destruction of the Divine Realm."

"Divine perhaps, but fallen," Moëlia said. "Queen Astéamat wishes me dead."

"Queen Astéamat is not your enemy and never was. Hear my plea and withdraw the Dragons ere the entire Queendom is wrecked. Your assault voids the last attempt at a balance between good and evil. If Emoria falls, evil is victorious. Know you not that without Emoria, Gormoth gains much power?"

"I know this, save that Gormoth is not the Enemy. King Azezakel wants peace, and we shall help bring it to him. Then peace will come. All resistance must fail."

"Alas!" Ishtarion said. "Azezakel's arms are indeed long, and his tongue anointed if he lets you believe this. Great is his wizardry, and dark his magic."

Then the Dragon spoke out loud and with force, in a voice for the entire Astar to hear. "Women of Ayasis, break the curse Azezakel has put upon you. The King of Gormoth is a liar and a Dark Lord. Believe him not. Be strong and think! Come to your senses and call your Dragons home. You are all spellbound!"

The Queen did not show onto her balcony to face the Gold Dragon, but her thoughts continued, "Dragon Ishtarion, I order you to leave our Queendom."

"I go nowhere ere the Dragons are back home. No longer am I a War Dragon, but I might need to revisit the old days and my own ways in these times of Great Evil. Tempt me not!"

"Threaten me not! You do what you must, but if you use fire, we shall send fire onto you just the same."

"You speak with the tongue of the Black King. Only he, or those under his influence, use such wording. Wake from your trance, Queen. Yet I came here not to threaten but to negotiate and plea to your mercy. Withdraw the Dragons and I will leave. It is not in my power to save Emoria, only to ask you to be reasonable. If you send the Dragons home, there might yet be a little hope. Let them stay, and we all go down with Emoria. If the latter is your choice, I need to set Ayasis on fire to prevent worse to betide."

"Very well, I shall withdraw my Dragons, but then you must keep your part of the bargain and leave."

"This I will do," Ishtarion said. Still, something was askew. She turned her gaze to the north and behold! Afar, at the top of a mountain, sat a red Dragon, eyes locked with Ishtarion's. The beast said naught, albeit she emitted no threat to the Gold Dragon. Why was the red Dragon sitting there alone, away from the rest? Why partook she not in the onslaught?

Ishtarion waited, sitting like a frozen statue on top of the Astar Castle, akin to a monstrous Gargoyle, but with a golden shimmer; an apparition no one had watched for thousands of years.

Then they returned, and there were many: In a long horizontal line, the Ayasisian Dragons soared swiftly toward the city. The Gold Dragon sent another thought directly to Moëlia.

"You have kept your word, Queen of Ayasis. With that, I shall leave, as promised."

"Leaving you shall!" Then, apace, a thought came back. "But you are not returning home."

Little did Ishtarion understand how deep the curse was on these indigenous people. In came the Dragons, encircling Ishtarion at the top of the roof, preventing her from leaving. Then, out of the balcony below, a row of bowmen trotted, and swift on their aim, they sent a cascade of arrows toward the unprepared Gold Dragon. Shrieking in pain, and in a great rage over the betrayal, Ishtarion flapped her wings and ascended to the sky above the encircling smaller Dragons. She knew she was badly wounded, but she yet had strength, and she could overcome. She opened her engulfing jaws and breathed out a massive flood of fire, hitting the Dragons who were closest. In one flush, four were in flames, jerking, and then falling onto the streets below, dying.

But the Ayasis Dragons did not stay idle. In unison, they shot out cascades of fire onto Ishtarion. Some hit the target, despite her attempt to dance and dodge, and she was terribly burned. Yet, despite age and diminishing powers, the Gold Dragon endured. More Dragons succumbed to her rage, and the rest were reluctant and pulled back in fear. Ishtarion took advantage of their retreat and deep-dived until she was in line with the balcony. From there, she spat out her fire and eradicated the row of bowmen.

Slowly, she felt her strength weakening, but refused to

withdraw or give up. Then, in her peripheral, she saw the red Dragon on top of the mountain flying in with great speed. Of all her enemies, she feared the red Dragon the most. She was more powerful than the rest, almost equal to herself.

But the red Dragon did something Ishtarion had not expected: she defended her. Gaining new strange, Ishtarion attacked the Ayasis Dragons with great fury, and the red Dragon fought by her side against a deadly enemy. But if death would come, Ishtarion thought, the two of them would die together, and pridefully so.

―

Like small oases in an immense wasteland, a few trees still stood in the once so magnificent Enchanted Woods. Most of the fires had burned out, and smoke rose in serpentine patterns. Gone were the birds and their unique songs, once so magical and divine. Vanished was the wildlife that could not survive the lower density into which Emoria had fallen. What had sprouted into abundant life was now a waste and mere memories of bygone glory. Away forever were the majestic Elementals, for the Queendom they upheld was no more.

From hither and thither, Mazosians came to join with their Queen, where she sat in anguish on top of the rock. Their once steady and light gait was now heavy and burdened with sorrow and despair, and no one spoke as they stood before Astéamat. They were great in numbers, for only a few Originals had succumbed to the fire, but none held their head high. Thus they stood when the Queen awoke to the devastating reality that would, from thereon, be the world of existence.

From afar, a great number of beings approached. They were giant and massive in stature, and their heavy gait cracked the dead gray trunks and branches as they strode, spread about everywhere. Swiftly and with purpose, they walked, and their steps were many paces long. The Emorians feared them not, for they knew who they were.

Soon, the entire group of gigantic creatures stood before the Queen and her people. The huge being in their lead bowed and swung his arm.

Hail to you, Queen Astéamat of the Divine Queendom of Emoria. I am Arraok, Lord of the Ÿadeth-Oëmin, whom peoples of the world call Giants or the Zemlins, "Men of Great Stature."

Queen Astéamat gazed at the enormous red-haired and red-bearded Giant before her, and she sent back a thought package to the Lord. *Hail, Lord Arraok. I remember you well from eons agone, and I wish I could welcome you to his world, but if so, it would be deceitful. I pity you, for you were better off asleep within the Mounds.*

She paused and made a sweeping gesture. *See what has become of my Queendom! Little did I expect such betrayal. I have been naïve.*

Inside the Queen's head, the Lord Arraok's voice was deep and vibrant, akin to a mountain, when he answered.

Mournful is the sight of this that once must have been but which I never witnessed; but in our awakening, we expected not to come back to paradise. We have a task to perform before the End of Days, and this task, we shall accomplish.

Aye, it is Destiny. You shall do what you must do, for even that must be Destiny. Yet no one knows the outcome of your doings. The world is pleased to have you here, even though the hope for us all is next to naught now when Emoria is fallen.

With due respect, Milady, we are heading for Gormoth, and our departure is eminent and immediate. All Yadeth-Oëmin who were asleep had the same dream: At the time of our awakening, the Resistance, of which we are part, is mobilizing, and the Last War is nigh. There is no time to linger. We will enter Gormoth from the south, and we shall demolish the Watchtowers and clean the southern gates into Gormoth from enemies, so others can enter the Dark Land from that direction. Then we shall continue over the mountain passes and storm Grincast, Azezakel's Fortress.

He paused to meet the Queen's gaze. Astéamat saw the concern in the Giant's large eyes. Then Arraok communicated again.

What are your plans, Milady, if I may be so bold to ask?

The Queen took a long time to answer.

Since I created Emoria, the Originals who followed me there were aligned with the density I encapsulated, and those who remain stand here before you now. Once we were skilled warriors. We were the Mazosians, the Female Warriors of renown. But Emoria is no longer, and encompassing us is the world we wished to change. I failed. But the war is not yet lost, unless we believe it is. Though Emoria can no longer keep a sense of balance, we can still be useful. As Mazosians, we shall once more go to war to assist the peoples of Taëlia. Our purpose must be to distract the Fallen Kings, so those who can make a true difference can find their way. There are Divine forces at play here—both of good and of evil. The essence of the war between these two forces is based on magic. Powerful magic has been given to one human as a sword. But this sword is not made to slay, but to spare. It is an arduous task to accomplish, and only someone flawed can achieve this. The one chosen must pull himself up from the darkest depths of his own mind and be strong enough to resist temptation. This is our greatest weapon.

Unless the world has changed in our favor since we fell asleep, this seems an impossible task, Arraok said.

Not impossible, but unlikely. Yet this is our greatest hope. Therefore, the Lord Arraok, we Mazosians will join you.

—

Furious and bitter was the battle betwixt the Dragons above the capital of Ayasis. Below, humans watched in awe and fear, but no one intervened, for it was futile. The Golden and the red Dragon fought courageously side by side, whilst Moëlia's loyal Dragons attacked from many directions at once. The red Dragon was young and skilled, and she could dance through the fire cascades from the mouths of the charging beasts. But Ishtarion was slower, and flames hit her ancient body over and again. Brave she was, and despite the excruciating pain, she killed a third of the Dragons alone.

But her strength failed her, and now she retreated; for she wished to tell Queen Astéamat about Moëlia's ultimate betrayal. In her flight, the Ayasis Dragons chased her across the Windy Mountains, out of Ayasis, but then they returned to Astar, letting the Gold Dragon go.

With immense willpower, Ishtarion flapped her giant wings and flew above the Heath of Hithos. But soon, the last of her strength failed her, and she lost height. With her sharp eyes, she could see the burning forests of Emoria, and it was not very far away.

To no avail, she wasted her remaining energy to put the last leagues behind to reach her destination, but her body was heavy and worn; and the wounds took their toll on her. Below, she saw great waters, and she presumed it was Moonlake, if that was what it was still called. Like a refugee who had been running for so long that legs failed to carry, the wings of the once mighty Gold Dragon failed her, and she fell like a shooting star. In a haze, she saw the water underneath approaching. With a splash that sent water into the air a hundred yards or more, Ishtarion the Great fell into the Moonlake on the northern shore, with her massive body halfway covered in water, and with her giant head resting in the sand ashore. She sighed, no longer feeling the pain that had been so intense, and with a last effort, she flapped her wings, trying to ascend. But she was too weak, and she closed her eyes, waiting...

As if in a dream, she suddenly heard the flap of wings above her head. *The Ayasis Dragons found me, after all*, she thought. *But it matters not now...*

With some effort, she opened her eyes once more, and before her sat the red Dragon, watching her. Again, Ishtarion sighed and then gasped for air before she said, "Who are you, red Dragon? Why came you to support me?"

"My name is Cloudwing," the Dragon said. "I am the Lead Dragon of Ayasis."

"Then why did you risk your life for me? Am I not your enemy?"

"You are not," Cloudwing said. "It is an honor to meet you. I knew not about your existence ere this day. And it is even more of an honor to fight by your side. Ayasis is no longer my homestead, for it is doomed and corrupted."

"Brave you are, and as mighty in battle as I used to be." A vague smile showed on Ishtarion's face, but then the pain came back, and she moaned, and green blood poured through her gaping mouth. In agony, she coughed.

"Yet, save you I could not," Cloudwing said. "What can I do for you? And may I know your name? I wish to know, so I may not forget."

"Brave you are, and as mighty in battle as I used to be." A vague smile showed on Ishtarion's face, but then the pain came back, and she moaned; and green blood poured through her gaping mouth. In agony, she coughed.

"Yet, save you I could not," Cloudwing said. "What can I do for you? And may I know your name? I wish to know, so I may not forget."

"I am Ishtarion, the last of Gold Dragons that once roamed

the world. And for me you can do naught. Albeit, for the world you can do much. I sense you are yet a young Dragon. Go find your Masterine and make a difference in these Last of Days, where aught effort counts. Do this, and it will please me, and I can leave in peace."

"I promise I will, Masterine Ishtarion. I wish I would have known you earlier."

Ishtarion closed her eyes again, and then she coughed, exhaled, and then breathed no more. But on her face, there was a smile. Cloudwing watched her die, the mightiest Dragons of all times, and big, blue tears fell on the sand below.

"Rest in peace, Ishtarion the Great," Cloudwing said.

Chapter 24
The Road North

HIGH LORD ARRAOK of the Ÿadeth-Oëmin stood next to his brother, Usbarg, gazing toward the distance. Relentless flames ascended from the Enchanted Forest of Emoria. The two Giants then glanced at each other, and their faces were grim. Their thoughts were not of a private kind, but could be heard by everybody in the camp.

We must not leave yet, Arraok said. *Emoria is swiftly falling into our realm, and it is now possible to enter through its gate. We must assist them ere it is too late.*

I think it is already too late, Usbarg said. *The entire Queendom is going up in flames.*

Then, at least, we must support the Queen the best we may, be it she is alive. We shall go there and then march to Gormoth.

Ismaril and Sigyn stood in disbelief. Sigyn wept openly, and Ismaril felt the lump in his throat. The shock was overwhelming and heart-crushing. The entire Queendom, the only spiritual oasis connected to this world, was going up in smoke.

"There went our inkling of a chance of victory," Ismaril said, speaking to no one. "How could Azezakel get into Emoria? I thought it was secure."

Kirbakin walked up beside him. "This is indeed the work of Gormoth," he said, "yet this is not Azezakel's work."

Ismaril and Sigyn both raised their brows. "Who then?" Sigyn said.

The Gnome shook his head, and his forehead was even more wrinkled than usual. Ismaril thought he looked much older.

"There is only one who could have done this," Kirbakin said. "Queen Moëlia…"

Sigyn gasped. "How is that possible? Why would she do that?"

"She is compromised and under a spell. She knows not what she is doing, and now there is no way back."

"But how could she enter Emoria?" Ismaril said. "She has no access to that density."

"Right, she does not," the Gnome said. "But she possesses something that can. Her Dragons."

"But how…?"

"The Ayasis Dragons once belonged to Emoria in an era long gone when Ayasis and Emoria were yet on good terms. Although a chasm built between them over time, they were never bitter enemies. Thus, after Emoria had ascended in frequency, Queen Astéamat sent her small Dragons to Ayasis as a gesture of goodwill, and to defend Ayasis against enemies. The Dragons had ascended together with Emoria, and thus could operate both in Taëlia and in Emoria. Little did Queen Astéamat know that one day, her generous gift would work against her. The Dragons of Ayasis executed Gormoth's plan to destroy the Divine Queendom. And they used Queen Moëlia to do it for them by manipulating her to send in her Dragons. And that is the end of it. I see not how it could be any other way."

Sigyn had to sit.

"A curse…," she mumbled. "But even if so… how could Queen Moëlia do something like this?"

"Underestimate not a curse," Raeglin said, now having entered the group. "Especially if it comes from Gormoth."

"But can it not be overridden?"

"I know of no way."

"And now, she is forever our enemy," Ismaril said lowly, and his eyes turned cold.

"And her potential redemption is not for us to decide," the pilgrim said.

"They killed the Gold Dragon." Sigyn's voice rang, tormented and bitter. "I know they did, for I can feel it. Ishtarion is dead."

Kirbakin, the only one in the group who could know whether this was true, sighed and kept silent.

———

That same day, the Ÿadeth-Oëmin gathered and equipped themselves for their march to Emoria. Meanwhile, Raeglin and the Nomads, Kirbakin, Ismaril, and Sigyn, prepared for the road north to the frozen lands. But Sigyn spent time in thought, and thus, she spoke.

"I would rather follow Lord Arraok and his men to Emoria. My heart is aching, and my hope is ruined. I want to see that land one last time, and I want to know what happened to Ishtarion." Her eyes glazed over with tears. Ismaril pulled her close and gave her a warm embrace, and he held her while she let her grief out. At that moment, he felt how her stomach had grown from the pregnancy.

When she stopped weeping, he said to her, "Even I wish to return, but this is not our fate. And better it is if we remember Emoria as it was rather than how it is now. Let us take our magic memories with us for the rest of our journey. We will need something to cling to when the frosty winds bite, and when all seems impossible. Time is of the essence, and we are running short. Our immediate destiny lies northward, and our fate is in the east. We must go now."

She looked up and met his eyes, and she kissed him gently. "I know," she said. "I know…"

A desolate northern wind swept over the hills when, on top of the highest mound, two large groups had gathered. One comprised a great number of Giants, in stature far exceeding the second group of Nomads. *It must be a remarkable scene for an outsider,* Ismaril thought. Yet he was glad the Giants were not his enemies. *Beware, Gormoth!*

The Ÿadeth-Oëmin marched down the slope at increasing speed, and the humans watched them enter the valley, only to vanish among the trees in a forested area. The sound of their heavy feet against the ground slowly faded, and thus they were gone.

"Make sure you all have the warm clothes you need," Yomar said. "If someone is missing something, now is the time to tell me. It will be mighty cold where we are heading. And now, there is no more time to waste. Follow me!"

———

Soon, the Mounds of Sleeping Giants shrunk behind them, and they were out on the wide-open plains. With summer still in its prime, the sun was merciless on the wayfarers. For long they strode across open terrain without vegetation, save a few bushes here and there, dry and tilted, as if they wished to tip over and rest. Raeglin, in the lead, scouted hither and thither, never comfortable to move across open land. Occasionally, they spotted wild animals running in this and that direction, but always at a safe distance from the company.

Here were no roads, and they often must stroll over uneven land, making for an arduous journey. Now and then, they stumbled upon a narrow animal path, which they could use for a while, until it changed direction, and they must abandon it.

The pathless wilderness made for slow travel, with horse-drawn carts bumping into elevations, knocking into rocks and other obstacles. Most were on foot, save a few on horseback, carrying elderly Nomad males and females. Others, who were not fit for a long walk, sat in the carts among the food supplies. Ismaril noticed the children were strong and healthy, running about, chasing each other in play, without a care in the world. Ismaril pitied them and envied them, for they knew not about the hardships ahead; but he envied them for being so carefree, wishing he was like that.

Closer to evening, when the sun sat low in the west, the air had turned colder, and they got the first taste of winter. That night, they encamped on the open heaths.

After most of the men, women, and children had gone to sleep, Ismaril and Sigyn remained by a campfire, joining Raeglin and Yomar. Away, Kirbakin sat on a rise, his short legs crossed, playing a melancholic tune on his flute.

"By tomorrow night, we may encounter snow," Raeglin said. "Then we must abandon the carts."

"Yes, I am aware," Yomar said, most unwilling to speak on the subject.

"I know your thoughts," the pilgrim said. "What to do with the elderly, and the women and children? You are a Nomad, so you understand the conditions we must face the farther north we get. What plans have you?"

The Nomad pointed to the northeast. "Over there, in the yonder, are the Weather Mountains. Though I never visited that region, I have had it described to me by well-informed sources. A cool and fresh river cascades down the mountainside at a place hither of the snow line. There, we must leave some men, carefully chosen for taking care of those in need. They can create a community there, whether temporary or stationary."

His eyes showed a trace of sadness when he continued. "We know not the outcome of the war I render inevitable, but if my army succumbs in battle, perhaps the small community left behind can create a new future here. In these lands, there is much prey, and timber enough to build a village. Unfortunately, I must leave some of my strongest men, whom I would prefer to have assisted us in combat, to help create the community and make it grow. Hopefully, one day, if we are victorious in battle, the survivors can return here and join."

Raeglin nodded and put his hand on Yomar's shoulder. "It is a good plan. I believe the new tribe will have a good chance of surviving if fate has it."

The group then sat in silence, listening to the crackling from the campfire. Ismaril followed the tiny sparks extracting from the firewood, shooting out into the air as it heated. There was a tiny breeze from the north, making the smoke dance, only to be eaten by the night sky. To and fro, some of it passed Ismaril's nose, and he inhaled. The smell of smoke took him back in time to the Wolfman War, when he and the soldiers sat around campfires in the mountain passes, hungry and with battle fatigue, struggling to stay warm. A strike of agony hit him when his thoughts wandered to the time of the murder and the blade he stole. He grabbed Gahil's hilt and squeezed it hard. A deadly blade it was; yet its purpose was not to kill. And amid all, he, a simple scout with a murky past, was chosen for a task the mightiest warrior would shun away from. Despite what he had learned since the war, he still did not fully understand.

The rest of the group was silent still, each in their own thoughts, and Ismaril closed his eyes. The sound of the fire crackling increased in volume, and from afar, Kirbakin's flute played another sorrowful tune. And Ismaril thought that perhaps the Gnome's flute playing extracted memories and induced the silence. Perhaps they all needed to reflect. He was wondering what his three friends were thinking.

Then he and Sigyn said goodnight to their friends and fell

asleep.

On the next day, the landscape changed, turning hillier. The wind changed direction to the south, making the temperature more comfortable. A few leagues ahead, the Weather Mountains summits ascended; and as they came closer, they witnessed massive eagles soaring up the mountains and descending into the canyons, diving for prey. Pine and fir first grew sparsely and then turned denser around them and up the mountainsides.

Then Yomar, who had taken the lead, stopped and gave a sign to the followers to gather round him. From the hill where they stood, they gazed out in wonder over a most astonishing valley, embedded between sturdy mountains on either side. In the midst ran a busy river, winding alongside, disappearing among the mountains farther down. Because of the mountains, winding and bending, the wind here was next to nil.

"That must be the Green River," Yomar said, and his voice was full of enthusiasm. "Is this not a perfect place to build a settlement? Here is water; the worst storms will spare you, and there is plenty of prey. What say you?"

And so it happened that those who could no longer follow stayed there to establish a new community, and men of strength stayed with them. But when Yomar and the rest of the Nomads, fit enough for battle, were ready to move on, the departure was bittersweet. Some men, not chosen to stay, were forced to leave their loved ones, and many bitter tears were shed.

"Woe to us all," they said. "And curse the Black King, who forces us to leave our families behind to battle him!"

The men promised to return soon, but they knew they made promises on uncertain terms, and most of them would likely not see their families again. Yomar wept, but not all his tears were of despair; he was glad he had found a new home for his people, amid all hardship. With eyes that were wet, he looked about in all directions and saw the beauty and the vast wilderness, and he was pleased. He knew his brothers and sisters would thrive here once they got things settled. And the elderly people were left in expert hands.

Thus, the Nomads, whose fate was not to stay, but to go to war, departed from the others. So, they strode off down the canyons and up the hills toward the cold and snow in the north, and then farther into unknown lands. Yomar walked first, thus hiding his tears from the others. He did not look back.

Chapter 25
The March of Giants

IN GREAT NUMBERS, THE Ÿadeth-Oëmin and the Mazosians marched to war. Behind them, they left a devastating wasteland. Smoke still covered the previously spirit-enriched forest ceiling like a dark, merciless cloud that would never truly disperse. This signified the end of an epoch, and the destruction of this oasis increased the magnitude of evil in Taëlia.

Queen Astéamat, striding at the front with Lord Arraok, understood that by entering these lower realms, she was changing. She had returned to the mindset resembling a time prior to when Emoria transformed into the spiritual realm. Now, she was a Mazosian warrioress again; the fighter mentality had returned, and it dropped her frequency. Yet she gave it merely a fleeting thought since she did not care. She knew her people felt like her; the Enemy must be stopped ere the entire MAEDIN would descend to Hell.

Northeast, up Anzabar Road, they marched relentlessly, and with little to no rest. They crossed the open heath, a quiet and unstoppable army of a kind the world had seldom seen. Those who saw them coming turned and ran for their lives, were they friends or foes; but the Giants and the Mazosians paid them no attention; their focus was on more distant places.

Without entering Northgrave, they crossed the bridge over the Great River Anzabar to the south and entered Kaz-Maír, the

Yadeth-Oëmin's ancient territory. From Zebadhim, Yongahur's men watched the seemingly endless line of warriors whom they lacked the manpower to beat, and they hurried to lock the gates. Arraok and Astéamat could not tell whether King Yongahur was in Zebadhim as they passed, and they did not stop to find out. As they crossed the Eccasion River, north of Elchamar, they passed south of the ruins of Avazin.

"For a long time, these ruins have stood like skeletons, whipped by hollowed winds in a deserted wilderness," Astéamat said, and her voice was low and sorrowful. "In a lofty place, such as Emoria, it is easy to forget. Here once lived a proud people, friends of the Mazosians of old. But many centuries have passed since this prosperous town was alive."

Arraok nodded. *I remember, too,,* he said. *What became of them?*

The Queen sighed. "An army from Gormoth attacked them... The Wolfmen charged at night, and they came in large numbers. Men, women, and children whom they did not slaughter in their sleep, they took as prisoners. After unimaginable torture, the brave men of the tribe finally gave up, no longer capable of seeing their women and children being slaughtered before their eyes. So, they made a pact with the Black King, and they became the Er-Ekhanim; the 'treacherous people,' who up to this day are serving the Enemy."

Did they act wrongly, Milady?

Queen Astéamat sighed deeply. "You would need to ask them," she said.

They left the ruins behind. Thereby, Astéamat knew they were visible from the Watchtower at the border of Gormoth.

"Let them see us come in wrath," the Queen said. "They may send their Dragons upon us, but as devastating as they might be, fear them not. Divine Dragons I cannot defeat, but Azezakel's beasts I can battle."

It gladdens me to hear, Milady; Arraok said. *The Dragons were my biggest concern.*

"Then use the strength and the fury of your men to break into Gormoth, and I will take care of the flying Worms if they show up. We shall start with conquering the Watchtower."

The next morning, the army reached the Highroad to

Gormoth and marched straight toward the Watchtower. As the hours passed, the weather got crispier, snow lay thick and glistering under a clear sky on either side of the Highroad, and a chilly sun shone. Closer now, the Watchtower arose from the mountainside, as an abominable construct out of place, blocking the way into Gormoth. Yet there were no signs of activity from the tower.

Then Arraok pointed at the top of the tower.

Behold! he said.

Astéamat followed the direction of his brawny arm and saw a murder of crows leaving the peak of the Watchtower, flying east.

"The Watchtower is summoning the Dragons," she said. "No doubt."

Let us hasten our steps; Arraok said.

Soon, the mountains surrounded the army to the left and to the right, and the weather changed suddenly. An icy wind swept from the north, whipping up the snow from the ground, hitting them straight. The temperature was by now far below freezing, but they continued relentlessly forward. The winds turned stronger, so the Giants walked three abreast with several more light-weighed Mazosians behind, sheltered from the winds by the massive bodies of the Ÿadeth-Oëmin, who could, with some effort, withstand the fierce winds.

"This is Azezakel's work," Astéamat said. "Here, his magic determines the weather. We have now crossed the borders of his land."

Before them, the Highroad got narrower until only two Giants could walk abreast, and the mountainsides ascended far up on both sides, protruding like sharp knives and swords from the snow-embedded sedimentary rock. The Queen remembered this narrow path since time agone, but now it was narrower, making it difficult for any intruders to enter Gormoth without consent, since any intruders were easy targets from the Watchtower. Arraok looked from side to side, and then up toward the silent, threatening tower. He sent a thought to the Queen, who picked up on his anxiety.

I dislike this. It is too quiet, and we are vulnerable here…

The Queen stopped in her tracks and gazed toward the tower. The magic necessary to build this fortress was immense, and this she knew. It was built by someone who was almost her equal in the Divine Realm. Even Azezakel was her creation, and he learned from her once, whilst the Universe was young, and when he was yet loyal to her.

The tower was raised directly out of the bedrock as a lofty extension thereof. Small windows, with lights as yellow as the slits of Dragons' pupils, stared out into the open in four directions to ensure they missed nothing. A massive stone wall, also raised from the bedrock, surrounded the tower on either side, blocking the way, so no one could pass without permission from Hútlof himself, the horrifying and pitiless Werewolf; the Chief Commander of the Southern Watchtower.

Why do they not attack? And where do we go from here? We can come no further, and we are targets where we stand, caught in a trap!

"They need not attack us," the Queen said. "They could, but they will not. Oh, how well I know them! Remember, Arraok, that these godlike Dark Kings are my children, and their minions are thoroughly trained to follow the same mindset as the Dark Kings. They are biding their time, for they wish to be the observers rather than actors; thus is their mindset. They want to watch us succumb to what they consider a mightier threat than that of the tower."

Arraok gazed at her with big eyes.

What threat?

"*That* threat," the Queen said and pointed at the sky.

For the common man, they were merely small spots in the sky, impossible to distinguish, and barely noticeable, but for the Mazosians and the Giants, these moving targets were as visible as if they were merely a hundred feet away; for their eyes could see far and clear.

There are many of them.

"Aye, about fifty, but see how reluctant they are. Know that their eyesight is as good as ours. They understand well who we are, and they know not what to do, circling around up there."

They fear you.

"And they fear you, too."

Lower and lower they circled, the terrifying Fire and Snow Dragons of Gormoth getting braver. Arraok and his men had trusted the Queen, but now, he doubted the situation and the ability to be victorious. Not even a legion such as his own and that of Queen Astéamat could withstand an attack from fifty Dragons. But the Queen's voice, now purely as a thought inside Arraok's head, was calm and confident.

Let them come.

The glorious army of Giants and Originals stood still. The wind subsided, the temperature dropped, and the silence was overwhelming; no sound from the tower, no wind… each Dragon moving in circles, building a formation, shaping a grander circle.

We only have swords; Arraok whispered inside Astéamat's head. *Swords do little against Dragons who can spit fire and ice.*

"Worry not," the Queen said. "There is no use for weapons here. This situation requires acts of magic. Leave this to me and my warriors."

The Dragons descended faster now, and soon the first Dragon swooshed close over the army, flying rapidly across the entire canyon where the soldiers lined up, in line, one by one, but neither fire nor ice did these Dragons exhale. Astéamat knew they were being tested.

Are you not going to do something?

"Wait until the next round. They are merely trying to scare us. Do not let them; they feed from that, and they make you weaker. Yet I want them to feel confident and careless, thinking we are not a threat to them. Then they will strike."

Is that supposed to comfort me?

One by one, the Dragons passed close above their heads, so close that they felt the wind and heard the flap of their wings. When the entire formation had passed, the beasts rose in triumph and ascended into the sky.

"Fear not," said the Queen. "Here they come once more!"

In the next moment, the Dragons shot down like projectiles from the sky, and this time, they were charging. So eager to kill were they that they must exhale fire and ice from their enormous fangs long before they came within reach enough to do harm. Astéamat followed their every movement, but she said none. Instead, she sent a telepathic message to all her warriors and to the Ÿadeth-Oëmin.

Be prepared! We can do this!

The most eager Dragons descended first, and they were all

Fire Dragons, much quicker to fury than their subspecies. Queen Astéamat waited until their fire was almost in range to hurt them, and then she gave her command to the Mazosian warriors.

The Ÿadeth-Oëmin raised their large shields to protect themselves against the ice and fire attacks. They knew it would be fruitless in the end. Even the bows were worthless, for the archers were easy targets in the small passage betwixt the mountains.

When the fire from the first Dragons almost licked their heads, the Originals used their magic. All at once, they stretched their arms toward the fire. A strange language came over their tongues and behold! The fire blazing from the Dragons' throats bounced back in reverse, burning their heads.

"Watch out!" the Queen cried, when one Dragon after another smashed into the mountainsides and fell into the canyon, burning to death. Some landed on top of Giants and Mazosians, crushing their bodies. Others saw the threat in time and avoided the dying beasts. One Dragon blazed its fire over a few Giants, setting them on fire. There was nothing anyone could do to save them.

At a great speed, the Dragons retreated once more into the sky, circling around at a safe distance. None of them seemed eager to charge.

"Quick!" Astéamat shouted. "Attack the tower ere the Dragons regain their courage!"

With the Queen and Arraok in the lead, the army ran as fast as their legs could carry them the last few hundred yards toward the tower. While running, a flurry of arrows welcomed them from the wall, and both Giants and Mazosians, falling behind, dropped dead or wounded. But the army pushed through. Arraok, now ahead of Astéamat, and in the company of other Ÿadeth-Oëmin, stormed the gates of the Southern Watchtower. Great was the impact when they ran into the iron gates with spears, giant swords of hardened steel, and massive stones thrown at the obstacle, and so furious were they that they created several dents in the crack between the two closed iron doors. With unbelievable strength, a line of Giants pulled one gate open enough with their bare hands to get inside. More Giants came to aid, and ere too long, both gates were bent unto themselves, and the way into the tower was open.

In like storm winds, they ran, loud and proud. Dodging the

rain of arrows, the best they could, the Mazosians had now caught up with the long-legged Ÿadeth-Oëmin; and once again, Arraok and Astéamat entered side by side. A foul odor met them inside the Watchtower, a stink of excrement and filth. There was no floor, for the gates led down under the surface of the earth, and the Giants' heavy feet sank into gray moss. Opposed to them, a dozen rusty iron stairs led up to a platform; a divider, where stairs dwindled upward in two opposite directions. An endless line of Giants and Emorians ran up there, splitting themselves into two groups, eager to combat Wolfmen and what else might dwell in this goddess-forsaken place.

Arraok was about to follow, but Astéamat stopped him.

"Wait," she said. "Behold the opening to the right under the stairs. My intuition tells me something is hiding in there."

The Queen stopped some of her warriors and told them to stay. Soon, two dozen Mazosians stood by their Queen, waiting for her orders. She pointed at the opening. "We are going in," she said.

Taking the lead, Queen Astéamat entered what seemed to be a cave. The overhang of green and gray grew halfway from the top of the cave gap to its midst on sturdy branches, but beyond the gateway, there was only darkness. Queen Astéamat, heeled by Arraok, entered the unknown, both having their swords drawn, moving slowly. The rest of the Mazosian followed in line.

There was no air moving in there, and it was pitch dark as if the tunnel led right into the Underworld, and perhaps it did. The odor from the castle yard subsided, replaced by a smell of soil and roots, which covered the trail and the entire tunnel. They followed the path for a few minutes. The Queen halted and a "Husch" came from her lips, loud enough for her crew to hear. They all stopped, and Astéamat listened carefully. To ensure no one could hear her, she sent thoughts into Arraok's mind, so that only he could hear.

There is someone in here!
I know..., Arraok said.

Both had excellent hearing, and somewhere ahead of them, they heard footsteps on the muffling soil.

How far away? Arraok asked.
Close.
Sounds like a single being.

Astéamat squeezed the Giant's arm and gave the sign to continue. Although it sounded like only one being, they could be mistaken. The Queen's senses were now on full alert, and although she did not mention it, she noticed the steps had stopped. She slowed down some more, and then she cried out, "Who is there? Heed my call and present yourself!"

For a while, it was as quiet as it could be in a tunnel made of mud; there was no echo. Now, something was moving again, and it was close by.

"Present yourself in the name of the Queendom of Emoria!" Astéamat said.

"Do not kill me!" an anxious voice answered. "I mean no harm. Have mercy on me."

"Then tell me who you are!" the Queen said.

"My name is Agon, and I am human! If you hold your charge, I will light a torch."

The Queen sheathed her sword, reached for her bow, and put an arrow on the string. In the next moment, the voice in the dark lit a torch, flickering in yellow and orange in the dark tunnel. Before them stood a young man in his teenage years, dark-haired, and slender. His eyes were black in the fire from the torch, and the garment he wore was shifting between brown and black in the flames and the shadows. His face expression emitted fear, and his breathing was shallow, eyes wide open.

"I am unarmed," he said.

"Agon?" The Queen relaxed the bow and gazed at him closely. "That means 'friend.' What are you doing here in Gormoth's watchtower?"

"I was kidnapped," Agon said. "They took me… the Wolfmen."

"Where are you from?"

"Bluehaven, Madame."

"Are there more like you here?"

"No."

"Then, why you?"

"Wrong place, wrong time. I was running away from home, and they found me."

"Why did they not kill you?"

"I don't know."

"How long have you been here?"

"Five years."

"What use do they have for you? And why do they let you run free inside the tower?"

A swift but strange snarl came from Agon's throat. Someone else than the Queen might have missed it, but she did not. She once more raised her bow and aimed it at the young boy.

"You are not whom you portray yourself to be," she said and tightened the string. "Now tell me who you really are!"

"You do not want to know!" Agon's voice now descended to a lower register, and his voice became a threatening growl. "How dare you intrude? This is my tower!"

Next, the young boy seemed to increase in size, until he grew taller than Arraok himself, and his skin grew hairy. The entire body of the slim teenager turned muscular and huge in merely a few seconds. Before them he stood, the Werewolf of the Southern Watchtower.

"I am Hútlof, and you will be my prisoners ere this day has descended! In Hell, you will rot as surely as I am standing before you! Damned are you all, and you shall see the light of day no more."

The Queen hesitated not. Her string sung, and the arrow left the bow at a speed that human eyes could not recognize. The arrow hit Hútlof in the chest. He moaned and growled, but swiftly pulled out the arrow and broke it with his hands. Then, he threw it back at Astéamat in disdain, and a wide grin cracked his fury face, making his yellow eyes glow.

"You disappoint me, Queen Astéamat of the fallen Emoria. Do you think I do not know who you are? Divine but fallen! I am fallen, too, but I will become Divine. Thus, Azezakel has told me. Hence, we are opposed, but I am the stronger of us two. Your time is up, Queen. The Queendom is lost, and little did we do; your own people destroyed it for you."

Hútlof's laughter froze the blood of the Ÿadeth-Oëmin. The Queen again felt the sadness of what had played out in her Queendom. Evil is the victor when friends attack friends. Hútlof was right: She was without a Queendom now, and she had descended. A sting in her heart told her the world was worse off than she had thought.

"Believe not that I fear you," Hútlof said. "Your arrows do me no more harm than if you would shoot me with tiny needles.

Do not fool yourself, for I am Hútlof, and never forget my name. It shall haunt you until the day you are all less than a memory."

And do not fool yourself, either Hútlof, Arraok said, noticing the Werewolf's surprise when a thought entered his mind. *For I am of the Ÿadeth-Oëmin, and you know not what we can accomplish!*

With that, Arraok took a step forward and attacked the Werewolf, a worthy opponent. The Giant growled, the Werewolf growled, and furious was the battle between the two in the narrow tunnel. As the attacker, Arraok had the advantage of surprise, and Hútlof fell backward, almost losing his posture. But he recovered, and the two opponents were then equal in strength. The Giant lifted the Werewolf from the ground and smashed him against the tunnel wall, which did him no harm. In return, the Werewolf, showing his yellow teeth and drooling mouth, buried his fangs in Arraok's shoulder. Arraok cried out in pain, but used his giant fists to smash into Hútlof's head. The Werewolf backed off for a moment but seemed not affected by the blow. With an ear-shattering outcry, he lifted the Giant with his brawny arms and threw him back toward his own army. Then he laughed viciously, ran into a side tunnel, and disappeared.

Confused, and with a vertigo, Arraok got to his feet, rumbled and tumbled, affected by the bite in his shoulder, which bled furiously, mixed with a greenish-yellow liquid.

"You were bitten badly by a Werewolf," Astéamat whispered. "We must get the poison out."

"Let us follow Hútlof and kill him!" the Ÿadeth-Oëmin said.

They could not see it in the dark, but the Queen shook her head. "Let him go. He knows these tunnels better than we do. One day, he will be faced with his fate. There shall be justice!"

Arraok, trying to remain conscious, fell to his knees.

"We must go back and help our fellows to take the tower!"

The Queen caught him and laid him on his back. Arraok sighed in pain.

"Damned are the times when I cannot even heal you," she said.

Arraok smiled, but it was joyous, "I do not mind, my Queen. I know where I am going. Why do I want to linger when eternity is waiting? I have done what I could, and I did it with pride. Leave me now, for the poison is taking its toll, and I am burning."

The Queen wiped his sweaty forehead with her hands. "Worry not, brave Arraok. The Tower is already taken. Wolfmen and Birdmen cannot withstand your kind, nor can they withstand the Mazosians. Go, my friend, and we shall meet again beyond this realm."

"I fear not, my Queen," Arraok said. "I had hoped to stay until the end, but there are many amongst my people who can take my place."

After that, Arraok spoke no more.

Chapter 26
Wilderness of Ice and Snow

The sun pulsated in the sky above a dazzling, frozen landscape, shining over a well-trampled animal trail that meandered through the deep forest between white trees, encapsulated in glistering ice. Chilly air hurt Ismaril's lungs with each inhale, and each exhalation was like the smoke of an Ice Dragon's breath. The snow crunched under their feet, and a wide, endless forest surrounded the small army of Nomads. Sometimes, they climbed a hill along the way, but when reaching the peak, there was nothing to see but trees, enveloped in eternal snow and ice.

Sigyn, riding one of few horses available, sometimes bent over, gasping for air with her hand over her belly. Ismaril kept an eye, but his mind could not let go of worry.

"Are you alright?" he asked.

"Yes, I'm fine," she said. "Tired, but that's all. It is the pregnancy. I'm blessed, though, for I am on horseback."

The frozen landscape was like cotton to the wanderers' ears; no sounds magnified here, and Ismaril had spotted no animals in the entire day since they entered the Frozen Forest, and there was no birdsong. When he asked Raeglin and Yomar, none knew what to expect.

"Yes, yes, I know," Kirbakin said. "I am a Gnome and an earth spirit. Clearly, I should know the answer to your question. Yet I do not. There are other earth spirits who would know more about the Frostlands, whereas I know only what I have been told, which is little. There were and are, I suppose, Icemen living here somewhere. We are trying to find them."

"You mean we are trying to make them find us?" Ismaril said. "Finding them seems as unlikely as finding a peaceful place in Grimcast."

The Gnome's mischievous eyes glanced at him.

"Eh… yes. Was that not what I said?"

"Then we should make more noise," Ismaril said. "Why are we all so quiet?"

"There are more than Icemen in these frosty lands," Raeglin interspersed.

"If so, they must not breathe at all," Ismaril mumbled to himself. "This place is eerily silent."

When the sun sank behind the tall firs and pines, the Nomads encamped beside the trail. Ismaril looked around. *I guess this place is as good as any;* he thought to himself. *Everything looks the same around here.*

"Set up the tents," Yomar commanded his men. "And sleep close together, for it will be a chilly night. Millions of trees surround us, but none will do for fire logs. Frozen wood does not burn well."

Ismaril helped Sigyn off her horse. She looked better now, yet she was not herself. Thus, he told her to sit on a rock while he set up the tent. Then he grabbed her by the waist and helped her inside and into her sleeping bag. He opened his backpack and fumbled among the stored necessities.

"I hope I can find something that is not frozen." He smiled, but his eyes did not. They glanced at his partner, and he knew she picked up on his concern. He was torn between speaking or not, for he feared the answer. What was wrong?

He found a brown cloth bag, closed with a black leather ribbon. He opened it, and his fingers trembled. Inside, there were thin pieces of dried meat, frozen but edible. He broke a piece and handed it to her. She smiled back at him, waving her arm.

"Save it, please. I am not hungry."

"But you have eaten nothing today. Think of the child."

When she reluctantly accepted the meat and took a tiny bite, he took the courage to ask, "Tell me. What is wrong?"

She locked her eyes with his and opened her sleeping bag.

Despite the cold, she pulled up her garment and showed him her belly.

"Look," she said.

He looked. "Yes, I see it," he said. "Our baby seems to do well. You are getting much bigger."

She hurried to pull down her garment again.

"That is exactly the problem," she said and grabbed his hand with both of hers.

"What do you mean?" he asked.

She sighed. "I wish not to remind you, but have you not seen a pregnant woman before?"

"Of course I have, and you know it. Why pointing that out?"

"Because you should know this is unnatural. Less than two months have passed since I got pregnant, unless I have lost track of time. The fetus should not have grown this big already."

Ismaril sat in silence for a while, feeling the heartbeats through his temples. "Maybe… perhaps time in the Underworld is not the same as here. Altogether, more time may have passed than we are aware of?"

She caressed the beard, which had now grown long and bushy. "My dear Ismaril," she said. "Even that I have considered. It does not add up. Something is wrong—"

"—Do not say that!" He squeezed her hand gently. "Everything will be fine." His gaze flickered. Then he said, "Although… I have noticed you are not well."

She nodded and lowered her gaze. "Yes, you are right. I am unwell. I'm so tired, Ismaril."

"But is that not a part of being pregnant?"

"Yes, but not like this. It is like the baby is eating me up from inside. Like it's sucking me dry."

He felt hopeless and afraid. "Is there anything I can do? I wanted you to return to Lindhost to give birth to our baby, but you wanted nothing to do with it. You wanted to be with me. I blame you not, but now it is too late, unless we both return, and I will help you get there. Once you are safe, I can return to complete my destiny. There is still time."

She shook her head. "You have your destiny, and I have mine. My destiny is to be by your side until the end, whatever the end might be."

"But how can you if you are ill and with child?"

"That I know not. I can only follow my destiny."

He swallowed, and said, attempting to sound enthusiastic, "What if we can break our destiny? What if destiny is our goals and drives, yet we can choose side trails? Who decides our destiny?"

"You know that. It is the Queen of the Heavens. She created us."

"Yes, she created us with a destiny in mind. But since creation, much has changed. Were the Dark Kings a part of her plans? Was this suffering something she wanted us to go through? No, we know she did not. The Queen blessed us with seeing Emoria before it fell, Sigyn. Even Queen Astéamat's destiny is not tangible. You and I can change things…!"

"I believe you," she sighed, and Ismaril watched her eyelids getting heavier. "Yet, how do we know *when* to change our destiny and when we should not?"

He couped his hands over her cheeks and looked her deep in the eyes. The smile on his face was real this time. "Now, listen to you. Since we started this journey together, you have been nothing but an encouragement to me when I was about to give up. That kept me going. Now I am the one encouraging you."

"Perhaps it's payback time." They both laughed.

"Well," he said. "I am here for you, and we shall go through this together. We know nothing about what will betide. I take it you wish not to go to Lindhost now, so let us then continue. I will ensure to keep you safe."

But she heard him not. She was already asleep.

He glanced at her chest, where a piece of dried meat was sitting. She had only had one bite.

The next day was like the day before. White, frozen forests continued endlessly, broken off by animal trails leading in different directions. The farther north they came, the steeper the drop in temperature, until it hurt to breathe.

Ismaril walked beside Sigyn, holding the reins, keeping a good eye on her. She seemed better after a night's sleep, and she ate some breakfast, which gave her some energy. Now she sat upright in the saddle but spoke very little.

"Behold!" Yomar stopped and pointed at the sky. "That is not an eagle!"

Kirbakin cupped his hand over his eyes and gazed. "It is not," he said. "That looks like a… Dragon."

"We must leave the trail," Yomar said, preparing to inform the rest of his men. But Raeglin held him back.

"The Dragon is leaving," he said. "It has already seen us. Whomever it spied for will soon be informed about our presence here. Friends or foes? We shall see."

There was little conversation that day. As they strode on, the entire army kept close watch on the surroundings, as if they were expecting Snow Trolls to jump out from behind every tree. But all was peaceful as the hours passed.

Not until in the afternoon, some men thought they saw quick movements among the trees on the left side of the trail. The Nomads stopped several times and waited for something to happen, but there was nothing. The apparent movements immediately stopped when the Nomads stopped.

Thus it continued for an hour or two, until a Dragon showed up above them once more, then another one, and another one. Soon, the beasts covered the sky and circled lower and lower.

"Ice Dragons," Raeglin said. "These must be Ice Dragons."

The Nomads grabbed their bows and put arrows on the strings, pointing their weapons toward the sky.

Movements again between the trees.

Some Nomads spun around and pointed their arrows toward the perceived movements. Tension. Steadying their positions.

As the Dragons flew lower, the archers were ready to loosen.

"Hold it!" Raeglin cried. "Someone is riding the Dragons."

"Icemen!" Yomar said.

While the Ice Dragons swept closer and closer, hundreds of figures stormed out from the forest, screaming loudly, with axes and swords raised, charging toward the Nomads.

"Wait! Don't shoot!" Raeglin commanded.

When there was no violent response from the Nomads, the figures from the forest stopped, positioning themselves in a long, horizontal line, yet with their weapons ready to use.

Ismaril lowered Gahil and studied the men from the forest, while also monitoring the Dragons above. The woodmen were a head taller than any of the Nomads. They wore thick coats of brown or black bearskin, and their faces were pale as in death, and their thick beards, as well as their braided, white hair, were white as the surrounding snow. There they stood in silence, waiting, with glowing red eyes watching their every move.

The Dragons stayed in the air, but continued to circle, emanating their power to intimidate.

Raeglin put his sword back in his sheath and took a step forward toward the woodmen with his arm raised.

"Hail, men from the north," he said. "We have come in peace."

The woodmen remained silent for a while, studying him from top to toe.

"Who are you?" one of them said with a voice as frosty as the winter itself. "And why you trespass on our lands?"

"My name is Raeglin, this is Kirbakin, the Gnome, and these are Nomads, led by Yomar here—"

"Nomads? Why so heavily armed?"

"That is a long story," Raeglin said. "The times require it. They do not mean to use them against you."

"Perhaps so, or perhaps just smooth talk. All of you, hang bows on your backs and return arrows to the quivers. And put the swords back in sheaths. We have you under watch, and if you make suspicious move, Ice Dragons will kill you fast."

Yomar nodded, and his men obeyed.

"We are at your mercy," Raeglin said. "We have no wish to fight you. Are you the Icemen?"

"That is a term used by some, but not us. We are Idum-Gharaphír, Men of Frostlands."

"Splendid! You are the ones we are looking for. Please take us to your king."

The spokesperson's eyes narrowed as he stared at the pilgrim, and his face turned grim.

"I know not what kind of errand you have with us, but we shall bring you to leader, and he will decide what to do. And be careful, for my men do not think twice before they use weapons if necessary."

The spokesperson waved at the Dragon riders above and pointed to the northeast. During their stride to the Icemen's abodes, the Dragons followed aloft.

The extended company departed from the main trail and turned in the appointed direction. The Icemen kept a fast pace, even for Ismaril's taste, used as they were to the climate and the harsh conditions this far up north. Surrounded by a few of them, Ismaril noticed how sturdy they were, and though warm fur trousers covered their thick legs under the bear coats that reached almost to their knees, he could envision powerful leg muscles, accustomed to walking through deep snow.

Sunset arrived late in these regions, and when the sun finally descended in the west, it spread beams that split against peaks of tall mountains, now visible above the tree line. An icy wind kept sweeping from the north, creating icicles in the men's beards and hair. Ismaril instinctively put his gloved hands over his face to avoid frostbite.

As the night approached, Sigyn again got weaker and bent over in her saddle.

—

That night, they set up a camp in a densely forested area to get shelter from the howling winds, and the Nomads set up their tents. To his surprise, Ismaril noticed the Icemen had shovels stuck into holsters on their backs, with which they dug holes in the snow. In these holes, they could keep themselves warm and sheltered from the winds.

Ismaril and Raeglin helped Sigyn into the tent and the sleeping bag. She was shivering and talking to herself, but her shivers were not because of the cold. Ismaril removed a glove and put his bare hand over her forehead.

"She has a fever," he lowly said. "I don't know what to do."

Raeglin had a grim look on his face. "She has a difficult pregnancy. I must ask the Idum-Gharaphír if they have a healer among them. In these white lands, there are no herbs or plants I can use."

He disappeared for a while and returned with one of the tall Icemen, who bent down and watched Sigyn's face for a moment. He opened her sleeping bag and laid his massive hand on her belly.

"This woman very ill," he said. "Why you bring sick woman on long journey?"

Ismaril shrugged. "I… we had no choice. Long story."

The Iceman locked his red eyes with Ismaril's. "I sense you her husband. You should care for her better."

"Not husb…" Ismaril did not complete the sentence. It mattered not whether he was her husband. The Iceman was right. He should have insisted on taking Sigyn to Lindhost, or even better—to Merriwater. There was nothing to say.

The Iceman grabbed Sigyn's cheeks and started massaging them. She continued mumbling in her fevered state, unconscious.

"Put snow on fire and melt," the Iceman said. "Then bring to me. And bring spoon."

Ismaril got up and rushed outside to fill a soup bowl with snow. When the snow had melted, he returned.

"Can you help her?" he asked anxiously.

"How I know before try?"

The large man went outside and wetted a piece of cloth in the snow to put on Sigyn's forehead.

"This will help," he said.

From a pocket, he took a thin piece of yellow bark from a tree, unknown to Ismaril, but not to Raeglin, whose face lit up.

"Ah!" he said. "Bark from the Perrion tree! I knew not that it grew so far up north. Excellent!"

The Iceman glared at him, curiously. "No such," he said. "This from Reander tree."

The pilgrim nodded. "Same thing," he said to Ismaril in a low voice.

The Iceman crumbled the bark until the pieces were as tiny as dust and sprinkled them into the bowl with water. Then he stirred the mix with the spoon and filled it up.

"Open her mouth," he said to Ismaril, and then he poured a small amount of the mix into Sigyn's mouth. Then a little more, and some more upon that, until he paused.

"That is good. Enough now."

The Iceman stood up and gathered his things, preparing to leave. Ismaril looked first at Sigyn and then at the Iceman.

"Hold on. She is mumbling, and her fever is yet high. She is not better!"

"You must be patient. If not better tomorrow, we give her more." Then he left the tent. Ismaril's heart raced.

"Why is there not any improvement at all?"

Raeglin put his hands on his shoulders.

"Grab your sleeping bag and lie next to her," he said. "The Perrion bark will hopefully work its way through her system during the night. Tomorrow, the fever should be down. Now then, go to sleep. We will probably start early tomorrow morning."

Raeglin left and Ismaril spread out his sleeping bag beside her. But he could not sleep. He listened to her rapid but shallow breathing and watched her head turning left and right, as if she had tormenting nightmares. When he put his hand over her forehead, it was bathing in sweat.

Around midnight, Sigyn's mumbling stopped, and her body stopped moving about. Yet her forehead was hot and wet. Ismaril lay back in his sleeping bag and stared at the tent ceiling. Suddenly, her fast, shallow breathing stopped. Ismaril rushed up. His blood froze, and he could feel his own heartbeats in the temples.

"Sigyn!" he cried and shook her. "Sigyn! Stay with me!" She did not respond. "The Iceman poisoned you!"

He lay her down on her back again and put his ear to her chest. First, he heard nothing, but then he noticed her chest moving up and down. She was breathing, but now it was deeper, with a steady rhythm. He bowed his head in relief, and he wept when the tension left him. This was a good sign.

He did not fall asleep until daybreak, when it was almost time to get up.

———

The Iceman returned to the tent early and woke Ismaril with his presence. He flew out from his sleeping bag and approached Sigyn. Her eyes were open, and a vague smile cracked her sickly face when she saw him.

"Ismaril…," she breathed.

"Aye, I am here," he said and took her hand, noticing her skin was not as warm this morning. "Try not to talk. I'm glad you are awake…"

The Iceman sat down and attended to her. She pulled away from the large man and anxiously glanced at Ismaril.

"Worry not," he said, calmly. "He is a medicine man who has helped you through the crisis."

She relieved her tension and let the Iceman do his job. He looked into her eyes, touched her forehead, and rubbed her cheeks.

"Good," he said. "Better today. Fever gone. But not well. When we get to great village, better help there. Until then, keep her warm and give of my elixir now and at midday. We will be at village 'fore evening. No food, only elixir now."

Ismaril nodded and grabbed the bowl. "Thank you!"

The Iceman bowed slightly and left the tent.

———

Raised in an ample canyon, surrounded by the blade-sharp White Mountains, it stood—Idum-Gharaphír, the major city of the Icemen, a place carrying the same name as the tribe. From jutting rocks above, Ismaril gazed out over a seemingly endless, slithering pattern of houses and cottages, all of them built with white timber. It blended with the snow so that the entire city at first seemed invisible, only to manifest like a mirage before his astonished eyes. No walls and no gates blocked the entrance; instead, a frozen river ran in parallel with the building blocks, shooting up on both sides. Ismaril, the old war scout, thought to himself that he, in this environment, if journeying across the mountains, might have missed the city, had he not already known of its presence. Where was the defense? He could not resist asking an Iceman.

"We need no gates, and we need no walls," came the answer. "We are protected in other ways."

As they descended toward the city, Raeglin whispered in Ismaril's ear, "Dragons. The Dragons protect them."

"In city people shall host your men," the leading Iceman said to Yomar. "Late it is, and soon the sun sinking in the west."

Sigyn had fallen ill once more. Hopelessly, Ismaril saw her bend over on the horse's back, struggling to stay upright again in the saddle. Ismaril drew the reins until the horse came to a halt and swung himself up in the saddle behind her, holding her so she would not fall off the horse. Almost unconsciously, he grabbed her harder than was necessary, merely to feel her closer.

The leader of the Icemen said to Ismaril, "Your shield maiden will be attended to by best healer. You two stay in Eywerin's house."

―

Eywerin showed herself to be in mid-life, a head taller than Ismaril. With a thick bone frame, intense red eyes, and a face carved like the sturdiest of men, she gave a stout impression. He had noticed other women as they strode through the city, and this appeared to be a common trait amongst these people. Whatever their origins, the Idum-Gharaphír were one with their environment—almost as if they had shaped it. Tall they were, men and women alike, durable like natural-born warriors. Yet, they came across as peaceful and friendly. Eywerin was not different: Her hair was as white as that of an elderly lady, but she was not old but fair, and the hair color did not make her look of any age. It fell, long and thick, down her back, and was set up at the top. To Ismaril, it could not look any different, or it would not fit her.

By now, Sigyn had fallen into a feverish coma, and her body was hot. Ismaril locked eyes with the healer, and although hers were sharp and determined, the reflection of his own gaze in hers was frightening and appeared foreboding. Was Sigyn and her child dying?

"Lay her there," Eywerin said firmly, pointing at a bed by the wall. Ismaril carefully laid her on her back. Amidst the room, the house being only one large open area, a fireplace was burning, spreading a comfortable warmth within the abode. The healer placed an iron bowl over the fire, filled it with water, and crumbled many herbs and plants into the pot,stirring it with a large wooden spoon. Then she let it heat, and whilst waiting, she examined her sick guest without uttering a word. With her fingers, she opened Sigyn's eyes and studied them for a moment, where after she glanced into her mouth.

"She is pregnant," Ismaril whispered.

"I know." Eywerin lifted her head and glared into his eyes. Ismaril now saw her intense gaze showing signs of concern. "But there is more, is it not? A curse, I can feel."

Ismaril swallowed hard, and a wave of terror washed over him.

"Aye," he said hurriedly. "Is she—"

"Maybe I can save, maybe not. If you had not come, no save for her."

"What is happening to her?"

Eywerin sighed deeply. "I know not. I have great knowledge of curses, passed down from ancestors. Yet, I have seen nothing like this. Who put this curse on lady?"

Ismaril hesitated, afraid the healer would reject Sigyn if she knew. But he understood he had no choice. No one else could help her now.

"A demon from the Underworld," he said in a low voice as if he did not want the healer to hear him.

His answer seemed to repulse Eywerin. "Suspected that. I shall not ask you how that came about. I know enow."

"Can you help her?"

"We shall see."

The healer forced the mix down Sigyn's throat while saying a mantra in a strange language. Then she grabbed a long, yellow pipe, crumbled some herbs into the bowl of the pipe, and lit it. She opened Sigyn's mouth, drew a puff, and blew it into her throat.

"Now, hold her arms down with your strength," Eywerin said to Ismaril. "Hurry ere it starts!"

Confused, Ismaril did as being told, grabbing his shield maiden's wrists, and holding her down. Next, there was a low-pitched growl coming through Sigyn's throat, and her face shifted. With great strength, she tried to get loose from his grip, and Ismaril had trouble holding her down.

"Do *not* lose grip!" the healer said.

Sigyn opened her eyes and stared into Ismaril's. His own eyes widened in shock, and his skin crawled when he noticed her gray eyes were bright yellow and her pupils slit like a serpent. The low growl turned into a loud, demonic scream. Her beautiful face turned into a snarl, and the skin was pale like a corpse. The strength in her arms increased, and Ismaril must put all his weight on to hold her down.

"Let go of me, or I shall devour you!" she spat in a distorted and raspy voice. Ismaril noticed how his arm started shaking. He looked at Eywerin, despair overcoming him.

"Hold her until it is over!" the healer said.

Sigyn's eyes jerked in spasms, and the skin on her face tore apart, squirting blood and green slime over Ismaril's face. He cried out in horror, but kept his grip. Her skull bone became visible underneath, and she screamed in pain. Tears of hopelessness filled Ismaril's eyes.

"Sigyn! Wake up!" he shouted. "This is me! It is Ismaril!"

Sigyn continued screaming and jerking, but then she stopped fighting, and her muscles relaxed. The inflated skin came together and healed, and the blood on her face evaporated. A great calm came over her, and she fell into a deep sleep. Ismaril let go of her wrists and ran to his feet. He took a few steps back, gulping.

"What in the deepest Hell was that?" he gasped. His body was shivering.

"Demon she carries," Eywerin said in a sad voice. "She will be fine, after good sleep. Herbs do the work, and she is herself tomorrow."

"Will she relapse?"

The healer shook her shoulders. "The demon still there. I cannot heal this woman. The power that holds curse… too strong. I can do very little against such evil."

"What will become of her?" Ismaril whispered. It was as if his entire world fell apart, and the deepest loneliness he had ever suffered encompassed him. His staunch ally, the woman he had come to love, also with child, was possessed, and there was no help. Inside, he cursed the day he was born, and he cursed the world that had come to this.

"I cannot say," Eywerin said. "Can only keep it in check. Will give you potent herbs to bring on journey for her. I fear you will need them."

―

All night, Ismaril sat by Sigyn's side, getting little sleep, but when the dawn broke, he nodded and fell into a shallow doze. When he awoke, she sat in her bed, watching him. He flew up from his chair.

"Sigyn! You are awake! How do you feel?"

She looked confused. "I feel fine. It seems I slept for a long time. Why are you so excited that I am awake?"

"Because…" Then he hesitated, and he did his best to hide his sadness and his worry, although his heart ached for her and for their unborn child. There was no use in making her concerned, too. "Because your sleep was uneasy. I only want to know you are alright."

She smiled. "Yes, I am alright. I feel rested. She sat, and she kissed him dearly. "Have you really been sitting in that chair all night?"

"Well, I…"

Eywerin interrupted them, coming in through the front door with some additional plants and herbs.

"Here," she said. "You have difficult pregnancy, lady. These herbs help you and the unborn."

Ere too long, an Iceman entered the house and bowed before the two guests.

"If you both are ready, our Chieftain and Council now want to see your leaders. The Lord Yomar said you two should come. There will be breakfast in place."

―

The Chieftain and his Council held the meeting at the City Lodge in the midst of town. Ismaril and Sigyn were told it was the largest building of all, but its size was far from impressive. No houses were large in Idum-Gharaphír, save for being high in ceiling to host the tall Icemen.

After having entered the lodge, a short hallway took them to a larger room, the room of the Council. In the far end, a fire crackled from a round fireplace built with stones and pebbles and insulated with clay. A series of small windows lined up horizontally against the wall to the left, carefully assembled to keep the cold out. Amidst the room was a long table of sturdy oak, and around it sat Yomar, Raeglin, and Kirbakin, side by side, facing five Icemen on the opposite side. They all stood up when Ismaril and Sigyn arrived. Raeglin hurried in Sigyn's direction.

"You look better today," he said, and his stern expression lightened up considerably. "Your face has color. Kirbakin and I were visiting you, unbeknown to Ismaril. But you were in good hands—in better hands than the Gnome and I could provide."

"Thank you," Sigyn said. "I feel fine. Why is everybody so concerned about me?"

"Come, sit!" Raeglin said and showed Sigyn to a chair. Ismaril took a seat beside her.

The table was decorated with the most delicious dishes. There was grilled meat, vegetables, and fruits in abundance, and the room smelled of warm, freshly baked bread. And there were several carafes of red and white wine.

"I do not understand," Ismaril said, overwhelmed and salivating. "How can you grow vegetables and fruit in this climate?

The Idum-Gharaphír, appearing to be the Chieftain, sitting amidst the group of the council, seemed amused and proud when he said, "We have good greenhouses, always heated. There food thrives. Bargo I am, and Chieftain of Idum-Gharaphír.

The group ate in silence, and when the last guest had emptied their plate, the Chieftain hit a mallet.

"Now time to talk," he said. His eyes locked on Ismaril's. "It appears you are important for future Taëlia, yes? Honorable Ismaril Farrider? Around you, it all circles…"

Ismaril shifted in his chair, uneasy, but said nothing.

"Well," Bargo continued, "Master Raeglin told me your errand and who you are, and the trust to put in you. Now we all must decide how to proceed."

"Sigyn Archesdaughter and I were absent through such a discussion," Ismaril said. "I know nothing about what Master Raeglin told you, and we know nothing about you—except Eywerin taking good care of my shield maiden. Will you help us, or will you not?"

"My apology," Bargo said. "I need to give background. For many long time, our people have lived here with ice and snow, where no one else wants to live. Why? My ancestors tired of living with wars and conflict. Everybody wanted their way. Always murder, killing, war… No good. We cannot live in such way. Understand me? We migrated north to be left alone. No war, only us. Harsh weather—yes! Hard work to survive? Yes. Many died, but we had Dragons. We still have same Dragons. They live more years than we. They spit frost and fire. Long ago, they were common but hard to tame. Now they are gone from world, but ours are yet here at service. They keep bad folks away, and we can live in peace. This all we want—peace. And be left alone. Understand me? No war, no more conflict. Only us. Has worked well for many a long year. Now, not even Dragons can keep evil out."

Bargo paused and stared, unseeing.

"What has changed?" Ismaril asked.

"Everything," Bargo said. "Our lands have been attacked, and we had wave of plague. *They* came with it."

"They?"

"Wolfmen, Birdmen, Ulves, and Tall People."

"The Giants?"

"No, not them. Others… from Gormoth."

"The Dark Lords?

"Aye." The Chieftain sighed. "We drew them back, but they returned. Many good Idum-Gharaphír dead, defending. Great grief. But we have strong army, and we have Dragons. But we are peaceful people, and don't want war. Only live in peace."

Ismaril nodded. "I understand. I apologize for bothering you. But the world is coming to an end. The Final War is coming, and it is coming soon. You can stay here, and you will most likely not be attacked for a while. Gormoth is preoccupied elsewhere. But eventually, war will come here, too."

Bargo made a hand gesture. "No, no, you being right.

Nowhere to hide. Snow and ice will not veil us, and the cold not protect us. Best defense is attack. We live in Taëlia, you live in Taëlia. Both vulnerable, both responsible, both the same. We Idum-Gharaphír happy you have come."

Ismaril tilted his head. "Which means…?"

"It means Idum-Gharaphír is going to war! It means we have Dragons. You are going to Gormoth. We go together!"

Ismaril looked at Raeglin, and they both smiled.

"Perhaps there is yet a chance for Gormoth to fall," Raeglin fell in with a smile from ear to ear. Then he turned toward Bargo. "There is little time, and we must travel soon. We must reach Gormoth fast, but I know not how we can enter enemy land the quickest from here."

Bargo embracingly opened his arms. "By air and by sled. I have enough Dragons to carry most of my army. The Strait of Aldaer is narrow and frozen, and we can attack Gormoth from north. You take sleds and wait for us in Wasteforge. From there, we join forces."

Raeglin stood. "Thank you, Chieftain Bargo," he said. "You and your men are giving us hope. When can we leave?"

"You said time is an issue," Bargo said. "Two days I need, and then we go!"

Chapter 27
Wasteforge

WHEN BARGO MENTIONED SLEDS, Ismaril could not imagine what they would be like, or how they would carry the entire Nomad army. Soon enough, he found out. Not until the morning of departure, he saw them lined up outside the village. Made of light wood, they almost floated upon the layers of snow, and each one could carry at least ten men.

But it was not until Ismaril noticed the sled dogs he gasped the most.

"What are these?" he asked an Iceman closest to him. "They are monstrous. These are no dogs."

"Nay, not dogs," the Iceman said. "These Frostwolves. Only here in the north they live, and we have them tamed. Strong and reliable when domestic. Ferocious and deadly when wild. Fear them not. They are loyal and quick on feet."

There were two black-furred, giant beasts pulling each sled, and they sputtered and slashed with their jaws toward each other in frustration. *Domestic?* Ismaril thought. *They act as if they were just captured from the wild.* By accident, he locked eyes with one of them, and its eyes were red as wildfire, staring back at him as if the beast could and would eat him in one mammoth swallow. The Frostwolf pulled back his lips and showed two rows of dripping yellow fangs. *I'd prefer the Dragons,* Ismaril thought.

The Iceman noticed Ismaril's discomfort, and he laughed. "Worry not," he said. "Iceman will lead each sled."

It was decided that all Nomads should travel in sleds in advance across the frozen Strait of Aldaer, further into Erbash, through Wasteforge, and enter Gormoth from the northwest through the passes of the Iron Peaks. The plan was to wait in the mountain pass for the force of Frost Dragons that would not start their journey from the Frostlands until the sled army was close to the Gormoth border; for they were fast in the air, ridden by Icemen. The distance between Idum-Gharaphír and the Iron pass at Gormoth's border was about fifteen leagues, and with the rapid sleds and the strong Frostwolves, they estimated the journey to take two to three days, depending on the weather. Once assembled, the Dragon force and the sled army would instigate a joint attack on Grimcast, Azezakel's fortress.

Sigyn was yet sleeping when Ismaril left to inspect the sled lineup. She was feeling better when they both went to sleep the night before, but his mind was occupied with all the uncertainties.

At that moment, a familiar voice reached him from behind.

"Good morning."

He spun around and saw her there, walking toward him, steady and with a faint smile. She was indeed looking better, although pale, but she could rest on the sled. He met her midway, and they held each other in silence for long, and he closed his eyes, feeling he got warmer and warmer from her body heat. For a moment, it was as if they merged into one, and he wished not to let go.

"You are feeling better," he said. It was a statement, not a question.

"I do," she whispered. "Oh, Ismaril, I know not what was wrong with me, but these people are excellent healers."

He said nothing, for he knew not what to say. A wave of gladness swept over him after noticing her improved condition, but a deep sadness simmered underneath, knowing she was not healed. To his surprise, he realized the open wound from having lost Maerion and Erestian was healing, and he felt closer to Sigyn than ever before. Perhaps her illness contributed to that his love for her increased. His shield-maiden she was, but also so much more. His heart warmed up every time he thought about her now, and he wanted to be with her evermore. It was a liberating experience to let go of the past and realize who he had here before him.

Ere too long, the village awoke and became alive. Master Raeglin and Kirbakin were happy to see Sigyn in such good shape this morning.

"Time to leave," Yomar said to his men. "It will be a chilly journey, so I heard, and that is especially true as we cross the Strait. In the north, we will have the Ocean of Ice, and if the winds are blowing from the north, we will have little shelter, save for the thick fur blankets in the sleds. The Idum-Gharaphír have provided us with warm clothes that shall suit us well in Gormoth, and for this, we are grateful. Now, beloved people of the Nomad tribe, we are going to war. We know not whether we can surprise Azezakel and take his fortress, but if not, we shall die in the attempt. Now, let us mount the sleds and start on our quest."

Ismaril sighed. A battle against Gormoth he feared not, but in hopes of success, he was not. Perhaps the many Dragons could make an impact, but Azezakel had Dragons, too, and ferocious ones at that. His thoughts once more went to Sigyn and the baby. What were the chances of them returning to Lindhost and raising a family? Next to none.

Ismaril stepped up on the front sled and gave Sigyn a hand. To his surprise, the seat was comfortable, and the thick blanket of bear fur was indeed warm and would be of great help when traveling over the Strait. Beside them, on either side, sat Raeglin and Kirbakin, and behind them, Yomar took a seat, surrounded by his closest men. A stout Iceman entered the coach box, grabbing the reins, and the Frostwolves growled, eager to set off on the journey.

Bargo entered Ismaril's sled and glanced at them, one by one, and he said, "Farewell for now. Lucky trip, and Goddess, be with you. We see you in couple days."

The Iceman on the coach box flapped the reins, and the Frostwolves took off at such speed that the company flew backward in their seats. Quick were they, and soon they had left the village of Idum-Gharaphír behind, and the snow-clad mountains surrounding them became lower until they turned into a wide and open plain. It took some time to get used to the bright sunlight that reflected on the snow; for here, everything was white, even the few trees that grew sparsely. Farther north, land transformed into ocean, which continued as far as their eyes could see; but even the ocean was at a freeze this close to the shore.

Ismaril turned to Raeglin. "Do you think we can trust the Icemen?" he said. "Perhaps the Dragons will not come to our aid?"

"I believe we can trust them," the pilgrim said. "Bargo was serious about joining. He knows what is at stake. War he does not like, but he understands that without the aid from him and his people, we stand no chance of defeating Azezakel. He gave us sleds to ride in, furs as blankets, food, and Icemen to ride the sleds. The Dragons will come."

"Yet I have little hope," Ismaril said. "Azezakel's armies are enormous."

"Perhaps so, but we will not be alone. We are not the only army approaching Gormoth."

Ismaril raised his brows. "That I did not know. Who else?"

Raeglin laid his hand on Ismaril's shoulder and spoke into his ear, "Ravens, dear friend. Ravens. Yomar knows how to summon them, and so he did. They brought news, indeed, and the news reached us last night. Thus, we have had no chance to brief Yomar's army, but we will. King Barakus got a message from Rhuir, where Prince Xandur and Prince Exxarion have occupied Khurad-Resh. Hence, the king has gathered all men in his kingdom that can yet fight, and he is heading north to assist. With Barakus on the march from the south, us from the north, and the princes from the east, we yet might stand a chance. Once we are out on the plains of Gormoth, if not earlier, Azezakel will spot us, but if we are quick, we might charge them ere they can build a defense. I know our chances are slim. We can merely do our best, and thus, we will."

The Nomads reached the Strait in the early afternoon on that day, and as they were told, it lay frozen, covered with thick ice and a thin layer of snow, since most of it had blown off from the icy winds hitting and swirling around and about.

"Our lucky day," the coach said. "Only light wind coming from southwest."

The Frostwolves slowed down, not to slip on the ice, but soon the entire army landed safely on the far side of the strait and entered Erbash from the eastern shore. For a while, they followed the coastline, and Ismaril could hear the roaring from open water way yonder, albeit all they could see was leagues of frozen sea.

"Some say the Ocean of Ice continues endlessly to the north, and there is no end," Kirbakin mused, and in a funny manner, his beard stood out, stiff and frozen. Yet, there was that mischievous smile on his face, always present to various degrees.

"Do you believe that?" Sigyn said.

Kirbakin laughed. "Nah. People let their fantasy run when they have no answers. Of course, there is an end."

"But if there is an end, what is beyond it?"

Kirbakin shrugged. "Who knows? No one has been that far out and returned. There are no true stories about the edge of the world. Maybe it is round?"

Sigyn laughed. "Aye, that would be the day, silly Gnome. How would that work?"

Kirbakin chuckled and nodded. "I was only joking."

Later in the afternoon, they reached the Mountains of Wasteforge, with pointy peaks standing in line like majestic guardians, blocking the way. The wind had changed and now hit from northeast, freezing cold. Behind massive clouds of black and gray, the sun was hiding, and within short, snow fell, blanketing the white flatlands. The wind increased in power and hit the travelers like knives of ice. Ismaril and Sigyn pulled the blanket higher to cover most of their faces. The bad weather seemed to have no effect on the Frostwolves, and they continued southward with an increased strength. A broad road meandered toward the mountain peaks thither, mostly kept clean by the howling and churning winds. But now, when the snowfall thickened, it covered some of it.

"This is an end of luck," the coach cried from the coach box, as he flapped the reins faster to make the wolves speed up. "We must get to Wasteforge before evening, or we are in trouble. Mountain pass somewhere ahead. Cannot see much in this weather. Must follow road!"

Cascades of snow swirled around them as they flew through the landscape at an astonishing speed, and when Ismaril turned around to look for the line of sleds behind, he saw nothing but a wall of snow.

Then something extraordinary became visible before them between two peaks.

"There it is!" the coach said. "The mountain pass."

A towering construct, gray and lonesome, stood raised at their front, with a wide, arched opening amidst, and with icicles hanging from the top. Keeping speed, the sled passed through the opening and continued along a narrow pass, as if one mountain had cracked and created a wedge between. Because of the dense snowfall, Ismaril could not see how far up the mountains stretched, and he was like a reed to the wind, which could lift into the air at any time.

Once on the other side of the pass, they entered Wasteforge from the north. Here, several mountain ranges surrounded them, giving them shelter from whipping winds, and as the afternoon turned darker, it snowed no more.

"It will soon be dark," the coach said. "We encamp here."

The coachmen parked the sleds in a circle to keep any potential wind out and set up their tents for the night. The next afternoon, they ought to reach their destination at the Iron Pass, where they would wait for the Dragons.

Dazed after a long day's ride, Ismaril and Sigyn got off the sled. Ismaril followed his shield maiden with his gaze, and she noticed it.

"Worry not," she said. "I'm doing fine, and I mean it."

Ismaril breathed a sigh of relief. Perhaps he could relax for a while, carrying a little less worry.

———

At daybreak, loud voices outside the tent woke Ismaril up. He quickly checked on Sigyn, who peacefully slept beside him, and he hurried outside to see what befell. Most of the camp was up, and many fingers pointed out over the plain, where a solitary man stood a few hundred paces away. He stood sturdy, with legs apart, dressed in rags, and a dark hood covered his head and his face, and a long, black beard fell down the man's chest. He wore no fur and no warm clothing, but it seemed not to bother him. From his belt, a long sword was stuck within a silvery scabbard. Over his shoulder, he carried a longbow, and many arrows stuck out from a quiver on his back. Ismaril, being a scout, immediately looked for more footprints, in case the stranger had company, but the only footprints visible were those of the stranger.

"Who is there?" Yomar cried. "Name yourself!"

There was no reply from the visitor.

"What do you want?" Yomar asked.

The stranger stood there, as if carved in stone. Ismaril felt a lump in his stomach, and he gazed to get a better look at the man.

Then he approached him. Yomar grabbed his shoulder, trying to hold him back, but Ismaril shook him off and walked toward the stranger. Reluctantly, Yomar, Raeglin, and a few Icemen followed in his path to protect him if needed.

About 20 paces away from him, the odd man spoke, and his voice was loud and assertive.

"Come no closer, heathens! Let not your impurity contaminate me!"

Ismaril stopped. There was something familiar with that voice… But how could it be? He had never met this man before.

"The end is nigh!" the stranger continued. "God is here, and God is good. I am soon to join him, for this is the end of time, and all those who are not of his people shall perish and wither, like dead leaves crumbling in the wind. You are all abomination, and your impurity is such that you cannot repent, for you come armed and hostile to King Azezakel's country."

"Who are you?" Ismaril said.

The preacher hesitated and tilted his head, cut off guard by the voice. He curiously studied Ismaril, and two wild, crazy-looking eyes stared back at him.

"I am Hoodlum, God's emissary and prophet. God is telling me to kill all heathens or force them to leave. You cannot pass here. I am the gatekeeper."

"And how are you going to stop us?" Yomar said, amused.

"With this!" Hoodlum said, and suddenly, an entire army of Grimms manifested behind him, growling, and spitting yellow gall on the ground, so acidic that it melted the snow with a sizzle. Ismaril backed off, and behind him, he heard the Frostwolves growling in great fury from the camp. Even the Icemen shrieked when they saw the monsters from Hell take form before them. Ismaril swallowed. The Nomads outnumbered the Grimms, but did it matter? Who could fight these hellish monsters? A gatekeeper, indeed.

"Until now, I have been the *meek* prophet, and I have done little harm, save for where harm was due. Now, those days are gone. To Grimcast, you are heading, thinking you can go to war against God, you servants of the Hellish Goddess, who have killed everybody I have ever cared for? But God Azezakel will destroy you all, of that I am convinced."

"Back off, Ismaril," Raeglin said. "He is correct; we cannot pass here."

But Ismaril did not listen. He took two steps toward the preacher, and then two more. It was as if a higher force was driving him. No fear overcame him anymore, and he continued to approach, slowly. Then the stranger charged. With an animalistic growl, he ran forward toward Ismaril with his sword raised.

"Wait!" Ismaril cried. "Hold it!"

Hoodlum stopped a few inches from Ismaril's face. Again, he raised his sword to sweep it across Ismaril's neck, but in that moment, he held back, and Ismaril noticed the indecision. Hoodlum's mouth opened wide, and he gasped.

"Turn around. Go," Hoodlum said, but his voice was weak this time as if he did not mean it. Then he dropped his sword, and the two men locked eyes and stood like that. In the background, Ismaril noticed the Grimms fading in and out of reality until they all vanished. Slowly, he pulled back Hoodlum's hood until his head was bare. The preacher let it happen. The ragged man tried to speak, but no words came from his lips.

"Is this really you?" Ismaril whispered. "By the Goddess, is this really you? I… I thought you were dead! What has happened to you?"

Hoodlum remained silent.

"Yes, it *is* you! Zale, my old friend!"

The stranger broke free from his trance and took a few steps backwards, and then he shouted from the top of his lungs, "Nooooo!"

"Do you not recognize me? It is Ismaril, your best friend! I can barely recognize you, but I know it is you. Do you not remember?"

The stranger put his hands to his temples, and his face was distorted. "No, I…"

"Wake up!" Ismaril stepped forward and rocked the man back and forth until the distorted face smoothed out. Then, Hoodlum fell to his knees in the snow, and big tears rolled down his cheek. "Nooo!" Then he wept, and the agony he emitted was more than Ismaril could bear. He wept as hard as Hoodlum.

"Is… Ismaril?" Hoodlum cried in disbelief. "What is happening? I am falling apart!"

Ismaril fell to his knees before his old friend and hugged him hard.

"Zale, do you remember the portal? You disappeared, and we all thought you were dead. I am so happy you are yet alive. Please, come with me to the camp. You and I have so much to talk about."

"Zale? Is that my name? Yes, that is my name. But Hoodlum? Who? Why?"

Ismaril helped his old friend to his feet, but Zale was so weak now that Ismaril had to almost carry him back to the camp. As the two passed Raeglin on their way back, the pilgrim stared at Zale in awe, as if he refused to believe what he saw. But so bad was Zale's condition that he was in no shape to talk or interact. Ismaril helped him to bed and let him sleep. Rumors spread quickly within the camp, and Sigyn and Kirbakin joined Raeglin to watch over their old friend, whom they could barely recognize. Yomar, who had known Zale, entered the tent, and he recognized him.

"We shall stay here for another day," Ismaril said. "We must let our friend rest."

Yomar nodded, "Then so it shall be!"

—

Numbering four, they watched over their old friend that night, and they slept in fits; and there were Ismaril, Sigyn, Raeglin, and Kirbakin. When Zale woke up, many hours later, Ismaril and Sigyn were on watch. When noticing them, their old friend gasped and crawled backward in his sleeping bag, and his eyes were big and horrified as those of a hunted prey who knew it was going to die.

"Easy, old fellow," Ismaril said and put his hand on Zale's leg, which made him freeze in his movement. Then he relaxed some.

"Ismaril…" he mumbled as if he were in the midst of a fever rush. "Sig… Sigyn? What is happening? I do not remember. I am so confused."

"Who is Hoodlum?" Sigyn asked.

"That is me," Zale said. "I mean… I do not know."

Ismaril put his hand on his old best friend's bony shoulder, thin like that of a starving man.

"Do you remember the portal? You were with us, and we were at the Gormothan border, trying to find the Book of Secrets. The snow was outrageous… You left and walked into some kind of portal and were gone. We all thought you were dead!" Ismaril swallowed hard, and his eyes got wet. Sigyn was already crying.

Zale scoffed and drew his breath. "What is wrong with me? Yes, I remember vaguely. Then I do not. Next thing I remember, I was in a forest by myself in Urandor, far from Gormoth. I had a head injury. Hard to remember my past. Parents killed by Originals. The only name I knew was Hoodlum."

"Magic!" Ismaril said. "When you went through the portal, you must have forgotten your previous life, and you were reborn as someone else… as Hoodlum. No memories."

"They are coming back," Zale said, panting. "Merriwater… my home. My true home… not the Forest of Tambar…"

Ismaril nodded. "Aye, and we were… are best friends, remember?"

Zale broke into tears, sobbing. "What have I done?"

Ismaril focused, "What *have* you done?"

And Zale told him the entire story of his time in Urandor, how he was forced to leave, and the pirates. He told about the transition he went through with them, and the Grimms, who killed the pirate crew.

"After that, my memories are vague," Zale continued. "I wanted to join King Azezakel's cause. I hated the Goddess. Her people killed my parents!" Zale raised his voice, and his face turned red in anger. "Death to the Queen of the Heavens! Azezakel is King! He is the King of Kings! Our Savior!"

Zale got out of his sleeping bag and stood raised before them. He stretched his arms in a cross-like manner, and he stared at his old friends in a frenzy. So loud was his voice that Raeglin and Kirbakin entered the tent. Zale noticed them, and he stopped his preaching, pointing at them with a trembling finger.

"I know you," he said, and his voice turned into a whisper. "But your name I cannot recall."

"Raeglin—

"—Kirbakin. Remember me, the curious Gnome? With the flute?"

"Aye… I remember. Are you joining Azezakel, as well? No, wait! What am I saying? I am living in two worlds!"

Zale headed for the tent entrance, but Ismaril caught him and held him. "Wait, my friend," he said. "It matters not to me the things you have done. Your actions have been spellbound and dark. Stay with me, for you are waking up from a trance. We will help you."

Zale roared like a wild beast and showed his teeth. Although underfed and bony, he showed astonishing strength and lifted Ismaril where he stood and threw him across the tent, tossing himself on top, locking a grip around his throat. The other three rushed to assist Ismaril, who could not fight back against Zale's immense power. Although they all worked in unison to loosen Zale's grip around Ismaril's throat, they could not unlock his powerful hands. Raeglin did the only sensible thing, using the hilt of his sword, and smashing it across Zale's head. Zale cried out like a wolf in pain, fell over, and lay still.

Ismaril's face was pale like ice, and he gasped for air until the color of his skin returned.

"Is he... dead?" he said anxiously.

Raeglin shook his head. "Nay, unconscious. I will get a healer. This is something I cannot reverse. Zale is possessed, and he is dangerous."

Soon, the pilgrim came back with a healer from the Iceman tribe, who looked at the newcomer with great concern.

"This man complicated," he said. "Dark magic, dark power."

"Can you help him?" Ismaril asked, while pacing to and fro.

"Dark magic strong. I can diminish, not cure."

The healer crumbled some leaves between his fingers and forced them into Zale's throat, while ranting in an archaic language.

"He wake up soon. This will be helpful, but not a cure."

—

When Zale awoke, he was much calmer.

"We are all happy to see you, Zale," Sigyn said.

"You are supporting the Queen?" Zale said.

"Aye."

"But why? The Queen's Order killed my parents. If she is good, why did she let that happen?"

"Zale, she did not," Ismaril said. "That is part of the curse that was put upon you when you walked through the portal. Before we parted, you were with us, and we worked for the Goddess. Somehow, the portal gave you false memories. Do you remember your life before you showed up in Urandor? Think about it."

Zale sat in silence for a while before he spoke. "It is very vague and hazy. I thought it was because of the head injury. Have I lived in a lie all this time? The pirates…"

Zale wept. "I was born with a gift. I could talk to animals and call out for them, and they would come to me from afar; and I never harmed them. Suddenly, I could not summon them anymore. Instead, I summoned the Grimms in their place, as my mind turned darker. They are horrifying, and I know not how to rid myself of them. I am cursed."

"If you could speak to animals, that was a part of the curse," Kirbakin said.

Sigyn took his hand. "You are with us now. I think you will slowly heal. We understand it must be confusing."

Raeglin spoke for the first time. "We want you back. Will you follow us to war against Azezakel and his Dark Lords?"

Zale nodded. "Aye, I will. I know who I am now, but an immense dark cloud is hanging over me, and I cannot wash it off. Tell me, where are the others? Where are Gideon and Holgar? I can't remember."

Ismaril lowered his gaze. "They are both dead. I am sorry. And both their deaths are on me."

Then Ismaril told Zale about their adventures since they separated at the portal. He spoke of the Underworld, the desolation of Emoria, and of the Giants. He told him about Sigyn's pregnancy, the Icemen, and their reunion with Yomar and the Nomads.

When Ismaril was finished, Zale sat for a while, pondering what he had been told. Then he rushed up and grabbed Ismaril's arm so hard that Ismaril grunted in pain, and Zale's eyes were wide, sprouting terror and agony.

"I saw it!" he said, and his voice cracked. "They are creating hybrids. Half human and half Wolfmen. Up in Ironhall! I came from there now… They take bones from dead humans and somehow use them to create monsters, twice as strong as humans. I know not what is wrong with me, but I thought the hybrids were a good thing, Ismaril. A good thing… do you understand? I was so lost. I thought I was God's preacher."

"You are lost no more," Ismaril said and grabbed Zale's shoulder. He said nothing about it, but creating hybrids from human bones eerily reminded him of how he was forced to dig up bones in the mounds around Eldholt for the Wolfman up on the hill. Those bones must have been of a special interest to the Wolfman crew. It seemed so long ago now, and Maerion and Erestian were yet alive. So much had happened since. That Wolfman was killed by his own people, but apparently, he wanted to create his own army, and he had help from people Ismaril knew from the Wolfman War. It made sense now.

"It is already past noon," Raeglin said. "We must move on so we can meet the Dragons from the Frostlands."

Chapter 28
Two Dark Kings

ELPHAZ WAS A LIVELY TOWN at the root of the Dragon Mountains in western Rhuir. The harbor stood on thick, wooden stilts and had many ports, where Gormothan warships lay docked, bobbing and swaying on the waves of the river.

Various races populated the town, all in service to Azezakel the Black. There were Wolfmen, Birdmen, human-like people, tall, sturdy, and grim; and there were Werewolves, stinking abomination, strange creatures, and species with no names. Everywhere was commotion, with grunting beasts elbowing themselves through the crowds to show their dominance. It was not uncommon to see corpses thrown into the alleys after deadly fights, or they were rolled away into the gutters until the odor of rotten flesh was so prominent that someone must drag the dead bodies to the docks and throw them into the river.

Elphaz was, among other things, a training center for new mariners. Tomlin and Iorwain had been transported there by the order of Hútlof, the Werewolf Commander of the Watchtower; and they were immensely miserable. But as Iorwain said, "At least they give us firewater to drown our sorrows. Tastes awful, but it does the job." Tomlin was not so sure, for it was easy to get too drunk to work.

"Be careful with that, lad," he said to Iorwain more than once. "Your life may depend on it."

But Iorwain always brushed it off with a laugh, and to prove his comrade wrong, he continued gulping the ill-tasting brew. Tomlin was more careful.

They put the two pirates to work immediately after entering Elphaz. A Birdman, standing 7 feet tall and made by muscle alone, commanded them to enter a warship.

"I am Senior Captain Ulash Gunn, but you will address me as Your Excellency. Fail to do so, and I will crush your worthless skulls with my bare hands," he said. No one doubted he could.

Well on deck, ready to be trained hands-on, Tomlin waited for the first command, but when uttered, his jaw dropped.

"This deck needs cleaning," Gunn said. "Sweep off the blood and guts from the weaklings who failed to defend themselves in fights, and then scrub the deck with hand brushes until it shines. You are done when you can see your own reflection in it."

In his usual manner, Iorwain could not be quiet. "But Your Excellency…" His jaws snapped closed when he saw the Senior Captain's stare, making the pirate shiver. "I mean, I'll start right away… Your Excellency."

Tomlin had already grabbed a bucket and a broom and Iorwain pursued. Then they scrubbed at an unprecedented pace, while the odor of rotten guts simmered through the air.

"That's better," the Birdman said. "And do not slow down, for now I have seen with my own sharp eyes what you can do."

Gunn hesitantly left the deck and went into the captain's cabin. It took a while before the two recruits dared to slow down, but since the Birdman remained in his cabin, they stopped with their choir.

"Have you noticed we're the only recruits on the ship?" Iorwain said.

"Aye, I'm not blind."

"That's not what I mean. But does it mean we are the only two cleaning the whole ship?"

Tomlin was not in a good mood. "Now your brain works. It took you a while."

"Hey! You are the one who put us in this misery."

"And if you don't shut up, I'll put you out of it, too!"

Iorwain mumbled something unintelligible between his teeth, took his bucket, and continued working on another section of the deck, away from his comrade. There, he discovered a severed human head behind a barrel. He screamed and took a few steps back in disgust. Flies were buzzing around the decomposed head amidst a pool of dried blood.

"What the hell am I to do with this? It's been lying here for days, perhaps a week."

"Throw it in the river. That's the custom here, haven't you noticed?"

Iorwain grunted, lifted the head in disgust, and dropped it over the rail. The splash when the head met the water must have alerted the Birdman, for in the next moment, he stormed out on deck and studied the two recruits, back and forth.

"What was that?" he said.

Iorwain, who yet appeared ignorant of the dangerous situation they both were in, was in a grouchy mood. "A severed head I casually found among the rest of the filth here," he said. Tomlin held his breath.

Gunn closed in on Iorwain until his yellow beak was merely a few inches from the pirate's face.

"Don't do that again," he said. "Not that close to my cabin. At least *try* to use your brain. Or perhaps your head wants to join that one?" Gunn pointed at the water.

"How would I have known…?"

Gunn grabbed a whip from a holder by the mast and swung it at Iorwain. It hit him over his right arm, and then over his left. The pirate screamed in pain, which seemed to make the Birdman even more furious.

"I should drink your blood—all of it!" he said. "But then I would most likely inherit your stupidity. No, thanks to that. And never forget to address me as Your Excellency!" The next two raps from the whip snatched across his thighs, and Iorwain fell to his stomach, protecting his head with his hands. The next snatch landed on his hands, immediately leaving bleeding, swelling wounds on the outside of his palms. The pirate screamed in agony and excruciating pain.

"Hútlof was right," Gunn said. "He knew you were the most worthless of you two. You will not survive here for long with your attitude. Get back to work, worm. I want to see you work harder than you have ever done in your life."

Moaning and groaning, Iorwain came to his feet, pearls of sweat dripping from his forehead. He grabbed his broom and continued sweeping.

"And you over there! What are you staring at?"

Tomlin was fast to get back to work again, clever to say nil.

In Rhuir, the summer was in its midst, and the sun was creating heatwaves rising from the deck. The recruits bathed in sweat, and their clothes stuck to the skin. Hours later, one of the humanlike creatures entered with two small barrels under his arms. Without bothering to meet the glances from the thirsty sailors, he dumped the casks on the deck.

"For you," he said and left.

Iorwain frowned. "Who are these people, anyway? They look human, yet they do not."

"It's because they're not," Tomlin said. "If you keep your ears open instead of your mouth, you might pick up on a thing or two, like I do. I heard they are human hybrids, particularly created to be sufficient soldiers in the war."

"Hybrids? Between what?"

Tomlin shrugged. "Humans and… something. How would I know? Never mind that now. Let's see what's in the barrels."

Iorwain reached for his saber, but remembered that they had surrendered their weapons before the Wolfmen escorted them to Elphaz. He needed something sharp to open the lid to the barrels with.

"Over there," Tomlin said and pointed at the rail. Close by hung a barrel opener made of oak, wedged at one end.

"Aye, look at that," Iorwain said after he had opened the first barrel. "Just when I thought I was going to die from thirst."

"Firewater, indeed," Tomlin said. "But of a much lesser quality than what we're used to—"

"Who cares? Where are the mugs?"

"No mugs. I guess we'll have to cup our hands or put our heads into the barrel."

Iorwain laughed and did the latter. His face disappeared into the liquid, and it took several seconds before he pulled back. His face and beard were dripping with firewater. Tomlin was about to cup his hands when the human hybrid returned and threw them a tin mug each.

"Phew! It's strong stuff," Iorwain said. "Stronger than what we're used to."

"Well, then you've had enough already. We'd better get back

to work."

Iorwain seemed to have forgotten the pain from his wounds, and he swung the broom in broad sweeps and called out an old pirate song.

Drink now brother, drink your brew
Toast together with your crew
Drink all night and next day, too
Let's bring forth the worst in you.

Board the ships and set the sail
Pull the plank o'er the rail
Thunder, plunder, yell, and hail
Come buccaneers, fill up your ale!

Tomlin was nervous that the pirate song was not to Senior Captain Gunn's liking, but the Commander showed his face no more that day. In the evening, he came out on deck without glancing at the two pirates, heading toward the plank to return to town. When the Birdman had his back toward the two recruits, Iorwain, far from sober, spoke.

"Ex'use me, Your Excellency. Where do we sleep this beautiful night?"

Gunn stopped and spun around. Tomlin could not stand his squeaky bird voice. "I like you not, Iorwain. One of these days, I might kill and eat you. Both of you sleep on deck. And at the first sign of dawn, you continue cleaning. I want it finished tomorrow." He turned around and left the ship, shaking his head in disbelief, mumbling to himself, "What was Yongahur thinking when he recruited these idiots? Now I must take care of them. Is he punishing me?"

Iorwain filled up his mug again. "I guess we're done for the night then," he said. "Means you and I can throw a party. Have a drink, lad, then have two! We deserve it, me and you. Haha! I'm quite a poet myself."

Tomlin was not in the mood to "throw a party." He was deeply concerned.

"The Birdman is right. You're an idiot, Iorwain," he said. "Maybe I should call you The Revenger, after all, so they take you out of my sight. Might save *my* life. Why are you confronting the captain?"

Iorwain corrected him. "The *Senior* Captain if I may. Well, I'm not afraid of that scum."

"Perhaps you should be. And maybe being sober would change your mind and act with more caution."

Tomlin lay down with his back toward his comrade and swept the garment over his head. Tomorrow promised to be a long day.

—

Many days went by, leaving Iorwain drunk most of the time, but his good mood lasted not. The jolly manner soon turned into anger and bitterness, and when Tomlin refused to listen to his complaints, he muttered to himself instead. By the time the main deck was inspected and approved, Iorwain had taken many beats from Senior Captain Gunn's whip, and his body was sore and bled from several open wounds. Wet and dried blood drenched his entire garment.

"I'm going to kill for this," he said to Tomlin one day when they were cleaning the orlop floor.

"Why killing me?" Tomlin asked. "You did that to yourself. If you can learn to shut your mouth—"

"I will kill you for your stupid ideas. I wouldn't be here if it wasn't for you. But I am talking about Gunn. I will kill him. No one may treat me this way. Our crew didn't call me The Revenger for nothing."

Tomlin sighed and continued sweeping.

"Well, you're right in that we must get out of here," he said. "I doubt they will make us captains. Gunn just wants us to clean his ship, so it shines when he goes to war."

"And then he will kill us."

"Perhaps… or perhaps not. I doubt he dares to go against Yongahur's orders. Unless Yongahur tells him to kill us, all Gunn will do is to torture us and make us do work for him. He must have more than one ship, and we're to clean them all."

"I refuse. So, what's the plan?"

"I have no plan. Not yet. I'm thinking. Would be good if you, too, would do some thinking instead of drinking."

Iorwain groaned in pain. "If I'm to think, I need some more firewater." He filled his mug and emptied it in one sweep.

"Forget it," Tomlin said. "I'll do the thinking."

Soon, Iorwain was so drunk he could not stand, and he sank

down against the wall, half asleep.

"Sober up!" Tomlin said in an anxious voice. "I hear footsteps on the upper deck. Gunn is coming, but he's not alone. There are at least three pairs of steps. On your feet, lad!"

Iorwain tried to stand but fell over, landing on his back. Heavy boots squeaked on the stairs, coming their way. Undistinguished voices. It was too late to help Iorwain to his feet now, so Tomlin returned to scrubbing the floor. In his peripheral, he saw three creatures coming down the stairs. They lined up before the pirates, and Tomlin's heart pounded like never before, and his hand that held the scrubber shook uncontrollably.

"Stand up, Tomlin!" It was clearly Gunn's annoying bird voice. Tomlin let go of his brush and stood up in salute. Then his body froze, and his head started spinning. He felt all the blood disappearing from his face, and he wanted to faint. Before him stood Gunn, and on each side were two Dark Kings. One was Yongahur. The other one was unknown. Both were in armor as if ready for war. On their heads sat helmets with horns attached on both sides and with edges sharper than any sword. Their armor was shiny black, heavy, and with pointy spikes pouching from the chest areas, and they had long swords and axes stuck into their belts. The second Dark King looked even more intimidating than Yongahur, being a half-head taller than his brother. His eyes were like oceans of fire, orange and without depth. When he spoke, his voice was powerful and raspy and seemed to come from the Void.

"What do we have here? Explain yourself, Senior Captain!"

For the first time, Tomlin saw Gunn nervous and submissive. And he had reasons to be terrified, with Iorwain passing out on the floor.

"I... I am sorry, King Nibrazul," Gunn said. "That one over there has been nothing but trouble..."

Nibrazul, King of Rhuir. Tomlin swallowed hard. Rumors had it that his cruelty was unprecedented. He was the Lord of War, and he was Azezakel's most loyal son. Iorwain was in much trouble, but so was Tomlin. He could sense it.

Nibrazul walked up to Iorwain and kicked him hard with his metal boot. The pirate grunted but showed no signs of waking up. The Dark King and his brother exchanged glances.

"Are these the two recruits you mentioned?" Nibrazul said.

"Regrettably so," Yongahur said. "What about the other

one? That one?" The Dark King pointed at Tomlin, whose legs could, out of terror, barely carry him anymore.

"He is better," Gunn said. "He is doing his job well. It is that other one… Iorwain."

Yongahur stepped forward until his face was next to Tomlin's. He studied the pirate from top to toe and then grabbed his hand to look at his palm, which was sore with many blisters. The Dark King nodded.

"Good," he said. "His hands show he has been working hard. We shall keep this one. What is your name again?"

His mouth was so dry that he could barely utter his reply. "Tomlin, Sire."

"Ah, yes. Tomlin. I remember now. We may have use for you. We will bring you with us, together with other recruits. War is upon us, and many Elphaz soldiers must follow us back to Gormoth. This will soon be a ghost town, for everybody has gone to war."

"Always at your service, King Yongahur," Tomlin said. "But I thought you needed me as a mariner… as… as a captain."

"We need you elsewhere," Yongahur said. "We need all recruits we can get. Our enemies are gathering, trying to take Grimcast by force. They are idiots, yet we must defend ourselves so we can get the war over with as soon as possible."

Yongahur joined his brother, and they both stood over Iorwain, looking down at his snoring body. Nibrazul grabbed him around his neck and lifted him up in the air, studying him carefully, as if he were of some strange species, The pirate woke up with legs bouncing and kicking, trying to catch his breath two feet above the floor.

"Good morning," Nibrazul said. "I hope you slept well. Sorry to wake you up, but we just wanted to introduce ourselves. Then you can go back to sleep again—a long sleep."

The Dark King let go of his grip, and Iorwain hit the floor, rustling and wheezing. Then he looked up, and when he saw who was present, he sobered up immediately and crawled backward, away from the two Dark Kings.

"Still thirsty?" Nibrazul asked and picked up the pirate's tin cup from the floor and filled it. "Drink for your health, sailor." With great force, he smashed the mug into Iorwain's face. Such a blow it was that Iorwain swallowed many of his teeth. Nibrazul forced him to drink.

"Do you like our firewater? It tastes better mixed with blood, does it not? *Your* blood."

Iorwain coughed violently and spat out a mouthful of blood, with a few teeth in the mix. Then he screamed in pain.

"Should I, or should you?" Nibrazul asked Yongahur.

"Allow me," Yongahur said. "After all, I was the one making the mistake recruiting him, albeit I had my doubts."

Nibrazul stepped back, and Yongahur drew his sword, cold and black, followed by a swooshing sound when the blade caught fire and continued burning with a steady, blue flame.

"We all have our favorite weapons," the Dark King said. "This is mine. It's the Sword of Fire. Do you know what that means?"

Iorwain shook his head and wetted himself. "No… Please…! Don't kill me!"

"Worry not. I shall not kill you. See, that is not how this works. Therefore, I love this sword. I sleep with it. No, that is not true, for I sleep not. No need for that, and no time, either. This sword is not a killer weapon."

Iorwain started crying, confused and in terror. A few paces away, Tomlin stood watching in horror, helpless to intervene.

"This blade will merely kill your body, which will burn. When I bury it in your pathetic flesh, your soul will fly right to… Tell me, to where? Come on now, Iorwain, tell me. To where?"

"Please… no! Have mercy. I'll do anything."

"Too late for that."

Yongahur approached the horrified pirate and pointed the burning edge of the sword at Iorwain's chest.

"You are not answering my question, so I will give you the answer. You will go to Hell and burn in the Eternal Fire of the Damned." Yongahur lifted his sword, grabbed the hilt with both hands, and stuck it deep into Iorwain's chest. The pirate gave up an unbearable, otherworldly shriek, and then his body burned to ashes. Tomlin, lightheaded and in disbelief, lost his balance and fell to his knees, sobbing and vomiting.

"We are done here," Nibrazul said. "Bring that other one with you. We are leaving for Gormoth!"

Tomlin's trauma made him feel like his life force left him. He lost his will and cared little about where they took him when

≈ *Two Dark Kings* ≈

burly arms lifted him up and forced him up the stairs.

Chapter 29
Confrontation

Omar pointed to the sky in the southwest.

"There they are! The Dragons are coming!"

"They come in from a strange direction," Raeglin said. "One would expect them to approach from northwest."

"Perhaps they needed to take a detour?"

"They are changing course," Vlazír, a senior Iceman, said. "They now heading east."

Kirbakin, who had a better eyesight than any of the people in the camp, cupped his hand across his forehead to filter out the sun, and ere anyone came back with a monocular, he said, "These are not Frost Dragons."

"Wait!" Yomar cried. "More Dragons arriving from the north!"

"They are ours," Vlazír said.

But instead of encircling the camp from above and land, the Frost Dragons swooshed over their heads and continued south. So many were they that it took several minutes for the entire force of Dragons to pass; and each beast had an Iceman riding its back.

Raeglin returned with a monocular and directed it toward the first force of Dragons.

"The first force is Queen Moëlia's Dragons," he said. "They have flown from Ayasis."

"You are correct," Kirbakin said. "They must be crazy if they think they can attack Grimcast alone. Azezakel's Dragons outnumber them by many and are more powerful. Why such an ill-planned assault?"

"And it is strange that Azezakel's Dragons do not already counterattack," Ismaril said.

Raeglin shook his head, and his mood sank. "Nay, it makes sense, for Moëlia's Dragons are not charging, they are joining. The Queen is adding her forces to those of Gormoth. Remember, she has changed sides."

Yomar sighed. "Then may the Goddess help us."

"Fret not," Vlazír said. "Our Dragons are attacking the southwestern force. Our Dragons stronger than the others."

"Which saddens me more," Raeglin said. "Moëlia's Dragons are not evil; they merely follow their Queen's order. Many will die today."

By now, the Frost Dragons, swift in flight, caught up with the Ayasis force, and an impressive battle between beasts followed. Loud shrieks from excited and dying Dragons filled the air, although the battle befell many leagues afar. Ismaril needed a monocular to unveil what happened, but he could not find one. Instead, he listened to what Raeglin told them.

"There are cascades of ice and fire in the air," the pilgrim said. "There are many Ayasisians riding their Dragons, and there are many casualties on both sides. But the Frost Dragons are bigger, stronger, and outnumber their opponents… Yes, the Ayasis force is now retreating, but they continue their course toward Grimcast… The Frost Dragons are not chasing; they are turning around… coming our way."

He lowered the monocular, and there was concern in his voice when he spoke.

"I am afraid the air battle has drawn much attention in our direction. I presume Azezakel knows we are here by now."

"And forlorn is our surprise moment," Yomar said.

—

When watching the sky, the Nomad camp saw the broad formation of Frost Dragons rapidly come closer. After circling the air, they found proper places to land, and ere too long, the entire Dragon force had descended, and the Icemen stepped down, welcomed by the Nomad camp. It pleased Ismaril to notice how vast the Dragon force was. Combined with the Nomad army, they made an impressive battalion. The man count was not notable enough to be a major threat to Azezakel, but adding the Dragons...

Chieftain Bargo went straight to Ismaril's crowd, while his men walked into the camp to rest after the battle.

"Greetings," Bargo said. "We fought unfortunate battle. Lost five Dragons and five men, but enemy Dragons driven off. They returning to Grimcast. Strange it was. All riders females."

"They were not returning," Raeglin said. "Those Dragons and their riders were once our friends and allies. Azezakel won them over by boosting the Queen's pride and significance. The Ayasis Council is under a spell. The female warriors are Originals, or as far as that goes, so they think."

"Originals... hmm," Bargo said. "Matters not. They now enemies."

The small group of six, comprising Ismaril, Raeglin, Kirbakin, Yomar, Vlazír, and Bargo, retreated to a line of fires the Icemen lit while the group was talking. Once settled where it was warmer, Bargo continued.

"We saw much in the sky when flying here on Dragons. Flew high we did, a little to the south across Bay of Aldaer, and we saw a lot beneath. Many armies marching toward Grimcast; some from south, others from southwest."

"Did you recognize these armies?" Raeglin asked.

"Aye. There was massive army of giant men, much larger than us. Strange folks. I cannot say whether friends or foes. You say Originals join with Azezakel the Black, so these imposing men could be his legion."

"Well, this is good news," Ismaril said. "These must be the Ÿadeth-Oëmin, the Sleeping Giants! So, they made it into Gormoth." He turned to Bargo. "They are our allies."

"Good to hear, for they seem like powerful army. And there were more Originals with them."

"More Originals?" Ismaril said.

"Aye, female warriors."

Why had some Ayasisians joined the Giants? Had the Ayasisians split loyalties? Then it occurred to Ismaril. "Oh, they may be Mazosians. Aye, that must be so... The survivors from Emoria. This is more good news. We urgently need them."

"Two groups of Originals?" Bargo said. "Strange times we live in."

"And who came from the south?" Raeglin asked.

"Long line or cavalry and army," Bargo said. "I think King of Khandur. Must be. They rode under Khanduran flag."

"You bring us much hope, Chieftain," Raeglin said and stood up, excited. "Where were they when you saw them?"

"Oh, just south of Tower."

"Which tower?"

"Tower, watching the comings and goings in and out of Gormoth. It is in narrow pass between two mountains—"

The pilgrim interrupted. "The Watchtower! Alas! I hope the Khanduran army is strong enough to get through the mountain pass. The Watchtower is not a simple task to conquer. Many Wolfmen guard the entrance to Gormoth. I hope King Barakus has a plan."

"King can pass there. Tower demolished and abandoned. In ruins. I saw in monocular."

"The Watchtower destroyed?" Raeglin laughed. "Who did that, I wonder?"

"I cannot be sure, but perhaps Giants?"

"Yes! Aye! Of course! The Ÿadeth-Oëmin. This is a good day. It means Barakus can enter Gormoth that way. For the first time in years, I have hope."

"Aye, this is good, indeed," Yomar said. "Yet my concern remains. Grimcast must have noticed the Dragon fight and know that we are here."

Bargo shrugged. "Perhaps. Likely Azezakel noticed, but he will not start assault. He must address Giants and Khandurans, and he has not yet resources to battle my Dragons. I think Black King is nervous. And he knows not about Nomads."

"I hope you are right, Chieftain," Yomar said, yet unconvinced.

"On our way back here," Bargo continued, "we saw many Wolfmen and Birdmen storming out of mountain behind Grimcast. Hole in the mountain wall and tunnel… army came out. Many, many troops. They were running west over snowy plain. Perhaps to challenge Giants in battle."

"Very well," Yomar said. "Hence, we must break up from here now and head south to support the allies and hold the enemy off until Barakus arrives. We have little time to lose."

Chapter 30
An Unexpected Encounter

KING BARAKUS ONEARM stretched in his saddle, held back his horse, and commanded his troops to halt. Then he leaned forward, not believing what he witnessed. He had expected this to be the place for the first combat, but the Watchtower of Gormoth seemed deserted and demolished. He turned to General Rhain beside him.

"Lo!" he said. "Who did this? The entire Watchtower deserted and assaulted?"

"We had best wait here and send in some scouts," General Rhain said. "We must be clear it is not a trap."

Barakus sent in a few spies to explore the terrain, and the large Khanduran army encamped at the mouth of the mountain pass.

The king shivered. "This is an eerie place. The passage is narrow, and should the tower yet be manned, it is difficult to get through here. We will be sitting targets, trapped like desperate wolves in a cage."

Ere too long, the scouts returned, and they were out of breath.

"There is chaos ahead, Sire," one said. "Corpses everywhere. No one is alive over there."

"Corpses? Who are the corpses?"

"Wolfmen and Birdmen, my King. Clusters of them. But there is something else, and it is strange…"

"Speak. What is it?"

The scout hesitated. "If this was an outside job, there are no signs of who did this. No bodies of the victors. It almost looks like an internal fight. Yet, if such is the case, they did a thorough job of completely killing each other off."

"We must be careful still," Barakus said to his general. "There could be enemies remaining inside the tower."

"With respect, Sire," said the scout. "The gate to the tower is flung open and torn to pieces. If someone is in there, they had better flee at our arrival, for we can ride right in."

Barakus and Rhain both raised their brows, exchanged glances.

"Well, then we should find out what has happened here," the king said. "If the Goddess is with us, this might be our lucky day."

—

The scout was right. The gate was torn asunder, and a section of the cavalry, led by the king, the general, and a flag bearer, entered the tower yard. There, they halted and looked left and right. And behold! An astonishing sight met them. Many corpses of Wolfmen and Birdmen lay spread, some of them ripped into pieces by someone with supernatural strength. Others seemed to have been lifted like cuts of wood and smashed into the wall over and over, while some were crushed as if someone gigantic had merely walked over them. Everywhere was blood, guts, and dead bodies in droves; and they covered the floors and the stairs to the next level of the tower, where the king's men lost sight of them.

Barakus' face froze, and his muscles tensed. "Who did this?" he said to himself. "No creature I know of is capable of this."

"Creature or creatures," Rhain said. "There could have been many."

"Beware, for those who did it may linger."

The sound of hoofs clattered behind them, and a knight approaching from outside the gate rode up to the king.

"Forgive me, Sire. A few of our men saw something north of here. It looks like the remains of a huge bonfire."

The king and his men turned around and exited the tower. From there, Barakus gazed north to where his men had seen the ash mound. He stretched out his hand, and the general gave him his monocular.

"There is indeed a burned down bonfire uphill," Barakus said. "Or perhaps something else…" Quietly, he waved to the men behind him to continue up the slope to examine. When they arrived, Barakus dismounted. "It is still smoking, and the stink is unbearable."

The king brought Rhain and a few knights to inspect. He drew his sword and whisked about among the ashes until he found something that made his heart jump.

"Bones," he said. "This is not a bonfire; it is a funeral pyre. Yet behold the size of the bones. What are they?"

"Looks like Giants," Rhain said. "If so, where from? Are they friends of foes?"

"In these times, everybody who is the enemy of Wolfmen and Birdmen are allies."

"There is more," a knight said. "Behold this!" He pointed at another set of bones further into the mound of ashes. "These are bones of humans… I think."

Barakus inspected. "Alas! These *are* human bones. What is befallen here? But even these bones come from people taller than us. Ayasisians? None of this makes sense."

He stood in thought for a moment, and then he said, "Well, there is nothing left here to see. The road before us seems clear of enemies, and whilst it remains so, we should hurry on."

—

The cavalry continued north, past the abandoned watchtower, and the road drove them through the mountain pass that opened to a wide plain. Here, the mountain peaks on either side left room for a broader landscape, enveloped by a layer of deep snow. But like a river running through a white, dazzling scenery, a meandering path took them farther north, until it made a northeastern turn. Behind them, in the southeast, betwixt two mountains, another tower rose, grimly watching the long line of Khanduran knights.

"Why do they not stop us?" Barakus said. "No doubt they can see us from that tower. And why did they not involve themselves in the massacre at the Watchtower?"

"Perhaps they did," General Rhain said. "It is not unreasonable to think that the hordes of corpses we witnessed comprised both the guardians of the Watchtower and the beasts from the tower over there. Or perhaps they are busy elsewhere."

"And where would that be?"

Rhain shrugged. "Someone built the pyre, and they were not Wolfmen. The pyre was for Giants and slain humans, and thus, it was built by the survivors. Some of these marauders, who so efficiently killed an entire army of beasts, are yet among the living." The general locked eyes with the king. "We know nothing of how many they are, but they may be marching toward Grimcast."

"I wish we could detect their footprints on this path, but because of some magic, the road is clear; not a single snowflake on the ground."

"We also know nothing about how fast these Giants travel, and how far ahead they are. Mind you, the pyre was still smoking when we arrived."

Rhain looked through his monocular.

"I see nobody," he said, "but ahead the road is slithering and waning between massive mountain peaks. Another mountain pass to consider. Once we reach there, we must beware. If these Giants are unfriendly, they may have seen us and are waiting there to catch us off guard."

"There seems to be no other road than this one, so if we must fight, we shall fight, regardless of who our opponents are."

Albeit the snow dampened most sounds, this part of the journey was unnaturally silent, and no wind was rustling trees that were growing nowhere on this all-embracing heath. The only sound was from thousands of hoofs clattering on the frozen soil, a random neighing from a frustrated stallion, and the small talk amongst soldiers and knights. But because of the intimidating silence, most men kept their voices down. Above their heads, a white sun shot merciless beams of bright light, reflecting on the snow, making it difficult to see far.

It was late afternoon when King Barakus' cavalry approached the mountains on their east. Two colossal mountains ascended on each side of a wide mountain pass. On their left, and to the north, the Iron Peaks reached out, grandiose and menacing; and on their right, and to the south, there were the Snowy Mountains. Unbeknownst to the king, and not too long ago, Ismaril and his fellowship passed only about four leagues south, the way birds fly, entering the cave where they found the Book of Secrets.

The shadows were long when the cavalry rode into the mountain pass with the low sun on their back. They proceeded in silence as if afraid to awaken unbeatable mountain beasts. They were not yet halfway through when a knight riding behind the king hurriedly shouted, "Behold! Up there!" He pointed forward, up the mountainside.

Barakus sighted two gigantic creatures, resembling men of great stature, standing on a cliff high above them. The king's troops came to a halt.

"Archers to your mark! Unknown target ahead!" Barakus yelled. A great number of bowmen nocked their arrows and aimed at the two Giants, who kept guarding their position. Then, four more showed up beside the first two, fearless of the arrows pointing at them.

"Identify yourselves!" Barakus shouted.

The Khandurans were so occupied with focusing on the four apparitions on the cliff that they did not notice what was happening ahead. There, at ground level, an army of Giants approached from nowhere. The archers immediately shifted their attention to the new threat and kept their arrows nocked. Other knights instinctively drew their swords and axes.

"I am King Barakus of the Divine Kingdom of Khandur. Identify yourselves! Friends or foes?"

The crowd of Giants stepped aside to the left and to the right, creating a corridor between them. Through the division, a long line of tall females approached, until the woman in the lead stopped at the Giants' frontline. The king's eyes widened, and his heart pounded faster when he watched her. Slender and taller than any man, she was the fairest woman he had ever laid his eyes upon. With an inner light, she shone as if there was something divine about her, and intense and captivating was her gaze, emitting a light and ancient wisdom the king had never witnessed until that day.

"Hail, King Barakus of the Divine Kingdom of Khandur," the woman said in a deep, mesmerizing voice. "So, we finally meet. Long and wearisome eons have passed since your first king, Irvannion the Great, traveled south. I am pleased that you still address your Kingdom as Divine, for as such, I once dubbed it."

King Barakus and his entire legion of men held their breath and said nothing. The silence was deafening, and even the king found no words.

"I am Queen Astéamat of former Emoria. I *am* the Divine,

walking the earth."

The soldiers and the knights, close enough to see and hear the Queen, followed King Barakus' example and dismounted. One after the other, they fell on one knee and bowed their heads in respect and honor.

"Queen Astéamat," Barakus said. "Little did I expect to meet you in my lifetime, and even less here in the midst of Gormoth."

"All please rise," Astéamat said. "I am here, but happy about it, I am not. Emoria is no more. Our frequency is dropped, and we are once more the fierce Mazosian warriors, in ancient times so dreaded by Wolfman and Dark Kings, fleeing in terror when they sighted us. This one last time, we are on the march."

"Good news, indeed," Barakus said, and his stern face lit up, as if he were a child once more. "With you and your warriors combined with ours, hope increases tenfold. And may I ask, who are these giant men?"

"Friends," the Queen said. "There is much to tell, but not here. The Gormothan night will soon encompass us, and we must find shelter. King Azezakel is aware of our presence, but he has not yet attacked. His silence is mysterious, but I expect the stillness to last not for long. Yet we have time to talk before we rest. Follow me!"

It was difficult to find a place that could house such a vast combined army, but they vouched for staying in the mountain pass, and not out in the open, where the immense Fields of Treshandor stretched.

"Albeit they know we are here, we should not challenge the situation by making fires," the Queen said. "We must endure the night and try to get good rest, for tomorrow we may go to battle. There is no other way to reach Grimcast than marching across Treshandor, and there we are sitting targets."

Before they went to sleep, Astéamat told Barakus and his men about the awakening of the Giants, the destruction of Emoria, and the decision to join the Giants in battle for the sake of Taëlia.

"So you were the ones ruining the Watchtower?" General Rhain said.

"This is so. But we lost many good men and women there. And we lost Lord Arraok in the battle, he who was the High Lord of the Ÿadeth-Oëmin. Beside me sits his brother, Usbarg, to whom the title as the *High Lord of the Ÿadeth-Oëmin*, the Tribe of Giants, is passed."

Barakus' mind was filled with questions and concerns about the future. There was one thing most of them seemed to have forgotten about.

"Azezakel's Dragons," Barakus said out loud. "Our army is now vast and powerful, but how do we defend ourselves against the Dragons? I doubt not the Black King will summon them to battle early on to eradicate us all. I am surprised he has not done so already."

Queen Astéamat nodded. "I am aware," she said. "We have the archers, but lacking Dragons ourselves puts us in great danger. Yet we can only do what we can do and perhaps die in the attempt, be it our fate or not. As Mazosians, we have certain powers to fight the beasts, but these powers are exhausting to use and will weaken us."

―

The following morning came, sunny but glacial cold. The army was up at dawn, having a swift breakfast, and then getting ready for the last journey across the Field of Treshandor to Grimcast. Soon, they left the mountain pass behind and were out on the open field, stretching out of sight. A wide trail continued east, and there was no other way; for the snow on either side was too high to ride through.

They had not reached far ere they watched the sky filling up with what seemed like gigantic birds.

"Speaking of Dragons," Barakus cried. "There they are, and they are many. Woe befalls us all!"

"Keep moving," Queen Astéamat said. "Unfortunately, we cannot spread out; the road is too narrow."

"This means the Dragons can put us all on fire in one blast," Rhain said.

"Archers! Keep your bows nocked!" Barakus yelled.

"These Dragons are small," the Queen said. "They are not Gormothan Dragons; they are Ayasisian Dragons!"

Barakus grabbed a monocular. "Aye, and Ayasisian warriors ride them. This is Queen Moëlia's force of Dragons. What are they doing here?"

There was an underlying sadness in Astéamat's voice when she said, "They will not bother us—not yet. They are heading for Grimcast to join forces with Azezakel. They will be a problem for later. It is a shame it has come to this."

"Alas!" Usbarg said. "There are more Dragons coming from the northwest!"

"These are bigger," Astéamat said. "Much bigger. These could be Gormothan Dragons joining Queen Moëlia."

"No, they are attacking the Ayasisians," King Barakus said, still looking through the monocular. "There are riders on those Dragons, too, but they are... Frost Dragons? What are they doing here? And who are the riders?"

"If they are Frost Dragons, I can answer that," Usbarg said. "They are the Icemen from the Frostlands, way up north."

"Does this mean...?" Barakus nearly dared not complete the sentence.

General Rhain laughed. "It means we have our Dragons! They are attacking the Ayasisians, so the Icemen must be our allies, and if so, we must rejoice! I wonder what brought them out. They are a peaceful folk."

"First, let us see how the sky battle progresses," the High Lord Usbarg said.

The combat was short but intense, and Dragons and riders on both sides fell from the air. But soon, the Ayasisian Dragons retreated and continued toward Grimcast in reduced numbers, and the Frost Dragons turned around and flew back north.

"I hope this was not merely a onetime combat," Barakus said, and his enthusiasm dropped. "We need them. Heaven knows we need them..."

—

The great company of horsemen and foot soldiers, comprising Mazosians and Ÿadeth-Oëmin, left the mountains behind and entered the Fields of Treshandor. The snow lay thick, and with the mountains behind their backs, there was nothing to see, save for the endless white blanket of snow. A wide road, magically free from snow, cut the landscape in half, but even the road blended with the white field in the great yonder. The sky was free of clouds, and there was no wind. Under other conditions, King Barakus would have blessed the weather, but when riding amidst Gormoth, pleasant weather was more eerie than ferocious storms. Behind him, he heard his men chattering in a pleasant tone, but in their merriment, he did not join. He leaned over in his saddle toward General Rhain.

"No sign of enemies," he said. "No assails."

Rhain frowned. "I was thinking the same. This is unnatural. Why does Azezakel allow us, such a vast army, to pass unhindered?"

"It puts me more on the watch. Our men are merry, but I sense danger."

Ere the sun was in its zenith, the road split into two. One turned north, and a second meandered southeastward.

"Very well," the king said. "Now I know where we are, at least. The northern road leads to Móragu, Ishtanagul's fortress, and from there, it runs further to Ironhall. We must take the southeastern road to Grimcast. If we are not assaulted or otherwise hindered, we should reach Grimcast by tomorrow."

The only landmark showing the troop's progression through the never-changing plains was that the mountains behind them decreased in size. Besides that, everything remained the same, and there were no disturbances for the rest of that day, and there were no living creatures; it was as if the king's army was the only living people in Taëlia. By then, the merry voices from the troops had subsided, and most of them now seemed as concerned as the king and his general.

When the sun slowly sank behind the mountains in the west, the company stood before a second crossroads, both roads leading eastward.

"We must choose the right road," the king said. "I have studied many maps of Gormoth. The left leads to the Dragon Fortress, where I hear they train Wolfmen and other abominable creatures. The right road takes us directly to Azezakel's lair. Although sunset will be upon us anytime soon, I want us to continue for another half hour or so. It is against strategy to encamp at a crossroads where we can be attacked from three directions."

After some farther travel, the army encamped on the road, where the ground was free of snow. The sun had fallen, but many stars twinkled in the night sky above. King Barakus studied them, and his feelings were mixed.

"This place is almost idyllic, if it were not for the overhanging hidden threat cutting through everything here. I want extra men to keep watch throughout the night. I am dreadfully uncomfortable."

But the night passed without incidents, and thus befell a new morning with bright sunlight. There was still no sign of life; it was shrilly quiet.

As they journeyed on, the Dragon Mountains in the east grew bigger, covered with snow and ice. And it was not until before midday the troops sighted the first life; and it was the life sign they had waited for but dreaded. Something the size of small dark dots moved in the yonder from the north, growing bigger as they closed in. The Khanduran cavalry halted, and Barakus put the monocular to his eye.

"Alas!" he said. "That is a monstrous legion of Wolfmen and Birdmen, and they are heading our way."

"How far?" Rhain asked.

"They are yet many leagues distant, but they ride Ulves, and they ride through the snow, disregarding the roads. They know we are here, and if we stay, they will be over us in a couple of hours."

"I suggest we speed up and hurry to get to Grimcast ahead of them," the general said. "This is not the place to meet them in open battle; and we want to get to Grimcast."

"I concur," Barakus said. "We need all our men and women to storm Grimcast. That is our principal goal. We may fall on the way, but if they stop us before we reach Azezakel's castle, we have little hope of taking the stronghold."

The king, head high and broad-chested, roared his commands back through the lines.

"Brave men of Khandur, ferocious Mazosians of Emoria, and mighty Ÿadeth-Oëmin. The time for the ultimate battle is now at hand! Enemies are coming for us, but we shall not let them—not yet. Thus, we must advance faster to reach Grimcast ere they catch up with us. Follow me, brave peoples of Taëlia. Grimcast is merely a few sun movements away!"

Then he drew his sword to encourage his men, who followed suit, until the air sparked when sunbeams reflected the cold steel of the raised blades. The king gave up a war cry, repeated by his men down the line, and he buried his heels in the sides of his stallion. His horse neighed and rose on his hind legs, where after he set off down the road, ensued by the rest of the army.

Chapter 31
Azezakel's Voice

SWIFT AS THE WIND, King Barakus and his joined army crossed the heath toward Grimcast. But there was a swifter wind moving across the plain that day, beasts on sturdy legs and with murder on their minds. As the Ulves swept across, steering up flurries of snow where they ran, they closed in on the king and his allies. By the time Barakus' army reached the Grimgroves, where the dead trees stood dense and with many finger-long thorns protruding from their crooked boughs, the vast Wolfman-Birdman army reached there, too.

The king's men drew their reins and lined up before the fence of trees. A few hundred paces to the north, the enemy stopped, barely able to hold the Ulves back from charging. Thus, the two armies faced each other in silence, but no one charged—not yet.

King Barakus gazed aloft at the towers of Grimcast, sticking up like thick, sharp spearheads above the tall, dead trees. They were so close now. All they needed to do was to storm the castle, but first they needed to pass the tree fence, avoiding the dangerous thorns, and this must be done while a vast army of Gormoth beasts were charging. The king was uncertain what to do next, for there seemed to be no passageway through the murderous fence.

"Perhaps we should split our troops," he said. "Half the army keeps the Wolfmen busy, while the other half storms into the castle, trying to penetrate the wall of trees. But if that is our plan, we end up fighting the Wolfmen with only half of our resources, and they will outnumber us. Queen Astéamat, may I hear a suggestion?"

The Queen never had the chance to answer, for in that moment there was a movement in one tower. Barakus' body shivered when he looked through the monocular and noticed two figures on the balcony.

Silence fell over the plain when the two figures showed up in the tower. In the monocular, Barakus sighted a male and a female, both wearing black. The man had a patch over one eye, but the remaining eye stared right into the king's monocular. So intense was the gaze that Barakus gasped and removed the device. No one doubted who the two gestalts on the balcony were. Queen Astéamat took a few steps forward until she stood by the king's side, and Usbarg placed himself on the opposite side of King Barakus' white stallion. For the first time since he arrived in Gormoth, Barakus felt fear washing through him, and there was a deep sense of doom.

"Welcome to Grimcast!" the man in the tower said. "Hail, King Barakus of the Divine *Kingdom* of Khandur. We meet at last. And hail to Queen Astéamat, since I suspect you still call yourself that, although your Queendom is no more. Very regrettable, indeed, and nothing I would have orchestrated.

"But let me introduce my consort, Queen Ishtanagul, with whom I share the Divine Kingdom of Gormoth. As you may have guessed, I am King Azezakel. Some call me The Black, which is a great misnomer, and quite upsetting, in all honesty, unless they refer to my dress code."

Like rolling thunder, his voice sounded. It was so impinging and authoritarian that everybody in the line of soldiers and knights could hear him speak, and they listened.

Then Ishtanagul raised her voice, which was equally strong and clear. "Hail to you, my human children," she said. "For my children you are, in the progress of growing up; but the notorious and rebellious acts when coming to age must now end, for it is time to enter the adult world. We both welcome you, for as your parents, we understand your growth labor."

"Now, let us make peace," Azezakel said. "No harm will come to any of you if we can combine our efforts and work in unison rather than as enemies. Being your parents, we will continue watching over you, but in peace. A king of great ancestry you are, King Barakus of the House of Irvannion, and may your children rule in peace and succeed you through many generations, although I see them not among you here today. Join us, and we shall have a grand feast inside Grimcast, and then you can all return home. Your Kingdom will remain yours, so long as you abide by simple rules."

"We make no bargains with the Black King!" Queen Astéamat cried. "Slick is your tongue, King of Scorpions, but you fool no one anymore, save for your horrified servants."

"Queen Astéamat, Queen of Lies," Azezakel said. "While my children suffered because of the untruths you have spread in their midst, you cowardly hid with your murderous warriors in the forests of Emoria where no one was allowed entrance for millennia. Apparently, peace and freedom were for you and your peasants only, and not for those whom you consider your children. Hence, what right have you to speak here today, unless you are here to repent? The rest of us are discussing peace, but I know your kind. Peace means you must hand over your so-called children to their rightful parents—us. This you wish not to do; hence, war is your solution."

King Azezakel raised his arms in a symbolic embrace. "Listen to me, my children! This has all gone too far. For thousands of years, you have struggled to grow up and fought against your true parents, misled by a vicious queen who should have no power over you.

"Yet we are merciful and forgiving. One word, and we shall let even you and your Mazosians into our castle to celebrate. Thus, all shall be forgiven, and old grudges forgotten. For behold the Ayasisians! Queen Moëlia is clever and no fool; her people joined us, for the Queen came to her senses and saw the benefits of long-lasting peace. Therefore, I am asking you, Queen Astéamat, to follow in her lead."

"Glib as always," Queen Astéamat said. "And a notorious trickster at that. Perhaps once your voice was hypnotic and convincing, but now you sound like an aging crow, senselessly cawing. Your magic is broken, Azezakel. Your strength was how you projected your evil plans and agendas on someone else, blaming them for your own crimes and misdeeds. Thus, you lured the herds into your fold. But the glorious army of Men, Originals, and Ÿadeth-Oëmin has not come here to greet you and your consort, the Queen of the Damned, for we all know your kind. No soft tongues can change that."

"So, it is a war you wish for," Ishtanagul said. "If the humans were your true children, would you not want peace instead of war? Peace is what we, the true parents, offer our children. This should be enough for anyone to know whom to trust."

Queer thoughts ran through King Barakus' mind. For the first time, he doubted his own religious convictions. What Azezakel and Ishtanagul said made sense. *Why more killing? Perhaps we should listen? And why does Queen Astéamat want war? Have we all been deceived? Are we favoring the wrong Deity?* He noticed Azezakel watching him.

"Beware, glorious army of Men," Astéamat said, "for I am hearing it, too. The voices in your head are not yours. Alas! Throw them out, for these two are contaminating your minds."

In the distance, the vast army of Wolfmen and Birdmen stood idle, uttering not a word. Even the Ulves were patiently watching.

One after the other, King Barakus' men sheathed their swords and hung their bows over their shoulders. Those with lances drawn from long holsters on their horses' backs put them back in place. Even Barakus followed suit, until he suddenly realized what had betided. Why did everybody listen to the Black King and his consort? He turned around in his saddle and watched the endless line of soldiers behind him. Astonished, he noticed their empty eyes and dropped jaws.

"Men of Khandur," he cried. "Enow! Fall not for the malison, for it is of evil. Wake up, Knights and Soldiers of the Divine First and Second Cavalry. Lay down your weapons now at the mercy of these two usurpers, and you shall be forever slaves. Peace, we shall have, but not yet. Queen Astéamat is right. There is no peace treaty possible, no truce to gain from with these tricksters. They want us to think war is a human invention, and that they are the victims, ready to pardon us. Our ancestors wanted no war, but neither were they idle when Gormoth's beasts and Wolfmen in droves invaded our lands. These two are not our parents; they are our nemeses!"

When King Barakus saw his men waking up from their trance, he turned toward the two apparitions in the tower.

"Hold your forked, black tongues, foes of Men," he said. "It is our turn to set the stage now. We give you one last chance to surrender and give us Taëlia for good and send all the monsters you have so viciously created into the Underworld, and Heaven might consider your fate. Perhaps they show you a fraction of mercy if you surrender. Refuse our offer, and there shall indeed be war, and it will start here, today!"

Deep and confident, Barakus' voice came across, and he felt new hope rushing through him like a river on which a dam gave in and let the water force its way through.

"Listen to me!" the Black King roared. "Have I not shown you my goodwill already? Did I not sacrifice my men, letting you break into my Kingdom past the Watchtower? Did I not let you ride and march unhindered all the way to my Castle, despite the aggression you showed by trespassing? And did I not hold back my army from the Dragon Fortress, commanding them not to harm you? And yes, the Dragons. I sent them not your way. And behold my army over there. Many thousands of them, outnumbering you, and I have more in reserve. If it were not for my goodwill, you would not be here now. What else do you expect of me? What has the queen-that-was offered you? Death and suffering. Now, when her Queendom is naught, she is back among you, showing her true face. She is the Queen of War; do you not see? Monumental risks have I taken by letting you come here to the threshold of my Castle, trusting you will listen to reason. Do not disappoint me, my children. I have much faith in you. You are grown men now. Favor me, and show you are *real* men, not worshippers of a queen no longer worthy of her title. Do not act like stray fawns, confusing their true mothers with wolves, only to be eaten."

Barakus turned toward General Rhain and Queen Astéamat, and he whispered, "As soon as I give the signal, we need to divide our armies. Most of our people must attack the Wolfman army, among them a great number of Giants. And a group of us must try to penetrate the thorny fence ahead, if that is at all possible. I will lead the army to battle. General, you lead the invasion of Grimcast. Soon, I shall give the commands to our army."

"I will stay here with General Rhain," Astéamat said. "I have a bone to pick with this God-wanna-be and his queen."

"Also, I will stay with some of my men to help with the fence," Usbarg said.

King Barakus nodded and stood in his saddle, pulling his

lance with his only hand, resting it under his armpit. Then he raised his head high, and he said, "There will be no peace anywhere in this world until all the Dark Ones are defeated."

Then he pulled the left rein, and his horse faced the Wolfman army in the distance, and he turned toward his men.

"Be strong, Men of Khandur, Mazosians of Emoria, and Ÿadeth-Oëmin of the North," he cried, and his voice carried over the plain, so the Wolfmen could hear him, too. "We have defeated these ill creatures before, and we shall do it once more and for the last time! This battle is for peace versus slavery. The outcome decides what it will be, so fight well, brave men! Let a fourth of you stay behind and help General Rhain, Queen Astéamat, and the High Lord of Ÿadeth-Oëmin on their quest. For the rest of us, let the battle begin. Show no mercy!"

Thus, King Barakus Onearm raised his spear in the air and gave the command.

"ATTACK! FIGHT FOR THE FREEDOM OF TAËLIA!"

Chapter 32
The Treshandor Battle

THE ENEMY ARMY INCLUDED not only Wolfmen and Birdmen; there were also tall and sturdy Mountain Trolls among them, rising many feet above the head level of the rest.

King Barakus' cavalry, all of them with their spears lowered, rode into the enemy line with great courage. As the two armies clashed, it was brutal and loud. On one side, Wolfmen took the lead over the Birdmen and the Trolls, riding their Ulves at great speed; and on the other side, King Barakus' cavalry was way ahead of the rest of his army, and the steeds ran into the Ulv cavalry without weighing. Knights and soldiers fell off their horses from the clanking impact, and Wolfmen flew off their Ulves, while snow twirled about the entire battlefield, some of it white, some of it red from splashing blood. Loud screams of agony and death filled the air when swords and spears hit their targets on both sides, killing and maiming. In the lead, piercing his spear with great skill despite being one-armed, the king was an encouragement for his men, and they fought with both vigor and bravery.

The ferociousness of the Khanduran cavalry was so impressive that they broke through the enemy's lines like an unstoppable whirlwind of snow and ice, throwing Wolfmen and Ulves off guard, making it possible to advance and gain ground. Halfway through the lines, the rest of the allies, comprising Giants and Mazosians, reached the inner quadrant of Wolfmen and pushed further. Mazosian arrows sang, seldom missing their targets, and the mighty Ÿadeth-Oëmin, some using longswords, split the Wolfmen and Ulves in half. Another group of Giants used huge oak clubs that they swung left and right. Wolfmen flew off the Ulves' backs, crushed and torn into unrecognizable pieces before they hit the ground many paces distant.

King Barakus, in the lead, plowed forward through the enemy crowd, using his spear. But suddenly before him was a monstrous Stone Troll, crouching with a stone club in his massive grip. With an ear-shattering roar, the beast charged toward the king with his club raised. Instinctively, Barakus attempted to dodge the impact, but realized it was too late. So fast and ferocious was the battle that there was no time for fear, and he must trust his instinct in each moment. Then, instead of pulling aside, he sped up.

"Serve me well, my proud stallion!" he cried as he raised his lance. The Troll weighed not, and an impact was imminent. The beast swung his club so fast above his head that it was difficult to follow the movements, and Barakus knew that if that club hit him or his steed, it would be over. But there was little time to think about that now.

His powerful baryton voice cried out.

"Argh!"

Then he bent over in line with his stallion's head, still with spear steadily in a tight grip. He felt the velocity of the Troll's club when it swooshed a few inches above his head, and in that same moment, his lance pierced the Troll in his chest with such force that it went right through his thick hide and out on the other side. The Troll screamed and fell back. The king lost the grip of his lance and flew backwards out of his saddle and landed in the snow with tremendous force, gasping for air, coughing when swirling snow entered his lungs. When he came to his senses, he noticed his arm was numb and tingling, but he ignored it. Quickly, he got to his feet, wobbling, looking about. Merely a few paces distant, the Troll was on his knees, coughing green blood in the snow about him, yet not dead. When he saw the king, he snarled and grunted, and his yellow eyes emanated such hatred that the king backed off. He wished to draw his sword, but his arm was numb and useless, and possessing one arm only, he was unarmed. He tried to retreat, but his head was spinning, and once more, he fell in the snow. With heart pounding like a sledgehammer, Barakus saw the Troll slowly approach. The monster had lost his club somewhere from the impact, but his hands and arms were massive and could crush the king's head at first attempt. With the spear still pierced through his body and with green drool pouring from his grinning mouth and from the place the lance had hit, he closed in, one heavy step at a time. Barakus' head was still spinning. Desperate, he tried to get to his feet, but all he could do was get on his knees.

"King Barakus," the Troll growled. "You have slain me, but I shall get my revenge on you, and I will be the one who killed the King of Khandur." He was now standing over the king, coughing green blood in his face. Then he grabbed the king's throat and lifted him up in the air as if made of glass. "I shall slowly strangle you... and then remove your head from your torso with my bare hands..."

King Barakus could breathe no more, and his vision faded as his eyes wanted to pop out of their sockets. Then something unimaginable betided. The king heard a loud neighing from behind the Troll. Barakus attempted to focus one last time, and there was his stallion, standing on his hind legs, waving his front hoofs in the air, hitting the Troll in his head repeatedly at an astonishing speed. The Troll screamed in pain and dropped Barakus, who fell to the ground. The beast turned around to defend himself against the furious horse, who could no longer prance and fell back on all fours, now vulnerable to the Troll's assault.

Thus, the king saw his chance. Using his last strength, he got to his feet, noticing the numbness in his arm had subsided a little, and he drew his sword from the sheath. Voicing a war holler, he ran his blade into the Troll's back in line with where the heart would be. The beast gurgled, trying to catch his breath, while a cascade of green slush spurted out with each heartbeat. He wobbled twice, trying to stand steady, and fell to the ground in spasms. Then he died.

The king, still exhausted from the combat, locked eyes with his horse, and tears fell on his cheeks.

"Windfarer, my dear steed," he sniffled. "You saved my life." He stumbled through the snow and gave his stallion a long hug. Windfarer pressed his big head against his master's and snorted. All about them, the battle was raging, but as if struck by magic, no one attacked the man and his horse.

Recovered from the encounter with the Mountain Troll, the king remounted Windfarer and unsheathed his sword. When he glanced to the north, he sighted more Wolfmen on Ulves flashing across the plain; and the allies were losing their advantage, and many a good knight lost his life. On foot, Mazosians, furious in battle, slew Ulves, Wolfmen, and Birdmen alike, using bows and swords interchangeably, switching between them in a blink of an eye. Many were the enemies who hesitated to go near them. The Mountain Trolls, they saved for the Ÿadeth-Oëmin, in whom the Giants of the Mounds found worthy combatants. But after having clashed through the enemy lines at the first impact, the Gormothan resistance became stronger with their increasing numbers. The allies, yet fighting with great valor, could not hold back the charging masses of Wolfman-ridden Ulves. Once more, King Barakus' heart sank. And thus far, Azezakel had not bothered to send in the Dragons. Whether this was by arrogance or to discourage the Khanduran knights, he knew not.

Left and right, Khanduran fighters fell, coloring the snow red. Barakus, one arm strong, swung his sword with force and glory so great that it would have gone to the annals if someone had been there to engrave it. From the back of Windfarer, he beheaded, aimed, and pierced many Wolfmen on Ulves' back, and Birdmen fled when they saw his rage.

"For Khandur!" he hollered, charged with strength and power. "For the Queen of Heaven, and for the freedom of our people!" About him, his men repeated their King's war cry, and it gave them the strength they so much needed.

Then once more, the king was thrown off his saddle when an Ulv ran into Windfarer with tremendous force. The king flew and landed in the snow many paces away. The snow spun about him, but before he regained vision, he was to his feet, ready to fight to death if thus required.

This is when he saw it. In a churn of snow, something was coming in from the south. If these were enemies, the allies would be in deep trouble. Then he saw what it was, and he rejoiced. A vast assembly of horsemen galloped at great speed toward the battlefield, and some bore the Khanduran blue banner with the castle, the full moon, and the Dragon, while others rode under the Anúrian flag with the prancing unicorn on a green background.

Barakus raised his sword aloft and cried from the top of his lungs.

"Behold, the Knights of Anúria are coming to our rescue! Prince Exxarion is approaching with an immense army!"

And the Gormothan enemies heard his cry and paused in their assaults, glancing across the heath, and they sighted the horsemen in horror, for they were many. The newcomers crashed into the battlefield like an unstoppable blizzard. Tremendous was the impact when the strong Khanduran and Anúrian combined cavalries clashed weapons with the Gormothans. And they sang as they stormed forward, fearless and proud. There he stood, King Barakus of the Divine Kingdom, broad-legged in the snow, with a bloody blade in hand, watching the advancement of the incoming cavalry. And in the frontline rode his sons, side by side, in full armor—Xandur and Exxarion, swinging their swords left and right, and foes fled for their lives in many directions, unable to stand up against the wrath of the horsemen. Tears blinded King Barakus' eyes when he saw his sons united toward one sole goal; and once more, he raised his voice.

"Proud and brave Knights and Soldiers of the First and Second Cavalry of the Divine Kingdom of Khandur, assist your brothers at arms and destroy the Gormothan forces, once and for all. Victory is nigh! Woe to Azezakel, for this battle is our victory!"

As he watched with joy the advance of his two beloved sons, the King of Khandur felt the sting in his back, followed by a pain so intense that his head nearly exploded. To his knees, he fell, and warm blood poured down his back and from under his chest. His eyes went cloudy until he could barely distinguish his courageous sons riding toward him at great speed.

Father! As if from a long distance, the king heard Prince Xandur's voice calling him. Then the King of Khandur fell to his side, grunting, eyes closed, and a stream of blood poured from the side of his mouth.

—

Prince Xandur and his brother drew reins when they reached the place where the king had fallen, and they flew off their horses and crouched before his body. Xandur's heart broke into a thousand pieces when he noticed how badly wounded his father was. A Birdman's blade had pierced his back and gone through his body. Exxarion helped the king on his back, digging up a pillow of snow to elevate his head, reducing the blood streaming through his mouth.

"Father!" Xandur repeated, and he firmly grabbed the king's hand. Barakus opened his eyes, studying his sons, to and fro, with a vague smile betwixt strained coughs of blood.

"I am delighted to see the two of you together. It is too late for me to celebrate the victory to come, but you will both enjoy the New Age of Freedom… And you, Exxarion... Always proud and stubborn, having it your way. Yet perhaps that was not such a bad thing. To see you two together pleases me more than you will know. Now I can leave this world in peace."

"Father, we—" Exxarion said, but Xandur grabbed his arm and squeezed it hard. Exxarion did not complete his sentence.

"Yes, father," Xandur said. "We are riding together, and with joint effort, we shall defeat the armies of Gormoth. There is hope."

Barakus locked his cloudy eyes with Xandur's. "And you, my son, will now be King of Khandur and lead our two cavalries to victory. Effectively, you have learned your task under my supervision. I have little doubt you will bring our people to a new Golden Age and be its first king, just as Irvannion was our first king once. And during this age, I shall be the last.

"But even for me, there is joy. The pain where my arm used to sit has bothered me more than I have let you know. Soon, I will feel pain no more, and I shall join my queen and consort, who went before me."

"Father, you can yet heal," Xandur said, not noticing the tears in his eyes.

But Barakus spoke no more. His eyes were still open, but they were empty and stared into space. So died the great King Barakus of the Divine Kingdom of Khandur.

Then Prince Xandur cried. "Alas and behold! For a great king and father has fallen." And Khanduran knights who saw their king's body in death wept and cried out loud, and in their wrath, they returned to battle with new strength and purpose.

But Prince Exxarion shed no tears.

"The king is dead," he said, "but to me, he has been dead for a long time. I mourn him not, and I miss him less. For alas! I feel nothing."

Then he turned toward his brother, and he said, "So, how

do I address you now? As King Xandur?" His voice was sarcastic and chillier than the air about him.

"I care not how you address me," Xandur said. "But it bothers me you show no empathy, nor compassion. It is all about you, is it not?"

"Why must I mourn those who forsook me and supported me not, and who always put you before me? Forget him, I will, but forgive him in my heart I shall not."

"Those are bitter words, brother. I am glad our father never got to know the chasm still lingering between us two. Yet you almost told him had I not stopped you."

"What good does it do to stay here and argue? For you can never see things with my eyes. Thus, we are wasting time. The battle needs us. Out of necessity, we still must fight side by side for some time, but out of loyalty to you, my brother, it is not. My loyalty is to the Kingdom or Anúria."

Prince Exxarion remounted and buried his heels into the sides of his mare. "Hyah, hyah! Carry me well, my steed, to victory for the Kingdom of Anúria!" And into the confusion of armies, he rode off in a great hurry and was gone.

To bury him later, Xandur pulled his father's body aside and laid it to rest under a rock, where there was less chance someone would ride over him, and so he returned to the battle. Whilst galloping into the midst of action, he bent over on his horse and picked up the Khanduran banner from a fallen flag bearer, and he held it in his left hand, using his sword arm to slay wherever slaying was possible. Again, the Khandurans made progress, and astonished, the prince spotted the Ÿadeth-Oëmin on the battlefield, not knowing what they were. Relieved, he noticed they slew both Trolls and Wolfmen. Hence, they must be allies, and he welcomed them.

So great was the advancement of the cavalry that Xandur smelled victory in the breeze, albeit there were still many enemies around, and the Mountain Trolls made much damage to the lines of horsemen.

That's when he sighted the Dragons.

Discouraged, Xandur stopped, and his jaws dropped. Flying fast, they came in from the eastern mountains and reached the battlefield within a short time. There were silvery Snow Dragons of impressive size, spitting out icicles over the battlefield without distinguishing between friends and foes. And there were a few Void Dragons, targeting their victim with their pitch-black out-breaths of bottomless void and unlight, and with their in-breaths, they sucked the targets onto themselves and devoured them. But most of all, there were Fire Dragons, so ferocious and worked up that they spat fire with every breath, melting the snow on the ground and setting bodies on fire, knights and Wolfmen alike. For the Dragons, everything that moved was fair game. On the ground, Mazosians used their magic to counter the beasts, but here, at the core of Gormoth, their power was diminished, and they created no substantial damage.

The force of Dragons horrified the Khandurans and the Ÿa-deth-Oëmin, for against these beasts there was no defense, save for arrows, which made minor damage against such a force. Yet many Khanduran knights used their archery skills to target the giant reptiles in the sky, and some were successful enow to hit the beasts in the right places, and they fell, devoured by their own flames.

This always agonized me; Xandur thought to himself. *How can we defeat a force of Dragons?*

The confusion on the ground was total. Knights who had lost their horses ran into Birdmen, who fled to avoid the Dragon Fire and the icicles that were so solid, flinging with such force that they could pierce even the thickest armor.

"Woe! These beasts will kill all; friends and foes!" Xandur's voice rang over the battlefield as he watched the sky to dodge the fire cascades, the icicles, and the out-breaths of the Void Dragons.

—

Farther up north, yet many leagues from the raging battle outside Grimcast, the Nomads and the Icemen, some on sleds and others riding Frost Dragons, hurried south to help their allies from the west and from the south. Ismaril's mind was more on Sigyn than on any potential upcoming battle, for he had left her with a small group of healers and Icemen in the camp near the roots of the Iron Peaks. She had ferociously objected to being left behind, but Ismaril had insisted.

"You cannot go to battle in your condition," he said. "And we must not jeopardize the life of our baby,"

That had calmed her down, but she was not happy, and she wept.

"I hate to see you go to battle without me," she said to him. "For I know not if I shall see you again."

Then Ismaril tightened his jaws to prevent himself from weeping. He knew all too well she was right. There was no guarantee he would survive the upcoming days, but his innermost thoughts he shared not. Last, they hugged, long and hard, and he jumped on the sled. Soon, the camp and Sigyn were far behind. He tried his best not to think about their painful departure, but it was impossible to keep his focus on anything else.

Merely a few hours' ride across the plain, the army saw a flock of big birds aloft.

"Not birds," Kirbakin said. "Again, they are not birds. They are Dragons. And this time, they are not Ayasisian Dragons. These are Azezakel's beasts, and they are heading south."

Yomar's face whitened. "Then we must hurry. Our friends need our help!"

Chapter 33
Grimcast

Astéamat paced to and fro along the fence of thorny, dead boughs and branches. There were spaces between a few trees, barely enow to slip though, but with her first attempt to pass, the branches spread and closed the gap. Usbarg ran to her side.

"Let me try my club," he said.

The Giant Lord gazed about, stopping at a place of choice. He lifted his club and smashed it with swell strength in between two trees. Surprised, and with a quick scream, he dropped the club as it bounced back at him, doing no damage to the thicket. Muttering, he picked up the club and tried once more. This time, there was no surprise moment, so he kept the club in his grip. Again, it bounced off. In vain, he hit the boughs over and over, but to no avail.

"This is not working," he said, gasping. "This is not the way in."

The Queen stepped back and stretched her arms forward. Beams of energy moved through her hands into the air and hit the trees. Instantly, they lit up in many colors, but they refused to flare. As soon as she stopped projecting the energy, the trees returned to their old, dead selves again.

"There is a way," the Queen said. "There is always a way. A weakness in the magic, but I know not what it is."

"How was the magic created?" a Mazosian asked.

"This I do not know. Yet you are correct. The weakness in the magic is in the principles with which it was created. Therein the answer lies, and when we know, we have something to work with."

Astéamat looked about in many directions to avoid being assaulted by Azezakel's troops, but they were busy elsewhere, fighting off the Khanduran cavalry.

"Even if we can dissolve the magic and penetrate the fence, how do we know we can enter the castle?" Usbarg said. "Maybe there is more magic, and they can kill us all from inside Grimcast."

"There is always that possibility," the Queen said. "But I am prepared to take the chance. Knowing the Black King, he is arrogant to think the dead trees will keep him safe and us out."

But alas! Aloft, and on the incoming from northeast, the sky now filled up with Dragons, meandering, closing in on the vast battlefield there in under. The Queen's eyes, sharp as a large bird hovering high, sighted Gormothan and Ayasisian Dragons in unison, and they were many.

"Aiming for the battle," Usbarg said, for he saw them, too. "Why does Azezakel send no Dragons our way? They could easily kill us."

"He is playing with us," Astéamat said. "He enjoys the challenge of having us here to see how we proceed, feeling safe where he is."

As the Dragons swept over the battlefield and created great havoc amongst friends and foes, something remarkable befell. In the yonder, another force of gigantic Dragons occupied the sky, as many in number as the Gormothan and Ayasisian Dragons combined. Usbarg and the other Mazosians also noticed them.

Queen Astéamat smiled. "Not all Dragons are of evil. The latecomers are from way up north. They are Frost Dragons, and they are with us. This means Ismaril and the Nomads got help from the Icemen. They will even out the playing field."

In a great hurry, and on the back of the Frost Dragons, skilled Icemen approached and closed in on the battlefield. The wrath of the Frost Dragons was unmatched when they charged at their Gormothan counterparts. In groups, the Frost Dragons spat out cascades of air, so chilly that it froze the Fire Dragons as they flew, and they fell, stiff and helpless, to the ground, where they crashed. Ferocious was the battle between sky monsters on either side, and on the back of the Ayasisian Dragons, Queen Moëlia and her female warriors were positioned. Many of them fell from the sky that day together with their beasts and were dead.

A small group of Frost Dragons sighted Queen Astéamat by the tree fence and shrieked out loud to alert the Icemen riders, who immediately steered their beasts toward Grimgroves. Once they arrived, they circled aloft, and the Icemen gaged the situation, whilst Astéamat heeled them with her gaze.

Then one Iceman descended until he was close, so the Queen's group could hear him.

"Back off!" the Iceman cried from the top of his lungs. "Stay gone!"

The group on the ground removed themselves from the fence, and the Iceman gave instructions to his kins. Then, in line, several Frost Dragons flew along the fence of trees and blew massive streams of frost and winter over the dead trees. Thick layers of ice thus concealed them, and these layers grew thicker with each assault.

Then a crack. After that, yet another.

The Dragons ascended and continued circling about, whilst the trees cracked one by one. The ice covering their skeletal boughs and branches made the trees tremble when the layers fell off and broke into small pieces of glass-like, shimmering ice, splitting with tremendous force, shooting shards of ice here and there. One by one, the trees fell asunder, and branches broke off.

The Queen laughed. "Of course! That is the magic with which this wall of trees was created. Dragon magic! Azezakel used his Fire Dragons to burn the trees to death, and Ice Dragons to eternalize the fence. The Frost Dragons can undo it all..."

The cracking rumble when the entire fence breached overrode the screams and the clinking of blades crossing, arising from the battlefield. A horrendous scream of anguish soared into the air and carried on the wind northward when the spell broke, then faded into the yonder. Thereafter, the way to Grimcast laid open, and the Icemen returned to the battle to aid their comrades.

"Our time is come," the Queen said. "Let us take Grimcast!"

She drew her sword and ran toward the gate of Azezakel's fortress, heeled by the small assembly of Originals, Giants, and men.

But they could not reach all the way to the gates. Halfway,

they ran into a wall, invisible and solid as it was. Usbarg and his Giants used their strength and force and smashed the wall with their thick clubs; but the wall withstood the assault.

"Azezakel!" the Queen said, and her voice was loud and demanding. "I challenge you! Hide no more behind magic and closed gates. Come out and show yourself and prove you are as powerful as you proclaim!"

They were met by silence, and they waited. Then the Queen spoke once more.

"You cannot hide in there forever with your consort and partner in crime. Surrender both, and I might propose to spare your eternal lives and not waste them. Pull back your troops and come out as one."

After more silence, the gates suddenly flew open with a bang. An odor of death and rotten flesh swept in waves toward the occupants, penetrating the invisible wall. So strong was the stink that it caught everybody off guard, the Queen included. Then there was a cloud of smoke moving out from the gate opening, spreading over the yard, blinding them all; and their eyes stung and teared up. Then there was a swishing noise when the invisible barrier disappeared.

Out of the mist stepped Azezakel the Black, ghostlike and threatening, but he was coming alone. Amidst the mist, he stood, and he was tall, reaching as high as the tallest of the Yadeth-Oëmin. Black and shining was his armor, and despite its weight, his intimidating iron boots made no imprint in the snow. He wore no helmet, and there was only one eye on his grim face. His hand rested on the hilt of a heavy longsword, too heavy for any knight to swing. So massive and threatening was Azezakel's gestalt that many men and Giants gasped for air. Although one eye was patched, from the depth of the other, the Eternal Fire of Hell glowed.

"Look not into his eye!" Astéamat said. "Whatever you do, avoid his gaze! Only I, as the Queen of Heaven, can endure."

Then the mist dissolved, and now fully visible he stood, the King of Darkness and the Father of Abominations. Then he spoke, and his voice was deep and horrifying; yet his lips moved not.

"I fear you not, Queen of Nothing, and Mother of None. So, you think you have come to defeat me? Me? The King of

Kings?" He laughed, and the wind carried his poisonous laughter across the battlefield, creating much horror and hopelessness in both friends and enemies. "And how are you supposed to defeat me? I presume you are not so naïve as to assume I will surrender. Why would I? I am not the one at fault here. If you had left me and my sons, the Dark Kings, as you call them, alone, there would have been peace in Taëlia by now. But you turned my human children against me, and for that, there is no excuse, and no repentance."

"If these are your last words on the matter, there is no other way for me than to fight you."

"Aye, that is what it has come to. The mighty Queen NIN.AYA, known in her lesser form as Queen Astéamat, the World Mother, has once more in her pride and entitlement allowed herself to mingle with the lesser folks. But think not that she did so out of love and compassion, for neither of it does she possess. Had she not been invaded by the much mightier Ayasisians, who have now found their way home to me, she would still dwell in the lofty realm she so pridefully called Emoria."

Azezakel then turned to the group of mixed species before him.

"Only a handful of you gathered here are men," he said, and his voice softened, glossed over with a magic spell of empathy and compassion. "See you not that her loyalties are not to you, but to the abominations, such as the inferior Ÿadeth-Oëmin? For abominations they are, and as such, they should be cared for. And there are others… the Icemen, calling themselves humans, but are they? Or could they be a species favored by your 'Holy' Mother?

"Nay, your mother, she is not. If worthy of carrying the mother title, it would be as the mother of Giants and Icemen, not of humans. Come into my fold, men of Khandur, and go to where your home is; come to your true parents."

"You can fool us no more," one knight said, but his voice trembled. "We know where our loyalties are."

The Black King sighed. "This saddens me, and it will not end well, for this meager lady will bring you nothing but destruction. I wish not to fight, but if war is the sole option for saving my creation, so it shall be. Behold, my cheek is wet. See my tears falling, for it is for you that I weep."

"No!" Astéamat shouted. "Do not meet his gaze!"

But her warning came too late this time and was to no avail, for Azezakel's hypnotic voice and slick tongue had done the work. Almost all; men, Giants including Usbarg, and Mazosians alike; locked eyes with the Black King, and they instantly froze in position, unable to move an inch, and like absurd statues, they stood. Left was merely a handful of warriors who had withstood the temptation to meet Azezakel's gaze. Among them was the High Lord Usbarg.

But the Queen looked the Black King in the eye, and she flinched not; nor did his gaze affect her.

"Oops," Azezakel said. "It seems your servants are not to as much use as you thought. Now, what will you do?"

"I shall fight you, one on one," the Queen said. "You use your sorcery on those who know nothing about how it works. You are a coward, Black King."

"Coward, you say. But who is the coward, coming to my doors with an army against the two of us?"

"Then meet me alone in combat," the Queen said. "Use your magic if you will, and I shall use mine."

Azezakel laughed. "Little do you know about my powers these days. You have lost most of yours, for you have descended to this realm from that of Emoria. You are lost here, whilst this is my domain. I have gained much vigor since you saw me last."

"Enow! Let the combat begin."

A swift beam of blue energy emanated toward Azezakel from Astéamat's hand but dissolved and split in many directions when the King of Gormoth set up an invisible shield before him.

"I am not impressed," he said. "Try again!"

The Queen had merely tested her opponent. Like a boxer in the clearing, she felt her enemy out. Now, she sent higher energy toward Azezakel, and this time, it hit him in the chest. But all she heard was his laughter. The beam went right through and pierced the fortress wall behind him and split. Surprised, Astéamat backed off, for Azezakel's body dissolved before her gaze. *A projection!* she thought. The Black King was never there. But his laughter continued, echoing, desolate and hollow, between the fortress walls inside Grimcast. As if coming from the most unthinkable depths of the world, she heard his voice in the distance.

"Follow me inside, queen!" the voice echoed.

—

Not one moment too early, the Frostlands sleds reached the top of a small mound, and there, only a quarter league away, the battle was raging, and Dragons were blasting their fire and ice over the combatants. The Icemen, riding their Dragons, flew close behind the sled army, and when they sighted the disastrous situation near Grimcast, they set off in maximum speed to assist their comrades at arms, and the sled coachmen forced the large wolves to do their uttermost to speed up.

In the front seat of the first vessel, Ismaril felt the icy wind against his face as the vehicle sped up, and together with the Nomads and the Icemen about him, he drew his sword. He wished he could use Gahil, but he knew he could not. Beside him sat Raeglin, and Yomar stood up in the sled, pepping up his men in the luges following behind.

As the sled army with many warriors approached, Ismaril heard Khanduran knights cheer when they saw them coming, and the cheers were also directed toward the supporting Frost Dragons, now attacking Azezakel's beasts in the sky and on the ground. The impact when the sleds ran into the line of combatants was thunderous. The Nomads and the Icemen swung their weapons and cut enemies dead with their blades as the countless vessels, packed with soldiers, spread out in many directions.

But the battlefield was sad to witness. The Gormothan Dragons had caused great damage ere the Frost Dragons arrived, and dead Khandurans and Giants lay slain here and there, burned, or pierced by icicles; and the wounded cried out in pain. Likewise, many Wolfmen and Birdmen had met the same fate.

Suddenly, and without a warning, two Wolfmen, riding Ulves in a great rush, ran into Ismaril's sled from the side and tipped it over while it sped. Nomads, Icemen, and equipment flew hither and thither and settled in the snow. Ismaril rolled around and landed face down. He hurried to his feet, grabbed his sword in the snow, and looked about. The wolves who pulled the sled continued forward, but the sled was upside down, and not all Nomads made it out in time, and some were crushed under its weight. The survivors, some wounded, got to their feet, and Ismaril was happy to see Raeglin and Yomar among the survivors. He sat in the snow up to his shoulders, desperately looking for something.

"Ah, there is it!" he said, and his face brightened. "My flute!"

"Your flute?" Raeglin said. "You worry about flutes, while I am grateful to have my head on my shoulders." Then he scanned the battlefield. "I assume we must fight on foot from now on. And here they come…"

A group of Birdmen, squeaking with hacked voices, charged toward the sled survivors, who got busy fending off the foes. Ismaril's heart pumped up a flood of adrenaline, and the rage built up inside him. For a moment, a picture of Sigyn flashed by in his head, and he was wondering how she was doing. But he soon got too occupied to ponder. Swords clanked, arrows swooshed, and axes cut, and Ismaril beheaded two foes as they approached, then ran after a third. Their blades met, and there was clanging and clinking, moaning, and cursing. Ismaril dodged at the last moment, and an arrow from a distance opened a flesh wound on his cheek when it swooshed by. While out of balance for an instant, the Birdman saw the advantage. He ran into Ismaril with extreme force, and Ismaril flew backward and landed in the snow with the foe on top of him, and he again dropped his sword. Instinctively, he reached for Gahil's hilt, but stopped himself before he unsheathed it. He felt like he was being tested. He was forced to use his strength instead, now unarmed. The Birdman was strong, and Ismaril's stamina failed him when the bird creature's blade approached his throat. *Must get loose! He is too strong!* The blade scratched his throat. Blood pouring. Hope fading. *Sigyn, I am sorry! I failed you… I failed everyone.*

Then everything around him suddenly caught fire and stood in flames. The Birdman, badly scorched, screamed out loud with such a high pitch that it struck Ismaril's ears. The Birdman's clothes were in flames, and facing the sky, Ismaril sighted a Fire Dragon, randomly breathing his deadly flames here and there. Ismaril used his last strength and rolled the Birdman over, got up, and wrested the sword from the Birdman's hand. Without hesitation, he ran it into his enemy's heart. He found his own blade and grabbed it. Then he spun around to scan the scene. No one on the ground seemed to pay attention to him now, and he looked for what to do next.

Then he noticed the black Dragon with the red eyes, soaring low only a hundred yards ahead. On his back sat a tall man, clean shaven and with long, sandy hair. Ismaril's heartbeat doubled, and he felt dizzy, gasping for air when he realized who this man was. And he was coming his way.

Twenty paces from Ismaril, the giant black Dragon landed, flapping his wings a few times, burying his claws in the snow. The man riding him lifted his chin in contempt and locked eyes with the Lindhostan.

"Yongahur," Ismaril said, and his voice was but a whisper.

"Well met again," the Dark King said. His voice dripped from sarcasm, as usual. "I assume you must have expected to see me again sometime. Now that time is come. This is going to be between you and me."

Ismaril swallowed hard. *Not now,* he thought. *I am too tired.*

Yongahur dismounted the Dragon, who lifted his enormous head toward the sky and spat out a long, roaring cascade of fire.

"Oh, this is Guthrog the Black, by the way," Yongahur said. "My loyal pet." Guthrog turned his head toward Ismaril and took a deep breath. "No, Guthrog, do not scorch him. This is my battle, my boy. My joy. But you can stand by and watch." The Dragon growled from the back of his throat and showed his fangs. There were Wolfmen and Birdmen about, but they dared not approach the Dragon.

The Dark King loomed and stopped a few paces from his opponent, glancing at Ismaril's hilt.

"Ah, I see you are still possessing Iguhl, or what did you call the blade again? Gahil? Yes, Gahil, it is. You probably named it in a moment of pride and valor. Temporary, of course. Your courage seems to fail you now."

"You like to talk," Ismaril said.

The Dark King raised his brows. "Oh, you think I talk too much? Very well, we can do without the small talk and get to business. I was going to ask if you are ready to go to Hell, Ismaril Farrider, but the truth is you have no choice, and I do not care. Yet, why don't you show me what you can do with Iguhl?"

Then he drew his own sword, and blue and white flames emanated from its blade. Ismaril grabbed his hilt with both hands.

"No, no... scout. For that is all you are, am I correct? A scout, and a bad one at it. You are grabbing the wrong blade. Throw it aside. I want to see Iguhl."

"Then I must disappoint you. Gahil stays in its sheath, and you know very well why that is."

"Perhaps, but it would be the height of foolishness to fight me with a regular blade. With that toy, you can do nothing."

In his peripheral, he noticed Raeglin running in his direction with sword in hand, coming to aid. Yongahur saw him, too, and without looking his way, he raised his hand toward the pilgrim. Raeglin stopped in his tracks and flew back a hundred paces through the air, landing amid a group of Wolfmen.

"Does he not understand this is between you and me?" Yongahur said. "Draw your blade, Ismaril! I command you!"

Ismaril said nil, leaned forward, rocking from side to side with legs apart, still with both hands on the hilt of his sword. Focused.

"You coward!" Yongahur cried and charged. One sweep with the fiery sword, and Ismaril's blade broke at the hilt. The Dark King laughed. "See? What are you going to do now when Iguhl is your only weapon?"

"Not the *only* weapon," Ismaril said and pulled up a long knife, stuck into his belt. Yongahur sighed and lowered his burning sword.

"You must be joking."

"You want me to use Gahil, but I will not. This means you cannot kill me."

"Kill you? No. Doing something worse than that? Aye!"

Again, the Dark King raised his sword, ready to charge, but before he took his first step, he paused and listened, as if someone was talking to him. Then he sniffed about and sheathed his blade. Quickly, he returned to Guthrog and mounted.

"We shall meet again very soon," Yongahur said to Ismaril. "Now, a more important duty is calling for me. Yet prepare, for your hours are numbered."

Then Guthrog ascended and rushed to the east.

Chapter 34
Divine Combat

ASTÉAMAT, HEELED BY a dozen Mazosians, five Ÿadeth-Oëmin, and four Khanduran knights, stepped inside the Grimcast fortress. From the group that had passed through the hedge of dead trees, they were the only ones to avoid Azezakel's gaze. Now, they were watching their steps, walking down the main hall inside the fortress, illuminated by flickering lights from torches stuck into holders on the walls.

Soon, the Queen sighted a short stairwell, which appeared to be the only way forward, and she moved toward it. But before she reached there, she heard swishing noises behind her; and there were screams of pain and anguish.

From the walls, long metal blades swooshed out on either side and hit the intruders before the blades swiftly returned into the walls again and vanished. *The hallway was booby-trapped!* In horror, Astéamat saw her group of courageous warriors falling, and there was blood everywhere. Farther away, the gates slammed shut. The trap was closed.

The small surviving group, comprising the Queen, a Mazosian warrior, and a knight, watched the massacre in a trance, barely breeding, and they were all in tears.

"Alas!" the knight said. "Azezakel has much to count for. But how are we to defeat the Black King now with a group of four?"

"Let not fear possess you," the Mazosian said. "Mind you, we have the Queen among us. She is not impotent."

"Behold the walls on either side," the knight said. "There are cracks. The blades inside did not trigger. We were spared!"

"Or *I* was spared," the Queen said. "You merely befell to be near me. That saved your lives. It is me Azezakel wants to see."

"But why, when he had the chance to kill you?"

"As aforementioned, he is fond of playing games with what he considers his prey. And I am his prime victim." Then she glanced across the hall. "There is nothing we can do for our poor companions. No one survived the insult. From here, there is only one direction to go, and that is forward. Follow me and stay close."

The assembly walked up the short stairwell and landed in a small open area, dark, empty, and gloomy. A sparse window in the rear let a beam of sunlight in, illuminating a spot on the floor, dust reflecting in its pale luminescence. The odor of dead flesh hit them harder here, and a wave of nausea rushed through Astéamat.

Before them, two hallways continued farther into the castle: one leading left and one leading right. Dark and menacing, they stared at them like two hollow eyes, ready to swallow them up. Suddenly, the right hall was lit up by torches, flaring up with a swish, but no one special had set them alight.

The knight scoffed. "More cheap magic."

"Not so cheap," the Queen said. "He fooled us all when his apparition appeared outside. Think what you will of Azezakel, but for your own safety, underestimate him not."

The foursome, with weapons drawn, entered the hall. Here, everything was iron made, and walls, floors, and ceilings, and carved statues of malicious-looking Gargoyles and other horned monsters decorated the walls, holding onto the torches.

Then Azezakel's low-pitched voice rolled and rumbled through the hall.

"Almost there! Come forth, and fear not. I will not bite you."

The Queen stopped and turned around. "Remember to not meet his gaze," she said.

And so, the four companions stepped into the Black King's chamber. The apparition he had projected outside had been horrifying and threatening, but no one doubted that this was the real Azezakel, sitting on his massive Iron Throne. In his chamber, everything was of black iron, including the Throne and the King's armor. The chamber was sparsely lit by only a few torches placed in each corner of his hall, held by tall statues of sneering Gargoyles. The flickering from the fire created a ghostly atmosphere. Mixed with the foul odor and with the massive man on the Throne, it was an act of tremendous valor for the visitors to remain in the chamber. Yet none of the three would have had the courage to stay if the Queen had not been present.

Astéamat placed herself before the group to protect them. Then she locked eyes with the Black King.

"You are alone," she said. "Where is Ishtanagul?"

Azezakel laughed dryly. "Tricked again, I hear. The Queen is not here, and I need her not. She is still residing in the Nether Regions, the Underworld, ready to welcome you all personally when I am done with you."

"Showing your true face, at last," the Queen said.

"Or not. I told you I wanted peace, did I not? You refused my offer, and so we are at war. Wars are messy by necessity, but we can stop it at any time if you change your mind and cooperate. If this war continues to the bitter end, it is your responsibility, not mine. In battle, you have your methods, and I have mine. I might save your knight from the Eternal Fire because he is human, but the rest of you... Think this over thoroughly, former Queen of Emoria, for the consequences of opposing me are severe."

"You scare me not, Lord of Abominations. Your words reveal only your own fear. In me, there is none. Hence, I will give *you* the ultimatum once more: Surrender and I will look kindlier upon my judgment of you and your kind."

Then Azezakel stood. A flood of malice swept through the chamber, and the torches flared up and hissed like vipers. The Queen could almost have sworn the iron Gargoyles moved a little. Her companions gasped and stepped back, for so vicious was the King's appearance that the otherwise courageous warriors hid inside themselves like children.

"Then I challenge you," Azezakel thundered. "Show me your magic, Queen of Nothing! Feel this!"

And the Black King shot out a ball of swirling fire from his hand, aiming at Astéamat. She swiftly put up a shield bubble, and the flames dispersed and went out. The Queen countered with two bolts of lightning, hitting a shield akin to her own. A few mutual blasts buzzed through the air until they both realized they were equally powerful.

Like an enraged, gigantic bear, Azezakel roared, and he manifested a long, flaming chain he rotated above his head.

"These are the Flames of Hell! In these I shall frame you and send you into the Eternal Fire!"

Then he swung the enormous chain to capture the Queen. Once more, she set up the shield, and the chain rotated many turns around her bubble, but she withstood. Azezakel pulled the chain tighter around her cloak of magic and kept it there. The Queen noticed her energy bubble weaken. *I must get loose! My power is lessened… my strength is failing.* She closed her eyes and took the deepest breath she could accomplish. Then she screamed out from the depth of her voice, and it vibrated through the hall and shook her energy bubble, which began to vibrate faster and faster. She kept screaming. Then the bubble burst, and powerful energy was released and splashed like water dispersing from an exploding balloon. The chain of fire rattled and vibrated until one link broke, and the entire chain dissolved into thin air. The King flew back from the impact, but still stood. Still gasping for air, the Queen sent another lightning bolt toward her opponent while he was caught off-guard. The bolt hit Azezakel in the chest, and he fell to the floor, yelling in pain. Smoke arose from his armor, and he lay still. The bystanders gasped.

"Stay put!" the Queen told them. "This is my fight!"

She stepped forward, closing in on the fallen king, but she was prepared when he levitated into an upright position in a flash and drew a long, evil blade, glowing in red from dripping blood. Astéamat pulled her own blade, which glowed in blue and white, cold as ice to touch.

With great force, the Queen charged, and the two weapons clanked, sparks flowing.

"Hell is close! Prepare!"

The two Divine warriors fought ferociously. Azezakel swung his blade with an enormous strength, creating ripples in the air; but the Queen dodged, and he missed his target. She waited for the right moment, and when the King's chest was exposed betwixt two assaults, she pierced her cold steel swiftly. Once more, she hit his chest. Clank! The magic blade went through the armor and into his flesh. He screamed out loud and backed off. Black blood fell down his torso and hit the floor, where it evaporated with a hissing noise. He stumbled and put his hand over the wound, but then he stood tall again, now in a great rage.

"This is the only hit you will get on me!"

Yelling, he charged, and the two blades collided. His red sword splashed out blood from the blade, hitting Astéamat's eyes, blinding her. Realizing the danger she faced, she furiously wiped her eyes to get rid of the blood, but it was thick and sticky. Then she felt the sting in her stomach area. She was hit, and it was bad. Behind her, the bystanders cried out in anguish.

When she regained her eyesight, she saw Azezakel standing before him with a grin on his face. The Queen stumbled backward, sensing the warmth of her blood spreading through her garment, and she fell on her back. The world was spinning, and she lost her strength. *I wish I could have done better,* she thought. *I must find strength. I must complete…*

But she was too weak to stand. The knight and the Mazosian helped her sit against the wall, and they stayed with her. The gigantic Black King stood over them, pointing his blade at Astéamat. Then he spoke.

"Little did I know you were so easy to defeat. Tell me now, Astéamat, whether I am worthy of the title King of the Universe? No one can defeat Azezakel the Black!" Then his face turned stern and malicious. "Now I am bored with this game. It is time for you to go to Hell, queen."

Astéamat's three companions stood before their Queen with their weapons drawn to protect her from the Black King's demonic blade, ready to take the piercing for her, which Azezakel seemed not to mind. He raised his weapon to charge when he suddenly paused, and an expression of surprise came upon his face. He took a few steps back and put his hands against his temples.

"What… is happening?" he said, and there was a desperate tone in his voice. "I… I am getting weaker." The sword he held split into many pieces and vanished until only the hilt remained in his grip. He dropped it on the floor. "Something is wrong! My Dragons! What is happening to my Dragons? I feel them less. In them, I store my power. I am losing my magic. Yongahur! I summon thee! Assist me!"

Then Astéamat found the strength she had sought, and she raised her arms. "I told you your reign is over," she said, and a wave of vibrating energy hit the wall behind Azezakel. A thick fog was forming in the air, and it swirled faster and faster, until it formed a black hole in the midst. A massive force of energy pulled air into the gaping hole, and helplessly, Azezakel was drawn into it. He screamed in terror, but he was too weak to withstand the pull. "Noo…!" Then he disappeared into the hole and was gone. His scream in agony faded, the hole closed, and the cloud vanished.

The Queen sighed and closed her eyes. This act had taken everything she had left out of her. The knight rushed to a torch and put the blade of a knife into the fire to heat it up. Soon, he returned to the Queen and put the heated blade against her wound. The pain was excruciating, and the smell of burnt flesh spread through the hall. But it stopped the bleeding.

When the Queen had recovered from the worst immediate pain, the knight asked, "What happened?"

"I opened a gateway," Astéamat whispered. "A gateway to the deepest depth of Hell. There he shall stay until the end of all time with no chance of escape. That will be his destiny and his fate. Azezakel will not bother us again. I saw my chance, for he was weak enow to succumb."

Then she studied her friends, one by one, and she said, "The King is gone, but we have yet to gain victory. The war is raging, and the Dark Kings are still out there."

Then she lost consciousness.

Chapter 35
The Dragon Whisperer

NAISHA, THE FORMER SEER of the Ayasis Court, rode in the lead together with Princes Xandur and Exxarion. As fast as their steeds could take them, they rode to battle at the Fields of Treshandor. But when they left the mountains and were down on the plains, Naisha drew reins and stopped her mare, letting the rest of the army pass. Alone, and out in the open, she gazed at the sky.

A deep sadness filled her up when she sighted the Ayasisian Dragons in the air, high above, soaring over the battlefield in cahoots with the Dragons of Gormoth. There, one of them fell, and there fell another. She could not distinguish who was who, but they were all her friends, and she dearly loved them all. She knew them so well, and they would never team up with Azezakel of their own freewill; but they were loyal to Queen Moëlia, for in such a manner, they were raised and bred. These Dragons had their own minds, but when the queen so demanded, they must obey—thusly they were trained.

Instead of catching up with the Khanduran and Anúrian troops, Naisha chose another route. At a slow pace, she let her horse plod through the snow with great effort, in a north-westward direction. The Seer knew not what to do, but she was drawn to the Dragons. Were they still friendly toward her? If the Queen viewed her as a traitor, how would the Dragon treat her? She cared not, and she wished not to fight this ridiculous war anymore. All she wanted was to play with the Dragons, ride them, and hug their scaly heads. If they killed her out of loyalty to the Queen, so be it. She would rather let them kill her than some abominable Wolfman. This war was not for her.

Amidst the plain, she came to a halt. The snow was deep, and her steed was exhausted from plodding through it, braying and snorting. Again, Naisha gazed at the Dragons above. She felt a sting in her stomach. *I hope she is alive. Dear Goddess, may she still be among the living!* Then she hollered, and her voice transferred over the long and wide heaths.

"Cloudwing!"

She repeated her favorite Dragon's name once more, then glanced aloft in silence. The Ayasisian Dragons were there still, easily sighted. Suddenly, in from the south, separate from the rest, a solitary red Dragon came flying in. Naisha held her breath. Was this possible? Then the lonesome Dragon wobbled in the air and halfway spun around to join its companions. Someone was riding it, trying to steer the beast back to the battle. Despite the effort, the Dragon, seemingly by its own will, continued flying toward Naisha. Closer and closer, the Dragon came and soared and circled above the Seer.

Naisha could see the Dragon clearly now.

"Cloudwing! Is this really you?"

Naisha wept a flood of tears, trying to see through them. She could not. But she heard Cloudwing crying out loud, like any animal when they reunite with a beloved friend. Yet on her back, an Ayasisian warrior screamed unintelligible commands. The Dragon seemed not to care, and she landed close to Naisha in a swirl of snow.

When the snow had once again landed, Naisha noticed who the rider was. It came as no surprise, for Cloudwing was the Dragon of Dragons in the Queendom of Ayasis, loved by everyone.

"Queen Moëlia!" Naisha said.

The Queen drew her sword. "How dare you?" she said. "You, the greatest traitor in the Queendom's history, got the nerve to call upon my Dragon?"

Cloudwing, capable of speaking, yet finding no words, had big, blue tears falling down her scaly cheeks when she locked eyes with her beloved Naisha. It was obvious two loyalties drew her.

Naisha dismounted and kneeled in the snow before Moëlia. "My Queen."

"What are you doing? I am not your Queen anymore. I have expelled you from the Queendom, and you know it. Of all enemies I have, you are the worst, for in you, I trusted."

Naisha stood. "And you still would if Gormoth had not gotten Ayasis under its black cape. Was I the only one seeing through the deception? Really? My Queen, can you not see you are under a spell or worse?"

"Such are the words of a traitor," Moëlia said. "I will never forgive you, not now or future-wise. For stories will be told about you that generations ahead will remember. Children will ask their mothers to tell the story about Naisha, the traitor, who allied with Khandur." She stopped, looking for the impact. When none came, she said, "Now you must die, and I will go on records as your slayer."

Queen Moëlia dismounted Cloudwing and approached Naisha.

"My Queen, do not proceed!" Naisha said. "For you know not what you are doing. The Messenger sent by King Azezakel put a spell on you, the Inner Court, and maybe the rest of the Ayasis population, from what I can tell. You are the only one who can break it. If you do, the spell might break for all the Ayasis warriors, too, and they will see the truth. Azezakel is a trickster! Please come to your senses."

Naisha breathed heavily when she saw the Queen, whom she still loved, approach her with a blade drawn, and with a trancelike face expression.

"No, this is so wrong!" Naisha cried out. "I cannot fight my Queen, whom I have respected and consulted my entire life. Like a mother, you have always been to me, and you are my protector and guide. Sheath your sword. I beg you, sheath your sword…"

"I shall sheath my sword, but not until you lie dead in your own blood in the snow, slain by my very blade."

Naisha backed off at the same pace the queen approached, with own blade drawn.

"Kill me if you must," Naisha said, "for I cannot fight or slay you. For this is not you. Please wake up! There is still time."

Moëlia said nil. Instead, she sped up her pace, plodding through the snow, which was reaching up to her knees.

Then she charged. Two blades clanged and echoed through the silence. The Queen approached with great power, and Naisha saw in her eyes she would not leave until one of them stopped breathing. Naisha met the charges, blocking the Queen's assaults, but she did not charge back. Queen Moëlia continued slamming her blade against Naisha's, but managed not to create any damage. The Seer felt the impact of every hit against her blade, and slowly, her energy depleted.

Naisha missed the rock that stuck up above the snow as she backed off, and she found herself suddenly on her back in the snow. Moëlia hollered, ready to put the final piercing into Naisha's body.

"Do it!" Naisha said between clinched teeth. "If you must, do it. I will not fight you."

Queen Moëlia yelled, out of mind, like a wild beast, grabbed the hilt of her sword with both hands, and pointed the edge of the blade toward Naisha's chest to give her the final blow. Naisha saw the crazy eyes of the leader she had adored, and she closed her eyes, ready to die. *So be it. There is no future for me or for this world. It is all lost.*

But the sting from the Queen's sword did not come. Instead, Naisha heard a loud roar, and as a Seer, she perceived the powerful energies from a beast charging toward its prey. Then there was a terrifying scream of pain.

Naisha opened her eyes. Above her, she saw the wings of Cloudwing hovering over her, and trapped in the Dragon's jaws was the Queen of Ayasis. The Dragon roared, the Queen screamed, and blood splashed when Cloudwing bit across the Queen's torso. Moëlia gurgled helplessly, being at the mercy of the Dragon.

"Cloudwing! No!"

It was too late. Cloudwing had torn Moëlia's body almost in half. The Queen of Ayasis lay on the ground and moved no more. The Queen was dead.

Naisha got on her feet and ran toward the Dragon and the slain Ayasis Queen. Confused, she knew not where to start. Then she looked at Cloudwing and noticed that the Dragon wept.

"Cloudwing, why are you crying?"

Then the Dragon spoke for the first time. "She was my Queen, too. But I kept my word to Ishtarion."

Naisha dropped her sword in the snow and ran toward her favorite Dragon and hugged her with all her might. And thus, they wept together. But as they soon would realize, not all tears are of evil.

"Well met, Naisha," Cloudwing said. "No day has passed without me thinking of you. There is no Dragon of the Ayasis Court who wishes to join forces with Azezakel. But my brothers and sisters have been bound by duty. Now, the Queen is no more, and we are free. I believe the spell is broken. Ride me, Naisha, and let us regroup against Azezakel and his armies. Let us join against the Dragons of Gormoth. To behold! There are more of our species flying in from the northwest, and they are not friends of Gormoth."

Naisha hugged her horse and whispered into her ear. Then she smacked her buttock, and off she ran.

"You and I shall be together until death separates us," Naisha said to Cloudwing and mounted her. "Where are we going?"

"I am afraid we must go to war," the Dragon said. "Little did I know, but I think we must war for peace!"

Naisha mounted the Dragon, but before they took off, she uttered, "The winds are changing. Something is happening, and it is not of evil."

"So it is, Mighty Seer. The Dragons of Ayasis are changing course. Beware, Gormoth, for you have lost a powerful ally."

"But how do the Dragons know…?"

"They knew all the time, and you know that. We Dragons are loyal to the Court, but the Court and the people of Ayasis are waking up. The curse the Messenger put upon them is broken, for the anchor that held the curse intact was Queen Moëlia. Now that she is dead, your people can again see things as they are. Once more, you have your own people behind you."

Naisha smiled, but her smile was not merely of joy. This was good news, but Moëlia did not deserve her destiny.

"I think I will remain here with the Queen for a moment," Naisha said. "Stay with me for a while, Cloudwing, before we go."

Chapter 36
At the Camp

IN THE CAMP, LEAGUES AWAY from the intense battle, the group of Icemen (healers and guards) roamed to watch over Sigyn. Also amongst them were Zale and Kirbakin.

Sigyn lay in her bed, staring absently at the tent ceiling, for her mind was inattentive and with Ismaril. Although the baby growing inside her was precious to her, so was her man, and whilst praising the unborn, she also cursed the fact she could not be present as Ismaril's shield maiden. She was too weak. In a fleeting moment, she thought of sneaking past the guards, taking one of the few horses, and following in the path of the others, but she knew it would be foolish.

Her troubled mind cooled when the Gnome entered her tent. He sat down on the floor, at her side, with his legs crossed, looking into her eyes. His own eyes sparkled in the mischievous way that was so typical for him.

"Sigyn Archesdaughter, milady," he said and bowed where he sat. "How are you feeling today?"

"Much better now when you are here," she said, and the smile remained. "Any news at all from the battle?"

Kirbakin shook his head, "Nay, not much. We know very little, but the Frost Dragons chased off the Dragons of Ayasis, and now we have spotted clusters of Dragons farther away and closer to Grimcast, we believe. But it is impossible to distinguish between them."

~ At the Camp ~

Then he was silent and watched her again. She could pick up his worries and concerns regarding her and her health, but he said nothing about it. She laid her hand over his.

"Worry not," she said, trying to sound cheerful. "I shall be fine." But inside, she shared his worries, for something felt not right about her. It was as if the unborn was eating her. This was her first pregnancy, so perhaps it was normal, after all.

Then Kirbakin took his flute and played. Sigyn closed her eyes, and beautiful notes filled the tent, and so emotional and colorful were they that the young lady felt as if she was hovering outside her body, and her soul spread out across the entire tent and expanded to the outside. High she flew onto the mountains yonder, and all the while, the magnificent flute melody followed her and embraced her; and she and the music became as one. Her essence was so blissful and carefree. There was nothing that concerned her, for nothing could touch her. If she might only stay in this state forever...

It is astonishing, for I can fly; she thought, *and I can go anywhere.* This filled her soul with laughter, but it could not be heard, except by her, for here she had no physical body that could make a sound. Yet somewhere inside, she heard herself laugh.

Then she got the idea of hurrying over to the battlefield. Barely had she thought it ere she was there, flying high above the plain. Down there, it was turmoil. Soldiers, knights, Mazosians, Giants, and in the mix, many abominable creatures fighting for the Dark Land crowded the battlefield. Then a sting of anxiety, and the flute music sounded more distant. Her magnificent thoughts turned desperate, for she tried to find Ismaril in the chaos. Where was he? In great anguish, she watched combatants die here, and she saw their confused souls leave their slain, mutilated bodies. *Ismaril!* she cried out, although she knew he could not hear her if he was still among the living.

There he was, standing amid the chaos, close to a tipped-over sled. And there were Raeglin and Yomar, but she barely noticed them. Her focus stayed on Ismaril.

Swoosh! A gigantic black Dragon swept close to her and landed on the field near Ismaril.

Yongahur!

Briefly, Sigyn picked up on the Dark King's thoughts, for it seemed he noticed her soul-presence but ignored her. She tried to catch Ismaril's attention, but he heard her not. The flute music surrounding her turned darker, and fleetingly she wondered why Kirbakin had changed the tune so dramatically. Or had he? Maybe she was the one who changed it? She could not tell.

Then there was a strong pull, and she knew her soul was being called back to her body. With all her might, she resisted it, for she wished not to leave. If she could not be his shield maiden, at least she wanted to be at his side, whether he knew it and could see or sense her. Yet the pull was too strong to fight, and ere her essence flew off from the battlefield, she noticed another skirmish in the distance, and it was fought in the air. Thither, many Dragons battled: There were a great many Frost Dragons present, and a good number of Ayasis Dragons, and they all joined to defeat the vicious Dragons of Gormoth. And it seemed they were victorious. Why had the Ayasis beasts suddenly switched sides?

These were her thoughts when she returned to her body. She gasped for air with eyes wide, and once more, she experienced the pain and discomfort of the flesh; and she wanted nothing more than to return to being her essence. The flute music had stopped and was no more, but the Gnome was still by her side.

Sigyn sat up in her bed, breathing heavily, squeezing her fists around her blanket.

"Why did you bring me back?" she cried. "I saw him!"

"You saw who?"

"Ismaril, of course! He was there on the battlefield, fighting Yongahur. Now I know not whether he survived. Please send me back, Kirbakin."

The Gnome grabbed Sigyn's shoulders and gently forced her back into her bed. "I sent you nowhere," he said. "You merely responded to my flute. Aye, magical it is, but those who hear me play react differently. I meant for you not to go to the battlefield; that was your own choice. I shall not play more now, for you must not return to the combat zone again. It will only harm you in your situation, milady. Whatever you see there will be of evil, and we must focus on your healing. Anxiety is the worst hurdle to healing."

Sigyn sighed and closed her eyes. Tears wet her cheeks, but she knew Kirbakin was right. He kissed her forehead and left the tent when the healer entered.

"I will be back," the Gnome said.

~ At the Camp ~

Zale, sitting on a stone, rocking to and fro, noticed Kirbakin leaving Sigyn's tent and coming his way. He was uncertain whether he wanted company, fighting his inner battles more than the battle befalling outside. When standing before him where he sat, the Gnome's eyes were in line with his own.

"Zale, you are avoiding us," Kirbakin said. "How can I help?"

Zale kept rocking, facing the ground before his feet. His discomfort was excruciating, as if torn between two worlds, and betwixt there was a looming darkness, a sense of doom that wished to eat him from inside. He recalled the time with the Gnome before he lost his mind after going through the portal, but now he felt nothing. There was no affection, no compassion, and no love or empathy was there inside him. He cared not whether Ismaril would come back alive, and for Sigyn and her condition, he felt none. He had not visited her since Ismaril left. Yet his shame and guilt for not feeling anything was more intense than anything, and it gnawed upon him. He put his hands over his ears, and he wailed, "Alas! I know not how to rid myself of the curse that is upon me. I no longer care whether I live or die."

The Gnome put his little gnarled hand on the tall man's arm. Once, being so strong and muscular when they met last, Zale was now skin and bones. He wished himself back to Merriwater, where life was simpler. But he could not return—not in the shape he was in. He trusted no one, and least of all himself.

"Bear with it," Kirbakin said. "You are among friends now, and things will improve. Hoodlum is not who you are, my friend. Let Hoodlum find rest deep inside and let the true Zale come out. Each one of us is important in these devastating times."

"Yet I am sitting here being useless. I can do nothing to protect Sigyn, and you know it. I can do little in battle in the shape I am in. You should put me in a cage where I belong, for like an animal I am, and I know not how to rid myself of my torment."

"Be patient, my friend. Your time will come. Remain here with us and wait. I sense a purpose in you that is greater than both you and I can think of."

"No need to cheer me up, old Gnome. But I could use some of your music, nonetheless."

Kirbakin smiled and pulled up his flute, swung it through the air, and chuckled.

"Is there any better healing than this?"

Now he played a very different tune from before. It was upbeat and in a major key, with sharp notes heightening the etheric experience. After only a few bars, Zale stopped rocking and tuned into the music. Something inside him ripped apart, and he could more clearly see the two aspects of himself: his true identity versus the lie. But he still knew not which of the two he preferred. Both were safe in their unique ways. And he realized it was all about survival, and survival alone.

Then the flute melody took him elsewhere. Despite the upbeat, his mood sank into the deep, dark waters inside; and suddenly, he perceived the song as being dark and heavy, rippling the ocean of blackness that was weighing on him, and voices demanded attention. *My true course is Divine;* the voice of Zale said. *We are the Grimms, and we follow your commands—just tell us!* said the Hoodlum inside. *Tell us, and we shall destroy this camp… camp… camp!* Zale breathed heavily and started rocking again. *No!* he said. *I cannot kill Sigyn or Kirbakin. They are my friends!* But the voice of Hoodlum continued, *We, the Grimms, are thy friends and servants. Forget that not! Once you called us from the Beyond, and here we are. We shall help you gain control over everything. Let us serve, and no one can touch you. You are invincible, but only through us. Use us not, and death will come. Then we cannot help you, for then you are at the mercy of the Queen of the Nether, and she is a harsh judge. Rid yourself of all those about you, for they serve you not. Azezakel and her Bride are the only ones who can give you eternal power. Keep serving them, and you will…*

"Stop it! Stop the music!" Zale cried and lashed out at Kirbakin. In great fury, eyes wild, his hands got new strengths and tightened around the Gnome's neck. Kirbakin dropped his flute in the snow, taken by surprise. But a Gnome without his flute is not yet incapacitated. A whirlwind of earthbound energy sped up around him, and it spun with immense force in a circle, encompassing him, making Zale lose his grip. The Gnome was slung backward, landing a few feet from his abuser. Zale stood and ran to aid.

"I am so sorry," he said. "I knew not what I was doing."

Kirbakin got to his feet and brushed off the snow. "No harm

≈ At the Camp ≈

done, so long as I can find my flute."

Zale turned around, looking left and right until he found the instrument sticking up in the snow. He brushed it off and handed it back to the Gnome.

"Please leave me," Zale said. "I am dangerous."

"So am I, and so are we all," Kirbakin said. "I simply played the wrong tune. I am not too savvy with Azezakel's spells."

Then Zale gazed to the east, and his senses were on alert.

"Kirbakin, something is coming... It's coming our way, and it is southbound, rushing from the north," he said.

The Gnome froze and strengthened his senses. "Aye, I feel it. But whoever it is, it knows not we are here."

"But they will..."

Thus, they sat in each other's company until the sun had changed position. Then Zale said, "They have stopped. They are following a trail, but someone powerful can sense we are here, and they have halted."

The Gnome swallowed, thinking about Sigyn. Was she still safe?

"Aye! They are coming here," Zale said. "Gormoth troops. Few, but enough to defeat us."

"We must leave," Kirbakin said. "Or we will succumb. But no, it is too late..."

Again, Zale was torn. His first instinct was to protect their camp, but a yearning inside made him wish to join the intruders. And there were those voices once more. Grimms talking. *Destroy the camp!*

"Zale," the Gnome said. "Who are they? I cannot tell."

"Werewolf in charge," Zale said, half in a trance. "Wolfmen, Ulves. Too many..."

"How do you know?" Kirbakin asked. "I have good eyesight, but yours exceeds mine."

"Something I gained. Part of the curse, I reckon."

The Gnome ran back on his short legs to warn the others and prepare to leave or prepare for battle, but Zale sat solidly on his stone, facing the approaching enemy. His mind was wrenched between two loyalties, and he clenched his fists in frustration.

The Gormothan company quickly came closer. Behind Zale, all Icemen in the camp lined up, carrying giant shields and long swords, worthy of their stature, but they were few, less than seventy-five, with the approaching army numbering at least twice as many, half of them riding Ulves. Most impressive was the leader of the army: a Werewolf, almost twice the size of a full-grown man. Thick, brown fur covered his body, and his head and face resembled that of a monstrous wolf with eyes focused on prey. In one hand he held a long sword, and in the other a heavy club made of the most robust iron, and over his shoulder rested a long-bow. He and his army halted a couple of hundred paces from the Icemen, and their commander had a vicious grin on his face.

"I am Hútlof, Commander of the Watchtower," he said in a hissing voice. "You are trespassing into Gormoth, for I have not given you permission to enter." Then he studied the Icemen, curiously. "Never have I seen your kind before," he said. "You are not human. Who are you and why are you here?"

Then one Iceman stepped forward, and his name was Úk. He said, "We are Icemen of the North, and gates to Gormoth were open. No one guarding Watchtower."

"It may be so," Hútlof said, "but why does that give you the right to trespass? And what is your errand here?"

"No one on watch, so we take shortcut to Wasteforge. We come from Eshamblin, other side of Bay of Aldaer, trading in furs. Winter soon upon all. We might have merchandise for Wasteforgers, too, so we go there." This was a blunt lie, but all Úk could come up with at this crucial moment.

"Which side are you on, Iceman? Do you support the false goddess or the King of Kings?"

"Neither. A peaceful people are we, wanting merely solitude and peace. We care not about world's sorrows. We only passing through."

The Werewolf studied them suspiciously. "Peaceful, say you? Why then those weapons?"

"Roads dangerous. Must defend."

"And what about that one?" Hútlof pointed at Zale. "He is a human."

"I am," Zale said. "I was wondering aimlessly when the Icemen found me and took care of me. There are great healers among them. I have since then joined them." This was true.

The Werewolf came forth alone and inspected the line of Icemen. Then he turned to Úk again.

"I am looking for two humans," he said. "A male and a

At the Camp

female. That one over there does not fit the description. Their names are Ismaril Farrider and Sigyn Archesdaughter, and they are from Lindhost, south of here. If you can give us any tips, we might let you continue your journey through our Kingdom. Any knowledge of their whereabouts?"

Zale swallowed. Apparently, this monster and his army knew not that Ismaril was already in the battle only a few leagues off. At least Zale had now chosen his allegiance.

"We know of no such humans," Úk said. "This the only human we met on the road."

"And where is your trade?"

"All sold."

Hútlof scoffed. "Not a single fur left for sale? Very well. Show me the payment for the furs."

Úk was silent. He knew not what to say. Then Zale stood up and he said, "Food. They paid us with food and weapons."

The Werewolf approached Zale and lifted him by the neck as if he weighed nothing.

"There is something odd with you people," the Werewolf said and dropped Zale. Then the hairy monster turned to the line of Icemen.

"Let us through," he said. "We shall investigate your camp before we let you continue."

Zale was desperate. This must not happen, or they would find Sigyn in her tent, and the Werewolf knew what she looked like. If they found her, it was the end of them all.

"We sorry," Úk said. "This our camp. We allow you not to come in." And the wall of the Icemen got tighter. Hútlof turned and walked back toward his army. Halfway there, he spun around once more, raised his sword, and burst out, "Kill them all, and then we shall investigate. They are hiding something. Charge!"

Thus, the battle was raging. The two small armies clashed. There were moaning, roaring, screams, and clanking of weapons. Ulves were growling, and Wolfmen cursing. About him, Zale saw Iceman upon Iceman fall, pierced by swords and arrows from Ulv riders. The Werewolf broke through the line like a tornado, swinging both his weapons left and right, creating a passageway through the Iceman army. Soon, he broke through and rushed into the camp.

"Noo!" Zale rushed after him, attempting to aid Sigyn, who

most likely was alone in there, or perhaps in the company of a healer. He saw Hútlof ripping apart one tent after another, looking for whatever he could find. Zale took a shortcut and stopped near Sigyn's tent, hiding behind another tent close by, ready to confront the Werewolf if he came that way.

And there he was.

The monster had ripped every tent apart on his way through the camp, and now he closed in on Sigyn's. Zale jumped out and stood guard in front of Sigyn's tent.

"Here, but no further," he said with his blade pointed toward Hútlof. The Werewolf stopped for a moment, surprised, and then he laughed.

"Ah. So, the treasures are in *that* tent. Step aside, or I will chop you into a hundred pieces and spread you over the camp!"

"You must fight me first!"

"One man alone against me? Save your skin and run if you have any sense."

"Not alone," said a voice from inside a tent. But it was no man's voice; it was female. In the tent opening, Sigyn stood, pale and sickly, with her blade drawn. And beside her stood her healer with an arrow attached to his bowstring.

Hútlof's voice brightened up. "Look at this," he said. "It is my lucky day. Who do we have here if not Sigyn Archesdaughter? I had expected to find nothing, or perhaps some gold and silver at the most, but I found a much greater treasure. And behold, you are pregnant. Only Farrider is missing. I suggest he is in the tent. Is he a coward, sending out his woman?"

"I am his shield maiden," Sigyn said, and her voice was proud, although her face was dripping from sweat and fever. "Ismaril is not here."

"Then step aside, all of you, so I can approach. Obviously, I do not believe you. I shall be greatly rewarded when I come to Grimcast with my booty, and my failures will be forgiven. I need Ismaril alive, but I have no instructions about you, Sigyn Archesdaughter, or your unborn."

"Back off," the healer cried, "or I bury arrow in your heart—if you got one."

Hútlof took a few steps forward, and the bowstring sang. The Werewolf grunted in pain when the arrow hit his chest, just about missing his heart. He pulled out the arrow in fury. Blood spread over his fur, but it did not become him. Instead, he rushed toward the tent in a rage. Zale and the Iceman posed before Sigyn to protect her in her weakness, and they both met the Werewolf's assault. Bravely, Zale fought against this monster, whose strength was many-fold that of Zale's, and Zale's attempts were like an irritating wasp to Hútlof. With great force, the Werewolf slammed his club against Zale's blade, and he dropped it. The next blow from the club hit him on the left arm, and he fell to the ground, having lost all sensitivity there. An excruciating pain radiated up his shoulder and the left side of his body, and his head was spinning. Helplessly, he watched Sigyn and the Iceman fighting for their lives against an enemy that was too powerful for them.

"Stormcloud, I wish you were here," Zale said, having lost all hope. He wished to see his old friend once more before the end.

And lo-and-behold! Suddenly, he heard a loud neigh, and there stood his mare, his most beloved friend, close beside him.

"Yes, yes!" he cried. "Come on to me. I have missed you so much. Give me a hug."

The mare bent her head until her nose was merely a few inches from Zale's face. In tears of joy, he raised his right arm to grab his friend's head. But his arm went right through. Desperately, he tried again, but there was nothing to grab.

"Stormcloud, no! I know you are not among the living, but I used to be able to touch you. What is wrong?"

The mare neighed, but there was a sadness to her neigh, and her eyes were wet. In vain, and to no avail, she tried to kiss him, but the two could not connect. Then she slowly disappeared and was gone. Zale knew he would never see her again, and he screamed in grief, and so loud it was that Hútlof stopped in his actions to see what was going on. Zale continued screaming, louder and louder.

"Stop that, you idiot!" Hútlof cried, as he turned away from the other two and approached Zale to kill him first.

Then befell something most unexpected.

Out of nothing, a vast army of Grimms manifested around Zale. The Werewolf stepped back, and although tears clouded his eyes, Zale noticed the horror in the Werewolf's gaze. Patiently, the Grimms stood idle, facing the scene.

"KILL HIM!" Zale roared, pointing at Hútlof, and the entire army of Grimms from the depths of Hell attacked the Werewolf. He growled and screamed, and he swung his sword and his club about him, but he hit nothing. Sigyn and the Iceman screamed, too, for they understood not what was happening.

In less than a minute, it was over. On the ground lay the Werewolf, or what was left of him. Zale now felt his strength returning, and his rage was uncontrollable.

Swift as the wind, he ran back to where the battle raged between Wolfmen and Icemen, but he stopped before he fully reached there.

"Slay them! Wolfmen and Ulves! Slay them!"

When the Icemen saw the army of Grimms approach, they dropped their weapons and ran. "Alas! Forces from Hell!" they cried. "Woe to us all! We are doomed!"

But the assault was not directed against them. The Ulves threw the Wolfmen off their backs, so they could escape more swiftly, but no Ulv and no Wolfman bolted the Grimms that day. Soon, the battle was over. Grotesque was the scene, and the many pieces of Wolfmen and Ulves, severed, and with arms and legs missing, colored the snow red. Followed by a swooshing noise, the Grimms swirled up into the air, faster and faster, like the fiercest tornado, and then they vanished as suddenly as they arrived. Zale fell to his knees, and he wept.

Chapter 37
The Mind of a Demon

RELIEVED, ISMARIL WATCHED Yongahur and Guthrog vanish in the distance, landing somewhere near the Grimcast castle. Something urgent had called the Dark King and made him postpone their encounter. Ismaril knew nothing about what that could be. Anguish grabbed him, for he knew time drew nigh when he must confront Yongahur and Azezakel, and supposedly fulfill his mission. But how could he? His shoulders sank, and he felt so lonely. Who might help him on this fateful quest? No one.

As his mood sank, he glanced over the battlefield. Everywhere was death. As far as he could see, there was an abundance of bodies, like warrior ants crawling, desperately trying to stay alive, pulsing through snow that had turned from white to red; men and beasts alike swinging weapons aimlessly here and there, barely knowing whom they were hitting, friend or foe. But it mattered not; it was all about survival.

How had the world come to this?

Then he shrugged it off. These were the end of times. This must be the Last Battle that had been discussed for so many centuries. The Last War. He took a deep breath, rushing into the combat to do his part. He killed a few, but it was as if no one paid attention to him. Why was it so easy to slay? All the while, many enemies surrounded him, but as he swung his blade, no one seemed to notice him. It was almost as if he was invincible. Thus, he took a chance. He stopped fighting, merely standing there, idle and with his bloody sword limp by his side. His face was stained from other's blood, but he was yet unwounded. Thus, he did nothing but stand still.

About him, near and far, there were slayings and ferocious fights, but no one attacked him. Why? He took it one step further. He spotted a Birdman standing on his own, with no one close. Ismaril approached him and consciously stuck his blade into the Birdman's brawny arm without killing him. In pain, the beast screamed in a high bird pitch, looking about him to counterattack his assaulter, but there was confusion in his eyes as if he noticed not the one giving him the wound. Then Ismaril fully realized they could not see him. It was impossible for him to get killed here. Confused, he drew Gahil and faced the blade, all in black, as always. His heart pounded faster when he noticed the blade pulsated, and when his heart rate increased, the pulse of the sword followed suit. *This is significant;* Ismaril thought. *But what?* He knew that was a silly question, for inside, his entire soul screamed to follow Yongahur. He closed his eyes. *This is insane. Yongahur is most likely inside Grimcast, and so is Azezakel. How can I fight them both?* Then it was as if the sword spoke to him: *Fail me not. The time of reckoning is here.* Ismaril gasped, and shocked, he put Gahil back in its sheath. Then he stretched, brushed snow off his arms, and started walking toward Azezakel's fortress. As he closed in, Guthrog, the Dragon ascended and flew east, but without his infamous rider. Yongahur must remain in Grimcast.

The closer Ismaril got, the air turned heavier, and it was as if the air was standing still. It was difficult to breathe, and he knew not whether it was because he was frightened to death. Again, he wished Sigyn was by his side. Not because he wished to put her in more danger, but by now, he was so used to having her there that he felt empty and naked without her.

The road to the fortress lay open. All about, there were shattered old tree branches, and there was a path through it. Ahead, he saw the gates open as if he was invited. Then his blood froze. Spread out across the courtyard, many figures stood in frozen positions, weapons drawn. Initially, he thought they were bizarre statues, resembling Emorians, Giants, and men, but when he neared, he found they were living beings, frozen in their action. *Magic;* he thought. *This is Azezakel's work. How can we defeat* such a villain?

The noise from the battlefield, only five hundred paces away, faded like a dream, and all that existed was the fortress ahead. He stopped at the gates, and they were open. A stink of rotten flesh lingered in the air, giving him convulsions, and making him hesitate to move farther. *This is absurd,* he thought. *I am nobody. What am I doing here?* Not so long ago, he thought of his mission as something in the future, and he worried not so much about it. Now, the future had caught up with him. It was time to face his destiny, so what was he going to do with it? How could he confront divine beings, even thinking for a moment he could defeat them? If he entered this fortress, he knew he would either come out as the victor or he would not come out at all. He was not even certain about what he was supposed to do.

A verse from the Book of Secrets came to mind, but oh, so vague,

For all the wise and for the fool
for shadows dark, for those who rule;
for those which hope since long is gone
and joy is foreign, faith is none
For all those, shine, be a star
and light the Darkness, near and far.

He felt nothing close to being a star or a spark of light in the dark. Everything, even here in Gormoth, seemed brighter than him. He felt betrayed. Cold, alone, and lonely in the center of evil, expected to fight the most powerful beings in the world and yonder. Where was everybody? His aid? Even Sigyn was absent. His legs were shaking, his mouth was dry, and the terror and disbelief he carried was unmatched. He drew a second blade, one he had picked up from the battlefield, and prepared to either die or succeed; the former, most likely.

Then his focus shifted to his right. A hundred paces and a half away stood a man dressed in Gormothan armor with the Dragon and the sword painted on his chest in red and black; but his head missed a helmet. Ismaril studied him for a few seconds, as their gazes met, but he thought the man looked more like a rough sailor from afar rather than an Er-Ekhanim or a hybrid. The stranger merely stood there, staring at him, and his sword was undrawn, resting in the scabbard. Then Ismaril disregarded him, took a deep breath, despite the foul odor, and entered Grimcast.

The flickering torches on the walls made a ghastly imprint as he slinked forward through the hallway. Here everything seemed built of iron: the walls, the floor underfoot... the ceilings. In intervals, iron statues of Gargoyles and horned abominations from Hell stood, evil and malicious, holding torches. And there were sculptures amidst, eating other monstrous abominations. Ismaril shivered, thinking about the frozen people in the courtyard. Were the monsters he now faced statues or living beings, frozen in time?

Then he saw the bodies on the floor, bathed in blood, and he gasped in despair. He put on his headband to better see what there was to behold, and with a lump in his throat, he realized there was nothing he could do for any of them.

A short stair flickered in the torchlight, and he heard voices speaking in a conversational tone at first. Then, someone raised his voice, and Ismaril's heartbeat doubled. There was little doubt about whom the voice belonged to. Yongahur was still here.

He stopped and listened.

"You miserably queen of nothing!" Yongahur roared.

"I have been called that before," a female voice said. Ismaril was uncertain, but it sounded like Queen Astéamat.

"What do you mean my father is sent to Hell? You are lying. Why?"

"Worry not, for that will be your destination, too, Yongahur, king of no land. But it is not my destiny to send you there. It is designated to somebody else."

"You are dying, Astéamat. It is almost beneath my dignity to end the process. Yet I will. My flaming sword shall send you to Hell, as well."

"You may use your sword on me, Yongahur, but if you do, you will also put a curse on yourself."

It was silent for a while as if Yongahur was considering the Queen's words. Then the Dark King laughed. "You scare me not, for I am Yongahur, and fear is below me. Your words fall flat, for they are lies, uttered by someone who is about to die, and worse. Prepare for your last journey."

Ismaril clenched his teeth, took a steady grip around the hilt of his sword, and ran toward the stairs. He must save the Queen; this was the time to show courage. *He might send me to Hell, too,* he thought, *but I must not think of that now.* Up the stairs he rushed, and thus, he entered King Azezakel's chamber. Fleetingly, he spotted dead bodies on the floor. Only two figures seemed alive in the Great Hall, Yongahur and the Queen. Queen Astéamat sat with her back against the wall, and her chest was bloody. Above her stood Yongahur, tall, somber, and with his flaming sword in hand, ready to bury it in the Queen's wounded body.

Yongahur stopped his sword movement midair when he spotted Ismaril rushing into the hall and facing him, and for a flickering moment, Ismaril noted a sudden glimpse of surprise in the Dark King's eyes.

"Ah, Ismaril Farrider," he said. "I am impressed by your courage, I must admit. I expected you not to look for me, but it is just as well; you saved me the effort to find you. Brave or not, you are a fool for coming here. Should I end the process with your beloved queen first, or should I send you to Hell before her?"

He looked at the Queen, and then back at Ismaril, as if he were in doubt, although Ismaril knew he was merely sarcastic.

"The queen thinks you are the one to send me to Hell, so why not let the show begin with you? I want the queen to see me defeat you, and when there is no more hope for this world, and all she feels is despair, I will send her to Hell right behind you. She will pass, knowing it was all in vain."

Ismaril fought against throwing out all thoughts of hopelessness from his mind and raised his sword to combat the Dark King.

"Wait!" Yongahur said. "That is not Iguhl you are holding. Are you telling me you are about to fight me with a toy sword again? You are insulting me. Draw your real blade, Ismaril Farrider. How can you possibly defeat me with a regular sword? At least give me an ounce of a challenge. Draw Iguhl!"

Ismaril's feeling of hopelessness returned with Yongahur's words. The Dark King was right. How could he defeat him with this joke of a blade when his opponent used his flaming sword and had all the other advantages? His mind worked at a rapid pace now. *What shall I do? If I draw Gahil, I at least stand a slightly better chance. Why am I here when I know not how to proceed?*

In a trance, he heard Queen Astéamat's voice as an echo inside his head, weak but demanding. "Do not use Gahil," she said.

Yongahur laughed wryly. "Listen to her. You think she has

your best interest in mind? No! She wants you dead, Farrider. Everybody wants you dead. Do you not feel abandoned? All alone? No aid? Everybody else is suddenly busy elsewhere, so they do not need to face what you are now facing? Why does it matter what you do? No one cares about you. Use Iguhl. Do me justice. Kill me with Iguhl if you can."

"I will not use Gahil against you," Ismaril said, surprised he could keep his voice steady. "You know that. You want me to kill you with Gahil, so the world will be yours. Perhaps you may also free Azezakel in Hell if I kill you. And soon after, you will resurrect."

"There is another option," Yongahur said. "I kill you and send you to Hell with my Blade of Flames. Then I take your sword and make it mine."

"If you do, the fight will continue. Nothing will change, except I will be gone. My sword will not obey you—it will ultimately consume you, for like a mirror, it will bounce back your evil onto you and destroy you."

The Dark King burst out in a rage that made every cell in Ismaril's body vibrate.

"IGUHL IS NOT YOURS! IT'S OURS. WE FORGED IT!"

In awe of his sudden insights that he knew not whence they came, Ismaril continued. "You forged her, but she was never yours. The Unicorn was of a much higher Order than you. What you did was sacrilegious, and you sealed your own fate… And you know it."

Yongahur roared and raged out at Ismaril with his fire sword, ready to slay. Ismaril raised his own sword to protect his head, but the Dark King stopped his hand before it reached Ismaril's throat. Then he backed off, and the flames from his blade dissolved.

"You confuse me," Yongahur said. "If you refuse to use Iguhl, how will you possibly proceed?"

Ismaril stood silent, for he had no words. He knew not what to do.

Yongahur sighed. "Well, then try to kill me with your toy blade. If you fancy yourself with such importance that you believe you can save the entire world with a toy sword, have you really grown up, Farrider? Are you not yet the same ignorant and childlike person you were when you left Eldholt? Have you learned nothing on your journey, playing with toys still? You are in a different league now, pathfinder. Can you face it? Can you take the challenge? Mummy is sitting over there, against the wall, helpless. Are you going to run to her and hide under her skirts? It is too late, Farrider. You are here, and now you must play in my league. There is no way back. Fight me with your toy sword, and I will sure send you to Hell, or grow up fast and use the blade worthy of a savior."

Ismaril shook his head, focusing on his opponent with his sword, ready to use it.

"Very well," Yongahur said, and then he charged. His blade was again burning hot with the Fire of Hell, and the two blades met with a loud clank. Ismaril felt the power behind the Dark Lord's assault, and he tripped backward from the impact. Then Yongahur swung his blade once more, and Ismaril's sword split asunder. Only the hilt remained. He gasped and cried out in terror. He was unarmed, waiting for the finishing blow that would send him to Hell.

But the blow never came. Instead, Yongahur sheathed his sword with a grim glance at his opponent. The Dark King knew killing Ismaril was the last resort, for if he did, the world would go on as before, and the battle outside worked not in the Dark Kings' favor.

"As I told you, a toy sword." Then he started walking in the opposite direction and waved at Ismaril. "Follow me," he said. "I have something to show you."

"I prefer to stay here."

"Come with me. You will not regret it, I promise you. Indeed, you may thank me afterward. A last treat before you die, or a way to change your mind?" Then the Dark King moved toward the other side of the Great Hall, where there were massive iron doors, all closed. Ismaril drew his eyebrows together, confused. He glanced at the Queen, but she was almost unconscious. Reluctantly, he followed his opponent across the hall. Yongahur stopped in front of one iron door.

"Wait here," he said, and he opened the door and was gone. Soon, he heard voices from inside, and he stopped breathing. He recognized those voices. Could it be...? No!

Yongahur returned to Ismaril, and behind him walked two figures, weak and starved—a mother and her little child. Ismaril's jaw dropped, and a flood of tears fell down his cheeks.

"This... this is a trick!" he said, and then he wept.

"No trick," Yongahur said. "I swear."

"My... Maerion... Erestian!"

The woman wept loudly and bitterly. "Ismaril!"

He ran toward them and embraced them, and all three wept together for a long time.

"I can feel you. You are real," Ismaril said. "If this is a trick, it is the evilest trick. And Erestian! You have grown."

"We are real," Maerion said. "And you are real."

"But you both died in the fire back in Eldholt—"

"We did not. We were kidnapped. They wanted you to think we succumbed to the fire."

"But why?"

"Is that not obvious, Farrider?" Yongahur said. "It is called hostage. We knew you and I would face each other one day, and we might have some use for them in due time, we thought."

Ismaril could not let go of his loved ones, but his mind was in an uproar. It was surreal. Here he stood, in Azezakel's fortress, ready to be sent to Hell, while he had reunited with his beloved wife and child, both of whom he thought were dead. And close by, Sigyn lay sick in bed, about to give birth to their child.

"So, what will you do now?" Yongahur said. "Here is your lost family, and your toy sword is useless. Only Iguhl left. You have no choice but to use it."

"Never!"

"Oh, you poor fool. You had better listen to me. The Book of Secret told you nothing about my Sword of Fire, did it? The one that can send you to Hell. You never seem to grow up, Farrider. You are still the same fool you once were, and you have learned nothing; your blindness never left you. See you not that you have been working for us all the time? Did you not ask yourself the question of why the Book of Secrets was hidden in Gormoth? No, you did not. Instead, you chose to believe a joker for a warlock to tell you things that are false. You have been deceived, but I shall tell you the truth before we meet each other in combat again. But are you ready to hear it?"

Ismaril felt a sting inside. Although he had no reason to believe anything Yongahur said, somewhere deep within, he knew he should pay attention.

"Oh well, ready or not, here it is… the truth. Do you think we would have permitted you to enter the cave and to find the Book if it was not part of our plan? We made it hard for you, but not harder than you could make it. Have you ever wondered why you are still alive? You were told to be spared. My men could wound you, but never take your life.

"Who do you think wrote that passage in the Book of Secrets that only you had access to? We did. And do you believe we would let you survive your journey through the Underworld if it was not planned? We could have killed you anytime." He laughed smugly. "Did we give you a hard time? Were we treating you unfairly? Come on, we were merely playing with you. You know nothing about hardship, being a spoiled farmer's boy. We lured you into the Underworld, so you had that experience in mind when I kill you. I want you to know where I am sending you. Do you see it now? For us, it is a game, pathfinder. We are playing with you, like your children are playing with toys. It is for our amusement. Sometimes, we wish you were smarter, so you can give us a challenge. But not even your *mighty* queen is smart enough to see through us. It almost becomes boring after some time. But you have seen the Lake of Fire, and you know it is real. You also know this is where I will send you before this day is over. The question is, what action will *you* take? You have a lot to ponder in a very short time. Had you been wiser, the outcome could have been different."

Shaken up, Ismaril screamed, "You are lying! None of this is true!" But he sounded not as certain as he wished to. What if Yongahur spoke the truth?

The Dark Lord ignored Ismaril's outburst. "My father is locked up in Hell, but you know, that is not such a bad thing. What if your queen did me a favor, unbeknown to her? This makes *me* the King of Kings, does it not? I will take over here as soon as I have finished my business with you and defeated your pathetic army outside. Look around and think about it. Does what I say not make sense? You know it does. I am sure you have had a lot of questions on your journeys, but few answers. I am giving the answers to you now."

Ismaril felt desperate. "But what of Raeglin? Is he one of you? Does he know all this and lied to me all this time?"

Yongahur scoffed. "Master Raeglin. Oh, that fool. He is not

clever enow to see through us. The problem with the queen's folk is that they are too naïve, underestimating me. I am the mind behind this, Farrider, not my father. Aye, he thought he was, and I let him. But I am the architect, and thanks to queen Astéamat, I no longer must eliminate my father. She did it for me, not understanding what she was doing."

"If they fought, she probably had no choice."

"Now you start seeing the brilliance behind my plans. I have covered everything. Whatever happens, it benefits me. Not even my brothers knew what I was planning. I have already sent them all back into stasis. They are sleeping within this Palace, but this time, they will never wake up again. I am the only one left—me and my servant, the Wolfmen, the Birdmen, and other creatures I have at my disposal. But no competition. I am the real King of Kings. Is that not always how it goes? The one most brilliant takes it all."

"You are indeed evil," Ismaril said in a low voice, and his rage bubbled up inside him. "Why are you telling me all this? I am sure it is not because you want to unburden your black heart."

"Of course not. I enjoy planning and plotting, and nothing I do is without brilliant planning, so also with you. I have tested you, Ismaril. Thus far, I have been unsuccessful in having you use Iguhl, but I would not be brilliant if I had not developed plans within plans. After I have told you what I am now going to convey, you will understand the entire reason I have revealed all this to you."

Ismaril clenched his fists, having serious problems holding himself back from attacking Yongahur with his bare hands.

"Now listen carefully," the Dark King said, and the smug smile returned. It was obvious he enjoyed this. "You can do whatever you want to try to kill me, and I will send you to Hell, or you may refuse to fight me, and I will send you to Hell, anyway. The outcome on your behalf will be the same. Another choice is to use Iguhl against me. If you have the skills, and if you and your blade are synchronized, you may kill me. I shall die, but I will resurrect again, and the curse, or as you call it, the Prophecy, will be unfulfilled, and I will rule.

"Remain stubborn, and refuse to use Iguhl to fight me, and I shall kill your wife and your child right now, and I will certainly send them to Hell forever. Yet you possess free will, Farrider, which I will be happy to grant you. The choice is yours."

"The only one who is going to die here is you, you messed up a demon!" Ismaril shouted and ran against Yongahur to beat him to death with his fists. He never reached that far, but ran into an invisible wall and bounced back, floored.

"I should have mentioned my magic," Yongahur said. "How could I forget? Well, it would be cheating to use it when we actually do have our fight, would it not? So, calm down, and choose one option I gave you."

"Even if you kill my family, you cannot win," Ismaril said. "I can still refuse to use Gahil."

"This is true. If your choice is that I should kill your wife and your little innocent, adorable child, things here in Taëlia will continue as usual. Yet I have a chance to win long-term, though it would be more difficult for me. Do you suggest I kill your family and send them to Hell, then, to save the world temporarily?" He drew his flaming sword and approached Maerion and Erestian, both screaming in terror. Ismaril got to his feet and stood himself between the Dark King and his family with his arms outstretched to protect them.

"No!"

"I did not think so."

"But how can I save the world?" Ismaril said. "Either option is to your benefit."

"Was that not what I told you? Whatever choices people make, I win. However, I give my victims a few choices nonetheless, for I am curious what their ultimate choice would be. It is interesting to me, you see."

"You are sick!"

Yongahur shrugged. "It is all relative. Everybody is sick. I am merely trying to enjoy myself." His voice hardened. "Now make your choice. My patience is running out, and I am getting bored. The way I see things is that either you go to Hell alone, and I spare your family, or I let them go to Hell, and I let you follow. But you will not meet them again, not even in the Eternal Fire—I will see to that."

Ismaril could no longer restrain himself. All this life, there had been anger inside him he had often let out, and which sometimes had hurt others. Lately, he had learned to tame that uncontrolled fire inside, but now it came out unleashed. With a raw scream of rage, he drew Gahil and ran toward Yongahur to slay him. The Dark Lord's blade burned in blue and white, and Gahil's black blade shone, flickering in different colors from some inner, mysterious light, ready to defend herself.

"Now you are talking!" Yongahur said when the blades met. Flames and sparks flew from the blades left and right, and Yongahur backed off whilst Ismaril advanced, for such was his rage that it appeared to take the Dark Lord by surprise. Or did Yongahur want Ismaril to slay him?

Ismaril swung Gahil furiously as if he and Gahil were one force, and there was no distinction between the two.

"Very good!" Yongahur said between the blows. "Sword and master working together. That is what I want to see before you slay me."

The fight continued for a while, and one combatant dominated the other to and fro. Then, without a warning, Yongahur lowered his blade and pushed out his chest. Ismaril, still in a rage, prepared to end the battle by burying Gahil in his opponent until death took him.

But it did not happen.

To his surprise, Yongahur screamed in pain, and the tip of a blade came out from his chest, blood splashing into Ismaril's face. Someone had pierced the Dark King from behind.

Yongahur, ferocious, spun around and pulled the sword out from his body, after dropping his fire sword on the ground. There, behind him, stood the strange man Ismaril had spotted outside the gates.

"Tomlin, you idiot!" Yongahur roared. "You stinking pirate! What do you think you are doing? You think you can kill Yongahur?"

Tomlin backed off, but in his eyes burned an intense fire. "You killed my companion, and for that you must die!" he cried. "You are a monster, and you are right that I have been a fool. A fool for joining your army. I have sought for you, and now I get my revenge. You are dying, Dark King."

"Does it seem like I am dying? You cannot kill me, fool, for you are merely a simple and stupid pirate. You are the one to die." Then he ran Tomlin's own sword into the pirate's stomach. Tomlin moaned in pain and fell to the floor, coughing and spasming.

"There you can lie and suffer. Death will not take you until you have bled out. Before then, I will run my Blade from Hell into you."

Yongahur turned around to pick up his sword of fire from the floor, only to discover it was gone. Desperate, he looked left and right, but could not see it. All he saw was Ismaril standing there before him, staring at him. Then, from behind his back, Ismaril pulled out Yongahur's sword, hot and burning, and pointed it toward the Dark King, whose jaws dropped. For the first time, Ismaril could see fear in Yongahur's eyes.

"You may be brilliant in your own way," Ismaril said, and his voice was cold and assertive. "But you forgot to cover one thing in your planning, for there is yet another option. What do you think would happen if I kill you with your own sword? It will send *you* to Hell."

Yongahur, still unstable after being pierced by Tomlin, held out a bloody hand. "Wait! This is not the solution. We can discuss this and come to terms…"

Ismaril said no more. While advancing with the sword facing his opponent, the Dark King backed off, but fell over Tomlin's body. Ismaril sprang forward and put his foot on Yongahur's wounded chest.

"No! No!" The horror in the Dark King's wide-open eyes cannot be described. Then Ismaril ran the flaming sword into Yongahur's chest. His scream made the iron walls shake, and then it was quiet. What remained of Yongahur was an empty cape. His soul had traveled to Hell, and his body dissolved into nothingness together with his sword, which crumbled in Ismaril's hand. Yongahur needed no physical body in the Lake of Fire.

Then a beam of yellow sunlight came in from one of the small windows, reaching Gahil, yet lying there on the floor. Ismaril gasped when he saw the sword fall asunder, until there was only dust, and Gahil was no more. But something ascended from the meager rest of the sword. For behold, the apparition of a snow-white Unicorn soared from the blade, facing Ismaril. He thought he could see a smile on the Divine animal's face before the apparition dissolved and was gone. It was over.

In a corner of the hall, Maerion sat, shivering, and with their child in her arms. Ismaril sat beside them, and they hugged and held each other again. And it felt good.

"Fear no more," Ismaril said. "The Dark Kings are gone, defeated. I do not know what will happen now, but the root of all evil is gone, and that means something. Come with me. We must leave, and you need something to eat and drink."

On the floor on their way out, Tomlin lay dying. Ismaril glanced over to where Queen Astéamat was and noticed she was now on her feet. Thus, he kneeled before Tomlin and held his head up. Blood poured from his mouth, and he knew there was nothing he could do for the pirate—the stranger he had never known but who had helped him complete his mission and stopped him from using Gahil on the Dark King.

"I am in debt to you," Ismaril said. "In fact, the entire world is."

Tomlin coughed, and a vague smile came over his face.

"I am glad if I have done the right thing for the first time in my life. If things were not the way they are, I could die in peace, but I am going to Hell, with or without Yongahur's help."

"After your heroic act? You will not."

Tomlin coughed up some more blood, and he got weaker.

"You don't understand. My partner and I are under a curse..." Then he told Ismaril about the Ghost King they met in Barren Hills, and how the two pirates had promised to tell Azezakel to set the Ghost King and his people free. Now, they had failed, and the Ghost King's curse was going to take effect.

"Then I will promise you one thing, and perhaps that will pay my debt in full to you," Ismaril said. "I will see to it that the Ghost King's men will find peace in one way or another so that your curse can be lifted."

Then a big smile appeared on the dying man's face, and thus, he was gone.

Ismaril hurried over to the Queen.

"Well done, Ismaril Farrider," she said. Her voice was weak, but she had gained strength. "I will be fine," she said. "The exhaustion of fighting Azezakel and Yongahur, in combination with my wound, took all my energy. Now Yongahur is gone, as well, and my strength is returning."

At that moment, a group of soldiers ran into the Hall. But they were not enemies, but the frozen statues Ismaril had seen outside the gates. Yongahur's death seemed to have lifted the spell. They all attended to the Queen, who now was in good hands. Ismaril helped Maeron stand up straight, and he took Erestian's hand.

"Let us leave this terrible place," he said.

Chapter 38
Turning of the Tide

A DARK OVERLAY OBSCURED the battlefield, and there were horrific war cries from abominable creatures from Hell's bottom. Round and about were piles of dead bodies, and side-by-side, and back-to-back, Xandur and Exxarion fought for their lives. For each moment that passed, Gormoth was closer to victory.

"Alas! King Barakus has fallen!" Xandur roared to cry down the loud noise from the battle. "I, Prince Xandur, am now the High Commander of the Divine Kingdom of Khandur. Fight bravely, Knights and Soldiers. Fight well, Mazosians of the Divine Queendom of Emoria! Swing your clubs, Mighty Ÿadeth-Oëmin! Ere too long, our fury and our fight for Freedom shall make us victorious!"

But the High Commander spoke too soon. Barely had he uttered these words before his own hope faded once more. He grabbed his brother's arm and pointed to the sky.

"Behold!" he said. "More Dragons! And there are both Azezakel's kind and those from Ayasis."

Unstoppable and deadly, the giant Hell Beasts swept fire and ice over the battlefield, not distinguishing between friend and foe. The larger Gormothan Dragons slew everything in their path to guarantee the extermination of all, their own army included. Everywhere, tall flames rose when bodies went up in flames, only to go out when plummeting into the snow; but even the snow melted beneath them until the battlefield resembled a field teeming with craters.

"All is lost," Exxarion said. "We cannot endure such assaults for long."

Attempting a counterattack, Icemen on Frost Dragons charged toward the overwhelming airborne enemies, and merely for a while, they could delay total desolation. But then something remarkable happened: From keeping a tight formation with the Gormothan Dragons, the Ayasis force wobbled and diverted in many directions, breaking the formation. Thereby followed a great confusion amongst the airborne. Some Ayasis warriors steered their beasts closer to the ground, but the Dragons no longer spat any fire, and in the distance, Ayasis warrioresses shouted amongst their own, "What is happening? What are we doing?"

Then the large group of Ayasis riders created their own formation, and the female warrioresses spoke between them from the backs of their beasts. Prince Xandur could not distinguish what they spoke of, for their voices came from afar; but something extraordinary befell. Under one command, the entire group turned around to help the Frost Dragons assault Azezakel's beasts, now being attacked from two directions. Many Gormothan Dragons caught fire and were pierced with spikes of ice from the Frost Dragons. They spun in the air while they went up in flames together with their riders, and heavy, they fell from the sky and landed with a sizzle when fire met snow.

Xandur cheered together with the allies yet capable of fighting. "Ayasis has switched sides once more!" the king said. "They are slaughtering the Hell Beasts!"

"What in Heaven's name made them change their mind now?" Prince Exxarion said.

"I know it not, brother. Something happened to them. They woke from their trance. Thus, bigger events must have occurred. The power of the Dark Kings is fading."

Prince Xandur scoured the battlefield, and once more he addressed his troops, shouting, "Find courage, brothers and sisters, for the tide has turned! Forward, forward! Victory is nigh!"

Then a loud shriek of anguish came from Grimcast, sending shivers down Xandur's spine, and all fighting on the ground paused. Aloft, Azezakel's Dragons answered the hellish screech, and one by one they fell from the sky without being assaulted. Desperate, they lay on their belly or on their backs like gigantic, dying insects, in a last despairing attempt to get to their feet. In vain, they flapped their enormous wings, but they were too weak to ascend. With their last long shrieks, they gave up their breath and were dead. All about, the battle had stopped, and friends and foes watched in horror; and many covered their ears, for the outcries of the Hell Beasts were loud and vibrant, driving the combatants half insane.

The Gormothan troops now ferociously let out their rage, and the assaults against Xandur's armies increased in strength since Wolfmen and Birdmen knew they must make up for losing the Dragons. Again, they tilted the battle in their favor, and many more good lives were spilled because of it.

Later, another shriek, louder than the first. The ground shook in its foundation, sweeping soldiers off their feet, and those who paid attention could see a beam of immense darkness leaving Grimcast, shooting up into the air, and darting toward the horizon. The shriek increased in pitch and the Blackness plummeted into the ground in the yonder. A massive cloud of snow erupted into the air when the dark beam vanished under the ground on its way to the Underworld. Yongahur's reign was over, and so was his magic influence.

In disbelief, Prince Xandur watched the scenario, not fully understanding how to signify the event. All he knew was that something dark and evil had just left Grimcast and flown across the land.

Then, suddenly, the Royal Ring on his finger heated, almost burning him. Shocked, he witnessed the solid band of his ring crack and the precious stone split. Then the entire ring crumbled into many pieces, turned black, and fell asunder before his eyes. Like soot flakes, the remains carried on the wind and were gone.

Xandur panicked. "What is happening? The Royal Ring turned to dust? This ring has wandered from father to son for many generations and has been one of the greatest symbols for our royal bloodline, going back to the great King Irvannion. What does this signify? The end of the Kingdom? Is Doom yet upon us, Exxarion?"

Then there was a great tumult. As that last shriek faded, panic broke out in the combat zone. Ulves threw their riders off their backs and ate them, struck by insanity. Then they aimlessly fled over the field, howling with their tails between their legs. Birdmen abandoned the battle and ran for the mountains, joined by other unnamable abominations. But none of them ever reached there, for from aloft, the Icemen and the Ayasis warrioresses chased them with their Dragons, and the refugees were all slain ere they came close to the mountains, prevented from vanishing into tunnels underground.

Left on the battlefield stood Prince Xandur and his allied armies, or what remained of them. For a long time, they followed the spectacle that befell before their eyes, untrusting of what they beheld. Then, a few cheered, insecurely at first, as if they were trying their voices, and then louder. More men followed, and soon there were cheers and hurrays everywhere. Soldiers and knights threw their weapons into the air and cast off their helmets, hugging and patting each other, crying, and laughing every other time. Xandur and Exxarion gasped and exchanged glances. As if the blackest of clouds had lifted from inside them, they too laughed until their eyes flooded with tears, and the two antagonists embraced, and they switched from laughing to weeping in each other's arms.

"My brother!" Xandur said. "What have we done to each other? We should not be fighting. We are of the same flesh and blood!" Prince Exxarion said none, but he nodded enthusiastically between the tears.

Then Xandur raised his voice so that it resounded above the delighted crowd.

"Rejoice, rejoice! For this is the day of Victory and Remembrance. Feel how the winds have changed! It is over! Gormoth has fallen!" Upon these powerful words, the cheering and the laughter increased in strength, and all survivors gathered around the new king to-be.

"We know not what has occurred," Xandur said. "Yet I understand the war is over. Something has befallen Grimcast. Evil has lifted, and this horrific place of evil is being cleansed!"

Yet there was a cloud in Xandur's sky: Where was Naisha? Up and down the battlefield, survivors now searched for fallen friends, and likewise were the Ayasis warriors, looking for their queen, who had vanished during the chaos. Xandur ran to and fro, up and down the theater of war, and in despair, he cried out her name, to no avail. Sweat broke out on his forehead. *She must not be amongst the fallen! She must not be dead! By the Goddess—no!*

And behold, for there before him now sat an Ayasis warrioress on a Dragon.

"Lady of Ayasis," Xandur said. "I know she is banned in your Queendom, and that Queen Moëlia wants her slain, but I need to find Naisha, your former Court Seer. I find her not among the living, nor among the dead. Allow me to ride behind you on your Dragon, and we shall go search for her."

"Although it is for Queen Moëlia to decide, I believe Naisha is no longer out of favor with Ayasis," the warrioress said. "A spell was cast upon us all, and we were not thinking clearly. Sit up with me, Prince Xandur. I must find our Queen, so we might as well scout together."

The Dragon lay down on her belly and let the prince mount her, and up they flew into the air. Xandur, on his virginal Dragon flight, had butterflies in his belly, holding onto the warrioress with all his might. In wide circles, they scanned the land, hoping to find signs of the missing females.

Distant from the battlefield, they spotted three dark dots in the snow beneath. The Dragon flew lower, and the two scouts now understood why both ladies were missing; they were together. But alas! One was lying down, perhaps wounded or dead, and the other sat by her side, head down. Watching them both sat Cloudwing, the Red Dragon.

So they landed, and the Ayasis warrioress and Xandur jumped off the Dragon's back and hurried toward the Queen and her seer.

"Queen Moëlia!" the warrioress said and kneeled before the woman lying on her back in the snow in her own blood. "What has here befallen? My Queen is dead! Naisha, what have you done?"

Beside the dead Queen, Naisha sat in tears, and she was sobbing. The prince rushed to her side and embraced her. The seer kept weeping in his arms, and he felt her body shaking and shivering, whether it was from cold or emotional turmoil—maybe both. Between the sobs, she tried to make sense of her speech.

"I... I had little choice," she said so that the warrioress could hear. "It was her or me. My Queen! My Queen is slain!"

The prince closed his eyes and inhaled. For now, he

understood why the Ayasis warrioresses had so abruptly switched sides in the battle: When their Queen died, the spell over her and her people broke. And Xandur cursed the Evil at its essence. The spell had caused betrayal and death, only to break with the Queen slain by her closest and trusted friend and her Dragon. And as fate had it, Naisha and Cloudwing had thus helped turn the tide, leading to victory. Yet for some, she would always remain the villain who killed her Queen, and for others, she would be the heroine, who helped save the world by waking her people from a trance that never befell her. And for the rest of her days, Naisha would be torn between the two.

"Alas!" Xandur said. "Aside from all the grief and despair over that which has befallen, a bright light is looming. And it is spreading and expanding. For what was cast with ill intent became our hope, became our victory. Despite the devastating sacrifice, you are my heroine, dear Naisha."

She beheld him through her tears, but rejoicing, she could not.

Xandur then lifted his gaze and witnessed the sparse trees about them shed their coats of snow; and to the east, blocks of ice and snow slid down the mountainside, rumbling and tumbling, leaving the bedrock naked.

Yet another spell was breaking, and the seasons were about to change.

Chapter 39
A Heroine's Last Journey

IN A SHALLOW CAVERN, by nature carved out from the mountainside, some surviving Emorians had made a temporary abode. In the midst burned a small fire, keeping the inhabitants warm while the snow outside was rapidly melting. From the entrance, Ismaril beheld how the ground, previously covered with deep snow, turned bare. To his astonishment, the soil swiftly swallowed up the white dissolving blanket, leaving the fields dry rather than overflowing with water. *Azezakel's magic;* a voice said inside him. *No, it is Queen Astéamat's work;* said another. *She is reestablishing order and dismantling old curses and spells.* Queen Astéamat had almost completely recovered after the Dark King and the King of Kings were defeated. Her strength had returned, and she was now out on the battlefield, helping the wounded heal.

Beside Ismaril sat Maerion, weak and thin from a long term of starvation and dehydration. She drank a little and ate less to let her belly adjust to a regular diet again. Erestian had been more properly fed during the imprisonment, but only because his mother had given him most of her rations. Even from the little she ate, she seemed to gain strength.

"I never thought I would see you again," Maerion said, and her eyes were wet.

He removed a lock of her dark hair from her face and looked her in the eyes. "I had given up hope a long time ago. I am yet in shock to have you by my side. So much has happened since we last saw each other. It feels like a lifetime ago."

"Yes, and you have changed," she said. "There is a maturity about you that was not there before. You have grown. But I also notice a deep sadness, and your restlessness is still present. In your face, there is little joy. Does it not please you to see us? And after all, have you not saved us from the Dark Kings?"

"Have I? They deceived me, Maerion. Everything was planned to begin with, but not by the True Divine. The mastermind behind my mission was the Enemy; it was Yongahur. And we all fell into his trap, including the Queen of Emoria."

"Yet I do not understand. The Dark Kings are defeated."

"So it is, but only because of an oversight by Yongahur. Circumstances had it I could make use of his mistake. I have a lot to talk to my so-called friends about. I no longer know whom to trust. No longer am I certain that it is, in fact, over. Whom have I served?"

"Doubt it not, Ismaril. Queen NIN.AYA is the Queen of the Heavens."

Ismaril gazed across the plains with distant eyes and spoke as if in a trance. "I doubt it not," he said. "I merely doubt people around me. Who is who? Is there an even stronger force lurking, of whom Yongahur was merely a puppet? And is such an enemy walking in our midst?"

"Yongahur has put a veil over your eye, my love. He had that ability. I was his and Azezakel's prisoner for a long time, and I know their character. They can make us believe anything."

"Aye. I only need to sort things out." Then he said no more, but his gaze remained absent.

She looked at him, concerned. "What bothers you, husband? Your mind is in a faraway place, and your heart seems not with me and Erestian. Tell me your thoughts."

Ismaril sighed. "I know not how to tell you, and I have hesitated, for I do not wish to hurt you."

"Now you are worrying me…"

After a moment's silence, he continued. "As I conveyed to you, I assumed I had lost you and Erestian forever, and the Goddess knows I have grieved, and She knows I have since then searched for revenge. I have thought about you constantly, awake and in dreams. My grief has tormented me and eaten me—

sometimes to the extent that I have made fatal mistakes and hurt those around me whom I love. Some died because of me. Little have I spoken to others about the torment inside that I have endured. The little I told them was the little I wished to confine. I blamed Yongahur for your death, and I swore not to give up until I had killed him." He paused and glanced at her, and tears filled his eyes. "I kept my promise, and I even got you back; you and my beloved son. Yet I am torn…"

"But why?"

Now he locked eyes with her, and he wept, and his voice shivered as he went on. "On the journey, I have had a shield maiden. Her name is Sigyn Archesdaughter. You know of her. She and I went through so much together, but we never *knew* each other until a long time had passed. We carried mutual feelings, but we had both lost loved ones in the Battle of Eldholt, and we needed to heal. I made her pregnant." He took a deep breath and noticed the excruciating sadness on Maerion's face that glazed her eyes with tears, and she sobbed. Ismaril's head pounded, and the lump in his throat was so big that he could barely say another word. Each part of him was breaking into pieces, but he forced himself to continue.

"Alas!" he cried. "I slew the Dark King with his own blade, and I even got my family back, yet there is a dark cloud hanging over me. Yongahur's curse is still lingering, Maerion."

"Where is she now?" she asked, and her voice was sterner and more demanding. "Is she still with child, or is the baby born?"

"She is in a camp nearby, and she could be in labor at any time. I needed to leave her there because of my mission, and I know not if the baby is born. I only know that when I left her with the healers, she was very ill. She was close to giving birth, yet she was not yet due. Something was wrong."

She buried her face in her hands and wept. Beside her, Erestian beheld her mother weeping, and his own lips started trembling. Ismaril took him in his arms and rocked him. "Easy, Erestian, easy," he said. "Everything will be fine. Daddy is here now, and mummy is here. We are a little sad, that is all. Do not worry. Daddy loves you." But he told him not whether he would stay.

Ismaril caressed Maerion's hair and shoulders, and thus she spoke. "What will happen now, Ismaril?"

"I must return to her to ensure she is alright," he said. "I cannot leave her there."

"Now I see why you have been so distant," she said. "Then go if you must. Will you stay with her? What about us? Your son?"

"I know not exactly how to solve this, for my heart is split in two. Of all the hardships I have gone through to complete my mission, this is the worst, even though the mission is supposedly fulfilled, and I got back what I thought I had lost. But I shall return, this much I promise. Wait here with the Mazosians. They will take care of you and Erestian until I am back."

"You will return, but you know not whether you will stay?"

He grabbed her head and gave her a long kiss. Then he kissed Erestian, who was now crying, understanding his father would once again leave. "I will soon see you again," he said to them both, and then he left the cavern without looking back. He could face neither his own pain nor theirs.

—

On the battlefield, men, Giants, and Mazosians had removed their own wounded brothers and sisters to places where they could help take care of their wounds. Others were piling up fallen combatants of friends and enemies and burning them in giant, separate funeral pyres. Ismaril then sighted a commander of sorts wandering to and fro, giving orders, and coming up with suggestions where thus needed. Ismaril approached him, and their gazes met.

"Sir, I am in need of a horse," Ismaril said. "I must return to the camp up north for a while."

The Commander studied the stranger. "And who are you?"

"My name is Ismaril Farrider, Sir."

A big smile came to the Commander's face, and then he laughed.

"Ismaril Farrider? So, we meet at last. I am Prince Xandur of the Divine Kingdom of Khandur."

Ismaril kneeled and put his fist to his chest.

"No, no," Xandur said. "I am the one who should bow down to you. Look around, Farrider. What do you see? I see Victory. It could not have been achieved without you."

"I am honored to meet you, Prince."

"Queen Astéamat told me you are here, and she told me what

you accomplished inside Grimcast. It appears your destiny and mine were intertwined."

"Intertwined? How so?"

The prince laughed. "We must gather in a group and tell our stories. Why not tonight over a campfire?"

"It would be a delight, but I must hasten. Someone needs me up north. May I use one of Khandur's steeds?"

"Of course! Choose any horse here, and you have my permission to use it. When will you be back?"

"That I don't know. Hopefully soon, but it depends on what I find in the camp. Yet I assure you I will return. This I have promised another, and this I promise you."

"Very well. Then I should go back to my business, and we shall soon reunite. I know of which campsite you speak, and have you not returned within a reasonable time, I might even visit you there."

"That would be an honor, Prince," Ismaril said and bowed down once more.

The horseback ride between the battlefield and the camp was indeed dissimilar from when Ismaril traveled the opposite way. The ground was now almost free from snow, and there was no use for sleds anymore. Above, a late afternoon sun was pulsating on its journey beyond the mountains in the west, and it was getting warmer. The breeze on his face was mild and fresh, and already, a few flowers sprung from the soil on either side of the road. There was no longer any doubt that these swift changes were Queen Astéamat's work.

Regardless of how much he pushed his black stallion, he could not reach the camp ere nightfall. Yet he was determined not to stop or rest until he reached his destination. Was Sigyn still alive? Had she given birth? Did she know the outcome of the battle? His anxiety increased the closer he came to the camp, and there was a knot in his belly. He drove his horse to his utmost, and the western mountains came closer with each hour. The wide heath lay open and void of any living creatures; there was only he on his horse.

When the sun vanished behind the mountains and it became dark, Ismaril was still on his way. Above him were now only stars and a waning moon, vaguely lightening the way, so he could see the silhouettes of the mountains drawing nigh; and it was past midnight when he stormed into a camp that was sleeping. There were guards approaching, not recognizing him at first, but then letting him pass. When he reached Sigyn's tent, he flew off his horse and rushed inside.

The tent was empty.

He panicked. There was her bed, and it was made and untouched. Everything else was in order, neatly organized and clean. But not a soul was there to greet him. His knees shook when the blood left his legs and gathered in his belly. His skin crawled as if he had ants, and he wanted to scream out his agony. Where was she? Was she dead? Was he too late?

"SIGYN!"

The camp woke up and got on their feet, and many realized who was calling out the name. The first in line to meet him in the tent opening was Master Raeglin, already returned from the battlefield. Ismaril stormed toward him and shook him, desperate and frightened.

"Where is she?" he cried. "For the Goddess' sake, where is she?"

"Calm down, Ismaril," Raeglin said.

Ismaril repeated his request, this time louder and more ferocious. "Where is she?"

"We must move her," the pilgrim said. "She was very sick, and her water broke."

"Is she... is she alive? And the baby?"

"She is alive, but the baby..."

Ismaril swallowed his cry, but his tears revealed his anguish.

"Take me to her!"

Raeglin spun around and started walking, heeled by Ismaril. Only a few tents away, the two men stopped, and Raeglin showed him in.

There was a smell of sickness in the tent, hitting Ismaril like a wall. Amidst stood a bed, and in it, Sigyn lay on her back, while healers gathered about her, one of them washing her face, using a cloth with cold water. He rushed to her side and grabbed her hand, whilst his heart pounded so fast and so hard that his chest nearly burst.

"Sigyn!" he cried.

She met his gaze. Her eyes, usually sparkling with life and

energy, now were dim and faded. The skin on her face was pale like the snow under a dim winter moon, her cheeks were sunk, and her lips were like dry clay. Her breathing was strained and wheezy, yet she gave him a vague smile, and her eyes regained a little of her luster.

But her voice was but a whisper.

"Ismaril, my beloved Ismaril... I am so sorry." And then her tears came.

He could barely keep his voice steady, but he wished not to show her his pain.

"Sigyn, my love. Why are you sorry? You have done nothing wrong."

The smile on her face faded, and she breathed heavily a few times, while still having her eyes locked with his.

"I have much to be sorry for," she said, but her voice was so quiet that Ismaril must get closer to hear her. "I am your shield maiden, and I could not be there with you when it really mattered..."

"Please do not worry about that. I am here, as you can see, and all went well. The Dark Kings are eliminated, and Taëlia is recovering."

The smile returned. "Aye, so they told me. I am so proud of you. So very proud. I wish to hear all the details from you, but maybe later. I am too tired for that now." Then her face turned gray, and a deep sadness fell over it. "You know of our baby?"

"No," he said. "I just arrived now. I only know... the baby did not make it."

She sighed shallowly. "Aye, but that is not all."

He felt another panic attack approaching.

"Sigyn, you need not tell me now," he said. "You can tell me when you are stronger."

But she squeezed his hand as hard as she was able. "You need to know."

"Then tell me."

"They delivered the baby yesterday, but it was not human."

He wanted to say something, but his voice failed him.

"It was... it was a monster. They did not let me see it. They did not want me to see it." She started sobbing, and then she moaned in pain. "But it was dead, and they have burned the body. We conceived it in the Underworld, remember? And then my curse…"

He held back from speaking, afraid to break out in a full crying spell, but his tears, he could not hide.

"Ismaril, my love," she said. "It is alright for you to cry."

Then he wept, and he wept. He bent over and put his cheek next to hers, and their tears mingled. She tried to hold him, but her arms were too weak to lift.

"The baby… it ate me up from inside. It destroyed me."

"Alas!" he cried. "Why is this happening? Can they heal you?"

"They say they might, but I think not. I am not getting better."

"Of course not. It is merely one day since you gave birth. It takes time to recover. But I will be by your side all the way until you are on your feet again. You will be well!"

She turned her head toward him and mildly caressed his cheek, and for a moment, she closed her eyes.

"When you get well… when you get *very* well, we shall go back to Eldholt, to our home. No more adventures. No more Wolfmen lurking in the mountains, no more raids. We can build a new community in peace and quiet." But he told her not about Maerion and Erestian. That had to wait. He could not burden her with that now. He hesitated what to do. In his entire life, he had never felt so helpless.

"You must sleep now," he said. "You are very tired."

Then her eyes widened, and the smile came back on her face again. "Ismaril," she whispered. She grabbed his hand, and there was enthusiasm in her voice. "Can you see it? Look!"

"See what?" he asked.

"There," she said. "It is beautiful, is it not? Everybody is so happy. Come, my love… We must go to them. I want to go there."

He sat up and beheld her. She looked at him, but her eyes were looking through him.

"It is so beautiful. And the music…"

"Sigyn… no!"

But she spoke no more. She sighed deeply and her breathing stopped.

"SIGYN!" he cried. "COME BACK!" He shook her, crying inconsolably. Then he lifted her and hugged her. "Please don't go!" She was still warm and so wonderful to embrace. He wished to sit there forever. No one must ever separate them. Behind him stood Raeglin and Kirbakin. Briefly, Ismaril glanced at them, and he saw the tears in their eyes.

―

They buried Sigyn Archesdaughter the following afternoon and they placed her grave up on a mountain, watching over a wide, magnificent valley, where a busy creek ran through the landscape. The entire camp attended, and many were those who could not stop crying as her body, wrapped in linen, was sunk into the ground. On top of her, they placed her sword and a shield, signifying the shield maiden she was. That entire day, an Iceman had spent his time carving in the text on her gravestone, and it read:

> Here rests Sigyn Archesdaughter of Eldholt
>
> A Heroine the world will no longer behold.
>
> Strong and brave was she, fair and wise.
>
> A shield maiden was she—a warrior's maiden.
>
> Rest in peace, beloved. Forever remembered.

When all participants had returned to the camp, and the sun was declining, Ismaril stood alone by the grave, and his body cast long shadows in the grass. He had no more tears, and he had no strength to weep. All he could feel was a vast emptiness; a loneliness stronger than any loneliness he had ever felt, and a big part was ripped away from him, and he knew it could never be replaced. From that day, he was only half a man. In his mind, he recalled their moments together, the dangers they resolved and outlived. He recalled her wisdom and her guidance, and he knew he could not have made it to the end without her. There was so much he wished he could have told her before she died, but it was too late now. When it was his turn to die, would he meet her again? But he was still young, and he must endure many more years in this world before he could see her again, if ever.

There, under his feet, she lay, his beloved shield maiden and partner. Her body was cold, yet he thought he could feel the warmth of her soul embrace him as if she were still alive. So strong was the feeling that he gasped.

"Sigyn?" he said.

Then it was like something light and uplifting swirled around him and wrapped him up in warmth and love. Soon the sensation left him, but when he looked at the night sky, a beam of swirling and dancing light ascended. It stayed there for a brief moment and shot off, absorbed by the blackness.

Chapter 40
The Council

FOUR DAYS AFTER SIGYN'S funeral, Ismaril fell ill. For three full days, he had been mourning his shield maiden, and he spoke to no one. He demanded a tent of his own, where he spent his time brooding. On the third day, he stopped eating, and on the fourth, he caught a high fever. Many healers came to see him.

"We know not what has fallen into him," an Iceman healer said to Raeglin. "We at a loss in struggle to help."

The pilgrim visited Ismaril in his bed, putting his hand on his sweaty forehead. It was burning hot, and Ismaril started an incoherent fever rant.

Raeglin frowned. "I think he has lost his will to live," he said. "No one can find anything wrong with him, yet he is rapidly declining. People can die of grief and a broken heart."

"So it is," the healer said. "For that, no cure there is."

The warlock sat in deep thought for a while. "I shall see what can be done, but currently, I have no solid plan. In the meantime, keep him cold to get the fever down."

Many ruminating thoughts tormented Ismaril's mind as he traveled between wakefulness and unconsciousness. Pictures flashed through his head; images of Sigyn, laughing, and of demons closing in, growling and showing their fangs, only to be gone in the next instant; and there were flashes of his old friends,

Holgar and Gideon, tormented in Hell. These images made him scream in his fever, and it woke him up. But soon, he fell back into his disturbing fever dreams again.

Then the tormenting images faded, and he knew not whether he was awake or still dreaming. His mind calmed, and a serene landscape, vast a beautiful, engulfed him.

There was a meandering gorge beneath from where he stood on a mountain path, and he beheld the magnificent view. A fast-flowing river rushed through thereunder, and a mighty waterfall released its forceful cascade of blue, foamy water from the mountains across the vale. Many birds were chirping about, and above him, a majestic eagle soared. And at his feet, colorful butterflies drifted from flower to flower. And there was a soothing fragrance of Spring, reaching his senses, mixed with the familiar and unique fragrance of fir and pine needles that covered the soil, heated by a friendly, warm sun. It reminded him of the fragrance in the forests around Eldholt. He took a deep breath and tasted the fresh air, only present at higher altitudes. Finally, he had found peace, and he was truly happy, perhaps for the first time.

In his hand, he held a walking stick made from an oak branch, and he turned his back against the basin and continued striding up the mountainside. Even so, he could hear the mighty roar from the cascade behind him. Yet he knew not his destination; he merely knew he must ramble on.

Up and up, he treaded, and the higher he ascended, the more he rejoiced. There was no one here but him, and he knew he must take on this journey alone. Yet it bothered him not, for it was a natural thing to do. He then rounded a corner, and there, the path ended abruptly. A deep chasm opened, reaching all the way to the bottom of the mountain, and far below he could see the features of another gorge and another river. High up he had stridden until several cotton clouds floated beneath him. In awe, he saw a golden bridge appear from nowhere, extending into thin air, and there, floating on the clouds, was a majestic emerald city to which the golden bridge led. His body filled with healing energies, and he wished to sing with pure exhilaration.

Enthusiastically, he crossed the bridge, ending in a vault or a portal, floating in the air before the entrance to the City of Joy. And there, before the vault, stood two fair beings, clad in white linen, adorned with gold emblems that emanated light, bright and healing. He could not tell whether they were males or females—perhaps both at the same time—and their golden hair fell on their shoulders. And in their sky-blue eyes, there was so much love and compassion, more than he could absorb in that unexpected moment. Their faces shone from the warmest smiles he had ever seen, and in their hands, they held scepters made of shimmering silver. And their bare feet touched no ground, for their bodies floated on the sea of air.

"Hail, Ismaril Farrider," said one soft-spoken, angelic being. "Thou have entered the gateway to the Emerald City."

He gasped, and his heart jumped with joy. "Where is this? Here is where I wish to stay for all Eternity. Will you let me pass, Divine Ones?"

"Not yet," the other angelic being said. "Thou time is yet to come, and thou must be ready to enter."

"But I am! I wish to be nowhere else but here."

"One day it shall thus be thy home, but thou still belong amongst the living for yet some time. Thus, thou must return whence thou came... for now."

"Who lives in this city?"

But the two beings dissolved before him, and so did the vault. He ran toward the city gate, but it slowly closed as he approached.

"No! Please let me in!" he cried, and despair fell over him where he stood. "I wish not to return!"

But alas! The Emerald City gently dissolved whilst he beheld it, and beautiful flute music filled the air about him. All despair washed off him, and once more, a great calmness embraced and soothed his soul, and he closed his eyes, listening to the soul-cleansing melody that expanded everywhere. The golden bridge dissolved under his feet, but he fell not. Among the clouds, and in the thin air, he stood, floating, while the music absorbed him, and he absorbed it.

Then there was a swooshing sound, and he gasped. An overwhelming heaviness engulfed him, and he opened his eyes. Confused, he looked about. He was back in the tent, lying on his bed. By the bedside, Kirbakin sat with his legs crossed, eyes closed, playing a Heavenly melody on his flute. Ismaril was back in his body once more, and he wished not to be there. Yet his fever was gone, and he felt better; but in his heart, there burned a consuming fire.

On the fifth day, two horseback riders slowly entered the camp. It was Prince Xandur, and in his company rode Queen Astéamat. Halfway through the camp, Master Raeglin came to greet them.

"Master Raeglin," Prince Xandur said, and his voice had a stern and displeasing overtone. "Thus, we meet once more, warlock. Remember, I banished you from ever entering Khandur again."

"That I remember," Raeglin said. "But this is not Khandur."

The prince in his saddle, and the pilgrim on the ground, locked eyes, sharing grave looks. Then Xandur's face cracked in a smile, and then he laughed. Raeglin followed.

"How silly," the prince said. "I believe the entire world must have been under a spell."

Thus, he dismounted, and the two embraced each other.

"Well met, Wizard of clothes-with-unmatching-colors," Xandur said cheerfully. "I am honestly happy to see you. Where is the mischievous, flute-playing Gnome you tend to carry about? Or is it perhaps the other way around?"

"He is here," Raeglin said. "You shall meet him soon. What is your errand, Prince? And yours, Milady?"

"We must form a small council," Astéamat said. "There are yet things to discuss, and we need to share our stories, so we all understand the times that lie ahead. I wish to summon yourself, Master Raeglin, but also Kirbakin the Gnome, and of course, Ismaril Farrider and Sigyn Archesdaughter."

"I told Ismaril we should sit by a campfire, and thus we shall," Xandur said. "It is my hope he is still here with you. He told me he would head this way, but he never said his errand, and he never returned to me."

Raeglin's voice was void of all previous amusement when he said, "Ismaril is here, but Sigyn Archesdaughter is not. She passed away a few days ago. She died shortly after childbirth. But the child was cursed, and so was she. Both child and mother died."

The Queen bowed her head in sadness. "That grieves me," she said. "I knew of her curse, of course, for she and Ismaril visited me in Emoria recently. The curse was too strong for me to lift, although I knew whence it came and who was behind it. Alas! I came too late, thinking there was still time to lift her curse after we defeated the Forces of Darkness. I could not do it prior to that. It must have been a premature birth."

"It was, Milady."

"Ismaril must be devastated," the prince said. "Now I understand why he was in such a hurry and why he wanted to borrow one of our horses."

"Ismaril has been very ill and walked through the valley of death," Raeglin said. "But he has returned, and Kirbakin played his magic flute by his bed until the fever broke. Ismaril has now recovered, but only in the flesh. His soul is yet tormented, and that is something Kirbakin's flute-playing cannot undo."

"Is he strong enow to attend the council?" the Queen asked.

Raeglin nodded. "I believe so."

"Then we shall hold it in a few hours' time, past sunset and around a campfire, in a place where we can be undisturbed."

Gathered around a sparkling fire outside the camp, they sat; Prince Xandur, Queen Astéamat, Master Raeglin, Kirbakin the Gnome, and Ismaril Farrider. The evening was mild, and the snow was gone. Everywhere, save for high in the mountains, the ground was bare and dry. Summer had reached Gormoth after millennia of ice and snow. Yet the fire created a pleasant atmosphere, with ghostly faces flickering in line with the flames. The logs cracked as they heated, and a thin smoke lifted and vanished into the dark. For some time, they gathered their thoughts in silence, where after the Queen opened the meeting.

"Welcome, my friends," she said. "I have chosen for you to be here because you have all, in your own ways, partaken in the effort to fulfill the ancient prophecy. I had also wished to bring Zale to the team. He is doing much better, from what I have heard, but he is still recovering. Personally, I know him not, but his story was conveyed to me close to this meeting. In haste, I excluded him for now and will brief him later.

"I want to start by articulating my condolences to Ismaril for his loss, which is not only his loss, but a loss for us all. Thank you for attending tonight, despite your grief. There are certain things we must address. It is not yet well known to all what befell in Grimcast and how the Dark Kings were defeated. Ismaril played the key role in achieving victory."

Ismaril stared into the fire, playing with a stick, and his face was numb and emotionless. "I wish for no celebration," he said. "If what I did must be known, tell people after I have left this place and returned home. This is not about me; I was merely a puppet in a play and apparently, unbeknownst, led by destiny, orchestrated by another. I was deceived. Hence, I failed, accomplishing nothing, and the glory should fall upon those who deserve it."

"But you did not fail," the Queen said. "I was there, and I bear witness. You, Ismaril Farrider, and no one else stuck the burning sword into Yongahur's body. If that had not been done, we would not sit here now. That was the only way to fulfill Prophecy. Had you not been prepared; the solution would not have shown itself. And yet, even if it would, you must have been emotionally ready to complete the task."

"If it were not for this pirate, Tomlin, who stuck his sword into Yongahur first, a heroic act, which he paid for with his life; I would, in my uncontrolled fury, have used Gahil on Yongahur, exactly as the Dark King had planned. I was on the threshold of ruining it."

"Yes, and that most likely would have befallen had you not made progress enough to change Destiny," Raeglin said. "You passed the tests, Ismaril, one by one; barely or not. You succeeded, and that is what counts. Tomlin in all honor, but only you could defeat Yongahur. Not even I or Queen Astéamat could have done it."

Ismaril shook his head. "Yongahur told me everything before I killed him. He conveyed the Book of Secrets was of his making and my entire journey he himself had planned and predestined. And like a fool, I followed his plan to the fullest." Then he stood, and his voice rose in anger. "My own foolish acts are on me, and they are many," he said. "But we have all been fools, have we not? Was it hidden from all of you that Yongahur was the mastermind behind preventing the Prophecy from befalling, and only barely could I complete the quest? Alas! We all thought Azezakel was my true target. Is that not so?"

"So it was," the Queen said. "According to the original prophecy, you should have killed Azezakel. The Prophecy was indeed Divine, but Yongahur cleverly altered it, hoping he could avoid his own demise and gain the Throne of the Heavens at the same time. Aye, he was clever, and he fooled us to a point, but not entirely. He never understood how he or his father were supposed to be killed, and that concerned him and gnawed on him. You see, the thing that was occult to him and missing in his plan was the exact thing he could not change—the nature of his death. He thought his death would come by the death of his father, and to prevent this, he tried to alter the Prophecy to gain his father's power. Thus, he hoped we were being waylaid, focusing on Azezakel when we should have focused on him, Yongahur. By transferring the power from his father to himself, he thought he could take advantage of the deceit and get away with it, and thus save his eternal life. But the power of the Prophecy was strong, and the outcome could not be altered, unless you, Ismaril, failed to do your job.

"When you and Sigyn visited us in Emoria, I knew many things, but I said little, for that would merely have complicated the matter, and likely interfered with your ability to complete the quest. It was imperative that you gained your own strength. You were never told precisely how to accomplish your goal, but that was by design. You, and only you, could find a way to proceed. It was not my task to tell you the truth as I knew it, including the distortion of the Prophecy; albeit it, admittedly, I knew not *who* had tried to alter it.

"What Yongahur told you was true in some ways, but he lied about the Book of Secrets. That book is Divine and does not originate with him or his father. All this said, I must also admit it scared me when I sent Azezakel to his imprisonment, yet thinking it was your task to kill him. I believed I had made a fatal mistake and jeopardized the Prophecy from fulfilling itself because of my own weakness and survival instinct in this incarnation. This was fortunately not true, something I did not know until it was all over and Yongahur was dead. Then I realized that, because of his intervention, Yongahur unintentionally saved his father from the Fires of Hell. Instead, that fate fell upon Yongahur himself. He needed your wife and your son as hostages, for he was afraid of you and of what you could do to him. The only likely guarantee he could envision was to kidnap your family."

Ismaril sat down again and fell into silence.

"So, you see, you failed not, dear Ismaril," the Queen said. "The Prophecy was solid. Details could be changed, but the core of the Prophecy could not. This is important to understand. The outcome played out as destined, with one exception: Azezakel was destined for Hell, burning in the Fire, but instead, I had to lock him into an energy prison in the lowest level of Hell from where he cannot escape."

"So, Yongahur is burning in Hell, and Azezakel is imprisoned," Ismaril said. "What of Queen Ishtanagul and the remaining Dark Kings whom Yongahur put back in stasis?"

"Hell is closed, and everyone and everything that resides there is trapped. At this moment, no one can enter, and no one can leave. Ishtanagul is as trapped as her consort. And the seven Dark Kings are no more. While you were here in the camp, Lord Usbarg of the Ÿadeth-Oëmin and many of his men entered Grimcast after Yongahur's departure, and they found the stairs leading down to a solid door. Using their combined strength and their solid clubs, they shattered the door and entered a chamber where the sarcophagi stood lined up. There, in stasis, lay the bodies of the remaining Dark Kings. The Giants destroyed the coffins and burned the bodies. These demons will bother us no more. In waiting to be called back to the surface and into their bodies in stasis by Azezakel himself, their dark souls reside in a certain part of the Underworld. Now, when their bodies have been destroyed, they have nowhere to return to. Thus, they are also trapped in the Underworld."

"All these demons must be terminated," Raeglin said. "Neither the Heavens nor the physical realms are truly safe until their dark souls are destroyed."

"This will be done," Queen Astéamat said.

"I have been to the Underworld," Ismaril said. "Not all souls there are of evil. Some were put there by the Dark Kings out of spite, or because they opposed them. These souls are not vicious and must be saved."

"They will," the Queen said. "That has already been planned."

"I have friends there who do not deserve such fate," Ismaril said. "What will become of them?"

"I am Queen Astéamat, and I am aware. Your friends will be released very soon."

"To where?"

"We shall discuss that in a minute."

"Then tell me what happened to the stillborn? I know it was

conceived in the Underworld, but who was the demon inside the embryo that killed Sigyn?"

"When the two of you visited us, I saw the curse," the Queen said. "Sigyn sent over mental images to me, unbeknown to her, of the tunnel and the light, in which a female entity appeared, falsely proclaiming your family was with her. But Sigyn saw through the deception, and the entity acted in vengeance. The demonic force told Sigyn they would meet again, and they did; for she possessed the embryo inside Sigyn with her dark soul and started feeding from her. But Sigyn was stronger than the entity thought, and the entity could not survive birth and must leave. That is the best explanation I have. Thus, the demon fell back into the Underworld. The entity in the tunnel was Queen Ishta-nagul."

Ismaril absently played with his beard. "I do not understand," he said. "Evil is defeated, and peace is established. We need not worry about Wolfmen, Ulves, Birdmen, or any other abominations. Taëlia is being cleansed. Why then do I not rejoice? Aye, I am mourning, but I feel even worse than I used to. And around us, everything looks and feels the same. I thought the clouds would lift, and we would feel happy."

"The changes are immense," the Queen said, "but Taëlia, as you know it, or the entire MAEDIN for that matter, will never return to what it once was when the world was young. A certain darkness will always linger, and not even I, in this incarnation, or as the Ice Queen, can do much about it. Therefore, a new world I have created for you; a Paradise that exceeds the former Emoria. It is an etheric world where you will gain eternal life. It is beautiful, Divine, and carefree. This is where I will send your friends and others who have suffered the torment in Hell and did not deserve it. When all those souls have been recovered and sent to the New Taëlia on a higher Heavenly plane, Hell will be destroyed and consumed, and all those souls burning there, be they Dark Kings, Queens, King Azezakel, Wolfmen, or others, will be terminated once and for all, and their souls destroyed. They are never to return."

"Fair enough," Ismaril said. "And Sigyn?"

The Queen smiled. "You will meet her in the New Taëlia one day."

"This is good news!" Ismaril said, and his enthusiasm

returned. "It must be soon, Milady."

"You have a family to take care of," the Queen said. "Maerion and Erestian are still alive."

"I know, but we can all go. I wish not to stay here. This world, despite its beauty, is a twilight world. I can never resettle here, not after all I know and have experienced."

"Yet you must, for thus are the rules. This world will still linger, so long as there are living beings left here. But from today, no one here can reproduce anymore. There will be no more offspring, save for animals and plants. When the last human, the last Iceman, the last of the Ÿadeth-Oëmin, and so on, have aged and died, animals and plants, no longer serving as food for the developed races, will be denied reproduction, too, and go extinct. When the last animal and the last plant are gone, this old Taëlia will be consumed and exist no more. All life will ascend to the Heavenly plane of the New Taëlia, which will be the paradise you have dreamt of."

Kirbakin chuckled. "I suppose I and my tribe, together with other Elementals, will be the absolute last to leave then," he said. "For we do not die like humans do."

"That is correct," the Queen said. "You will all be the overseers and balancers and thus experience Taëlia's last days."

"And I will be the last King of Khandur," Xandur said. "But what of you, Master Raeglin? And you, Milady?"

"I will return to the Heavens," Astéamat said. "NIN.AYA and I are one and the same. I am merely a physical incarnation of Her, another aspect, and I must return to her. My people will follow me to the Heavens, and so will the Ayasisians."

"And so will I," Raeglin said.

Ismaril sighed. "This is all well," he said, "but I am still young, and I have many years ahead of me. Even though I'll spend them with my family, these years will be long, and I know not what Maerion thinks about all this. Nonetheless, I must be patient, for one day, we shall all enter the new world."

Then he locked eyes with the Queen. "Milady, ere you leave our realm, will you still make time to free the Ghost Kings of their curse, so that Tomlin and his friend can leave Hell with the rest?"

"Thus I promised, and this I shall do," the Queen said. "All curses cast in this realm will be lifted. We should soon think about leaving Gormoth and going back to where we best belong. Most of the journey we can make together. If you and your family are returning to Eldholt, which I presume you wish to do, we of the Originals will accompany you all the way to Dimwood, where we will part. I and my people will continue to Barren Hill to lift the Ghost Kings' curse, and after that, we must leave Taëlia. Raeglin will come with us to the Hills."

"And I will follow you to Green Peaks, where my journey began," Kirbakin said.

"And I will lead my people back to Khandur," the prince said. "Ismaril, you and your family are welcome to spend some time in Ringhall, ere you return to your homeland. It would be an honor to accommodate you, and we might get to know each other better. And we must return King Barakus' body to Khandur, where he can get a proper burial."

"It would be an honor, Prince," Ismaril said. "Sigyn's body will remain here, where her life ended. She took the title of a shield maiden seriously, and I knew her well enough to understand that here is the place where she wants to rest. And now, evil has left the lands, and the land will prosper soon. I have thought of bringing her body home to Eldholt, but something inside me tells me not to. It is as a shield maiden she wishes to be remembered. Her lingering energy will be the protector of this land, and she will bless it and make it prosper."

The Queen nodded. "You are speaking wisely, Farrider. Yes, I feel this is what she wants, and that is what she will do."

Then Prince Xandur spoke. "There is something I cannot make sense of. After Yongahur's soul left his body, my Royal Ring crumbled into dust. I am not completely sure why, for it has been a treasured asset within my royal bloodline since King Irvannion. Yet it seems the ring and the sword Gahil were interconnected."

"I was going to get to this," the Queen said. "I am very aware of that ring, for it is Divine, as much as Gahil was Divine. You say the ring was a treasured asset, but do you know why?"

"I do not," Xandur said.

"Irvannion knew, for it was to him I gave the ring. It was a tool—a crucial part of the Prophecy. Your first king was clever, and he knew of the Prophecy. But the ring had only one purpose, and that was to destroy Gahil if the Prophecy was fulfilled. And once Gahil was destroyed, so was the ring. The two were intertwined."

"I suspected there was a correlation," Xandur said. "Hence, I mentioned it to Ismaril before he left to return to this camp."

"When Gahil was destroyed, I knew the Prophecy was fulfilled," Astéamat said. For thus it is said: If the sword turns to dust, all is done and completed."

The Queen studied the council members, one after the other, and she said, "I believe all has now been conveyed, and hopefully things are clearer. We all had a role to play in all this, but now it is over, and the bits and pieces are for me to bother with. I suggest we end here, and tomorrow, we head back to Grimcast. The Yadeth-Oëmin will most likely join us on our journey south and depart halfway, going north with the Icemen. The sleds are on bare ground and are of no use, and the Icemen cannot walk home the same way they arrived. There are Dragons who can take some of them, but the rest will ride with us until we reach the Bridge of Elchamar, and from there, heading north. There are many vacant horses at their disposal since many good soldiers died in the battle. We have more than enow for the Icemen to make use of."

With these words, the council dispersed, and they all could use a few hours' rest; for the next day, they were riding to Grimcast, and Ismaril would return to his waiting family. But before he went to bed, he visited Sigyn's grave one last time to say goodbye. He knew he would never see this place again.

Chapter 41
Another Time, Another World

ISMARIL SAT ON THE PORCH in his favorite rocking chair, gazing out over Silverlake. His thoughts were wandering, as they always were these days; his troubled thoughts never ceased. Still, they were sometimes pleasant, and he smiled to himself at the images in his head, but mostly, his memories were haunting, and he was restless.

Yet he should feel privileged.

When he, Maerion, and Erestian returned to Eldholt so long ago now, they had nothing to come back to. Yongahur and his Wolfmen had burned down their house, so they had lived with a neighbor until Ismaril had built a new house with a glorious view over Silverlake, just outside town. For over twenty-five years they had lived there now, and his wife and son loved that place. He smiled when he thought about how happy his family was to move in there. It was like anyone's dream, yet he had never felt at home. Lindhost was his country and Eldholt his home, but nothing was the same anymore.

It was a perfect summer morning. The sun was shining, and it was not too hot; a mild breeze swept in from the east, carrying scents of forest and water from the lake to the veranda where he was sitting, rocking. Beside him sat Maerion in her own rocking chair, working on a cardigan for Erestian. She was still her old, talkative self, but Ismaril spoke very little these days, caught up in thoughts as he was.

Then his gaze caught a young man walking up the path from the lake, carrying some fish he had caught. Ismaril smiled wistfully, always amazed at how tall Erestian had grown. He was now a young lad of twenty-six, strong and healthy, and he had inherited his mother's brown hair. Ismaril recalled him as the toddler he was when the company left Eldholt on their quest, and it felt so close in time, yet so long gone.

"Mother, father," Erestian said, and his gray eyes were sparkling. "I have some lunch for us." He disappeared into the house for a moment, and Ismaril heard his voice from inside. "Father, we should go up the mountains hunting. We haven't been there for a while."

"Aye, we should," Ismaril said. "We certainly should."

"How about today? Look at the weather. It's a perfect day for hunting deer."

"Certainly looks like it." These days, hunting with Erestian was what he enjoyed the most, and that thought got him in a better mood. "Well, get ready then, and we shall leave."

—

Up the mountainside they strode, father and son, equipped with arrows and bows. They chatted about this and that until they had left the village behind and allowed the forest to embrace them. Then they kept silent and moved slower. These woods were teeming with wildlife, and if they were quiet, they would soon spot some game.

Suddenly, Erestian stopped and held his father back, and he whispered, "There, I hear something…"

The two hunters stood as still as they could and barely breathed. Something was certainly out there, and it was moving toward them. Ten paces ahead, the path made a sharp right turn, and thickets of pine and fir blocked their view. They left the trail, took cover behind the trees, and strung their bows, waiting.

But what came around the bend was not a deer; it was a man. He was dressed in a long, gray cape, and he covered his face under a hood. The two hunters could distinguish a thick, gray beard under the hood. Around his waist, he wore a scabbard attached to a leather belt, and from the scabbard, the hilt of a sword stuck up. With the arrow still attached to the string, Ismaril returned to the trail, with Erestian close behind.

"Greetings, old man," Ismaril said, and the stranger halted

twenty paces away. "Are you heading for Eldholt?"

"I am," the stranger said.

"Forgive our weapons, but we are on a hunting trip. We are not hostile."

"Neither am I. Perhaps you can help me. I am looking for Ismaril Farrider. Does he still reside in Eldholt?"

Ismaril froze, and his grip around the bow tightened. "What do you want with this man?"

"By studying your reaction, I can tell you know him," the stranger said. "Ismaril knows me, but not in many far-gone years now have I seen him. In a strange way, you remind me of him…"

"What is your name?" Ismaril said.

The stranger pulled back his hood and exposed a bushy beard, and his hair was abruptly cut at the shoulders. Hair and beard were both gray, and his facial hair covered most of his weather-bitten face. With the hood removed, he no longer looked as old as he first appeared; perhaps around the same age as Ismaril. His brown eyes were awake.

Ismaril gasped. "That face I can never forget," he said, and he chuckled. "Zale Anórin?"

The stranger jerked. "Is… Ismaril?"

"Indeed!" The two men ran into each other's arms, and they hugged and patted each other's backs, breaking out in mutual laughter.

"By the Goddess," Zale said. "I could not recognize you. It has been so long. Your hair is gray, and you are clean-shaven."

Then Zale glanced at the young man and said, "Is this… Is this Erestian?"

Proudly, Ismaril walked over to his son and put his hand on the young man's shoulder. "He sure is," he said. "Almost the same age we were when we started our journey to Gormoth."

"Erestian," Zale whispered. "You were just a toddler. Perhaps your father has said a few words about me over the years? Do you know who I am?"

"Aye, he has," Erestian said. "I know about you. An honor to meet you."

"What is your errand?" Ismaril asked. "Has something happened?"

"Has something happened?" Zale laughed out loud. "By the Goddess, it has been twenty-five years. Many things have happened over such a long time, but nothing alarming or extraordinary. I am merely here to visit."

"Well, if so, follow me back to the village, and we shall talk."

After having dinner on the veranda, Ismaril suggested he and Zale should go to the lake to continue their conversation. There, they made a fire, and Ismaril lit a pipe.

"My old friend," he said. "So, you are with the Nomads these days?"

"I am," Zale said. "Yomar is alive and well, leading his people." Then he chuckled. "I know he always told us the Nomads have no leaders, but everybody is following him. It is a good thing, though, for he is wise, and he is a survivor. After the Ending War, I returned to Merriwater, as you know, and I stayed there until my parents both died. Before you and I went on our mission, I loved Merriwater, but everything felt different after I came back. I was restless and unhappy. It was like it was no longer my place."

Ismaril nodded and sighed. "I know that feeling."

"Aye, our experiences on the road may have made us wise in some ways, but we also lost our sense of belonging, did we not? After Queen Astéamat saved the innocent souls from Hell and destroyed Hell, together with all demonic entities roaming there, my curse finally lifted. I can still not remember all the things I did while in a trance, thinking I was someone else named Hoodlum. And I prefer not to think too much about it, either. It is too hurtful."

Ismaril put his hand on Zale's knee. "Aye, you are back to being your old self again; the friend I knew in my youth."

"I am happy to hear you say that. But I have changed. I am constantly restless, and I never took myself a wife, knowing I could not do her justice. These days, I no longer have things in common with most people, bar those I traveled with within your company. I sold the house and went on the road again—alone. This was many years ago now. I had no goal or destination in mind; I merely wanted to be in nature, and I wanted to know what befell all those I once knew but were scattered with the wind.

"Then I came to think about the Nomads, and I felt the yearning inside me grow. I had to find them, and a good place to start, albeit far away, was by the Weather Mountain, where

Yomar left his people once upon a time when your company went to the Frostlands. And alas, I found their tribe settled there, where Yomar had left them. Many of them were permanent settlers, but Yomar was seldom with them. He has always been a restless Nomad, like what I had now become. I found him on the Northern Path, close to Wildwood many moons later, and I have traveled with him and his closest men ever since, and it suits me well. This is the best way for me to spend the rest of my life before I die and go to the New Taëlia. It is difficult to wait for that day, alas! I may have many years left. And what about you, my friend? Are you doing some traveling?"

"Nay. None whatsoever. I am as restless as you are, but I have a family. I have traveled no more than a few leagues from Eldholt since I returned, and then only to the neighboring villages. My days of traveling are over, and I have mixed feelings about that. Yet, there is nothing for me to see out there. This world appeals to me no more." Then he locked eyes with his old friend, and he said, "This is something I have only told Maerion, so you are the second to know. When I was almost dying at the Iron Peaks up in Gormoth, following upon Sigyn's passing, I had a vivid dream. But I think it was not a dream—it was somehow real. I was standing before the gate to Heaven or something, and there was a beautiful city, floating in the air. But two angelic beings rejected me and said I must go back. And here I am, many years later. Since then, I have had very similar visions in my sleep often, and each time I was told to return here. I begged them to let me stay, but I could not. Yet I think the reason I could not stay there was because I stopped myself. I have a family, and I must not leave them behind. Therefore, I have been rejected. But I am torn and split in two, Zale. I am in two places, and it tears me asunder." He squeezed Zale's shoulder and moved his face close to his. "Do you think... Do you think I have been seeing the New Taëlia?"

"It is not for me to say," Zale said. "I could not possibly tell, but I understand they have been mysterious experiences. One day, you will go there to stay. What does Maerion say about your visions?"

Ismaril's eyes teared up when he said, "I love Maerion, and I love my son," he said. "Yet I feel disconnected. Like you, I am no longer the same man I used to be. Although Maerion and Erestian have had their share of tormenting experiences at Azezakel's and Yongahur's mercy, it is yet different. We no longer have much to say to each other, and I am seldom truly present around them. It grieves me, for they do not deserve such treatment from me, though I know not how to act differently. And Zale, my dear friend, after all these years, I still miss Sigyn. We went through so much together. She is always on my mind, and I am praying I will see her again."

"I feel your pain," Zale said. "Yet your family needs you. What else can you do? It is not beneficial to take our own lives; this we have been told. It might jeopardize our entrance to the New Taëlia. Our energies will not match."

"I know, and I have no plans to end it like that." Then Ismaril changed the subject. "Zale, tell me! Do you have any news about those we once knew? After all, you have been on the road for so long."

"I do. That was one reason I have traveled. It showed that Yomar had much news on the matter. As you must know, Prince Xandur is now King Xandur of the Divine Kingdom of Khandur, the *Last King*, as he calls himself. I visit him from time to time, and he is an excellent ruler. He made peace with his brother and gave Prince Exxarion Anúria in the north, and he declared Anúria a sovereign kingdom. Thus, Exxarion is nowadays King Exxarion. I have not met him since the Ending Battle, but rumors have it that the Anúrians like him, for he has changed. So many of us were cursed and spellbound under King Azezakel's reign, and most of us were unaware. When the veil lifted, many people changed for the better. King Exxarion was one of them.

"We both met with King Zarabaster of Rhíandor before we took on the journey home. He sailed back to his homeland with his remaining crew, and from what I heard, he passed away shortly after from the effects of wounds he received in the battle. His eldest son is now ruling Rhíandor.

"After Queen Moëha's death, the Ayasisians stood without a queen. Most of them departed from Taëlia in the company of Queen Astéamat and the Originals, but some remained here and returned to Ayasis. Among them was Naisha, the Seer, and they crowned her the new Queen of Ayasis. She and King Xandur see each other often. It is no secret how they feel about each other, and although they are not of the same stock and can't unite in matrimony, they are very close. The King told me they both look forward to being together in the New Taëlia. Naisha has chosen to depart when King Xandur's time in this world is up.

"The Icemen are still living up north with their Dragons, but their tribes are decreasing in number, of course. A quarter of a century has passed, and so have many of the Icemen. Usbarg and the Ÿadeth-Oëmin settled around the Weather Mountains, close to the Nomad tribe, and although I knew him not back when, I have come to know and appreciate Usbarg since. I would not dare say we are close friends, which is not his fault. I have been on the road most of the time, preventing me from getting to know him better. He looks the same as during the Battle—the Ÿadeth-Oëmin age slowly, and I suspect they shall be the last species leaving Taëlia, save for the Elementals.

"I am afraid this is all I know. I have yet to meet with Kirbakin, but I trust he is still residing at Green Peaks with the other Gnomes."

"Thank you, my friend," Ismaril said. "This was much more than I expected to hear from you. I am glad to have gained this knowledge, for it eases me, and I can be at peace with that part."

Zale stayed with Ismaril and his family for another few days, and they went hunting together, bringing Erestian with them. Then Zale got restless, and Ismaril departed from his old friend. He watched Zale disappear up the mountain and among the trees. This was the last he saw of him in Taëlia.

———

Six moons later, the vision came to Ismaril in his dreams once more, but this time was different. Instead of the two angelic beings guarding the portal, a tall female dressed in a golden dress greeted him. Her hair was as white as linen, and on her head rested a splendid crown of white gold. and her body seemed to appear and vanish to and fro as if transparent. When he gazed into her eyes, he beheld the stars of the Universe twinkling back at him. He kneeled without thinking about what he was doing, and he bowed down, for the light this female emanated was so powerful that he could not face it too long.

"Please stand, Ismaril Farrider," said the female. "Do not fear me."

Then Ismaril stood and confronted the light she emitted and embedded him with. Everything around them disappeared until there were only the two of them in an empty void. But it was far from an unpleasant feeling. He wanted to stay here with this being forever, although forever was not the correct word, for no time existed, only eternal bliss.

"I am Queen NIN.AYA," she said, but her lips did not move. Her voice came from inside his mind. "But I am also Queen Astéamat and the Ice Queen." In an instant, she changed shape and form to resemble the Queen of Emoria. "Welcome to the gate into the New Taëlia. I understand you have been suffering, and the yearning to get here is wearing on you. Now you are welcome to join us at any time you wish. But first, go back once more to your family and return together. Offer them to follow."

The apparition vanished and Ismaril stood in a magnificent meadow with flowers in many colors, majestic mountains in the yonder, and a wide ocean to his right, and the smell of saltwater lifted his soul. Across the meadow, a magic forest grew tall and enticing, but he did not recognize the trees. They had leaves in all colors of the rainbow, and on the branches and among the leaves, birds were chirping and singing. He stretched out his arms in pure joy and he cried, "I am blessed!"

Then the vision faded, and he woke up in his bed.

—

Many days went by, and he hesitated to tell Maerion of his recent vision. One afternoon, while they sat in silence on the veranda, Marion spoke.

"Ismaril, tell me what is on your mind. For years, your thoughts have been wandering, but now more so than ever before. Do not be silent. Speak to me."

"I had another vision," he said in a low voice, and in it was a trace of sorrow. "But this time it was different. The Queen of the Heavens invited the three of us to transcend if we wish to."

She looked at him, and she sobbed. "I suspected it," she said. "I know how much you want to leave this place. You have never truly been present here since we returned from Gormoth. Your mind is not with us; it is with Sigyn, is it not? You are not happy here with us."

Ismaril did not know how to best continue, and his eyes teared up. "It grieves me," he said. "I love you and Erestian dearly, but I must be honest. My heart is with Sigyn, foremost. She has been on my mind every day since she died. While she and I went through all the hardship on our journey, we were both so busy surviving that I failed to realize how much she meant to me. Since her passing, I have dreamed of uniting with her. It torments me, for it is not fair to you and Erestian. After my journey long ago, I have alienated myself from everything and everybody in this world. I have tried so hard to hide it from you, but to no avail. Come with me, Maerion. Let us all transcend, for it is my hope… no, even my conviction, that if we all arrive at the New Taëlia, things will be different. We will all think differently. I have been there; I have tasted it. There, no one needs to choose. We can all be together, for it is not like here. In the New World, there is no suffering."

Her tears increased, but she kept her voice steady. "I am no fool," she said. "All these years I have known this. Of course, I have. You should go to her, Ismaril. You must go where your heart belongs, and it is not with us. We do not share your visions and experiences. Thus, we know not what awaits us, and therefore, your words fall empty. You have lived almost fifty-three years in this life, and you may have many years left to live if you choose to do so. Yet I know you cannot stay that long. Erestian and I both have known for many years that this day would come, but we choose to stay until our lives here are over. Then, we shall see what befalls. Meanwhile, you get time to spend with Sigyn should you meet her again. I know that is what you want, and I can do nothing about it, and neither can you. You must go, Ismaril."

Then she went inside, leaving him alone, and he wept. For hours, he wept, but he knew he could do nothing else but transcend. Deep inside, he had known his family would not follow—not yet, and it grieved him. He loved them, but he had drifted apart from them, at least in this life. With his eyes closed, he prayed it was going to be different there, but he could not know for certain.

A few days more, he waited, until one day, he told Maerion and Erestian that he would transcend the following night; and again, he begged them to come, but they declined.

"Then I shall stay," Ismaril said, firmly.

But Maerion shook her head. "No, my love, for my love you are. You must leave. You cannot live with us for many decades to come when your mind is not here. I have seen how hard you have tried, and both I and Erestian know you have done your best. Yet it is tormenting for you and for us if you force yourself to stay for our sake. Besides, Erestian is a grown man now. It is time to say goodbye… for now. It is alright, for it is what it is. And perhaps you are right in that things will be different there."

Thus, they hugged, and they wept in each other's arms, and like so many times before, Ismaril's heart broke into pieces.

He transcended that following night.

———

Once more, he stood in the beautiful meadow. Behind him was the Emerald City, shining in a Divine light, and his joy and happiness returned. Gone were his worries and his weight in the old Taëlia. He thought of Maerion and Erestian, but no longer did he experience the unendurable burden of immense sorrow. He knew now that once they arrived, all would be fine.

One by one, he met those who went before him. The first encounter was with Holgar, and the second with Gideon, and they were joyous reunions, indeed. Everything here was so light, and there was no physical or emotional pain, only an overwhelming wish to create. Create what? Anything. Here, no words were uttered, for everybody spoke with their minds. Thus, there were few misunderstandings.

Repeatedly, he asked about Sigyn, but he got no direct answer. Although this was not a world where worries were common, this concerned him. It was the only cloud in his sky.

One day, he went into the forest, and he came to a lake. He got to his knees to drink. Like in a mirror, he saw his reflection in the water, and he rejoiced, for here, in the New Taëlia, where no one grew old, he had regained his youth, and the picture that stared back at him was an image of himself when he left Eldholt and went on his journey. Once more, he was in his mid-twenties.

As he studied himself, he saw another reflection in the water. It was vague at first, but became clearer. It was the face of a young woman with long, dark-blond hair and big, gray eyes, and they beheld him. He gasped, and a wave of bliss and exhilaration washed over him. He flew up and spun around.

"Sigyn!" he cried, and he wept. But these were happy tears. "My beloved Sigyn! I have missed you so!"

"I have missed you, too," she said, and they embraced.

It was impossible to say how long they stood like that, embracing, crying, and laughing, feeling each other's presence.

Then Ismaril exclaimed, "Lo-and-behold! You look the same as I remember you. I am so glad you never saw me aging in the old world. And look at your eyes that used to be so sad. They are sad no more."

"It is because I am no longer sad," she said. "Here is nothing to be sad about. I have even met my husband who was killed in the Eldholt raid, for he is here. But he knows about us and knows I have been waiting for you. He does not mind. It is different here; there is no jealousy."

Then she giggled. "Come, let me show you around. I wish for you to see the places I love the most."

Thus, they spent the day in each other's company. There was so much to say, but most of it felt irrelevant now. Here, every life was lived in the present moment, and the past, no matter how tormenting, bothered no one, for they were now memories alone; experiences and lessons learned. It was here and now that true life began.

As they sat there on the shore, and the sun was sinking, Ismaril took Sigyn's hand, looked her in the eyes, and smiled. Then he gazed out over the ocean, and he said, "I am happy to be home."

★—★

MAPS

For a free, resizable overall map of Taëlia in full color, go to **https://wespenrebooks.com/2021/09/11/detailed-color-map-that-goes-with-the-book-download-here-for-free/** to view or download.

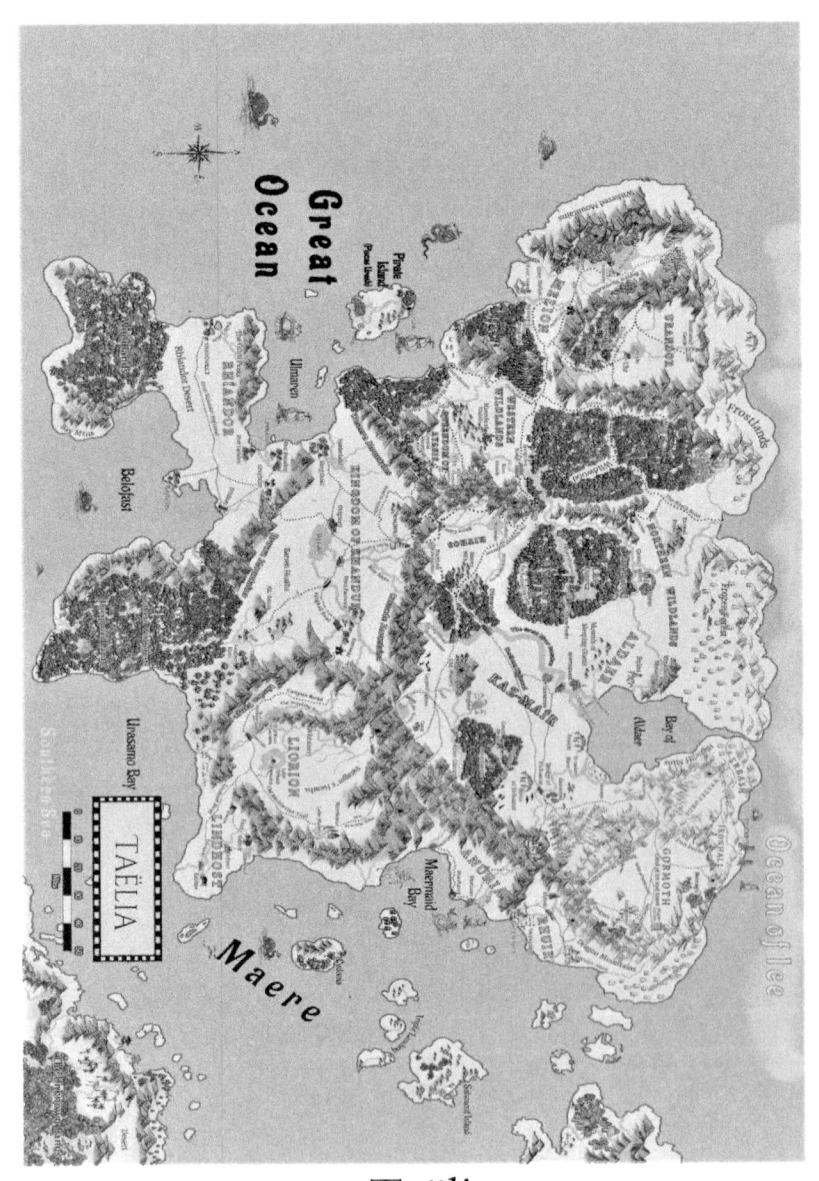

Taëlia

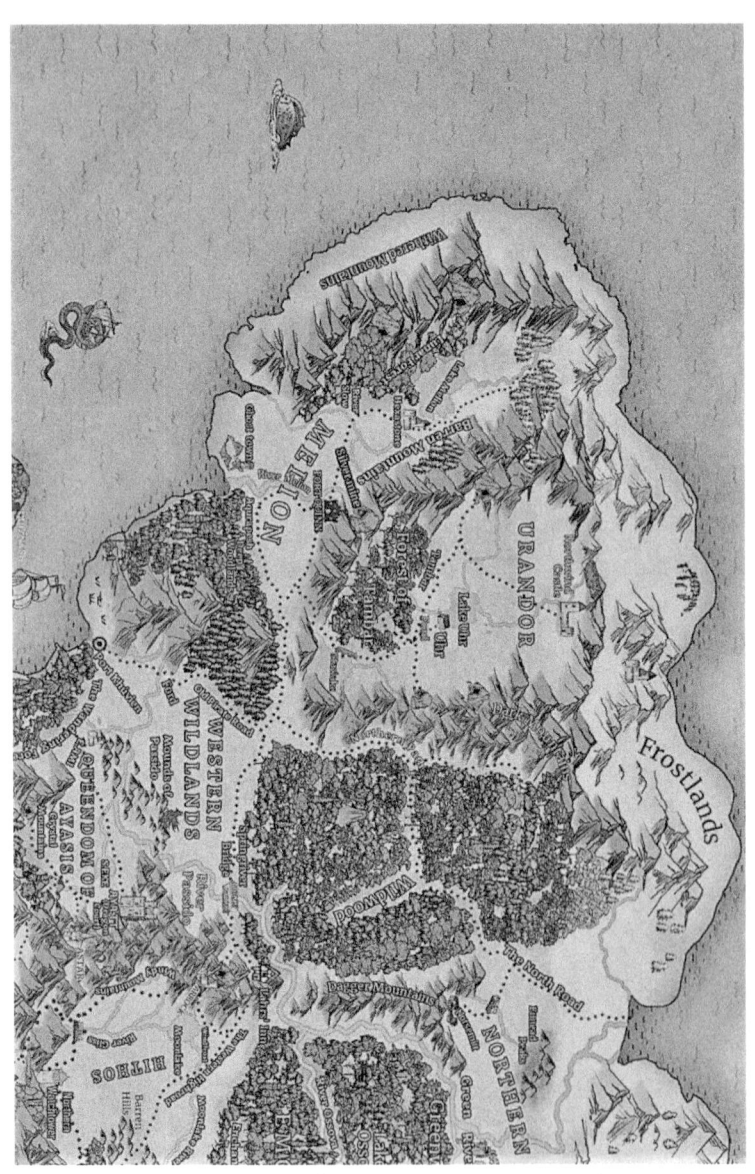

Northwestern Taëlia

Southwestern Taëlia

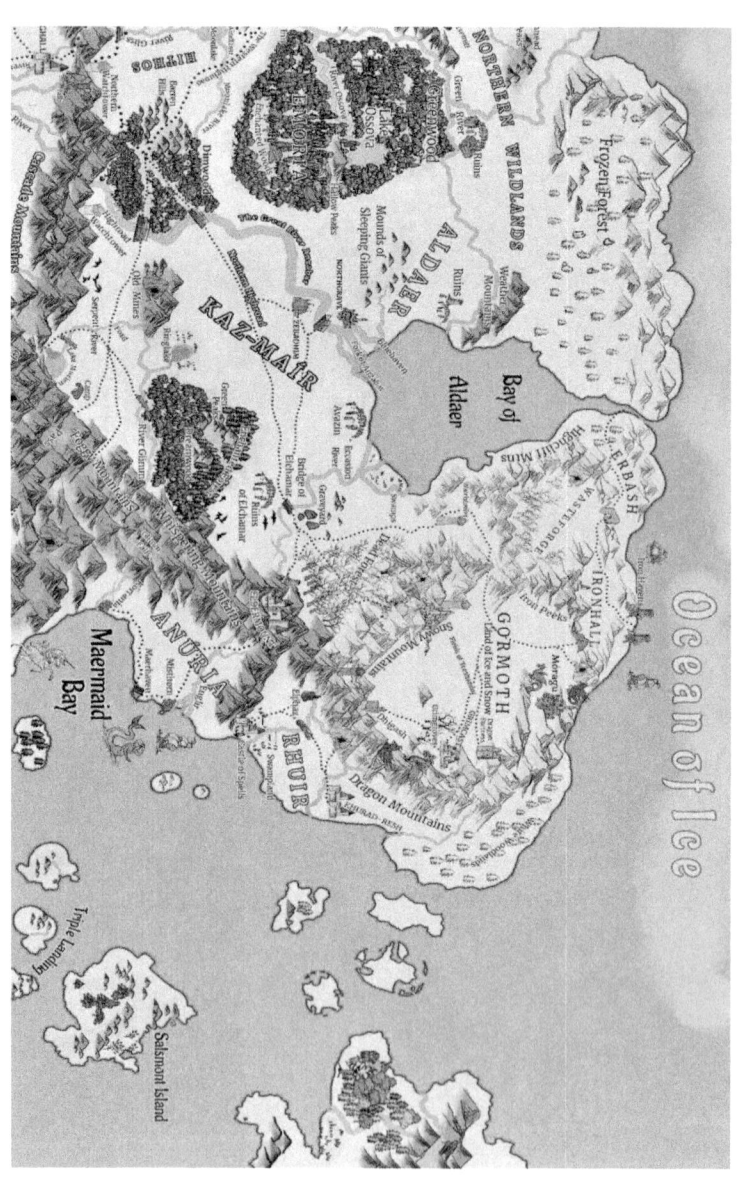

Northeastern Taëlia

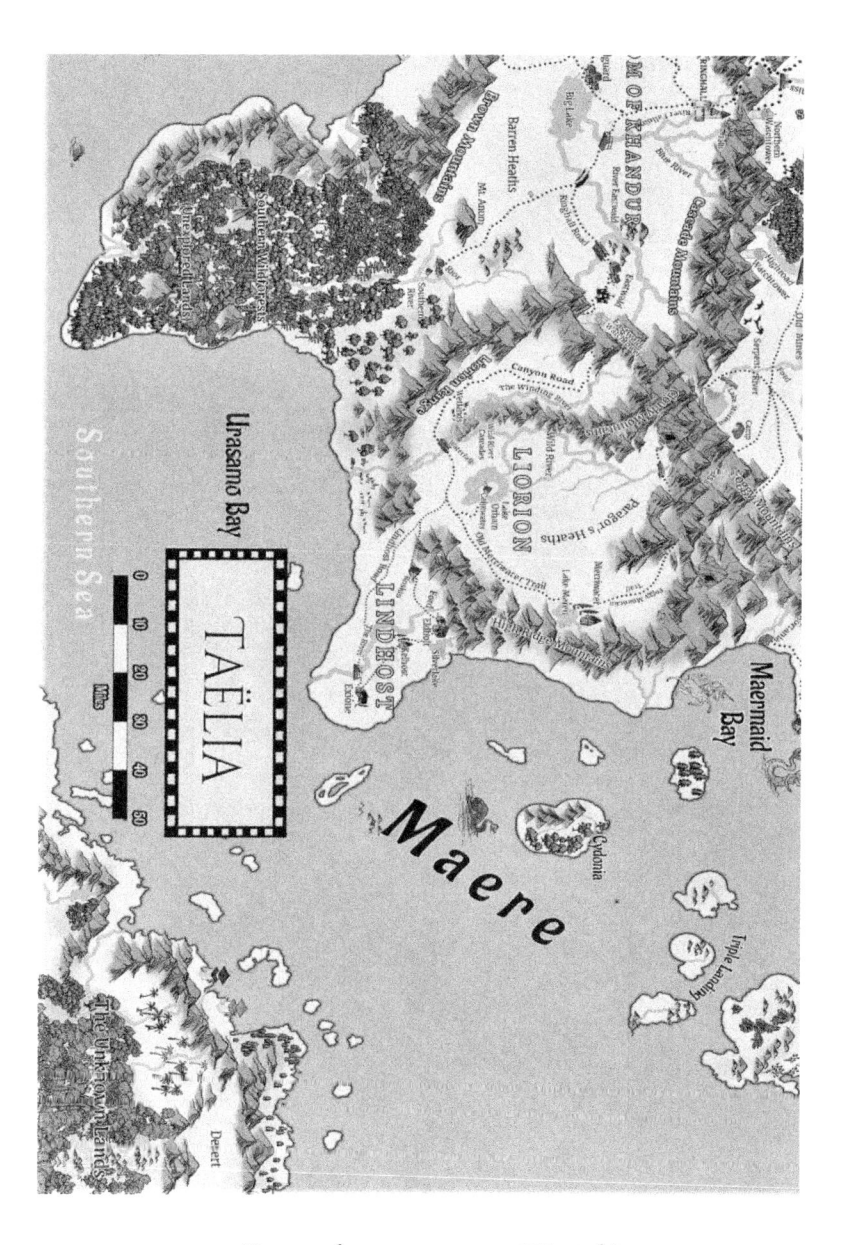

Southeastern Taëlia

Printed in Dunstable, United Kingdom